An impossibly perfect young woman appeared in my novels *Charisma* and *Brontomek* and generated a lot of fan mail. People asked if she was based on a real person; and if she was, what a lucky guy I was to know such a woman. Well, unfortunately she was not real, and I emphasized this point by having her disappear into nothingness at the end of each novel. She was an impossible male dream. Her physical appearance was based on the movie star Susanna York (a clue to that is her fictional name Susanna Lincoln) but her personality was all my own erotic imaginings. She puts in a guest appearance in *Flower of Goronwy*, the story you are, I hope, about to read. It is not my usual kind of story and the basic premise gives rise to possibilities that require a much longer book. I feel there are too many issues arising, too much conflict and there are parts of it that are much creepy for my taste. It also has a strong sexual theme, unlike my usual writing which tends to have a strong love theme.

One thing hasn't changed. I'm still a sucker for a happy ending.

—Michael Coney

Flower of Goronwy

Flower of Goronwy

Michael Coney

First DIP Edition

1 3 5 7 9 10 8 6 4 2

ISBN
978-1-848637-77-1

Layout by Jaharisam

Printed and bound in England by T. J. International

PS Publishing Ltd
Grosvenor House
1 New Road, Hornsea
HU18 1PG, England

e-mail: editor@pspublishing.co.uk
website: www.pspublishing.co.uk

CHAPTER 1

MISTRAL WATCHED THE TALL MAN from behind a clump of bushtrap. She'd been crouching there for some minutes now, her pet stoag at her side, and her knees were starting to ache. Wilfred was getting impatient, snuffling and shifting as the bushtrap began to wrap its tendrils around his stout legs. "Down, boy," she whispered, her hand digging into the coarse fur of his neck.

When would that man find the dead body?

It was late morning of the short Goronwy day and the sun was hot on her back, and her macabre joke was getting a bit tedious. Half an hour ago she'd stumbled across the body of a man lying beside a stoag trail, face down. She'd known he was dead right away; his wound was very nasty, laser-inflicted. Well, that was humans for you.

She sometimes forgot she was a human herself. And looking north, it was difficult to imagine humans had ever set foot on this world—if you ignored that stupid guy ambling along the old stoag trail as though he had all day. The mountains rose spiky in the far distance; in between lay a patchwork of aeolus fields. They constantly changed shade from light to dark and back again as the millions of flowers making up each field reversed their petals. This alternately heated and cooled the fields, causing air to flow from one field to the next, carrying the scent of the flowers to the myriad pollinating insects. And bringing the scent of the man to her.

Like most humans, Mistral was sensitive to the powerful pheromones of the planet Goronwy's creatures. But she'd been born on Goronwy and so her senses were preternaturally acute; moreover, she refused to take the antifero pills used by other humans failed to block reception of the emotions around her. Unusually, she was even affected by human pheromones. So she'd suffered from wild mood swings as a child, until she recognised what caused them and learned to control them—after a fashion.

And now she could sense how that man felt.

He was depressed and frustrated, and trying to work out some problem. Poor guy... But sympathy would be wasted. He was an employee of the Samaritan Organisation, who were responsible for screwing up her world. A bloody bureaucrat like her father— damn him!—making capital on the backs of her friends the gorons. And the worst thing was, the Samaritans pretended to be good guys, helping out.

Well, it had been a black day for the gorons when they'd requested help from the Organisation fifty years ago.

She glanced behind. There was nobody else in sight; the five domes of Samarita dozed in the sun a kilometre away. Lady river, flowing so slowly past them, glowed dully, sunlight glinting on the gelatious surface. It was a fine morning for a Samaritan to discover a body.

Then the sense of shock reached her on the aeolus winds.

It affected her like a rush of adrenaline. He'd found the body. In fact he'd fallen over it in his preoccupation and was busy picking himself up, dusting his gold uniform legs. He looked a nit-picking, prim kind of nerd, late twenties probably, a key-punching zombie, one whose tidy world would be blown to pieces by such a gruesome find. She sniffed the wind, eager to gauge his subsequent reactions.

Horror and sorrow, mostly. Well, that was refreshing, anyway. Too often people derived a nasty glee from the misfortunes of others, which was one of the reasons she didn't get along too well with members of her own species. This guy seemed unusually straight. Not so straight as a goron, of course. Those little men were gems. They never lied, never cheated, and certainly never murdered . . .

Discovery! The man was looking directly at her. She must have raised her head, a stupid thing to do. Naturally he'd be looking around for help.

"Hi, you! Over here, quickly!"

What an idiot! There was no need to hurry; that body had been dead for hours. She rose slowly to her feet and eyed him coldly across a fifty meters of aeolus flowers.

"Why?" she shouted back.

"Don't argue! Come here, quickly!"

Accustomed to command, apparently. Well, he wasn't going to command her. Calling Wilfred to heel she strolled easily toward him, the succulent aeolus petals squishing under her bare feet.

Bryn Trevithick, Director of Ecology, was a very unhappy man. He'd been on Goronwy only sixty-two days and was wondering if he'd made a mistake in taking this job. A couple of years ago he'd been looked on as a high-flyer, the youngest Director in the Organization. Then came disaster at Annecy, his previous posting, and his career had stalled. So he'd jumped at the chance when he'd received the warpwire from Murdo, the alien Director of Personnel at the Samaritan Organisation project on Goronwy, offering him the job.

Maybe they'd put down the Annecy fiasco to youthful inexperience and decided he deserved another chance. Perhaps Ivor Sabin had put in a good word for him. Ivor had been his deputy on Annecy and he'd been here on Goronwy for two years. At first he'd thought it odd that Ivor hadn't taken the job of Director himself, but now he was beginning to think the crafty little guy had known exactly what he was doing.

Because Trevithick had discovered that his new job was the pits. The database was a shambles and it had taken him until yesterday to make some sense of what had been happening for the last fifty years. And now he almost wished he hadn't. His department was probably the most important in the Project, yet research had been marking time. Apathy was everywhere. The only bright spark was young Gary Docksteader, and even he'd had a fit of weirdness first thing this morning.

Gary had slipped into his office quietly and handed him a piece of paper. On the paper was written the words, in ill-formed capitals: WALLS HAVE EARS. MEET YOU IN THE STORAGE DOME.

Trevithick had had other priorities, less bizarre, but eventually he'd gone to the storage dome, a big open-plan place with no interior walls and consequently no ears. Docksteader had not been there. Trevithick had come across Martha Sunshine, the big and blowsy Director of Entertainment, instead. She was checking some drums of fertiliser stored together with a stack of theatrical backcloths and props—God only knew why, but he was tired of asking dumb questions.

"Seen Gary Docksteader around, Martha?"

She'd been startled. "Do you always creep up on people like that, Bryn? Gary? Yes, I think I saw him over by Hydroponics maybe an hour ago."

Jonathan Cook, Director of Sustenance, was showing a team of gorons how to change the growing medium in a ponics tank. He'd seen Gary, too. "He poked around here for a while, yes. Then he went outside."

So Trevithick had wasted half the morning looking for Gary, his mood steadily deteriorating. Around noon he'd started on a brisk walk along an animal trail through the aeolus fields to calm himself down. It had taken him some minutes to get past the brown wasteland created by the application of Trent's Vivicide fifty years ago. Fifty years ago! Why was it that a herbicide banned on Earth for centuries could still be used to clear ground on other worlds? Well, it wouldn't be used any more; the Galactic banning of Trent's five years ago had been one of the major achievements of his career.

Since then, things had gone steadily downhill for him . . .

Recently he'd gotten into the habit of awakening in the middle of the night, worrying about the job. He needed to exercise more. He'd call Martha later and find out about Samarita's facilities.

Meanwhile . . . he tripped over something and fell full length.

Angry with himself, the liquid from crushed aeolus leaves quickly soaking into his uniform, he scrambled to his feet. And saw the body.

At first he thought it was just somebody sleeping in the sun, face down. He began to mumble apologies, without receiving any response. He bent over the figure and gently lifted the head back.

It was Gary Docksteader.

A dark slash ran across the back of Gary's gold uniform just above the hips. Although the wound looked deep, very little blood showed. The heat of the laser beam would have cauterised it and melted his clothing into it. Trevithick swallowed heavily and stood, looking around for help.

There was a young girl looking over the top of a bushtrap not far away. "Hi, you!" he shouted. "Over here, quickly!"

She stood up. She had a stoag with her, one of those odd six-legged Goronwy beasts. He hoped it was under control. She still stood there, gazing in his direction.

"Why?" she called.

For God's sake, was she half-witted or something? Maybe he should have her transferred to his staff; she'd fit right in there. "Don't argue!" he shouted. "Come here, quickly!"

He heard a rustling sound, and for an instant thought Gary wasn't dead after all. Then he saw a bushtrap tendril snaking around an ankle. The tendril tightened and Gary began to slide away. Trevithick dropped to his knees and tried to disentangle him. No good; the tendril was a centimetre thick and stronger than his fingers. And he had no knife. He took hold of Gary's leg and braced himself, digging his heels into the ground.

"The bushtrap'll get you and all, if you do that." A shadow fell over him. The girl had arrived.

"Do you have a knife?"

"Maybe."

"Then let me have it, will you!" He snatched it from her hand and began to hack away. Meanwhile another tendril began to caress his own leg. He knocked it away and resumed sawing. They said that if more than two bushtrap tendrils got hold of you, that was the end. These plants captured their food live; like most Goronwy plants they were monoradicals, wide-spreading but with a very small central root system. They carried potential fertiliser to the centre of the plant and allowed it to rot there and feed the roots.

Belatedly the girl began to help, kicking away approaching tendrils with her bare feet. Trevithick finally freed Docksteader and dragged him clear, deliberately shielding the body from the girl's line of sight. He made it too obvious.

"Afraid I might faint or something?" she asked sharply. "I seen more bodies than you've had hot dinners, Mister."

He straightened up and looked at her for the first time. She was slim, medium height, wearing a dirty green dress with short sleeves, and what he could see of her body was none too clean either. He couldn't see her face; a lank cascade of jet-black hair fell past it to her chest. She looked maybe sixteen, seventeen. She smelled as though a shower would do no harm.

He found himself saying, "Why aren't you in class?"

She lifted a hand and parted her hair. A furious green eye stared at him. "Why aren't you at work?"

Angrily, he asked, "How old are you?"

The eye was joined by another as she parted the curtain of her hair further. He guessed immediately that her reply was not going to be acceptable. "What's the matter with you? Did I ask *you* how old you are, Mister? Some bloody nerve. You called me over here, remember? So what do you want, huh?"

"I'd like you to go over to the domes and get them to send an ambulopter out."

Her pet stoag had got himself lassoed around the neck by the bushtrap. The girl took the knife and bent to cut the animal free. Small, neat breasts showed beneath the neckline of her dress. "They can handle bushtrap around their legs, easy," she said. "But they

6

can get strangled this way." She glanced up. "And stop looking at my tits, will you?"

"I wasn't," he snapped, flushing with guilty anger.

She straightened up. "You want something to look at," she said loudly, "I'll give you something!" She threw her head back and raised her hands as though about to toss her hair back over her shoulders. Then she seemed to think better of it, and dropped her hands. "Forget it," she muttered.

"Now will you go and get help for me, please?" he said quietly.

She shook her hair back into its customary curtain. "Come, Wilfred," she said, and set off across the aeolus fields with long strides, the short green skirt fluttering in the winds. He watched her go, regretting the hostile turn the conversation had taken. Moving with a dancer's grace, she stepped around clumps of bushtrap and finally disappeared into a dense thicket, Wilfred following her with the weaving gait of his species. He was a big animal; he must have weighed almost two hundred kilograms.

Trevithick waited. Time passed.

Occasionally he was forced to kick tendrils away from the body, and on two occasions vespas, the huge Goronwy wasps, came to inspect him. But they were more interested in the giant flowers at the centre of each aeolus field and after fanning him with their wings they darted away. He began to glance at his watch more frequently as the short Goronwy afternoon fled by. Once a copter rose above the domes, winking like a red star in the low sunshine, but it headed south toward Ladysend. Finally the sun neared the horizon of the flat western plain and he was forced to face facts.

The girl had let him down.

Or possibly he'd let her down, with his insensitive, patronising questions. He'd probably been quite wrong in sensing hostility in her from the start; she was likely shy with strangers.

But it didn't alter the fact that the ambulopter wasn't coming.

Eventually he made the decision he'd been dreading, and bending low, he heaved the body of Gary Docksteader onto his shoulders. It felt all wrong, hanging oddly and dangling because the spine had been severed by the laser burn. Before he'd gone the first ten meters he was forced to pause and gag. Then, settling the body into the most comfortable position he could manage, he stumped off toward the domes of Samarita.

Mistral was still hot with anger as she pushed her way out of the thicket and into the small garden she'd carved from the wilderness. What a prat that guy had been! Absolutely typical of the dome bureaucrat. If only she'd kept her head down from the start. With nobody to vent his panic on, he'd have been running round in circles out there. Better still, he'd have been food for the bushtrap. Well, there was no way she was going to help him out with an ambulopter. From now on, he was on his own.

The garden calmed her, as usual. This was her private place, completely walled in by bushtrap with just that one winding route through. It had never been seen by human eyes, apart from her own, of course. The row of Earth-type trees was laden with cones this year. She touched a dipping branch and caressed the cones. Maybe she'd raise seedlings and plant them around the evaporation ponds up at Ladysmouth; that would give the gorons something different to look at. Slowly she walked the length of a row of cabbages. Yes, they were fattening up nicely, green and solid. All her vegetables were doing well. This was good soil, and she looked forward to a harvest of good food. The fools in the domes didn't know what they were missing. All their food was grown in tanks and processed so that a carrot didn't look like a carrot any more. It was all mushed up with other stuff and stamped with a number, A26 or whatever. Ugh!

Nothing like a sense of superiority to restore the temper. Smiling to herself, she dropped into a pit at the south end of the garden and, ducking her head, made her way along a sloping tunnel. Reaching a branching she hesitated then, calling Wilfred close to heel, she dropped to her hands and knees and lit an oil lamp she took from a nearby alcove. Then she began to crawl down a low, narrow stoag tunnel, pushing the lamp before her.

It was dry and sandy in there, rich with the smell of stoag. She reached a junction where tunnels radiated in all directions and, forming a trumpet with her hands, shouted down one diagonally to the right.

"Hi, fellows!"

She fancied she heard an answering snort, or maybe not. Stoags were a tad stupid, even she had to admit that. She crawled on until she reached a place where the tunnel widened into a big chamber. In the flickering light she saw at least six stoags digging, shoulder to shoulder. She moved aside to allow a seventh stoag to back past her, pulling a mound of loose sand down the tunnel for disposal. Disposal of sand was one of her biggest problems. A massive cone of yellow sand on the surface would be something of a give-away.

The stoags worked on, sand spurting out from between their hind legs. They were expert diggers with four forward paws equipped with sharp claws. And she had them well-trained too; they'd been digging all morning without her supervision. Then, as she watched, one of the stoags hesitated. She heard a metallic squeal, as of claws scraping against a hard, smooth surface.

Perhaps this was what she'd been waiting for. "Stop!" she called. "Come!"

The stoags stopped digging and began to shuffle back from the face, turning awkwardly in the confined space, rearing up and climbing over one anothers' backs. Mistral crawled forward, holding the lamp before her. The sandstone was scored with a multitude of vertical grooves from digging, but in one area, near the centre of the face, the lamp caused a bright reflection. She crawled closer, raising the lamp.

Yes. They'd reached metal. She ran her fingers over the smooth surface and tapped it with her knuckles. No doubt about it, they'd reached their goal at last.

The stoags glanced at her curiously as she let out a whoop of delight.

CHAPTER 2

"**GARY DOCKSTEADER WORKED FOR YOU, I BELIEVE.**" The voice boomed echoingly, as from a bottomless well. Tillini, Director of Security, was one of the Project's muscans. Trevithick stared at the sexless alien angrily. Would he ever get used to these strange creatures? He'd seen enough of them with Outward Ho on Annecy; he hadn't realized they'd infiltrated the Samaritan Organization too.

Tillini was clothed only in a brief wrap, a sop to human notions of decency. The gross body was elephant gray and elephant huge. The peculiar mind was excruciatingly logical and totally dedicated to the good of the majority—so people assured him. Tillini resembled an overweight hippo bulging over the arm-rests of a muscan chair; in short, Tillini was bigger than most.

And no fool.

"I asked you," said Trevithick slowly and carefully, "if you've seen the girl. Or if any of your staff have seen the girl. Or know anything of her whereabouts. That, Tillini, is priority number one."

"There is little point in talking at cross purposes. You were seen carrying the body of one of your employees. You have made no attempt to clear yourself of the possibility that you killed him. Murder must surely be, as you put it, priority number one."

"The girl may be murdered too, for all I know."

Rob Mauser, one of Tillini's all-human staff, spoke. "Easy, Bryn. This girl you're talking about—she sounds like Mistral Greene.

You've met Ralph Greene, Director of Engineering. His daughter. Well, I have a pretty good idea young Mistral can take care of herself."

"Maybe. So why didn't she report the body and have your people send a copter out?"

Mauser chuckled. "That's Mistral for you. You probably put her back up. You're a pompous bastard when you want to be. So she thought: What the hell? and went home to her burrow. Now just answer Tillini's questions and you'll be out of here in no time flat."

Trevithick considered. Yes, it was possible the girl had simply gone home. She had an irresponsible look about her. To her burrow? Well, she certainly looked as though she lived in a burrow. He'd have to question Ralph Greene about her. And for the present, there seemed to be no alternative to submitting to the interrogation of this gigantic alien.

"In reply to your earlier question, Tillini," he said carefully, "You already know the answer. Gary Docksteader is—was—one of my staff. A valued member, I might add."

And so the question and answer period dragged on. He got home at midnight.

The matter of Docksteader's value came back to him during breakfast in his Ladyside apartment the following morning. It would have been more accurate to have told Tillini that Docksteader was the *only* valued member of his staff. The only one with any sense of urgency. The rest of them seemed to be in Samarita for the sole purpose of drawing their pay. And that even applied to Ivor Sabin, who hadn't particularly impressed him on Annecy either.

Breakfast finished, he unlocked the safe, placed a box of back-up disks carefully in his briefcase, and walked out into a perfect Goronwy summer morning, testing the door to make sure it was securely locked behind him. Half an hour later he was seated at his terminal, checking up on the qualifications and personnel appraisals of his staff.

Why hadn't he done this before? Frankly, he'd shrunk from it. He'd felt he should take his people as he found them, rather than relying on the friendships and prejudices of past Directors. But the seed of suspicion that had sent him walking thoughtfully among the aeolus fields soon flowered into a full-blown anger as he viewed the files.

Because the screen showed the situation in Ecology was far worse than he'd thought.

Janine Starseeker, Director of Earth Sciences, peeled the film from her face and examined herself in the mirror. Not bad. Not bad at all. She'd pass for fifty if the sun wasn't shining—well, fifty-five, maybe. Fifteen years younger than her physical age, anyway. That woman in charge of Health—what was her name?—Susanna, had done an excellent job.

But—and it was a big but—you couldn't halt the physical aging process. Correction. You *could* halt the aging process, but you weren't allowed to. The technology was there but the treatment had been outlawed after consultation with other species. Death, it had been decided long ago, was a natural and useful process allowing human evolution to continue within controlled limits, and resulting in a dynamic and progressive society. Room at the top. A continuous cutting away of dead-wood. Deadwood such as she, Janine Starseeker, overdue for retirement and working on borrowed time through the kindness of the Organization, because what the hell would she *do* if they shipped her back to Earth? She hadn't seen the place for forty years. All her friends were here on Goronwy.

So she got older, she felt more tired and her body hurt more when she crawled out of bed in the morning, no matter how many facials she underwent. God, what a drag life was for an old woman!

How old was Susanna? Now there was a thought. She looked to be in her mid-twenties, but she didn't seem to have aged a day since her arrival on Goronwy four years ago. And her position: Director of Health Services. Pretty damned good job for a woman of that age. Rumored to be the child of genetically altered parents, too. Could it be that immortals walked among them secretly, laughing at them?

Well, probably not. But nobody could deny that Susanna was

perfectly beautiful in a healthy, bouncy way; and remarkably good at her job, too. All she needed was a good man, thought Janine, whose own man had died ten years ago. But Susanna seemed in no hurry.

Coincidentally there came a knock on the door at that moment and a good man entered: Bryn Trevithick. Now *there* was a real gentleman. Always dressed well, never late for work, and she was quite sure his apartment was spotless. Thirty-six, although one might think he was older. A fine catch for any girl. Yes, things had looked up in Operations since Bryn's coming.

"Janine, may I have a word?" The poor man looked worried.

"Sit down, if you've got time." Would he notice her facial? He sat neatly, none of the sprawl affected by some of the junior members of his staff. He even hitched up his uniform pants to preserve immaculate creases. Obviously he'd been used to wearing expensive organic fibers on Earth. She left her desk and sat in the chair opposite him. "Something to drink? I have a good local mead."

"No, thanks." He seemed to be wondering where to start. The Goronwy morning was short; maybe he'd suggest they had lunch together. It would be good for her morale, sitting with a young man in the canteen. At last he said, "I've been looking through my staff's personnel files."

"Oh, yes?"

"Gary died yesterday, you probably know. He was my best man. At least, it seems that way to me." He rubbed his eyes tiredly. He looked exhausted. Rumor had it that he'd been with Security until midnight. "So I thought I'd see what else I've got. I haven't even caught up with reviewing all the projects we're involved in, yet."

"It takes time to settle in." She felt herself smiling sympathetically.

He leaned forward. "Janine, why are we so poorly staffed in Operations? You have just one assistant in Earth Sciences. I have thirty-two people in Ecology. Twenty-eight of those were born on Goronwy. I'm not suggesting that makes them stupid, but it does mean they haven't had the benefits of education on Earth."

She said quietly, "I know what you're saying. The fact is, there's no formal education in any of the Operation sciences on Goronwy. Not in Earth Sciences, Engineering or Ecology."

He looked shocked. "Why not, for God's sake?"

"Not enough pupils. You can train to be a cook, or a Personnel Officer, or a finance clerk—any of the Support jobs. Support is big. Operations is small. It's the nature of the beast."

"So you're saying my people learned on the job?"

"That, and home study courses. The Guilds allow a special dispensation for people born off-Earth. Didn't you talk to your staff about their qualifications?"

He shifted uncomfortably. "Well, you don't exactly go around asking people how they got their Guild membership. They can be sensitive about that kind of thing."

"With good reason."

"And there's another thing I found out. I went back a few years and followed the careers of some past members of Ecology. And I found that the best qualified people had either been fired, or transferred elsewhere."

"Elsewhere?"

"To Samaritan projects on different worlds. You see what that means? A good ecologist isn't wanted on Goronwy, but he might be ideal for a project somewhere else."

He'd certainly been doing some digging. Should she tell him what she'd overheard one of his staff saying to another? *Our new Director? He won't rock the boat. Didn't you know? He was broken by the Annecy business.* No, it wouldn't be fair. Why upset him more? Staff always gossip about their bosses, but she was beginning to think Bryn Trevithick was tougher than his people realized.

Instead she said, "Your predecessor is still on Goronwy."

"Marik Darwin? Yes, so I believe. He held the Directorship for six years." He paused thoughtfully. "He must have fought a few battles before he left. Murdo tells me he quit on a matter of principle. I'm going to have a chat with him the first chance I get. He may be able to tell me what's going on around this place. Here we are, supposed to be helping the gorons with a biological problem, but we don't have the biological knowledge to carve a turkey."

"Have you talked to your assistant?"

"Ivor? Not about this, specifically. He's too busy keeping the projects going." He sighed. "Sorry to trouble you, Janine. I guess I just needed a willing ear. There's nothing you can do about this, and I'm sure you have enough problems of your own. I'll get out of your hair."

She kept him as long as she could, chatting of this and that, but eventually he left and the small office seemed empty with-out him. But not for too long. Half an hour later a tap on the door announced Susanna, Director of Health Services, blonde with a heart-shaped face and a wide smile, and possibly genetically enhanced.

"So . . ." she said, regarding Janine's face closely. "Looks good to me. Should last a few more years, eh?" She sat in the chair recently vacated by Trevithick, crossing strong legs with a swirl of full white skirt.

Janine didn't want to talk about years. Regarding the somewhat flamboyant figure, she asked curiously, "Don't you ever wear your uniform?"

Susanna laughed. "You want to know why they give us uniforms, with all those little pips and symbols? To reinforce a class structure the Samaritan Organization pretends doesn't exist. So piss on uniforms, that's what I say. I don't need little gold blobs on my shoulder to prove I'm better than five thousand other people." She smiled her broad smile. "Neither do you."

"I rather think I do, these days," said Janine sadly.

"With your nice new face, and all that? You look great."

"The face is fine. It's the morale that needs a lift." And it didn't help, subconsciously comparing herself with this beautiful creature opposite. "I'm deadwood and I know it. And yet I'm a Director. This means I have nothing to strive for, nothing to look forward to. It's demoralizing. I've been demor-alized for a number of years now. I don't have the guts to retire voluntarily. Why in God's name doesn't the Organization fire me or something? I really *believed* in the Goronwy Project, you know. But I don't think I've contributed anything for years."

"My God. What's brought all this on?"

"Bryn Trevithick," she admitted frankly. "I'm thirty years too old for him. He was in here half an hour ago."

"I *thought* there was a lingering warmth in this seat. So you fancy the guy, do you? I haven't had the chance to speak to him yet, but I don't think he's my type. A tad too serious. A man who goes by the book. Ah, well, one day I'll hear the clanking and rattling and the thudding of hooves, and a knight in white armor will snatch me up and carry me off on his charger. Somehow I don't cast Bryn Trevithick in that role. Too bad." Susanna shrugged, clearly not too concerned. "So. Aside of the gulf in your ages, what else did you discuss? I'm interested."

"We didn't actually discuss the gulf." Janine described the conversation and Trevithick's misgivings about his staff.

Susanna listened with wide-eyed attention. If only her eyes weren't so goddamned *blue*, thought Janine. If only there were some flaw in that perfection.

"Perhaps I should tell you," said Susanna at last, "that Trevithick may have good reason for concern. Even his own presence here follows the pattern. He screwed up royally on Annecy by all accounts, and yet here he is, Director of Ecology on Goronwy."

"I don't believe the rumors about Annecy," said Janine flatly. "He's a meticulous kind of man. Like you said, he goes by the book. The Annecy thing has got to be exaggerated somehow."

As she finished, her terminal uttered a beep. She left her armchair and pressed a function key. "Public announcement," she said. "We may as well hear it."

"Probably the lottery draw," said Susanna as she joined Janine at the desk. They watched the screen together . . .

After a couple of minutes Susanna whispered, "My God. Maybe I was wrong about that guy."

The conversation with Janine Starseeker had lit a fire in Trevithick's belly. He hadn't mentioned the fact that he'd looked up her history too, in the files; and that of her only assistant, Gwendoline

Oxblood. And he'd learned that Janine was well qualified for her job whereas Gwendoline's training had been in the nebulous area of social studies.

He'd looked up the other Operations Director: Ralph Greene of Engineering. Here the picture had been quite different. Greene had a staff of over one hundred. Why the contrast between Engineering on one hand, and Ecology and Earth Sciences on the other? Was it because Engineering was responsible for the maintenance of the Goronwy Project's machinery and services, whereas Ecology and Earth Sciences devoted themselves to solving goron problems? In other words, was the Goronwy Project more concerned with looking after itself than meeting its objectives?

The answer to that question could be scary.

Back in his office he activated his terminal and sounded the alarm for a Department round table discussion. The tiled screen showed a mosaic of empty desks. Then people began to show up, hurriedly and guiltily, having heard his distinctive signal. He regarded the screen, collecting his thoughts. About two dozen faces stared back at him anxiously, wondering what had brought this on. A round table call just before lunch could only mean an emergency. And emergencies were unpopular in the relaxed environment of the Ecology Department.

Ivor Sabin, dark-haired and saturnine, spoke. "Everything okay, Bryn?"

"No," he snarled, surprised at the venom in his own voice. "Everything is *not* okay. You can forget about lunch, all of you." As he spoke, a few other compartments of the screen filled with worried faces. "And this discussion is going out public, all domes. I want any Samaritan who happens to be watching to hear exactly what Ecology is doing toward fulfilling our purpose here on Goronwy." That should shake them up a bit, he thought. Once the word got around the domes that dirty linen was being washed, people would call one another to the monitors. And then his staff would find themselves trying to justify their work to several thousand fascinated viewers.

"You can't do that, Bryn," whispered Sabin, appalled.

"I've done it. We're going out live. As from now."

"But—"

"Right, let's get on with it," said Trevithick firmly. "I've called this meeting in the interests of cooperation. If we're to solve the problems of Goronwy we've each got to understand our contribution to the overall picture. We want no duplication of effort, no overlaps in responsibility. I'll run through the current situation, then I'm going to ask you each in turn to summarize, briefly, the purpose of your research and how it contributes to the overall objective. Later I'll be inviting comments from any Samaritan, of any Division, Branch or whatever. All right?"

A screenful of sullen nodding. To the right, a digital read-out showed 7% of the population of Samarita was already tuned in.

"This is going to take all day, Bryn," said Sabin faintly.

"And most of the evening. Now," he ran his eye across the screen seeking a lamb for his slaughterhouse, "Tom Feather. Before I begin, maybe you can tell everyone what you consider the role of Ecology to be."

The elderly man, gray-haired, lantern-jawed, blinked unhappily. "Uh. Well, we all know the gorons appealed to us for help, how long ago was it? Fifty years ago, I guess. That's what the Samaritan Organization is for, helping intelligent species in trouble." His voice rose defensively on the final words.

"Perhaps you'll remind us what particular trouble the gorons are in," prompted Trevithick gently. "Some of us seem to have forgotten." He glanced at the digital display. 17% audience. Looking good.

"Their hive-mother is sick. We call her Lady river. Maybe she's dying." Feather's delivery was becoming jerky with nerves. "If she dies, it's the end of all the gorons."

"And our objective?"

"To cure her, I guess. What else?"

"Thanks, Tom," said Trevithick. "You've got it. As you say, what else could we be here for, but to cure Lady? Okay. I'll run through our findings so far. Some of us may not be familiar with all of this."

It all centers on Lady River. We think Lady started as a kind of underwater queen bee, living in the big central lake. There were other Ladys. The males were mostly workers bringing food to her, probably weed and plankton. The earliest fossils we've found look like a kind of newt. We think there were guard males, and maybe warrior males. With more than one Lady there'd have been territorial wars over fishing grounds."

There were no interruptions as he described the increase in population over the millennia, the growing scarcity of food. Gorons crawling onto land to catch insects. The final war—there surely must have been one, although it wouldn't have been fought by gorons looking as they do now—and the single victorious Lady.

"She would have been the best-protected Lady, probably backed into a stream so her flanks couldn't be attacked."

"How big was she then?" asked somebody via the link.

"Pretty big. About the size of a terrestrial blue whale. And from then on, with all the males in the lake devoted to feeding her, and no enemies, she got bigger still, fast. Her stream backed up on the plain not far from Samarita and formed a lake. Then the lake overflowed and the stream flowed the other way, southward to the sea. There was nothing to prevent Lady growing bigger still, except food. The workers began to go further onto the land. And that's when the big change came."

He described how the newt like males, crawling around the fringes of the lake, discovered the firepots. Probably the first discovery had been of a toppled firepot, and the newt tried the remaining puddle of nectar and enjoyed it. And Lady enjoyed it too, when it was disgorged into her vast maw. "In fact she enjoyed it so much, she got into the habit of eating males who didn't bring nectar. So there was pressure on the newts to stand upright, and even to climb, so they could drink from the firepots. And over a few thousand generations, they evolved better means of doing it, and the ones that didn't, died off. The successful ones looked much like the gorons do now."

"How did they get to be intelligent?" came a question. It was becoming clear that the Project employees' knowledge of Goronwy's development was sketchy, to say the least.

"Who knows what triggers the development of intelligence? Our best guess is, it happened during competition with the vespas. They have their queens just like Lady, and they drink the same nectar. There would have been battles at the firepots while the gorons were discovering ways of avoiding being stung to death. This took survivalist cunning. Maybe that developed into intelligence. And after that, it was simply a matter of Lady spreading downstream, getting bigger and bigger, until eventually her tail end reached the sea."

Trevithick took a deep breath. "So then, naturally, Lady began to age, and get sick. Everything ages. It has to happen, or nothing would evolve. When the gorons realized what was happening they got scared and contacted the Samaritan Organization for help.

"So here we are. Helping. Or are we?"

CHAPTER 3

"**A**LL RIGHT, BACK TO YOU, **T**OM. Perhaps you'll share the details of your research with us."

Tom Feather gained confidence. He knew his job. "I'm involved in field studies, mostly. You haven't been here long, Bryn, so you probably haven't had a chance to observe the aeolus plant, for instance. It has the most fascinating musculature, somewhat similar to the terrestrial Venus flytrap. Currently I'm recording the time-lapse between the two colour phases according to ambient temperature and time of day. I'm getting the most surprising results." He was warming to his theme. "Would you believe the plant actually seems to *tire* with successive colour changes on days of intermittent cloud cover? And I'll tell you something else . . ."

Watching the earnest face as the man talked on, words from the far distant past began to run through Trevithick's mind:

He said, I hunt for haddock's eyes
Among the heather bright,
And work them into waistcoat buttons
In the silent night.

"Yes, I'm sure that's all very relevant to a cure for Lady," he said dryly. "Perhaps you'll explain to everyone just how relevant."

"It is absolutely vital," said Feather, "for us to understand fully the details of Goronwy's ecology, otherwise how can we begin to appreciate the factors that may account for Lady's sickness?"

Sabin broke in. "I should point out that all projects are approved at Board level, Bryn."

Trevithick eyed the screen sourly. People were beginning to look smug. The outside viewers had jumped to 33%. He'd lost the edge of his anger. He was in danger of making a fool of himself.

"Just one last question, Tom. How long have you been doing this?"

"Oh, three or four Goronwy years," said the man with obvious pride. "That may sound a long time, but there are an infinity of weather factors to consider, to say nothing of the differing subspecies of aeolus."

Disappointed with the glibness of the answers, Trevithick was in the process of selecting his next victim when he caught sight of Feather visibly relaxing. Quickly, he said, "Oh, by the way, Tom. How have your results been integrated with our main thrust of research on Lady herself?"

Feather looked aggrieved. "That's not for me to say, Bryn. Integration is what we have a Director for."

It was a good reply and it garnered a lot of chuckles. Trevithick felt himself flush. "I haven't been here long enough. Ivor, your comment?"

Sabin was clearly uncomfortable. "Actually, Tom's research hasn't yet reached the integrable stage."

Integrable? Was there such a word? "You mean nobody's using his stuff. All right," he said quickly, using the override to mute Ivor's retort, "Let's move on. You, Farra. A progress report, if you please."

It emerged that Farra, a dark-haired woman of about Trevithick's age, had been seconded to Security's Audit arm for the past year, checking catering records.

"Don't they have auditors of their own?" asked Trevithick.

"Oh, I'm not complaining at all, Bryn," she said. "I took a course in auditing. It's interesting work, and I really feel I'm making a contribution toward our presence here on Goronwy."

"And is Lady any healthier as a result of your contribution, Farra?"

She looked puzzled and didn't reply. Trevithick made a conscious effort to understand her thinking. There was something strange going on here. Or perhaps it wasn't strange at all; perhaps he was witnessing the normal evolution of a bureaucracy over fifty years. One by one his staff gave their reports, and at one point the outside viewers peaked at 57% before the sameness of the reports bored people and they began to switch off.

When the last staff member, one Ida Summers, had shared her interest in the dung constituents of the pied vespa with them, his temper had subsided to a kind of dull despair. Two of his staff, Lara Wing and Seth Rill, were working on research connected with Lady. The rest were playing around compiling a mammoth encyclopaedia of goron wildlife. Well, he couldn't blame them for obeying orders, and they obviously thought they were doing a great job.

But what had his predecessors been thinking of? And Ivor Sabin had been standing in since Darwin quit without getting a grip on things. He looked at the clock. It was early evening. Outside viewers stood at 24%.

"I'd like to thank you all," he said woodenly. "As you probably realize from the drift of my comments, I shall be making some changes in direction to place more emphasis on Lady herself. He wanted to shout *You stupid bastards! Hasn't any one of you the sense to see we've wasted fifty years farting around while Lady is dying?* But instead he said mildly, "I feel two people is rather a small team to be working on the core problem of Lady."

"Three," said Tom Feather.

"Three? Who's the other?"

"Gary Docksteader. He's not here at the moment."

Somebody said quietly, "Gary's dead, Tom, hadn't you heard?"

Feather looked shocked. The notion of death hung in the air, silencing people.

Finally Trevithick said, "So back to the big question. Here we are, but have we helped? Ask yourselves, you people who've been feeding one another, and looking after one another's personnel records, paying one anothers' salaries, and maintaining our machinery, and our health—all funded by Earthaid, who think the

Samaritan Organisation is a worthy cause. Have we helped the gorons and their hive-mother Lady river?

"Or have we just become a self-interested, self-centred colony, like Outward Ho on Deganwy?"

It was the comparison with of Outward Ho that sparked the outrage that followed, outweighing any soul-searching that might have resulted from Trevithick's more important points. Outward Ho was interested only in profit. Whereas the the humans here on Goronwy were Samaritans. They were good guys. The name said it all. Trevithick had insulted them.

It went down in history as the Ecology Confessional. About halfway through the broadcast, Susanna left Janine, went to her office and picked up her things, then hurried along the darkening street to her Ladyside apartment. A few gorons trotted here and there; members of Clan Service going about their tasks before everything closed down for the night. The lights were already on at the Passing Barge Inn and she was tempted to drop by for a glass of mead, but decided against it. The Confessional might come to a sudden, catastrophic end. The power might conveniently go out, or Trevithick's staff might go on strike, or sinisterly-uniformed members of Security might burst into Trevithick's office and drag him away, kicking and screaming.

And she wanted to catch the end of the show.

She reckoned herself a good judge of character, but she'd never been so wrong as in her estimation of Trevithick. He was a refreshing change from previous Directors of Ecology. And that sluggishness over the past two months? It must have been a methodical approach building up to the moment when he pounced. The cunning young fox.

Back at her apartment she dimmed the windows, poured herself a glass of mead, sat down at her home terminal and switched on. And there onscreen was Brent Twigg, typical Ecology loser, describing his progress in mapping the distribution of the bushtrap beetle and its natural enemy, the stoag dung fly. He would publish his findings any day now. Terrific. The three last members of Ecology staff followed, then Trevithick accused the Project of becoming self-serving, and all hell broke loose.

The public outcry lasted until midnight. Susanna watched in fascination as employee after employee voiced their outrage at Trevithick's comparison with Outward Ho, conveniently ignoring the main issue: the lack of progress in fifty years. Most of the complainants were recent immigrants and relatively low on the totem pole. Idealists, no doubt. Attracted into the Organisation by the brochures.

In time, they'd become just as complacent as the oldsters, happy to preserve the status quo. The last angry face had faded from the screen. She poured herself another glass of mead, went to the window and looked out. Lady flowed past, black and slow. A tiny light gleamed half a kilometre to the south. There, an aged goron would be committing himself physically to Lady, becoming food for her, his life's work finished. She crossed the room to the opposite window. The occasional street lights showed no pedestrians. Beyond, the domes loomed huge and speckled with lighted windows. There would be alarm and despondency in those domes tonight.

Then she sat back to consider the situation. The good news was that Trevithick's show had shaken people up. The bad news: What would happen to Trevithick now? Would he go the way of Gary Docksteader? There were forces at work on Goronwy, forces who did not stop short of murder, so it seemed.

The stakes were getting uncomfortably high.

But there was an alternative scenario. Supposing Trevithick survived to represent a constant thorn in the side of the enemy, whoever they were. Now if that were the case, they'd show their hand, sooner or later. Trevithick was the key, and an unexpect-ed one.

How could she ensure his survival?

With the possibilities neatly catalogued out in her excep-tion-al mind, she fell asleep in her chair.

———

The following morning Trevithick arranged a field trip with Ivor Sabin and the two people who had been working directly on the problem of Lady's sickness: Lara Wing and Seth Rill. He felt drained and defeated after a poor night's sleep. While he waited for them to show up, he took his glass of nectar onto the balcony at the back of his office and leaned on the rail above the sloping wall of the dome and some forty meters from the dirt road below. He did this every morning before starting work. Trevithick was scared of heights, and he found it useful to contemplate the possibility of the balcony rail collapsing. The adrenaline rush sharpened his mind and set him up for the day's work.

Four of the other five domes making up Samarita were in view, linked by spidery open walkways; Goronwy's atmosphere and climate were very similar to Earth. The only significant difference was the powerful pheromones emitted by the gorons and other social creatures, which eluded the domes' air filters and could play havoc with the emotions. Most humans took antifero pills against these.

A vespa buzzed into view and alighted on a balcony nearby. Trevithick kept a wary eye on it; the brutes were two meters long and their sting killed. Even a drop of their poison on the skin could cause a nasty burn; it was a powerful acid.

But they were the only dangerous life-forms on Goronwy—apart from certain humans as yet unidentified. The gorons themselves were peace loving. Their tight social clan structure may have seemed odd, but it was all very logical to them, and it worked well.

Or it did, until Lady fell sick.

Lady flowed beyond the domes, hive mother to all gorons, a gelatinous ribbon of life stretching from the huge central lake to the sea, a total distance of four hundred kilometres. The siting of Samarita had been chosen to suit the gorons. Seventy kilometres from the lake, it was the traditional point at which they fertilised Lady, and the lowest point at which they fed her. It could be said that Lady started to die from Samarita onwards. By the time she reached the sea, she was beginning to disintegrate.

Trevithick could see the gorons' shacks clearly from his balcony;

little wooden structures with leaf roofs, all brown and weathered by the sun. The ground around the domes was brown too. The plant life killed by the application of Trent's Vivicide had never come back. It had been found to affect animals as well as plants, although there was no concrete proof that it was affecting Lady.

The gorons bustled to and fro, members of every clan coming to Samarita, either to die, or to feed Lady, or just passing through on their way north. Some would be members of Clan Service, permanent residents who looked after travellers or, in a few cases, worked in the domes.

In his short time on Goronwy Trevithick had heard stories of ex-Samaritans who befriended gorons and, before long, went native. They lived in goron-like huts and philosophised their lives away. They cut themselves off from human contact and became, so it was said, gigantically fat. So fat, in fact, that the gorons began to see them as queen bees similar to Lady, and fed them nectar, which made them fatter still.

And when their hearts gave out, the gorons loaded them into coracles and rowed them out onto Lady, and tipped them in. Lady was always ready to receive them, although she had difficulty absorbing human cells and frequently rejected them after a brief sampling.

It might be an idea to see Marik Darwin soon, before all this happened to him.

The nearby gorons seemed to be happy on that day following the Confessional. Their pheromones were drifting past the balcony, and had the effect of improving Trevithick's mood. Maybe it wasn't such a bad morning after all. Just as well he'd forgotten to take his antifero pill in the rush that morning. Refreshed by the pheromones and the fear of falling, he went back into his office.

His fellow-passengers for the morning's flight sat there, glancing at him and at one another other apprehensively. Sabin, Wing and Rill. He activated his terminal and refreshed his memory on the latter two. Both had graduated from the Samarita School of Sociology within the past year. That meant they knew next to nothing about their current job. And they were barely out of their teens.

Ten minutes later they were seated in a small copter, following the sluggish path of Lady as she flowed south across the plain. Seth Rill sat at the controls, looking at ease—perhaps at little too casual. Trevithick sat beside him, Sabin and Lara Wing behind. At intervals they would see a goron barge heading southwards with its load of nectar. No wake trailed behind; Lady's surface was too viscous and the barges moved at little more than walking pace. In the far distance, the ocean showed as a thin luminous line across the horizon.

It was strange, thought Trevithick, how he felt no vertigo in this situation. As though the copter cabin was another planet with its own physical laws. Far below, he could see the Ladyside trail on the west bank, with stoag-towed barges making the laborious four-hundred kilometre journey upstream from Ladysend to Ladysmouth. The barges might have been beetles on a map. There was no sensation of fearsome height.

"I have to tell you, Bryn," Sabin broke a long silence, "that was an ill-advised ordeal you put us through yesterday. A lot of our people are very unhappy about it. Extremely unhappy. There's been an incalculable effect on staff morale, as if Gary's death wasn't enough. And there will be repercussions from elsewhere, believe me."

Trevithick twisted around. "To hell with staff morale," he snarled. He'd heard enough negative comment recently. "What's the good of morale if our direction is all wrong? And as for repercussions from elsewhere, what exactly do you mean?"

"Well, as I said previously, all our projects were approved by the Board at one time or another. When you criticise our direction, you're criticising the Board's judgement."

"That's my problem, Ivor."

"I just wish you'd spoken to me before taking this step. We'd have been able to sort something out, I'm sure. Now the staff are all pissed off and everything we do is going to be questioned by outsiders."

Sabin could be right. It was one of the worries that had kept Trevithick awake through the short Goronwy night. Had he acted too hastily? Had he in some way been lashing out in revenge for the grilling Security had given him over Docksteader's death? If so, he'd chosen the wrong target.

"It's done. What's the point in talking about it?" He allowed Ivor a moment to scowl and brood, then turned his attention to the young woman. "So, Lara. Last night you told us you were working on data gathered from the lower reaches of Lady, right?"

"About twenty kilometres north of Ladysend," she said brightly. "The location will be coming up soon."

"And what was the data?"

"Results of the analysis of samples from the decaying areas. There, see! There's the first of them."

The surface of Lady had changed. Now she resembled a frozen river beginning to thaw in patches—except that the patches were a yellowish colour.

"It doesn't look good," Trevithick observed. Rill reset the controls and dropped them to within a hundred meters of the surface.

"They're like pools of pus," Lara Wing explained, wrinkling her nose in disgust. "They spread as she approaches the coast, until a few kilometres from Ladysend she begins to fall apart."

"What were your findings?"

"Lady's system for production of phagocytes is breaking down. The pus comes about when Lady's equivalent to our white blood cells attacks an infection caused by a puncture in her skin." Brown eyes regarded Trevithick gravely. "Would you believe we actually used boats with *propellers* on Lady when we first arrived? Goodness knows what damage we did. Anyway, by rights her phagocytes should move in to scavenge the pus, but this isn't happening and secondary infections are setting in."

"Can we synthesise phagocytes and treat her?"

"I imagine we can."

"Who's working on that aspect, Ivor?"

The dark man looked uncomfortable. "Well, actually it's on the back burner right now, Bryn, but—"

"Top priority, Ivor. Select a team as soon as we get back to Samarita and let me have a working plan by tonight."

"But—"

"No buts. Just do it." Trevithick was getting very tired of his assistant.

They followed Lady down as far as the straggle of buildings at Ladysend. Most of these were grass-roofed goron huts, but there was a group of larger square buildings that bore the stamp of human architecture. They stood a little apart, facing the ocean, unlike the huts that clung to the west bank of Lady.

"That's the nursery and the school," said Seth. "Bridget Booker's babies." He chuckled. "The only ones she's likely to have."

"She's a very nice woman," said Lara reprovingly.

Seth's reply was to bank the copter steeply and drop to within ten meters of Lady. Patches of decaying matter flashed past as they headed back north. An unpleasant smell became evident. Lara closed her eyes, clearly troubled by the impression of headlong speed.

"Up a bit," said Trevithick.

"Sure thing."

Trevithick left his stomach somewhere around the fifty-meter mark as Seth keyed in an immediate altitude change. The copter ceilinged out abruptly at two hundred meters, lifting them off their seats for an instant. Trevithick began to form a dislike for the young research assistant.

"Okay," he said. "Now you, Seth. What have you been up to?"

"Well, Director, I guess I've established that the major cause of skin punctures in Lady is squitos." He lolled back in his seat, staring absently at the horizon, deadwood in the making. "I guess—"

"Don't guess, Seth," said Trevithick gently. "Either you've established it or you haven't. We all looked like fools last night. I'd like to think we learned something from it."

Seth Rill sat up and shot an aggrieved glance at Sabin in the mirror, as if seeking support. "Yeah. Well, you've seen the squitos, they're all over Lady in the reaches around Samarita. They lay their eggs below her surface and at the same time they squirt a shot of gunk in that sets up a mild infection. If they didn't do this, Lady'd move in and absorb their eggs the same way she absorbs gorons that jump in. He scratched his sandy hair. "Helluva problem. We could try to kill all the squitos, I guess. Easy enough to spray them, so long as we didn't spray Lady at the same time. Hardly the ecological way out though, is it?"

"Any other ideas?"

"I guess not."

"Check into the squitos natural enemies, large and small. We don't want to upset the balance of nature here, but that doesn't mean we can't tilt it a little if it means less eggs laid in Lady."

"The termites—the gorons, I mean—they use some parasite to keep squitos off the barges. Crabs, we call them."

"Look into it. Now, what about Docksteader? What kind of progress had he made?"

Seth twisted round and looked at Lara. She looked back at him blankly.

"You mean you don't know? Didn't you think it was your business to find out? Has nobody ever told you about team-work?"

Sabin had withdrawn into his shell for a sulk. Lara was gazing at Trevithick wide-eyed, as though he'd come up with a bold new concept.

Eventually Seth spoke. "I guess he was doing okay. He was all excited a couple days ago. He didn't say why."

"He was working on the aging process," volunteered Wing, coming out of her trance. "Lady ages just like us, and some people reckon that's what her problem is. She's just dying of old age." She glanced at Trevithick guiltily. "A lot of people in Ecology think that."

"It's kind of demoralising," said Seth. "Kind of makes a fellow wonder, what's the use?"

Trevithick controlled his temper with an effort. These people had to be won over diplomatically. "Thanks for your help. Be prepared to review your projects with me in detail this afternoon. And Ivor, you and I had better take a look at Docksteader's work." As they began to descend toward the Samarita pad, he said, "And by the way. I'll expect every member of Ecology to show up for work in uniform from now on."

"Oh, shit, Director," whined Seth. "Nobody in Ops wears a uniform. It's what distinguishes us from Support."

"So make sure your Ecology flashes are stuck on. Then they'll know who you are, for what it's worth."

The copter touched down. They stepped to the ground and gathered around Trevithick apprehensively, as though wondering what discipline he might impose next. "Back to work, you two," he said to Seth and Lara. "Now, Ivor, let's go and take a look at Docksteader's project."

"Docksteader impressed me, the little I saw of him," said Trevithick as they made their way to the laboratories. "He struck me as the brightest of our people. I'll tell you this, but keep it to yourself. That story Security have released about his death being an accident is untrue. Gary was murdered."

"Oh, yes?" said Sabin

"You don't seem very surprised."

"I don't surprise easy. If Gary had been killed by a vespa, Safety would have been filling the air with warnings by now. Never step outside. Wear a bloody wet-suit in the blazing sun. Carry half a tonne of sting balm at all times. But they haven't. So his death wasn't from natural causes. So how did he die?"

"Cut in half by a laser rifle and left under a bushtrap. If I hadn't come along, that plant would have carried him off and pulled him into little pieces. So far as everyone is concerned, he'd have disappeared without trace. So what I want to know is, why Gary?"

"No idea. People liked him. He was good at organising events and suchlike. He used to help Martha Sunshine out in his spare time, putting on shows and things. Voluntary stuff."

"So he didn't have any enemies, and yet someone wanted him out of the way. And he was one of our best people. What does that tell you, Ivor?"

Sabin was looking very unhappy. "Politics?"

They entered the laboratory, a huge area with workstations clustered in the centre, benches and equipment along the walls. Most of the equipment extended into other areas behind the walls, where maintenance technicians worked. Only the interactive parts lined the lab walls; the tip of the iceberg, as it were. It looked as though the staff were all there; no doubt anxious to display enthusiasm after the Confessional.

There were many more workstations than staff; a sign of the gradual erosion of Operations Division over the years.

Docksteader's workstation consisted of a desk with monitor, keyboard, mike, proximation headset and a box of disks. Pathetic reminders were also in view: a mug with a picture of a pair of sparkling and obviously female eyes on it, a complex puzzle made of short rods and connectors, and a small hologram which, when Trevithick activated it, displayed a naked young woman.

"Anyone we know?" he asked.

Sabin shook his head. "Probably some girlfriend back on the Old Planet. I guess we'd better find out."

Docksteader had been one of the few members of Ecology to undergo their training on Earth, and had been here on a three-Earth-year tour. Trevithick regarded the hologram thoughtfully. The tiny image appeared to smile at him, then it waved and switched itself off. He wondered how often Gary had activated the device, and how the girl would feel when she received the warp-wire notifying her of his death.

Someone had put a bunch of aeolus on the desk, in a small pink vase. A nice thought. "Who did that?" Trevithick asked.

"One of the women, I guess. He was a bit of a lady's man."

This opened another avenue. "What about jealousy as a motive?"

"Maybe. I don't know. Ask the women."

"No, I was just curious. Investigation is Security's job. So let's take a look at his work, shall we?"

Five minutes later Trevithick had established that the directories containing Docksteader's work were all empty. All files had been deleted and only the directories themselves—which required Ivor's voiceprint to delete—were left.

Trevithick stared grimly at the empty shells on the screen. "Okay, Ivor. What the hell's happened to everything?"

"Search me."

"I may do just that. What's going on here? You've been in charge of this place."

Sabin was looking apprehensive. "Anyone could have done it."

"You mean there's no security? Hell, I rely on you to handle that kind of thing. Are you saying that anyone could have walked over to this workstation and simply wiped everything out? It was all protected with Docksteader's voiceprint, wasn't it? With you as an alternate, of course."

"People get round the voiceprints with audio tapes. It happens all the time. Nothing sinister, Bryn. People get sick and other people need access to their stuff. That kind of thing. Teamwork," he concluded with a faint grin.

Trevithick could feel the beginnings of a headache coming on. A glass of Goronwy mead would go down well right now, he thought. "Come to my office," he said abruptly. Minutes later they were seated in the supposedly soundproof office, although Trevithick was beginning to suspect the very walls by now, and with some justification. "I want you to tell me exactly what's going on here, Ivor. If I'm not satisfied with your reply, I'll have to reconsider your position."

"Fire me? What for?"

"Let me ask the questions. Now, Docksteader was working on Lady's aging process. Somebody murdered him. Somebody's wiped out his work. Therefore somebody feels threatened by Docksteader and/or his research. Who and why? Your move, Ivor."

"You were never like this on Annecy."

"I've learned my lesson."

"All right," said Sabin suddenly, "I'll give it to you straight. Let's suppose Docksteader had proved conclusively that Lady is incurable. Maybe she's simply dying of old age and there's nothing can be done about it. That would mean our purpose on Goronwy is finished. We can do no more. So we'd have apologise to the gorons, pack our bags and take the next shuttle out, okay? Well, more than half our staff were born here. This is their home. And now they've all got to uproot and never come back, because of Docksteader and

34

a bunch of tiny little electrical charges in his computer. Bryn, any one of them could have wiped that kind of data out and the others would have stood by cheering."

"Good grief. Would they have killed him for the same reason?"

"They might. Who knows? You're not talking just Ecology now. You have maybe three thousand candidates in Samarita. Bound to be a few weirdoes among them."

"Did he talk to people about his discovery? If there was a discovery."

"Who knows? He probably blabbed to a couple of the staff, and you can bet it spread from there. He never said anything to me, but he wouldn't have done yet, see? Not until he was cast-iron sure. He was that kind of guy."

"He'd have backed up his research on disks," said Trevithick thoughtfully. "I'll go and take a look at his apartment. And I think I'll get a warpwire off to Earth, tell them what's going on here. It sounds as though half Samarita doesn't want Ecology to come up with any answers. That means we have bigger problems than I realised."

CHAPTER 4

THE BIG WOMAN STOOD AT HER OFFICE window looking out at Lady and trying not to think about chocolate, or C2 as her food dispenser described it. Worry always channeled her thoughts in one tasty direction. Her present weight—so Martha Sunshine told people rude enough to comment—was an indication of how much she worried. Meaning how devoted she was to the job.

The current worry centered on replacing the late Gary Docksteader. He'd been a willing organizer, and always ready to understudy in those pathetic little shows Entertainment put on from time to time. Now Gary was dead. A lot of people would have wasted time regretting his passing, but not Martha. She had to find a replacement, and quickly.

There were some five thousand people in Samarita. You'd think she'd be able to rustle up a decent cast for a mystery play out of five thousand people. *Epitaph for a Muscan* opened in seven days time. But it was like trying to raise volunteers to explore a black hole. She'd never known such a reluctant, talentless bunch of layabouts. It was enough to make a woman turn to C2. Who would be Director of Entertainment in a hole like Samarita?

"Abigail, come in here, please."

Abigail Fern had been born on this godforsaken world and bore its unmistakable stamp. The pale complexion, the lank hair, the laid-back attitude. Even the weird handmade clothing. She'd read somewhere that Abigail meant handmaiden. What sort of a woman would have chosen a name like that?

The wretched woman gazed at her blandly. "Yeah?"

Forty years old and looking sixty. No make-up.

"You probably heard Gary Docksteader's been murdered. Well—"

But Abigail had assumed a dramatic pose, knuckles to mouth, eyes wide. "M-murdered?" she stammered. Maybe there was a place for her in *Epitaph for a Muscan*.

A minor error on Martha's part. One forgot that people like Abigail were not privy to inside information. "My mistake, I believe it was an accident. I guess I had our next production on my mind. Anyway, Gary's gone, and he leaves a gap. I'm going to need you to fill it until we find someone else. That means some voluntary work on your part. Distributing posters, handling tickets, maybe some work at rehearsals. You have a clear voice. You might take over Gary's prompting work."

Abigail was aghast. "I can't *do* that kind of thing, Martha. I really *can't*. You know how nervous I am, dealing with people. And *prompting!* I'd be *petrified!*"

The chocolate withdrawal was affecting Martha's temper. "You'll bloody well do as you're told, Martha, and that's an end to it. Now, what's the latest on *Barker Sam?*"

Instantly Abigail was transformed. In a hushed and excited whisper, she said, "A warpwire arrived just a minute ago." She flourished a piece of paper before laying it on Martha's palm like some kind of offering.

The gesture was almost unbearably irritating. Martha glanced at the short warpwire. YOUR MESSAGE RECEIVED RE BARKER SAM. SHOW WILL BE HELD OVER IN READINESS. KEEP US UP TO DATE WITH DEVELOPMENTS. PENDA, OUTWARD HO, DEGANWY.

"Isn't it *exciting!*" exclaimed Abigail. "I never thought Outward Ho would let us have the show. I mean, *Barker Sam* has broken all records on Deganwy. And, well, the Organization and Outward Ho aren't exactly the best of friends, are they?"

"*Barker Sam* is big enough to make its own bookings. It's no business of Outward Ho's where the show goes when it leaves Deganwy. They know that and we know that. We maintain a pretense of cooperation."

"So it's coming to Goronwy?" persisted Abigail. "I mean, we're really going to put *Barker Sam* on?"

"The *Barker Sam* people put it on, not us. There's a whole ship-load of them; it's a big show. We just sit back and watch it happen."

Abigail fluttered out and Martha turned her attention to more important matters. She activated her console, brought up a spreadsheet and began carefully to schedule possibilities and consider alternatives.

Manning Edlin, the Director of Communications and currently Chairman of the Board, was also considering alternatives. There were certain advantages in being Director of Communications. It meant that he was at the hub, able to control major events for the simple reason that most data leaving the planet of Goronwy passed through his department. And the same applied to arriving data, too.

He held one such piece of data in his hands at that moment. It was a copy of the warpwire that had so excited Martha Sunshine's secretary.

He considered it. Presumably Martha would bring it up at the next Board meeting. But it seemed the *Barker Sam* thing was going ahead, and this made him uneasy. Not that he minded an extravagant and entertaining show in Samarita; that was good for morale. It was the prospect of a large number of people suddenly arriving from off-world. Doing the tourist thing, befriending the Samaritans, uncovering things best left covered . . .

That had been a bloody stupid act of Bryn Trevithick's, that Confessional.

Suppose word got back to Earth? In particular, Earthaid. Suppose that benevolent but shrewd body heard that the Organization had been frigging around on Goronwy for fifty years without coming up with anything that benefited the gorons? Suppose the Samaritan HQ itself got to hear of it?

It would create a very unpleasant situation.

Edlin prided himself in his calmness under pressure. Big handsome face, steel-gray hair, erect bearing; he spent much of his off-duty time watching videos of himself, ever on the lookout for ways to improve his manner and his image. The rest of the time he spent in Martha Sunshine's fitness center. He was in great shape. According to Samaritan gossip, even his stools were sterile.

But the Confessional had caught him off-balance.

Damage control was called for. Should he notify the Old Planet before they got the news from someone else, such as some bloody *pierrot* from the *Barker Sam* troupe?

The problems of Ecology were not his. In no way could he be blamed, except indirectly as Chairman of the Board. When was *Barker Sam* coming? In a month's time? Six months? Suppose someone else leaked the story while his back was turned? He couldn't monitor every syllable that passed through his department. And there were a few items his people never saw. Martha Sunshine, for instance, had a special dispensation to send and receive warpwires directly. It was necessary; she was always communicating with distant worlds, arranging shows. Murdo, the muscan Director of Personnel, also sent and received stuff directly.

So that problem was insoluble, for the time being. But he could do something to forestall any fallout, at least. What he had in mind was a tad underhand, but Manning Edlin was able to tell himself that he was acting in the best interests of Samarita.

Ten minutes later a minor communications clerk knocked on the door and opened it without being invited. Edlin was speaking rapidly into his audio pickup. The large face of Murdo, Director of Personnel, loomed out of the screen. "Get out!" snapped Edlin.

Shaken by this uncharacteristic lack of control, the clerk reported back to his supervisor.

"Something's eating the Cool Ruler. Better keep our heads down for a while."

Shocked, Bryn Trevithick stared at the wreckage of Gary Docksteader's apartment.

All Samarita apartment blocks were built on the same pattern. Outside steps and walkways linked two-storey structures, perched on stilts to avoid flooding when storm water flowed over the top of Lady, as it frequently did. The size and basic furnishings of the apartment varied according to the status of the employee.

Gary's place was small, and it looked as though a herd of stoags had been turned loose in there. A table lay on its side, a cheap two-piece suite had been slashed to ribbons, two tall bookcases had been tipped over and the books, valuable collectors items, lay scattered over the carpet.

Lara whispered, "Who on earth would do a thing like this?"

Even the food dispenser, standard Organization issue, had been wrenched from the wall and pulled apart. Plastic bags of ingredients had been cut open and the contents dumped onto the floor.

Trevithick picked up a small china model of a terrestrial rabbit. It had lost one ear. Docksteader must have brought it from Earth. It was probably a good-luck gift from that girl in the hologram. He placed it gently on the only shelf that hadn't been torn from the wall.

"Whoever it was," he said, "my guess is they were looking for Gary's back-up disks." Everything had begun to fit together into a very sinister pattern.

"Do you think they found them?"

"I doubt it. If they'd found them there wouldn't be such a mess. They'd never have dismantled the food dispenser except as a last resort. My guess is they went away empty-handed, and they don't know where to look next. You knew him better than me. Where would you look for Gary's disks?"

She picked her way through debris and stood at the window, her back to him, watching Lady flow by. "I don't think I'd look," she said.

"What do you mean? They've got to be somewhere."

"No, they haven't. Like you said, I knew him better than you. He . . . was the kind of guy that didn't bother to back up his work. Yes, I know what you're going to say. It's against the rules. But Gary didn't think in terms of rules. He would get these bright ideas, and work in a kind of fever until he'd finished, maybe in the middle of the night. Then he'd just switch off his workstation and go straight to the inn, you know the Passing Barge? Everybody goes there. Backing up his work would never occur to him."

"The Passing Barge? Did he meet anyone in particular there?" Trevithick joined her at the window. An A-frame vessel was slipping by on the far side of Lady, stoags climbing the drive belt, goron bargee dozing on the foredeck. It was a peaceful scene, preferable to looking at the wreckage of the dead man's home.

"He might meet any of us, or none of us. We never bothered to make arrangements."

Trevithick tried to visualize the scene. Gary Docksteader, fired up as he often was, bounding into the goron inn where they'd raised the roof to accommodate human and muscan customers. Operations staff would be there, making merry. Would he join them, and drink with them, and hold forth on his latest triumph?

Maybe . . . or maybe not. Maybe they wouldn't be interested. Most of them would have put in a day's work, and as Trevithick had already discovered, their work didn't excite them. They would tend to put a damper on Gary's enthusiasm.

"Did he ever talk much to anyone else? Someone outside Ecology?" A picture was building up in his mind. "Someone he could bounce his ideas off? Maybe someone who usually sits alone? Maybe someone with a background in ecology but not active in the field right now?"

Lara looked at him, surprised. "You must have seen them talking."

"Seen who?"

"Gary and Lath Eagleman. Gary often talked to Lath, heaven only knows why. He couldn't have gotten much sense out of him."

"Maybe he didn't need to. I think all he needed was a willing ear." Lath Eagleman . . . Son of Samarita's first senior biologist, Paul Eagleman. Elderly, thin, incurable alcoholic and mentally subnormal to boot. It would be difficult to discuss Docksteader's research with Lath Eagleman, but he'd have to try.

There was little that could be done here, anyway. The apartment had been turned over by experts.

A recent conversation came back to him.

"You were born on Goronwy, Lara. You've lived with the Lady situation all your life. Suppose Gary had established that Lady's deterioration is irreversible, so there'd be no point in us staying here? How would you feel about packing up and leaving?"

"It'd be rather exciting, wouldn't it? To see somewhere else, to go and work on another world."

"And never come back?"

"Well, that might be kind of tough when I get older and start to feel nostalgic like old people do. But I'm only twenty. If you want to settle down, you don't join the Organization. You sign on with Outward Ho and go to live in one of their new colonies."

Her outlook was quite different from the norm suggested by Sabin. Refreshing. "Does everyone think like you?"

"Some of us. Seth Rill, for one. I know he doesn't come across too well, but he's a bright boy. Gary was bright, too, but he was trained on Earth, so he would be." She sighed, acknowledging the fact sadly. "He used to say Ivor Sabin stifled him. That's probably why Ivor doesn't know too much about Gary's work. Gary had learned not to show his hand. Yes, there are quite a few people who'd be happy to leave Goronwy. But that's nothing to the number who want to stay."

"And they'd do anything to stay here?"

She turned from the view and looked directly at him, brown eyes suddenly serious. "Yes. Anything."

He was about to ask her opinion on the lengths she meant by the word 'anything', when footsteps sounded on the stair outside. He caught hold of her arm and drew her into the bathroom. "Keep quiet," he whispered. Possibly the searchers had returned. If so, they would be discovered quickly enough. But before that happened they might overhear some snippet of conversation that would give some clue as to what this was all about.

They heard the door click open. There was a gasp of surprise. A female gasp. Then the door closed and the footsteps receded.

"Come on!" Trevithick hurried out of the bathroom and plowed through the wreckage to the nearest window. Bright sunlight gilded the dusty ground, and a woman was walking briskly away from the bottom of the steps. Shoulder-length golden hair swung as she walked, glowing in the sun. She wore a pale blue dress, knee-length, with a dark blue belt matching sensible shoes. She was strongly built rather than slim, with a narrow waist and muscular legs. She walked lightly but confidently, like a talented dancer.

Trevithick heard Lara chuckle. "You groaned," she said. "I definitely heard you groan with lust. Why, Director, how could you!"

"I did *not* groan. I was clearing my throat. Why isn't that woman wearing a uniform?" he asked sourly. No doubt about it, the rear view was enormously attractive.

"She's Manager of Health Services. I guess at that level you can dress casually if you want to. Her name's Susanna."

"Susanna what?"

"Just Susanna, so far as I know."

Risking derision from Lara he activated the window zoom, bringing the woman into close-up. At that moment she turned, blonde hair swinging. She glanced back toward the apartment. He felt a sudden thud in his chest as large blue eyes seemed to look directly into his. He caught a glimpse of an engagingly wide mouth with full lips, plump cheeks and a broad forehead, then she'd turned a corner and was gone.

He took a deep breath. "What's the Manager of Health Services doing snooping around a dead man's apartment?"

Again the knowing chuckle. "Hit you hard, did she? I believe she does that to men. Too bad. She's pretty fierce competition for the rest of us."

"Spare me the social chitchat, Lara. What was she doing here? By now everybody knows Gary's dead, Health in particular. They'll have charge of the body."

"Listen, I'd rather not talk about Gary any more." Her voice was suddenly quiet. "Anyway, I don't suppose she came for the same reason as us. She has no use for Gary's research."

Resolutely he tried to put that enchanting figure out of his mind, but the image of those eyes remained. Good grief, he hadn't been so affected by a face and figure for years. If ever. Odd that their paths hadn't crossed during the past two months. Maybe he should find some way of ensuring they did cross. He sighed. What was the use, anyway? He was a bit of a nerd, a failure at his last post, unimpressive physically, never particularly popular with women.

"I don't think she has a boyfriend," he heard Lara say mischievously.

"Not my type." He tried to meet her halfway.

"Then there's got to be something wrong with you."

"Forget it. Let's get out of here. This place gives me the creeps. I'll call Security and have them come and investigate. There's something pretty strange going on around here, Lara."

"It's taken you two months to find *that* out?"

He tried to slam the door behind them but the lock was broken.

CHAPTER 5

"**B**EFORE WE GET INTO THE MAIN BUSINESS of the meeting," said Manning Edlin, "an extraordinary item has come up." He waited for the buzz of interest to die down. "A few minutes ago a warp-wire arrived from the Old Planet that has an immediate effect on ourselves as the Board of Directors."

The weekly Board meeting. Usually an occasion of unmitigated boredom, although last week's meeting had been enlivened by a discussion of the Confessional. The directors sat at the long table. Some were human, some muscan. Bryn Trevithick sat between Janine Starseeker and Ralph Greene, representing the Operations bloc. Outside the window, the early afternoon sun glinted on the domes of Samarita. Business as usual. Nothing had happened in the last fifty years and nothing was likely to happen today, the members of the Board seemed to be thinking.

Until Manning Edlin, Director of Systems and Communications and Chairman of the Board, made his opening remarks.

"Get on with it," said Ralph Greene, Director of Engineering. "Don't keep us in suspense, man!"

"I don't know how best to handle this," said Edlin. "To put it bluntly it seems there's been an about-face by HQ in the matter of staffing. In particular, the Department of Ecology."

There was a sick feeling in Trevithick's stomach. "They can't cut my staff any further. Good grief, I'm down to the bare bones already!"

"Uh, it's not your staff, Bryn."

"What is it, then?"

"It's you. They've abrogated your contract."

The words took a moment to sink in. Trevithick's voice did not work properly as he said, "You mean they've fired me? Is that what you mean?"

"I'm very sorry, Bryn. I'm sure we all are."

There came a brief and amazed silence, then: "It's that bloody Confessional!" Greene shouted. "Somebody leaked the Confessional to HQ. Jesus Christ, they ought to be *glad* Bryn faced up to facts. I guess they're scared it puts them in bad odor with Earthaid. Well, you know what I think? They're a bunch of yellow bastards!"

"Steady, Ralph," said Edlin. "It has nothing to do with the Confessional."

"What, then?" Trevithick asked. He reached out. "Show me that warpwire."

Edlin hesitated, glancing round the faces. After their initial disbelief people were rapidly coming to terms with the matter, each in his, her or its own way. Now nobody would meet Trevithick's eyes. They were too busy examining the grain of the table: fine goron ironwood. It was a painful and embarrassing business, having a director fired. "I don't think so," said Edlin finally.

"This is ridiculous," snapped Trevithick. "I have to know why I'm fired, otherwise how can I appeal? Have some sense, Manning. I've only been on Goronwy two months. How could I have screwed up enough to get fired in that time? What am I supposed to have done?"

Manning Edlin looked uncomfortable, fiddling with his audio pickup.

"Well?" said Trevithick.

Edlin said, "I don't see any reason to air dirty linen in front of the entire Board. This is a confidential warpwire to Personnel from the Samaritan HQ on Earth. I'm relaying it to you, Bryn. It has nothing to do with the rest of the Board except, obviously, that it changes our composition."

"Then show it to me."

"If I show it to you now, you'll start disputing it. That will get us nowhere. Come to my office after the Board meeting. We'll talk about it then."

The Board meeting had only just started. The clock on the end wall showed 1417. The sun still shone on Samarita outside the window. Just beyond the domes Trevithick could see the brown roofs of the goron dwellings and beyond them, Lady river wending her slow and slippery way to the sea. The little he'd learned so far about the fascinating world of Goronwy was wasted, because he would soon be shipped back to Earth in disgrace. For the second time in two years. He knew only too well what had gone wrong on Annecy, but how had he screwed up this time?

He found himself standing; the others still sat. Janine Starseeker suddenly spoke, the words jerking out. "Disgusting! This is no way to treat anyone!" Everyone looked at her in amazement, because Janine was a shy person and almost invisible at Board meetings. "We should lodge a formal protest!"

Vorda, the muscan Director of Planning, said, "Without knowing the reason for Bryn Trevithick's dismissal I could not support such a motion. I fail to understand how you can propose it, Janine."

"I didn't mean . . . All I meant was . . . " Her voice trailed away.

Vorda continued, "Then I suggest we move on to the next item."

Edlin said quietly. "Leave us now, Bryn. I'll see you in about an hour."

Trevithick couldn't bring himself to turn around and walk out, just like that. The defeat was too great. "But I have an item on the agenda. The latest figures on goron births. It's important."

"Give Janine your papers. She can handle it. I'm sorry, Bryn. Please go."

There was no other way. Janine was crying. Ralph Greene's face was crimson with anger. The other humans wore varying expressions of embarrassment, regret and fear. *If it can happen to him*, they were thinking, *it can happen to any one of us*. And the muscans? Vorda (Planning), Murdo (Personnel) and Tillini (Security)? Trevithick couldn't tell what they were thinking. He never could. Maybe they didn't think unless they had to. Maybe they just switched their brains off until they were needed.

He gulped. His throat was bone dry. He couldn't have spoken even if he'd had anything to say. So he swung around and got out of there as quickly as he could. The door valve slapped shut behind him.

"Yes, I'd heard you'd been recalled," said Ivor Sabin. "Manning Edlin told me."

Recalled. Trevithick grunted cynically. That was a nice euphemism. "Did he tell you why?"

"No." Sabin looked embarrassed. Everyone was embarrassed, it seemed. Trevithick wondered foolishly if all this embarrassment could somehow be harnessed to good use, like putting together a petition. Sabin was forty-seven, thin with hollow cheeks and jet black hair. Trevithick always figured he dyed it to make himself look like Count Dracula. He'd been on Annecy when the disaster struck but, since he was not in charge of Ecology and therefore not the scapegoat, he'd been able to get another job easily enough. Trevithick, on the other hand, had spent two years on the beach until the Samaritan Organization picked him up.

"We've known each other a few years," Trevithick said. "You'd tell me if you knew anything, wouldn't you?" He began to shuffle the stuff on his desk, hardly thinking what he was doing. There wasn't much there. The disks containing his biological data on Goronwy life were gone. He reached for the keyboard.

"Uh . . ." Sabin was suddenly standing beside him, unnaturally close. Trevithick could smell his depilatory.

"What?"

"I, uh . . . I was told to make sure you didn't access anything."

"I haven't gone yet, Ivor. There'll be a period of notice."

"Personnel said you'd be leaving right away."

"I don't think so." There was no ship in orbit. The next available ship was the *Samaritan Trader*, due in about one goron month. Surely they'd want him to work his time out?

Or would they? Edlin had already made it clear he was no longer a Director. Did that mean he was no longer an employee, either? Was he supposed to spend the next month sitting in some goron bar on the banks of Lady, talking to the few Samaritan retirees who'd chosen to stay on Goronwy?

"Bryn, I'm just doing what I'm told. Now leave things alone, huh?"

"That's easy enough." His hands were trembling with outrage. "My disks have gone. I put them right there half an hour ago. Someone's taken them. You?"

Sabin was actually leaning his shoulder against Trevithick's, pushing him away from his own desk. "No need for unpleasantness, Bryn. You know the rules."

"No, I don't know the bloody rules! I've only been with the Organization two months since Marik Darwin walked out on you all. I've been supervising half a dozen projects and I would assume I have time to put things in order before I go."

"I'm sorry, Bryn." He put his hands on the desk, covering the untidy pile of oddments.

Infuriated, Trevithick strode across the room and spoke into another pickup before Sabin could stop him. The display remained dumbly blank. "Moved fast, haven't you?" he asked bitterly.

"It's the rules. There could be sabotage, you see. Of course, I'm sure you wouldn't do anything like that, Bryn. But some people, angry... bitter... You know what I mean."

"I know exactly what you mean!" He pulled himself together. There was no point in antagonizing Ivor. If he was going to appeal his dismissal, he'd need friendly colleagues to back him up. "Well, I don't have anything personal worth taking. It's all back at the apartment." He pressed the door button. "Be seeing you."

"Uh, good luck, Bryn." Sabin didn't offer to shake hands. The monitor would have seen it. Bryn Trevithick was bad company. He hurried along the walkway, fuming. It was too early to go hanging around Edlin's office. It was too early for a drink, too, but that didn't stop him heading for the Social Club bar.

The bar was almost empty; most people were at work doing

whatever good Samaritans did. All around him, five thousand humans and a few muscans were beavering away at their jobs, secure and happy, no cloud on their horizons. All confident that they were bringing salvation to the world of Goronwy and its intelligent and friendly little folk, the gorons. It gives them a warm feeling, thought Trevithick bitterly, being out here doing good, making a world safe for nice little guys. As for himself, he had no warm feelings that afternoon.

Neither was he confident that they were making the world safe for nice little guys. Well, too bad. There was nothing he could do about it now. He suffered the further humiliation of finding the autobar would not accept his voice, slipped coin into the slot, took a mead and looked around.

There was one other customer, a woman of about fifty. And she was weeping silently into her drink.

Normally he'd have felt compassion and tried to get her to talk about it, whatever it was. But today he was too wrapped up in his own problems. He sat there oblivious of the nearby sorrow, trying to get his thoughts into some kind of logical order, and failing. After an hour of this it was a relief when his visiphone buzzed. Edlin's big face appeared on the screen, skin glowing with health. "Bryn? I'm free."

"I'll be right there."

Edlin was examining his screen when Trevithick entered. To avoid being kept waiting—a typical Edlin ploy—Trevithick said immediately, "Okay. So what's all this about?"

Wordlessly, Edlin passed over the warpwire.

TO: MURDO, DIRECTOR PERSONNEL, GORONWY PROJECT.
FROM: CONWAY, DIRECTOR PERSONNEL, SAMARITAN ORGANIZATION, EARTH.
RE: BRYN TREVITHICK.

TEXT: DUE TO INTERNAL COMMUNICATION PROBLEM PERSONNEL BRANCH WERE UNAWARE OF UNSUITABILITY OF TREVITHICK FOR POST OF DIRECTOR OF

ECOLOGY, GORONWY. IT APPEARS TREVITHICK IS RE-
SPONSIBLE FOR THE DEATH OF OVER ONE HUNDRED
HUMANS ON ANNECY WHILE WORKING FOR OUTWARD
HO. INSTRUCT HE BE DISMISSED FORTHWITH.

"My involvement with Annecy was nothing new to them,"
Trevithick protested. "I told them. I could hardly keep it a secret,
could I? After I gave them all the facts, they agreed to give me a
chance."

"Who are they?"

"The people I talked to. Cotter, and the guy with the long nose,
what's his name? Jobbs. Good grief, Manning, the whole Annecy
business was common knowledge at the time!"

"Common knowledge in Outward Ho, yes. But maybe not at
Samaritan HQ. Annecy was an Outward Ho show. They play their
cards close."

"Well, I told Cotter and the others," Trevithick said obstinate-
ly. "And Ivor Sabin's been here for a couple of years; he was with
me on Annecy. I find it impossible to believe nobody passed
the information on." Something else occurred to him. "Anyway,
Cotter told me the Board here had asked for me personally. I
assumed Ivor had put in a good word."

Edlin leaned back in his chair and gave his well-known fleet-
ing grin. "Ivor is loyal, and I understand your predecessor Marik
Darwin mentioned your name, too. But Annecy wasn't mentioned.
So far as HQ is concerned, you've concealed relevant information
about your previous employment. That's serious. You can see how
people here would feel if they knew you'd been responsible for the
Annecy fiasco." It was the instant coldness of his expression
immediately after the grin that angered Trevithick. "There have
already been rumors. Maintaining morale on an off-Earth
project is of paramount importance," he said sententiously.
"Paramount."

"You haven't exactly got a killer in your midst. They held me
responsible for the Annecy deaths simply because I was in charge
at the time."

"So you were, in fact, responsible," said a new voice.

It was Albert Brassworthy, Director of Finance, sitting in the far corner with Murdo, the Director of Personnel. Trevithick hadn't noticed them.

"What's he doing here?" he asked, annoyed. Brassworthy was a pompous little jackass. The postname people chose on getting their Guild membership often indicated their personality rather than their profession. Obviously Albert had picked the name Brassworthy because he thought it sounded dignified and financially reliable. Shortly after Trevithick's arrival Brassworthy had questioned his unusual name; presumably he felt Trevithick should have called himself Bryn Oxygen or something equally puerile. Trevithick had told him it was an old family name and he preferred to stick with it.

And the little jackass, after a few seconds muttering into his calculator, had told him that if all his family, male and female, had always done that, every human being in existence would be called Trevithick by now. "And where would we be then?" he'd asked, eyebrows raised in mock alarm.

"Your dismissal from the Organization has financial implications, obviously," said Edlin.

"It has Personnel implications too," rumbled Murdo.

If anything, Murdo was worse news than Brassworthy. A muscan would be against him from the start. It would *always* do what it felt constituted the greatest good for the greatest number. Muscans were totally without sentiment and by human standards totally amoral. And they were very clever. He would be wasting his time appealing to the finer instincts of a muscan.

"Albert?" Murdo said.

Brassworthy was dictating figures into his wretched little calculator. He was never without it. "There's the initial interviews, and Bryn's expenses on Earth. And the passage here." Brassworthy clicked his tongue and raised his eyebrows, looking convincingly frightened by the total. "And his salary here, and the loss sustained on his aborted projects. Oh, dear me. Bryn's cost the Organization an awful lot of money."

Trevithick felt the tide of fury rising again. "And the cost of the passage home," he snarled. "That should bump your losses up a bit."

"The cost of the passage home?" Murdo queried. "I don't think we can run to paying that, particularly in view of Albert's figures. There's no precedent for it."

"What!"

"There has to be a limit to the loss we can stand."

The fury had turned to a sick feeling. "Edlin?"

"It's nothing to do with me, Bryn. Murdo's the Director of Personnel. I can't overrule its decision."

"Is it a decision? I mean, has it just made up its mind this minute or was it all planned? How much thought has it given this? Have you considered the kind of adverse publicity this would bring, Murdo? Stranding a human on an alien world?"

Edlin looked at Trevithick coldly. "I really couldn't allow wild stories to be strewn around the Galaxy. And as you know, I'm Director of Systems and Communications." He paused to allow the implication to sink in. "Anyway, I'm sure we can manage a small severance package."

"You've got it all sewn up, have you?" Trevithick could hear his own voice trembling, and despised himself for it. "I demand that you put this before the Board."

"I don't want to do that, Bryn. It would make you look bad in front of everybody. All the Support directors would vote against you; they're duty bound to accept Earth HQ decisions. Which leaves Janine Starseeker and possibly Ralph Greene on your side." He shook his head and pursed his lips. "Don't let's do it, Bryn. Don't let's do it."

"All right, then. Can I ask you three to reconsider the matter? Can we talk about it tomorrow, maybe?" Trevithick was uncomfortably aware this sounded like begging.

"It's Murdo's decision. I think he's made it."

Trevithick stared at them for a second, but saw no indecision on their faces. Their minds were made up.

They were stranding him in a world he hardly knew.

CHAPTER 6

THE SAMARITAN PROJECT LOOKED AFTER its executives well—until it fired them. Trevithick's apartment was luxurious. For a while he stood at the foot of the steps to his front door, his pant legs dampened by a mist of ripplegrass-flung moisture, wondering if his severance package would run to this opulence. *Mistral Greene went home to her burrow.* The words of Rob Mauser came back to him. Would he be forced to live rough like some of the other Goronwy humans who'd opted out of the Organisation? *Could* he live rough? He'd never done it before; how the hell did a guy set about it?

He could see Lady through the pilings supporting his apartment. The surface was grey today, misted by raindrops. Squitos squatted here and there, abdomens pulsing, injecting their eggs under her skin. The Organisation had fortified the bank here with a concrete wall to prevent her eroding the ground and undermining the nearest dome.

This reminded Trevithick of one of his first theories about Lady's sickness. She was a single organism, her mouth at the lake, her tail, or whatever one wanted to call it, at the sea. She grew southward, adding body cells between the lake and Samarita, forcing the older cells toward the sea where they died. So she flowed, at less than walking pace. And because her flesh was much denser than water, she eroded her banks much more severely than normal rivers. She got wider.

Was width a problem for her? Did the consequent slowing of the seawards flow cause dying cells to back up and infect new cells?

Trevithick was wondering about this, watching a goron barge working slowly downstream with a load of nectar for the riverside communities, when he became aware that someone was standing a couple of meters away, getting as wet as he was. It was the woman he'd seen in the bar.

"Excuse me," she said tentatively.

"Yes?"

"I wondered . . . Aren't you the Director of Ecology? Bryn Trevithick?"

It said something for the depth of his shame and despair that he couldn't bring himself to tell her he was now a mere ex-director. "I'm Bryn Trevithick," he said.

She wore cheap plastic rainwear with no hood. Rain had flattened her short grey hair to her scalp, accentuating the bony features. Her eyes were sunken, lids like hoods. When he'd seen her crying, he'd supposed she was an ineffectual twig of the deadwood that inevitably accumulates in a bureaucracy.

"I'd like to talk to you."

"Look, uh, I'm really very busy." It was a stupid excuse, in the circumstances.

"It looks like it," she snapped sarcastically. "This is important. We're getting wet standing here like this. Would you mind coming to the Passing Barge with me?" Her dark eyes hooded slowly like a lizard, and she turned away. Trevithick followed, telling himself he had nothing better to do.

He knew the inn; he sometimes dropped in there on his way home. It was run by a goron, Yon from Clan Service, but most of its customers were from the Organisation. Years ago it had been a barge staging point, but when humans began to drop by Yon's predecessor made some changes. He raised the ceilings, added human-size furniture and even a few giant muscan chairs. He decorated the timber walls with memorabilia of old Earth; photographs, ancient weapons and other stuff donated by Samaritans. He gave the place a name: The Passing Barge. He served mead distilled from goron nectar, and very good it was.

"We'll sit there," said the woman, pointing to a table in a secluded corner.

There were only three other customers at this hour. A couple of young gorons drank nectar at the bar, fortifying themselves for the nightmare trek to Ladysmouth. In the far corner the spare frame of Lath Eagleman lay in a deep chair, legs extended across the floor, his violin held awkwardly. He was playing the slow movement of Mendelssohn's violin concerto, as usual. That was how he earned his keep; that, and a minuscule pension.

The woman remained silent while Yon brought mugs of mead, then said abruptly, "You've probably heard of me. I'm Bridget Booker. The teacher from Ladysend."

"I've heard people speak of you. I haven't had time to look over the area properly yet." Again Trevithick caught himself pretending he hadn't been fired.

"Ladysend is on the coast where Lady flows into the sea. You can't call it the mouth, as you would a normal river, because the mouth is at the north end, at the inland sea. All gorons are born at Ladysend. About ten kilometres from the end they begin to surface from Lady in little wombs." Her voice became warmer, and he began to understand something about her. "I go out in a coracle to make sure they're all right and," she blinked the big eyelids, "I cull the damaged ones. I don't have to do that, but I can't bear to see ... There are more damaged ones all the time."

"I've seen your figures." It was one of the reasons the gorons had asked for the Organization's help in the first place. That, and the creeping decay in Lady's lower reaches.

"Then you'll know. I have a small group of gorons from Clan Birthcare to help me. When the wombs reach the place where Lady begins to deliquesce, they dissolve and we bring the babies into the coracles. You'll see it all, one of these days."

Trevithick said nothing. He was thinking how little he'd learned those past two months. He'd been sitting at his desk shuffling paper while the real things were happening outside the domes.

He'd been on the planet for the purpose of curing Lady, but he'd hardly looked at her yet.

She continued, "Later, when the children are old enough, I start to teach them. I teach them our language first. We haven't always done that, you know. Many years ago we pretended the gorons were ineducable, but later we found it convenient for them to be able to speak our language and use our facial expressions. It's easier than us learning theirs." Her tone was bitter. "So they hired me. And now I've been on Goronwy twenty-two years. Pretty well every goron you speak to has been taught by me. And I give them a brief education in other subjects too. Earth history, physics, biology, that kind of thing. Most of it's wasted, I'm afraid, because as soon as they leave me they join a clan and learn their life's trade from other gorons. Are you listening?" she snapped suddenly.

"Of course."

"You looked preoccupied. I'm telling you things you know already?"

"No, really, it's very interesting."

"Be patient, please. I was coming to the reason I wanted to speak to you . . . Oh, no. That wretched man Eagleman has seen us." Lath had laid down the violin, hauled himself to his feet and was weaving through the tables in their direction. "I'm sorry," she told him forcibly. "This is a private conversation."

Lath took it in his stride, swaying above them, placing his palms on the table to steady himself. "It's a bloody shame. He knew all about it, you know. His mistake was talking to the wrong people." His eyes focused on Trevithick. "You're new. What's it like on Earth these days? Oh, my bright eyes. Tell me about Earth."

Bridget stood, took him by the arm, led him across the room and deposited him in his chair. "That man's a disgrace to the species," she said as she returned. "What the gorons must think I don't know. To say nothing of the muscans. Anyway, as I was about to say—and speaking of muscans—today I was summoned before Vorda. They were kind enough to send a helicopter for me," she said acidly, "but how I'll get back is anybody's guess."

"And what did our Planning director have to say?"

"Very little. It just sat there gasping the way muscans do, and left the talking to that dreadful man Brassworthy. God knows I'm not a religious woman, but Albert Brassworthy has no soul!"

"None that I've noticed," Trevithick agreed with feeling.

"He started by talking about financial stringencies, but that was just an excuse for what he really wanted to say. Which was, they're cutting my budget. Imagine that! Have you any idea how small my budget is already?"

"No."

"Well, I'm the only Samaritan at Ladysend; there's my salary and an expense allowance I use to pay the gorons who help me. And the computer and communications equipment. Medical supplies, they pay for those. And that's it. My food, repairs to my apartment, the schoolroom, the hospital—if you can call it a hospital—all come out of my pocket. I have to break even or starve, so Ladysend is falling apart. And now they want to cut my budget."

"Where, exactly?"

"My expenses. They say I must lay off the goron teachers. They say that when Lady is cured, the Organisation will leave Goronwy so there'll be no need for the gorons to speak our language. But we're nowhere near finding a cure for Lady, are we?"

He hesitated. "Not yet. These things take time. We're following some promising leads." He wanted to get away, to escape from the false scenario into which he was being trapped. But Bridget Booker was not the kind of person to let go until she was good and ready. He'd have to come clean. "Look, there's something I ought to tell you—"

"Bryn, I love these little people." Her eyes were bright. "And imagine how they feel, ten thousand little folk with the same mother, and that mother dying? How they look to us to help them? They're born quite clever, you know, and they learn much more quickly than us. By the time they're five they're old enough to join a clan. The whole purpose of their lives is to sustain Lady. And Lady's dying. Can you imagine the communal guilt? Have you heard their songs at sundown?"

At sundown the gorons gathered on the banks of Lady and sang in their own language. Trevithick didn't understand the words himself but Bridget Booker knew goron. The music alone told him the songs were sad. They sounded something like Christian hymns. Samaritans would gather to listen, and he'd seen some of the more emotional employees crying. And while this was going on, old gorons whose time had come were rowed out in coracles, and committed themselves to Lady.

"I think I know what you mean," he said.

"The only good thing I can say for Brassworthy, is he's letting me keep my staff of midwives. That's what I call the ones who patrol Lady with me and look after the births. Vorda says that's our number one priority. It says we must maintain the health of the stock and cull the runts. It talks as though they're cattle, but I'll forgive it that because it's a muscan. I trust it more than Brassworthy."

"You're probably right."

The deep eyes were fixed on him, and now he got the impression she was seeing him for the first time. Previously her eyes had been unfocused, seeing Ladysend and Lady, and the little wombs drifting to the surface. "You chose an old family name. I like that. I've often wished I'd done the same. But I was young and proud of my profession then, and Booker seemed harmless enough." She smiled at last. "One of my colleagues called herself Helen Pythagoras. I'm sure she's regretted it ever since. Well, Bryn Trevithick, I'm going to ask you to help me."

"I'm not sure I—"

She was on it in a flash. "Don't you think it's important that we educate the gorons? Here we have an intelligent species, and because they have no written language and a single-minded purpose in life they're not using the brains they have! They could have cured Lady's sickness themselves generations ago, given the knowledge. They wouldn't have had to cry for help the way they did. And it was pure chance their cry was heard. They have no radio technology; a Galactic charting team discovered them. But you know that, of course." She rested a bony hand on his; her touch was cool. "All I'm going to ask is that you use your influence."

"I have no influence."

"Nonsense! You're the Director of Ecology. It's the most important position in Samarita!"

"I . . ." Yon was watching him from behind the bar, eyes grave. Gorons had exceptional hearing; he'd heard every word of the conversation. Added to which, they had learned to interpret human pheromones. Trevithick flushed. "I've been fired."

"You? Fired!" Her exclamation was so sharp that even Lath Eagleman jerked from his stupor. "Fired? Why?"

Trevithick wasn't about to explain Annecy. And anyway, he was beginning to wonder if that was the reason for his dismissal, or if it was simply that he hadn't fitted in, in some way. The Confessional, possibly. It sapped a person's confidence, being fired. "I'd rather not say."

She eyed him closely. "I'm beginning to think something funny is going on. They've dropped my education program, and now they've fired their top Operations director. You're a young man, Bryn. What are you, late twenties? You'll get another job soon enough. Myself, I'm fifty-two. I daren't rock the boat. Well, I'm going back to Ladysend and I'm going to organise those little people into a self-sufficient unit, and I'm going to teach them how to use my database. I have all the knowledge of our galaxy in there, solar powered. They're not just going to learn the basics. I'm going to aim for professional standards. And my guess is, we'll have the Lady problem beaten within five years or less. The gorons have short lives, but they learn fast. And when I'm dead their learning can go on!"

Her eyes shone with an almost religious fervour, her cheeks were pink and she looked twenty years younger. And her enthusiasm was infectious. Suddenly things didn't look quite so bad.

It wasn't until later that Trevithick's dark mood returned, and he saw this as evidence of how humans differed from muscans. Humans, he decided, could kid themselves.

There were three ways of getting to Ladysend from Samarita. The winding riverbank trail took about fourteen Goronwy days.

There were wayside inns for travellers, but the beds were built for the meter-tall gorons. It was possible to hitch a ride on a nectar barge, and that took about fourteen days too because, as Lara Wing told Trevithick, propellers were not allowed on the surface of Lady. The last option was a copter.

When Trevithick left Bridget she was calling Engineering. She was quite prepared to take a barge back to Ladysend because she figured Brassworthy might say the Organisation couldn't afford a copter. But as Trevithick mounted the steps to his front door he heard the hum of the motor, and was glad. He'd developed quite a liking for the teacher.

Then he forgot about her, because his voice wouldn't activate the door lock. He tried shouting, he even tried singing a few notes because the lock could be temperamental. No result. In a fit of frustration he kicked the door a couple of times. The noise brought a group of gorons to the foot of the steps.

"Stand fast." One of them called the traditional goron greeting.

"I can't get in," he called down to them.

This caused a bout of shuffling and repositioning. Gorons were like that. Being wholly social creatures they found it difficult to select a leader. Finally, one of the identical little humanoids said, "The Organisation deleted your voiceprint."

That was a shock. Trevithick could understand them deleting his print in the domes, but to lock him out of his apartment? Where did they expect him to sleep? The sun was already low.

"Why did they do that?" he asked.

"You don't work for them any more. The apartment belongs to them. On the other hand, your personal possessions belong to you. So we have them in our office. We were awaiting your arrival." Bridget Booker had taught them a nicely logical mode of speech.

"They're a lousy bunch of bastards!" he shouted.

This caused another fit of milling about. When it was over, a different spokesman had been elected. "They are saving Lady's life," he said.

Trevithick stared at them angrily. They stared back anxiously with innocent brown eyes. He swallowed his rage. They meant no harm. They were members of Clan Service, hired at minimal pay by the Organisation to look after employees' dwellings. The minimal pay aspect was incidental; gorons had nothing to spend it on anyway. They had no individual possessions. What they did have: the inns, the boats, the tools of their trade, belonged to the race as a whole. So they didn't need money. They accepted their pay in old-fashioned cash specially imported for the purpose, and nobody knew what they did with it.

Trevithick took his two bags of belongings and headed back to the Passing Barge. He'd get a bed from Yon for the night.

But when he arrived Yon had gone and a different goron was behind the bar. Trevithick knew he was different because Yon had a scar between his wide-set eyes as a result of a fracas the previous year.

"Where's Yon?"

The goron smiled at him. "Yon is thirty-two years old today. My name is Mana. Welcome to my bar. I'm sure we're going to get along excellently. Yon spoke very well of you."

The last bit was just politeness; Yon hardly knew him. The first bit came as something of a blow; he hadn't realised Yon was so old. He'd come to accept him as part of the scenery, and now he was gone. Tonight he'd be taking his last coracle trip. Things had changed a lot that day.

Mana said, "Perhaps you'd like to wish Yon well."

Now that was a nice thought. "I'll do that," Trevithick said. He might as well start getting used to goron customs. He'd be seeing a lot of them from now on.

Mana interrupted his thoughts. "Yon goes soon."

He took the hint, booked a bed for the night, and left.

It was getting dark. The riverbank was crowded. He'd expected a couple of hundred gorons with maybe a few humans and muscans. Instead, there were almost as many humans as gorons. Yon's clientele had turned out in force. Floodlights had been installed. At least five hundred people of three species thronged the narrow street between the shacks, and spilled out along Lady's edge. Those nearest Lady were mostly gorons, and several funeral coracles were being made ready. A knot of gorons stood a little apart from the others; he saw Yon among them. Others approached this group singly, clasped hands with each member in turn, exchanged a few words then gave way to the next in line. It was very orderly and not at all sad.

"Your first funeral, Bryn?" It was Martha Sunshine, the big woman in charge of Entertainment.

He nodded.

"I hear the Organisation gave you the old heave-ho," she chuckled. "Lucky guy. Golden handshake after two months, darling? That's some kind of a record. Do you have a bottle on you? This night air sure gives an old lady a thirst."

Trevithick couldn't help but smile. Martha wasn't old. She was no more than forty. But she put on an act in keeping with her job: a stagy red-hot Momma. He didn't mind. She was fun, and he needed fun that night.

He explained the situation.

"The dirty dogs," she said. "That's big business for you."

"What do I do now, Martha?"

"A few alternatives. One: you go native. Live in a shack, drink nectar and mead, die young. The gorons will look after you; you'll become an honorary Clan Service member. Two: you find some good-looking female Samaritan and shack up with her." She cast a knowing eye over the assembly. "Samarita is lousy with them, all itching to mother someone. Look, there's a toothsome possibility." She indicated a mop of golden hair in the crowd.

Trevithick had to chuckle. There was something infectious about Martha. Then the girl turned round and he stopped chuckling. He caught a glimpse of big laughing eyes and a wide mouth, a cute nose in a heart-shaped face, and the breath went out of him for an instant. It was the girl who'd looked in at Gary Docksteader's apartment when he and Lara Wing were there. Susanna, Director of Health Services. He couldn't see anything of her from the neck down, but he'd seen enough. Sex had reared its pretty head, and in his darkest hour, too. She met his eyes for an instant, grinned, then turned away talking to someone. She'd made his evening.

"You have good judgement," he told Martha.

"It comes of being in the entertainment business. I can spot them a mile off. It's not necessarily their looks; it's the way they carry themselves. A few girls have talent, ninety-nine percent don't. Susanna's got it. She could be a big 3-V star, or she could be a brain surgeon. Do you know her?"

"Not to speak to."

"I've tried to get her involved with our dramatic group, but she just laughs. I plant the seed in her mind whenever I see her, which isn't often. Funny how we tend to stick with people from our own departments, in Samarita."

He watched two gorons climb into a coracle. One took the oars, the other stood in the bow. The singing, which up to now had been a haphazard cacophony of several groups, suddenly came together in a harmony that made his eyes sting. A beautiful anthem rolled through the night. The oarsman began to row. The oars had no blades; they were simple poles to depress Lady's skin and skid the coracle along.

"I'd like to adapt this song for one of our live shows," said Martha quietly. "But it would seem wrong, somehow. Did you know I've persuaded Brassworthy to bring in *Barker Sam* from Deganwy?"

Trevithick was irritated. "We can spend a king's ransom bringing in a bit of entertainment, but we can't afford to send me back to Earth."

"You used to work for Outward Ho, didn't you?"

"Yon's next." He avoided the question.

Yon was already standing in his coracle. The previous boat was returning to shore. Yon's oarsman began to row. Humans began to clap. A few were openly tearful despite the cheery goron pheromones in the air. There was nothing sad about death to a goron; it was a thing of beauty, a returning to the mother that gave them birth. Yon raised his hand and the oarsman paused. Then, quite simply, Yon bent at his plump waist and rolled over the side. Trevithick could see the hump of him in the floodlights for a minute or two, then the surface was oily smooth again. The music rolled on. Another goron stepped into a coracle.

Humans began to drift back toward the domes. Trevithick lost sight of Martha and pushed his way toward Lady's edge. He needed to be alone for a while. As he passed among the gorons he stuck out like a lighthouse among the tiny folk, but nobody acknowledged him; no kind and well-intentioned human came to offer sympathy he didn't want. Someone turned out the floodlights and he wandered downstream unnoticed. He found a quiet spot near a cluster of firepot plants and stood listening to the music and thinking.

Tonight he'd sleep at the Barge. And tomorrow? He thought of Bridget and her problems. Perhaps he should make his way to Ladysend; she could do with some help. And so could the gorons; after all, that was why he'd come to Goronwy in the first place. With Bridget's data base at his disposal he could continue his research into Lady's sickness. Correction: he could start his research. For the last two months he'd been acting as a Director, overseeing but never getting his hands dirty. Perhaps the prospects were not so bad after all.

It was at this rare moment of rising spirits that he received a violent shove in the back.

He fell forward, windmilling his arms helplessly. The dark surface of Lady rose to meet him. He slapped into her face first, bounced and settled full length, face down. She was slightly warm, slightly sticky. The bank was only a meter away; there was no danger, was there? He tried to kneel, to turn round and grasp the overhanging ripplegrass. His knee sank into the resilient surface and he fell face forward again. He tried to claw his way around with his hands, but he could get no purchase. He rolled onto his back with difficulty; it was like lying on a warm and over soft waterbed. He shouted, but his cry was lost in the goron singing. Then he tried to row with his arms, to push himself shoreward like a coracle. But the bottoms of coracles were coated with a slippery vegetable oil. He was not. Struggling like an insect on resin, he stayed where he was, yelling.

Lady began to claim him; she exuded a penetrating opiate to ease the final moments of her guests.

Within a few seconds the lights of his brain switched off.

CHAPTER 7

THERE WAS A HUMMING IN TREVITHICK'S EARS. His world swayed around him. Everything was dark. He lay still for a while without thinking much; his brain didn't seem to be functioning very well. There was no pain; he felt relaxed and comfortable. He dozed for a while, then the swaying became bumpy and he was thrown about violently. He tried to extend his arms to cushion himself but nothing happened. He tried to kick, and failed.

He was paralysed.

He knew what that meant. Lady's fluids had taken effect. What would happen next? Was he in the process of being consumed like Yon, or would he be returned to the surface like a young and virile goron who had planted his seed? It didn't matter, he decided pessimistically. Lady took her nourishment in many forms, and humans had been known to offer themselves, and occasionally to be accepted.

Then he realised he was breathing. And that was odd, because he was supposed to be deep within Lady's tissues.

As he was drowsily puzzling over this, a cheerful female voice called, "If you can hear me, we just hit a spot of turbulence. It's nothing to worry about; I'm one heck of a good pilot. If you can't hear me, well, sweet dreams."

So he was alive, unconsumed and apparently above sea level. And the choppy nature of the turbulence suggested a copter. This brought Bridget Booker to mind, but the voice was not hers. It was younger and much more chirpy.

"You're probably wondering what's going on," the voice resumed. "We're heading north and just passing over the mountains. I can't see them because it's dark, but fear not. I know they're there. To your right is Goronwy's famous northern sea, the source of the slimy river known as Lady, into which you were pushed by persons unknown and from which you have been plucked by a team of gorons and myself. You may think of me as Susanna. We've never met formally, but I've seen you around. We are now descending toward my weekend cottage. Though humble, it's infinitely preferable to the depths of Lady. So I expect you to be suitably grateful when you wake up. Unless, of course, you are dead."

He mulled over this for a while. Soon the turbulence abated, the copter bounced gently and a cool breeze blew. It was still dark. Then as a pink glow appeared, he realised his eyelids were closed. He couldn't open them. He felt himself in motion again; a rapid but minor bumping. He was being wheeled along on a trolley. Then there were hands under his armpits, he heard a grunt and felt himself rolled onto something resilient.

"Lucky for you I'm a good strong girl," said Susanna. "Okay, I'm going to give you a shot. It's just an ordinary stimulant, enough to bring you out of this. Don't worry, I'm fully qualified."

Trevithick felt nothing, but in a moment found he could move his arms a little. He opened his eyes.

He saw a wide smiling mouth and a round chin. Big blue eyes looked down at him. Golden hair framed a perfect face. Yes, it was Susanna, whom Martha Sunshine had said could be a 3-V star or a brain surgeon. He tried to speak, but could only croak.

"I know," she said sympathetically. "You're trying to mumble broken words of gratitude. Don't worry about a thing; in five minutes time you'll be articulate enough to address the Board of Directors. You are Bryn Trevithick, Director of Ecology, aren't you? Croak once for no, twice for yes."

He croaked twice. It was a small deception that he could correct later.

"Oh, good. I was hoping I'd rescued a Somebody. You never know who you might pull out of Lady these days. Well, Director, you're not going to like this, but it looks as though people are out to get you."

He managed to raise his eyebrows.

She stood suddenly. "A shot of mead will loosen your tongue." She disappeared from view. With a supreme effort he rolled his head and saw her standing at a counter on the far side of the room. She wore a white dress with a wide blue belt; she was pouring mead into mugs from an earthen jug. She turned, saw him watching and smiled. "You look a mess. All covered in Lady slime. We'll have to get you into a shower as soon as you've recovered the power of speech."

A few moments later he was able to say, "Thanks."

"You're welcome, Director."

"Listen, I lied to you. I'm no longer the Director of Ecology. I've been fired."

"That's all right, I'm used to disappointment. For one thing, I came to Goronwy with good intentions." She didn't enlarge on this, but regarded him speculatively, head on one side. "How are you feeling?"

"A bit dopey. Okay, I guess."

"We have a lot to talk about, you and I. But this isn't the time. See if you can stand."

He succeeded, shakily. She took his arm and helped him to a small bathroom. He leaned with his hands on the washbasin, and caught sight of himself in the mirror. He looked terrible; his face was gaunt as though he'd been on a crash diet and his clothes glistened with muck. He felt weak and ashamed. "I'm sorry. I . . ."

"Let me help you out of your things." She loosened his belt and began to pull his pants down. He grabbed at them. "No cause for embarrassment, I'm a doctor."

"A brain surgeon, maybe?"

She glanced up at him, puzzled by the allusion. "No, I don't have the patience for all that fiddling stuff. A good clean amputation now, that's different. But it's mostly administrative stuff these days." She grinned, hauling his pants down to the ankles. "I don't often have the chance to get my hand in."

He didn't reply, but allowed her to take the rest of his clothes. He stumbled into the shower. It was the old-fashioned kind that sprayed water, but none the worse for that. He felt he could have slept a week, but there were so many questions he wanted to ask. He stood under the dryer, then Susanna brought him a robe and took him into the living room. They sat in deep armchairs with mugs of nectar. She'd gone suddenly quiet, staring into her mug, blue eyes thoughtful.

He looked around. It was a strange room, to a man accustomed to the clinical decor of standard outworld accommodation. For one thing, it was totally unsanitary: wooden walls, some kind of woven carpet, big cushions stuffed with God knows what, painted representations hanging everywhere. For another thing, nothing seemed to match up; clashing colours blazed around. It made him almost dizzy. Not the kind of place where you'd expect the Manager of Health Services to live; more like a Ladyside inn.

"Like it?" she asked.

"It's different. Who does it belong to?"

"Me, of course. Do you really like Organisation apartments?" There was mild contempt in her tone.

"I've never thought about it. They're all right, I guess. All you need is a place to lay your head down."

"No, Bryn Trevithick, that's not all you need. The kind of person who thinks that way is the kind of person who's totally lost when the bureaucracy throws him to the wolves. You must live your own life as well as the Project life. Otherwise the bastards will swallow you whole. You're lucky you were only in for two months. You got out in time."

This was disturbing talk. She seemed deadly serious; a complete contrast to her earlier manner. "You don't seem to have a very good opinion of the Project," he said.

She regarded him steadily. "You say you were fired, which is a point in your favour. But you could be lying. If you think I'm going to bare my soul on such short acquaintance, you can think again, Trevithick. Spies are everywhere."

"Spies? Spying for whom? About what?"

"Okay, so maybe I exaggerated. Or maybe not. Since I've been on Goronwy, funny things have been happening. Not much. Just little things, now and then, that make a girl think."

"What kind of things?"

She grinned suddenly. She had a nice wide grin. "For one thing, seeing an ex-Director of Ecology committed to the mercies of Lady."

"You saw who pushed me in?"

"I didn't see the actual shove, or any frantic windmilling of arms as you overbalanced. But a goron told me somebody was in trouble. Lucky for you, huh? When I got there, you were thrashing like a demented water beetle."

"Was anyone else on the bank?"

She hesitated. "There were some gorons with coracles not far off. I rounded them up and we formed a circle around you, and hauled you out. And here you are, saved."

She was hiding something behind the flippant manner, he knew. But she looked so delightful sitting there with crossed legs, showing a modest amount of thigh under the white dress, that he didn't want to spoil the relationship by close questioning.

So he said cautiously, "Why the copter? Why didn't you take me to the hospital?"

"You ask difficult questions, my good man. I just deemed it unwise, that's all. Wouldn't you rather be here, anyway?" She stretched her arms above her head, yawning, watching him all the time. "Not a bad little pad, huh?"

"Listen, thanks very much—" He broke off, hearing the hum of a copter.

"Okay," she said, "the forces of darkness have arrived. I guessed it wouldn't take them long. So it's time for you to do some trusting. Just remember there was an attempt on your life earlier this evening, so do as I say without arguing, right?"

"Right."

"Go up those stairs. You'll find my bedroom there, if that's any encouragement. Stay in there and keep quiet, no matter what you hear going on down here. Resist the temptation to make a grand entrance; it could be your last. Understand?"

Trevithick was not one to accept the commands of a stranger readily, but this time he heard myself meekly saying "Yes."

The world outside turned glaringly bright. Susanna's head was suddenly in silhouette. She cried "Go on up, and keep your head down!" As he made for the flight of stairs, bent double, he saw her run to the window and wave to somebody outside.

It was dark upstairs; the drapes were drawn. He could make out a large bed and a door, presumably leading to a bathroom. He sat on a cane chair and awaited events. His heart was pounding uncomfortably. Susanna had convinced him he was in danger, which was bad enough; but not knowing who the enemy was made it infinitely worse. Who was in the copter, and why did Susanna think its arrival was connected with him?

Voices downstairs greeted her. He heard her reply, "Hello, Rob. Hi Porky. This is an ungodly hour. What brings Security to my humble cottage?"

A male voice answered, "Sorry about the hour. There's been trouble in town. One of our people was attacked by gorons."

"My God, the natives are restless, are they? Who's the victim?"

"Director of Ecology. Trevithick."

"Is he hurt?"

"No idea. We can't seem to locate him. Apparently they pushed him into Lady, and when we got there he was nowhere to be seen. He couldn't have been absorbed that quickly, so he must have managed to get out somehow. Well, you know how Ladyjuice affects people. We think he's wandered off somewhere. We have to find him soon; he could die out there."

"Why would the gorons attack the Director of Ecology, Porky?"

Trevithick pictured Porky to be in his late twenties, slightly overweight like most Security humans, pink face, fair hair. With nothing to do in the dark except visualise, he went on to credit him with a square jaw, pale blue eyes, and a faulty zipper on the breast

71

pocket of his uniform jacket, which would be a shade tight under the arms.

"Who knows what's in a termite's mind?" he answered. "There's been rumours of trouble down at Ladysend, maybe it's spreading upriver. Maybe they're tired of Operations not getting anywhere. We all heard the Confessional."

"But Trevithick's trying to put things right. He wouldn't be a target, surely?"

"I see it as part of a general malaise," said Porky. "A general malaise," he repeated, clearly pleased with the expression. "I've been here seventeen years, and has a termite ever thanked me for my contribution to making our joint society work? Never. There's gratitude for you. Rob feels the same."

"And now," said another voice, presumably Rob, "attempted murder."

"There's worse to come," said Porky.

"Oh?" said Susanna, surprised. "What's going to happen?"

"Well obviously we won't know that until the time comes. But I can tell you, things are changing here on Goronwy."

"Have you caught the, uh, attempted murderer?"

"We sure have," said Rob grimly. "Well, let's put it another way. We've rounded up all the termites in the immediate area. Six of them. Wouldn't surprise me if they were all in it together. And that's another reason we need Trevithick, to identify his assailant."

"Well, thanks for the information, boys. If Trevithick shows up at my door, I'll tell him. But it would be a long trek for him, over the mountains. Now, if you don't mind..."

After a pause, Rob said, "Trevithick may be here already."

"I think I'd have noticed."

"Listen, I'm sorry about this, Susanna. But our monitors registered excess weight in your copter this evening. Now, Trevithick isn't in the domes, and we've checked all the apartments. There's, uh, a theory he may have stowed away on your copter. Easily done. We have orders to search your cottage."

"Over my dead body."

"Don't make things difficult, huh? It's for your own good. You wouldn't want Trevithick creeping around here. Ladyjuice can do funny things to a guy's mind."

"Who's orders are these?"

"Tillini. Our Director."

"I know who Tillini is, Rob, and I also know it's a bloody muscan." Susanna's voice was angry. "Maybe I can put up with you two referring to gorons as termites, because that's the way you're made and you don't know any better. But I won't allow my home to be searched on the orders of a sexless dugong with the moral sense of a dead mackerel. Now run off home and go to bed, there's good boys. Oh, and you can tell Tillini my excess baggage was two gorons I gave a ride to."

"I'd hoped we'd get through this without any hostility."

"You hoped in vain. You know me, Rob, and you know I mean what I say."

"Maybe we should call the Director," said Porky.

"Listen, Susanna," said Rob, and Trevithick could detect the unhappiness in his voice, "I'm in a spot. I don't want to call Tillini because it's already told me what to do. And I have to find Trevithick because we're holding six gorons without evidence."

"Let them go. Trevithick isn't around to press charges."

"I wanted to do that, but Tillini wouldn't let us. It said if we let them go we'd never find them again. It said we have to show the gorons that nobody is above the law. I think Tillini thinks the Ladysend problems could spread. It wants to nip them in the bud, to let the gorons know we mean business."

"We mean business?" echoed Susanna. "Good grief, we're supposed to be helping them! Now listen to me, you two. If I'd found Trevithick wandering around Samarita full of Ladyjuice I'd have got him to the hospital, quick. Obviously, I'm a doctor, remember? You have two choices. You can try to search this place by force, in which case I'll use this pistol on you—no, keep your hands away from your sides. Or you can go back to Tillini and tell him you've searched the place and Trevithick isn't here. I'll back you up on that. Well, boys, what's it to be? Unpleasantness and a few nasty burns, or peace with honour?"

"She's bluffing," said Porky.

Then he yelled with pain.

"Convinced? Here, it's nothing much. I'll dress it right now, if you like."

"Stay away from me!" Porky sounded scared. "Come on, Rob. Let's get out of here. She's crazy!"

Heavy footsteps sounded. Trevithick heard the door open. Rob said plaintively, "Why won't you let us take a look around, Susanna?"

"It's a matter of principle."

"I guess we can't argue with that. Okay, so Trevithick isn't here. We've done our job. No hard feelings?"

"Have a safe trip back. Bye!"

A few minutes later Trevithick heard the hum of the copter, then Susanna called. "You can come down now."

They sat down and he saw the two mugs where they'd left them on the occasional table. Had the Security men noticed them? He hoped not; he didn't want Susanna involved in something he was beginning to suspect was very nasty indeed.

Susanna saw the mugs too. "Enough of this nectar," she said. "It may be nourishing for the body, but it does nothing for the senses." She filled his mug with something paler and less syrupy. "You were in no condition to appreciate my mead the first time round. That's a real shame, but it will be rectified. Roll this round your mouth. It's the best; I keep it for special guests. Distilled by my own hands in the Pathology lab, guaranteed not less than sixty days old." A silence followed while she glanced at him from time to time over the rim of her mug. Eventually she said, "Convinced?"

She wasn't talking about the mead. "Maybe. Thanks anyway. I don't know what's going on, but I sure didn't want to go back to Samarita in the care of those two."

"They're not so bad. Like they said, they were obeying orders."

"The point is, why were the orders given? Why does Tillini want me? I don't work for the Organisation any more. And why round up six gorons on a trumped-up charge?"

She regarded him seriously. "To provide a reason for looking for you."

"Well, it was no goron that pushed me in. Whoever it was, shoved me at shoulder height. A goron isn't tall enough or strong enough for that. It was a human. Or a muscan. Surely Tillini would guess that."

"Exactly. And anyway, gorons aren't capable of murder. They're simply not that kind of animal." She sipped her drink. "Someone tried to kill you, and failed. They must have gone back to check Lady to make sure you were being consumed according to plan, and found you gone. Very disappointing for them. So now they have to try again. Maybe they're using Security to find you for them, or maybe Security and Tillini are behind the whole thing. And for all they know, you saw your attacker. You didn't see your attacker, did you?"

"No. I fell face down into Lady."

"Bryn . . . You realize this isn't just someone with a grudge, don't you?" She hoisted herself up in the chair and brought her legs underneath her, watching his face. "You realize this is much bigger than that?"

"I'm beginning to wonder. And I'm just hoping you haven't involved yourself too much. If Tillini suspects you've been hiding me . . ."

"Fear not, Trevithick. Rob and Porky won't say anything. It was just chance my payload was monitored, and Tillini will believe my story about goron passengers because I've done it before. It's a rotten trek up the canyon or over the mountains for the little guys, bloody dangerous, too. But they have to make it before they can fertilise Lady, because it's a rite of passage. If they can make it through the mountains, they're strong enough to breed with Lady at her mouth."

Trevithick felt his professional hackles rise. "But you're interfering with the natural course of events, giving them a lift."

"Yes, aren't I? But I'm just a doctor; I don't understand the ethics of your job. I try to prevent people dying. And when I meet a scared little guy who knows he's not going to make it, I see it as my duty to help."

"But if everybody gave them lifts—"

"Stop talking like a bloody ecologist. They fired you, remember? Let's talk about your problem. Persons unknown are out to get you. What are we going to do about it?"

CHAPTER 8

TREVITHICK PASSED AN UNCOMFORTABLE NIGHT on the chesterfield in Susanna's living room. It wasn't so much the slats beneath the cushions imprinting themselves on his anatomy, as the not-quite-subconscious listening for approaching copters. Every little sound caused him to jerk awake and stare into the near-darkness while he wove threatening shapes from chairs, the drinks cabinet and—most fearsome of all—his own clothes hanging lifelike on the back of the door

"Rotten night, huh?" Susanna regarded him critically as they sat at breakfast. "When am I going to see you at your best, Trevithick? Or is this the way you always look?"

The cottage had no food dispenser. It was a long way from civilisation. They ate organic matter prepared by Susanna in pans on an electric cooker; the concept was primeval but the food tasted fine. Trevithick didn't ask what it was. The sun slanted through the window, the gorons were busy on the inland sea outside, Susanna wore a loose-fitting yellow housecoat and everything looked good. He just wished he felt healthier. The combination of Ladyjuice, mead and sleeplessness had given him a slight headache. He had no reply to her question. She looked altogether too perky, grinning at his misfortune. He grumbled, "It's not you they're after."

They'd discussed the matter in depth last night, but later the mead had gotten in the way of clear thought. Susanna had disappeared when his eyes had closed for a minute or two, leaving the deliberations at an inconclusive stage.

She'd said one thing that stuck in his mind: "It's beginning to add up. If I'm right, your dismissal is part of the pattern. And the attempt on your life is, too." At least, he thought that was what she'd said, but he'd kept dozing off at the time.

Now he was alert enough to follow it up. "Last night you talked about a pattern," he said. "What did you mean?"

She paused, collecting her thoughts. "You've been here a couple of months or so. You probably think this Goronwy project is just what its name implies, huh? Samaritans responding to a cry for help. Good guys who bring the benefits of technology to people in trouble. As distinct from Outward Ho, which exploits other worlds for dirty motives of profit."

"Yes, that's what I think. The Organization's presence here proves it."

"So perhaps you should ask yourself a few questions. Like: how big is Operations Division compared with Support, here on Goronwy?"

"Maybe Support looks a bit top-heavy," he said. "I've wondered about it."

"And Lady is still dying." The blue eyes stared into his. "She is still dying, isn't she?"

Trevithick was thinking how lovely she looked, and how he didn't want to talk shop over the breakfast table. "We need a breakthrough," he admitted.

"Bryn, I watched the Confessional. If the evidence of current research is anything to go by, your predecessors were just frigging around."

"Well, I wouldn't say frigging, exactly. But the research hasn't been as logical as I'd have liked. Promising leads haven't been followed up." He didn't want to sound too critical of his predecessors. "It's a complex problem."

"Bullshit. We've had fifty years. How complex can a problem be? We have a dying life form, right? And we have all the advantages of modern technology, right? So ask yourself: what's missing?

And I'll tell you what's missing, Trevithick. The will to solve the problem."

"I've noticed apathy here and there."

"Now, I'm just a lowly Manager, but you rub shoulders with the Great—in fact you were a Great yourself until you tumbled into my hands." She chuckled with no evidence of sympathy whatever. "You spoke with gods, such as the members of the Board. Did they ever offer an excuse for their failure?"

"They don't see it as failure," he said slowly. "They just get on with their jobs."

"And how do they get paid?"

He thought about it for a moment. In the case of Outward Ho, salaries were paid out of revenue like any other business. But the Samaritan Organisation? "I know there are big grants from Earthaid. And the deal is, once the Organisation has put a world on its feet, that world repays the debt over the next few centuries."

"It all comes down to money, doesn't it? But there'll be no payback from Goronwy because the place hasn't been put on its feet. A fortune in Earthaid has been pissed away to no effect. Excuse my language, but we medical people tend to use medical metaphors. So what would you do in a case like that?"

"Hold an inquiry, maybe? " he suggested feebly.

"You might, but our people here wouldn't. They'd send encouraging warpwires and suck on Earth's tit until she lost her patience, then they'd look all hurt and bewildered."

"Maybe you're right."

"Lesson One in your reprocessing is complete." She grinned and drained her mug. Trevithick got up and walked over to the window, feeling his headache subsiding. Susanna had picked her site well; she had quite a view. The sun glittered on an endless expanse of blue water, and a light breeze ruffled the surface into silvery ripples. To the east lay the mouth of Lady, looking like any other river mouth except in the way the rippling water became oily smooth between low headlands.

Hundreds of one-man goron coracles milled about this area. These were the members of Clan Gatherer, feeding Lady. He touched the window zoom, magnifying the scene. He'd seen this once before, soon after his arrival on Goronwy, and it took some getting used to.

"Not for the squeamish," commented Susanna, standing beside him.

The gorons of Clan Gatherer looked for all the world like sea-sick little men. They would row to the fringe of Lady, choose a spot and ship their oars. Their faces would contort into an odd expression of disgust. They would clutch their plump bellies. Then they would lurch to the side of their coracle, lean over the gunwale and disgorge the contents of their stomachs into the water. The coracle would rock with the violence of their retching. Occasionally one little craft would tip too far and the occupant would fall overboard. Such an event was always greeted with howls of delight from neighbouring coracles. Their cargo discharged, they would scull rapidly back to the distant firepot fields, jump ashore, drink their fill of nectar and head back for Lady. They worked with the industry and devotion of ants.

"And yet they're intelligent," murmured Susanna. "Odd, isn't it? What purpose can intelligence serve in a society like theirs?"

"Not all their jobs are as mindless as Clan Gatherer's."

"True." She glanced at him, then away again. "Okay, enough of the chit-chat. I stuck my neck out for you last night, and I deserve some honesty. Are you going to tell me what really happened on Annecy or do you intend to keep me in suspense for ever more?"

Annecy... It was always going to haunt him. But she'd spoken as though she was ready to believe the official version was flawed.

Outward Ho made no bones about it; they were a huge profit-making corporation in the business of exploiting other worlds. By exploiting, this didn't mean they enslaved the local populations or anything so crude. They chose unpopulated planets. If conditions were not suitable for life, they operated robot mines and exported raw materials. If the world was near Earth-type, they founded colonies. Nothing wrong with that. They were simply going forth and multiplying, both humans and muscans.

Annecy looked promising: Earth-type, no intelligent indigenous population. Insects, fish, extensive plant life; that was all. Trevithick headed the biology team with Ivor Sabin as his chief assistant. They had a dozen or so scientists and technicians on the team, all good people. The exploratory party numbered over fifteen hundred; Outward Ho did not do things by halves.

Twenty-five days after their arrival a local virus they called Annecy 8 started laying people low with flu-like symptoms. The sickness lasted only a few days, then people were up and working again. No lasting effects, but people were dropping like flies and productivity suffered. Things started slipping behind schedule. And the schedule was God, when you worked for Outward Ho.

Within twenty days Trevithick's team had developed a vaccine that looked promising. They called it Annecy A12 and tried it out on a test group of ten people. The test was successful, but one had to be careful with alien viruses. They waited a few days to be absolutely sure, watching their ten guinea pigs closely. No adverse reaction. The Board began to pressure Trevithick to get moving.

Was that his excuse for what happened? Probably. A man with his history needed some excuse, otherwise how could he live with himself?

They began to vaccinate, starting with the lower administrative personnel. The Board seemed to think they were expendable. At the inquiry Trevithick used this as evidence that they knew there was a degree of risk. It didn't do him any good.

Within a day, those first vaccinated began to show severe symptoms; high fever and internal bleeding. They halted the program immediately and ran tests on the vaccine. They found it had mutated into something they later called Annecy 9, despite being stored at fifty-plus below zero. And Annecy 9 was a killer. Of the hundred and fifteen vaccinated on that first day, thirty-two were dead within three days. And worse, Annecy 9 was now on the loose, apparently contagious.

There was only one thing to do, and Outward Ho did it. The

entire exploratory party was evacuated and kept in orbital quarantine. During that period another forty-three of the original recipients died, plus fifty-nine others who had been in contact with them. But in about eighty days the virus mutated to a benign form, and fifteen days later began to die of its own accord.

That is a factual account of the Annecy tragedy.

There is a postscript. The Inquiry found Trevithick guilty of gross negligence, and he was fired.

"But the vaccine was produced from killed virus, wasn't it?" said Susanna.

"Of course it was. My guess is, it was contaminated after production. That doesn't make a lot of sense, but I didn't have time to run tests before we were closed down. People were only interested in destroying the remaining vaccine as soon as possible. They saw it as a threat to the human race. They were right."

"You must have had a pretty incompetent team."

"There were a hell of a lot more competent than my team here. If I'd had this crowd on Annecy we'd have wiped out the whole human race."

"So we have two interesting facts. One: Operations Division has been stripped to the bone, and Two, it's been staffed with incompetents. Ponder on that, Trevithick."

"And Three, I can't access our early research data."

"You can't access it?" she echoed incredulously.

"Either it isn't there or it's protected. There are areas that wouldn't respond to my voice."

"There'd be a password. You can't have access relying on voiceprints alone. What if somebody dies?"

"If there's a password, nobody seems to know it."

"I see what you mean about incompetent staff."

She'd got him thinking. Had he been set up in some way? "Edlin will know if there's anything funny going on. He runs the Board, more or less. I'll see him tomorrow and get the truth out of him!" He felt his temper rising.

"That might not be wise, Bryn. We went through all that last night. Someone tried to kill you, remember? They could try again. Best to lie low for a while."

"I hardly think Edlin pushed me into Lady. It was more likely somebody who didn't like what happened on Annecy."

"Listen to me. If you go storming into town saying people are just marking time on Goronwy to pull in as much grant money as possible, then people are going to get upset. Particularly if it's true. No, you sit tight and I'll do some snooping. I wonder . . ." She sipped her drink thoughtfully. "I wonder if you were getting a bit too warm for their liking when you were digging around in the data base. That could explain the hurried firing. That, and the Confessional." The golden hair swung across her shoulders as she turned to him. "Maybe that's why they hired you in the first place. Because of Annecy, not in spite of it. They wanted another incompetent to lead their team of deadbeats."

"Gosh, thanks."

"But they got more than they bargained for. They got a man anxious to prove himself, who was prepared to dig for facts. They got you, and you weren't about to sit on your backside until everyone pulled out."

"Exactly what facts might I have found?"

She glanced at him as though gauging his reaction in advance, then said, "Maybe Lady is incurable. We already know she's the last of her species. And she's an evolutionary dead end. Maybe there's nothing anyone can do. Maybe all that was discovered in the first few months on Goronwy and they've been hiding it ever since. For over fifty years."

"It's possible, I suppose."

"And I have an alternative. Maybe they found Lady is curable after all, and they've been hiding that."

"Also possible."

She nodded to herself. "You know what I think Samarita really is? It's a cosy little colony of bureaucrats serving out their time! You and the rest of Operations Division are just window dressing!"

It was all too fast for Trevithick. "There's one hell of a lot of assumptions in there."

"I've had longer than you to dream them up." She chuckled. "And I've been waiting for someone like you to come into my life. Now I have an accomplice to bounce ideas off without fear of ugly betrayal. Okay, so we two are the good guys. And there are others. Not everyone's delighted with the Organization's performance here."

"That's good to know."

"Okay," she said. "Let's think who might throw some light on matters, if pressed. I'm good at pressing people. Well, there's Lath Eagleman, for a start."

"Lath Eagleman? He's a nut case!"

"He's also the son of Samarita's first senior biologist. Paul Eagleman was fired after five years. I don't know why. He stayed on Goronwy," she grinned at him, "because they wouldn't pay his passage home, I bet. Then after a couple more years he just disappeared, probably as a tasty breakfast for Lady. That left Lath to fend for himself at the age of twenty-two."

"Paul Eagleman had no wife?"

"She left him before he shipped out from Earth. Couldn't face the journey, so they say. And once Paul was fired, the whole Goronwy trip became a waste of time for him. That would make a guy pretty sick, huh? In between his dismissal and his disappearing, there are two years when he probably told his son all kinds of rotten stuff about the Organisation. It might pay us to pry it out of Lath."

"Lara Wing suggested seeing Lath, too. She said Gary Docksteader often talked to him. But like I said, Lath's none too bright."

"It's worth a try. And then there's Marik Darwin, your predecessor. He walked out on the Project. Said he was sick of the whole shebang."

"Yes, I've tried to locate him. I thought he might be able to help me find the early data."

"He's often in the Passing Barge. He's become a bit of a thorn in the side of the Organisation. He leads a group of activist gorons."

"Activist gorons? I didn't know there was such a thing."

"They're low-key compared with activist humans. But their aims are pretty bizarre. They want to kill Lady and rid Goronwy of all intelligent life, including themselves. They see it as a cleansing. They reckon it'll happen anyway, so why fight it? It's dangerous talk, you know, in their kind of society. Any persuasive view can spread like wildfire, because they all tend to think alike."

"What's Marik doing leading a crowd like that?"

"I reckon he wants to get back at the Organisation. You know how gorons find it difficult to appoint a leader from among themselves. They need someone to show them the way, and that's what Marik's doing."

"Why doesn't Security stop him? He could undo everything they've achieved."

"And that isn't too hard, is it? No, Security seems happy to let him go his own sweet way. Which leads me to two conclusions. Either they think the group will fizzle out of its own accord because it flies in the face of all current goron philosophy, or Marik's secretly still in our pay."

"Paid for what, for God's sake?"

"Maybe working to destroy the group from within. To turn them round. Gorons have a terrific respect for humans, didn't you know? Marik can twiddle them round his little finger. And people wouldn't want Lady killed. It would remove their reason for being here."

For a moment Trevithick watched the gorons devotedly feeding their giant mother. "So what can we do about all this?"

"Talk to Lath and Marik, obviously. But first, we need to fill in the background." She glanced at the clock. "I'll do that this morning. I'll run a check on the Operations staff. You already know their qualifications, where they came from, that kind of thing. I'll try to dig out any unexpected links with Support. And if so, with whom, specifically."

"You can do that?"

She smiled her broad smile. "Bryn, when you get to know me better you'll realize I can do anything. But seriously, I have friends in strategic places. Friends who have a gut feeling something odd is going on, but who haven't been able to put their finger on it."

"Who are these friends?"

Suddenly serious, she said, "I'm not going to tell you. Bear with me, but you're kind of vulnerable right now." She glanced at the clock. "I must get going. You lie low today and don't open the door to strangers. I'll be back this evening. 'Bye!"

A couple of minutes later the copter rose into the morning sky.

And about two minutes after that, Trevithick heard noises downstairs.

CHAPTER 9

"**C**AUGHT SIGHT OF YOUR DAUGHTER the other day, Ralph."

Ralph Greene, Director of Engineering, looked up from his examination of the culvert hologram. Something was odd about the loading factors, but he could quite figure it out. That culvert was supposed to withstand any normal stress, and there were contingency plans for earthquakes. Hell, if anything went wrong, they'd have sewage backing up into Dome 4. Treated sewage, but inconvenient nevertheless. And no doubt the Support staff would enjoy themselves bitching and complaining about inefficiency of Operations.

His concern turned to pleasure at the sight of the visitor. The gorgeous Susanna, Manager of Health and looking as though she practised what she preached. She breezed into his office like a breath of spring air and sat down, showing plenty of leg, smiling in her sunshiny way. It was good to see a woman who didn't hide herself behind the unisex Samaritan uniform.

"You saw Mistral?" His heart had given the inevitable thump at the mention of her. "How was she?"

"I only saw her from a distance. I was in the copter. But she must have been in good shape; she was with a party of gorons trekking up Ladycanyon."

"Ladycanyon? My God." The canyon included about forty kilometres of narrow trail cut into the cliff face, with a fearsome drop to Lady far below. "What the hell would she be doing up there?"

"On her way to Ladysmouth, I guess. Never mind, Ralph, if she calls in at my place I'll give her a good meal and clean her up a bit."

He grunted. "Her weight and personal hygiene are the least of my worries. Her falling a hundred meters is a tad more serious." He ran a hand through his unruly hair. "Why can't she be like other Goronwy brats, and train for a job and all that? What does she have against the Organisation, and me, and everything? What kind of company are the gorons for a young woman?"

"You want me to answer those in order? I won't bother; it all comes back to the Project. She's an idealist and she hates the bureaucracy. And it's not all bad. Don't you see, she's the best ambassador the Project has? The gorons worship her. She has the potential to build bridges more permanent than anything you've ever built, Ralph."

"Well, great. I hope she stays alive long enough." The culvert caught his attention again, revolving between the projectors. "Uh, what can I do for you this morning, Susanna?"

"Your people built the communications system here, right?"

He frowned. This was a touchy subject. "Yeah. Part of it. Everything you can see. Everything that has good honest copper wire linking people together."

"Sounds as though you're holding back a teeny bit of information from your good friend here."

"I'll give it to you straight. We didn't install the bugs."

"The bugs?" said Susanna innocently. "You mean walls have ears?"

"And how. Every time we do any structural alterations, we find bugs. The very latest models; we don't have any equipment to detect them. Who'd have thought we'd need that kind of equipment in Samarita? I wish I knew what the hell is going on around here."

"You sound tired and dispirited, Ralph. Too bad. I need a favour."

"Anything you like," he said rashly. Those eyes did that to a man.

"Right, let me put something to you. If you want an efficient communication system, you need to monitor its use." She held up her hand as he was about to speak. "No, I don't mean you tap people's lines. I mean you just record the fact of the calls, so you know how many lines you need, and when they need beefing up. What I really mean is, somewhere there's a little counter ticking over whenever a call is made, recording where it's made from, and where it's made to."

He nodded. "There's a system, yes. A bit more complex than a counter ticking over, but yes, we have a system for predicting when additional lines are needed."

"I'd like to see it."

"See it? It's not a thing you see." A part of him was thinking how pleasant it was, explaining part of his job to a beautiful and intelligent woman. Another part was wondering what the hell she was getting at. "It all happens in there." Inaccurately, he waved a hand at the terminal. "And it just spits out a warning whenever lines are regularly overloaded."

"But it must record an awful lot of data before it can spit that warning out. That's what I want to see. The data. Where the calls are coming from, and where they're going to."

"But there are almost a hundred thousand calls in the average day. Like I said, you don't see that kind of detail. You see the results after the numbers have been crunched."

"Let's narrow it down. Most of the calls must be internal, within departments. All I want to know is, which Ecology employees have made the most external calls to other departments over the past two years, and who did they make the calls to. The top five, as it were. Can you do that for me?" She grinned irresistibly. "As a personal favour. I'm not above using my natural charm to get what I want."

He had to laugh. "I could write a program to do that in ten minutes. Ecology, huh? Anything to do with their departed Director?"

"Everything to do with him."

"Fancy him, do you? I'd have thought he was too straight-laced for you."

"There's no accounting for tastes." She stood. "Thanks enormously, Ralph. Just the top five people in Ecology making external calls, that's all I need, right? You'll let me have the figures this afternoon, then? Bye."

She breezed out before he could object to her schedule, the door valve slapping shut on the view of her attractive rump. Greene sighed. It was times like this, when a pretty woman had just walked out of his office and left that emotional vacuum like they did, that he began to think of Wendy, dead for two years now. Mistral had left home immediately after the funeral. Perhaps she'd only stayed as long as she did because of her mother. Did she really hate him that much? He'd tried to get her to take money for decent accommodation, and she'd refused. And when she'd had that terrible accident with the vespa, he'd offered to pay for facial treatment and she'd refused that too.

He was only thirty-seven, but thinking about Wendy and Mistral made him feel old and ineffectual. He stood and unlocked a cupboard in the corner of his office. For a few moments he regarded the contents and tried to make sense of what was happening around him, then he shut the door, heard it click securely and stood regarding it, sick at heart.

Like many people in Samarita, Ralph Greene had his secrets.

Back in her office, Susanna considered the situation. She would know more when the data came from Ralph. Or would she? There were plenty of reasons for interdepartmental conversations, ninety-nine percent of them totally innocent. But she was convinced that someone in Ecology had a relationship with someone in Support based on something more sinister than mere friendship. There was a strong and permanent link. And over a period of months or years, that link was bound to show itself in increased visiphone communication between certain people.

It was then that she realised that, without intending it, she'd already tipped Ralph Greene off as to whom she suspected one of those people to be. No matter. He'd see the figures himself, soon enough.

By a series of mental connections this brought her back to the tall and somewhat academic-looking Bryn Trevithick. What was the secret of this man's appeal? He wasn't her type, surely? He was altogether too straight and serious, wasn't he? Around this point in her meditations there was a buzz at the door and Rob Mauser entered, looking worried.

"Sit down and get it off your chest, Rob."

He perched on the edge of the chair, looking too young for the cares that furrowed his brow. "I've had a rough time of it with Tillini." He hesitated. "I thought the bastard was going to fire me. Supposing it did? What would I do? I hear they've stopped paying passages for people they fire."

He looked so scared that she took pity on him, but this was not the ideal location for intimate discussions. "Let's go outside for a breath of air," she said, and led the way onto her balcony, snapping the door shut behind them. "If it's Bryn Trevithick you're thinking of, I think Brassworthy had a very good reason for refusing to pay his fare back to the Old Planet."

"What reason?"

How far could she trust him? On the other hand, a few simple facts couldn't do any harm. "You haven't forgotten why we're here, Rob? And you're aware that Earthaid is picking up the tab? It's a hell of a big tab, and Earthaid thinks it's all in a good cause. There's naive for you. Now, what would they think if a fired Director of Ecology showed up on their doorstep, bleating about lack of effort on Goronwy?"

"They'd begin to wonder what was going on," said Mauser slowly.

"And they'd remember the previous Director of Ecology, one Marik Darwin, quit a short while back. In fact Directors of Ecology are short-lived on Goronwy. And then they'd start asking questions and tightening the purse-strings."

"Makes sense."

"So fear not, Rob. If you get the boot, the purse-strings will be relaxed in your case. So what's your problem with Tillini?"

"Porky talked. About our visit to your cottage."

"What did he do that for?"

"He's a jackass. And he's yellow, and Tillini scares him. So the next thing I know, Tillini's asking me: what's this about the Manager of Health Services holding you at gunpoint? Well, Susanna," he looked at her pleadingly, "what could I say? So now that goddamned muscan will be gunning for you, as well as me. I'm real sorry about it."

"I can take care of myself. It's Bryn Trevithick I'm worried about. I suppose Tillini's convinced he was at my cottage?"

"Well, even Porky thought that bit about you standing by your principles was kind of weak. And Tillini's built suspicious. I reckon muscans breed people specially for their jobs. It shouldn't be allowed. It gives them an unfair advantage."

"It's no big deal, though, is it? They just want Trevithick to testify against a few gorons. Even Tillini could hardly mount a manhunt on that basis."

He glanced over his shoulder as though expecting the elephantine Director of Security to materialise then and there. Satisfied, he dropped his voice further and said, "I don't know whether Trevithick was at your place or not. I don't want to know. But let's suppose—just for the sake of argument—that he was. You follow me?"

"So far." She found herself whispering too.

"Then for God's sake get him out of there. We're gearing up for a full-scale raid on Ladysmouth tonight."

"But like I said, Trevithick hasn't done anything."

"That's what you think."

Whispering fast and nervously, Rob Mauser gave her the latest chapter in the ongoing saga of Trevithick the fugitive.

CHAPTER 10

TREVITHICK HAD ASSUMED THE COTTAGE had only two floors, but obviously there was a basement too. The noises had stopped. Probably the intruder—if there was an intruder—had realised the cottage wasn't empty after all. Now everything was breathlessly silent, as though two antagonists were each waiting for the other to make a move.

At least it couldn't be the forces of darkness, as Susanna called the nebulous enemy. They would have charged in waving lasers. No, this was someone who didn't want to be discovered. Someone, perhaps, who wanted to search the house for subversive material or whatever. An enemy of Susanna's, rather than an enemy of Trevithick's.

Or possibly his imagination was playing tricks, fed by Susanna's theories. Perhaps he'd heard innocent outdoor noises and fashioned them to suit his fears.

A window on the south side of the cottage overlooked a neat lawn of ripplegrass, fringed with earth-type flowers and separated from the scrubby landscape by a wide border of flaming orange firepots. Trevithick could see the legs of a goron sticking above the rim of a firepot as he drank nectar, but that wasn't what he'd heard. A fat stoag stood six-legged on the lawn, munching stolidly on the ripplegrass while the tiny green fronds tugged ineffectually at its thick legs. That wasn't what he'd heard either. As he watched, the stoag defecated. The ripplegrass seized the dry turds and bore them toward the centre of the lawn to fertilise the limited root system.

No, what he'd heard had been a thump and a scurrying.

There was no vehicle outside that might have brought an intruder. There were no roads; just a trail leading away around the hillside, winding among the bushtrap scrub. Whoever it was, had come on foot. Which meant they were unlikely to be human. He went into the kitchen, and for the first time noticed a door in the corner of the room. He opened it. A flight of stairs led down to a gloomy basement lit by a small window in the south wall. He descended cautiously.

Several tall figures stood around; broad-shouldered and angular, apparently wearing cloaks, and utterly immobile.

Unnerved, Trevithick backed against the wall, heart pounding. He heard a slight sound. A scraping, creeping sound, such as a broad-shouldered and angular figure might make if it took a stealthy step forward. He felt behind for a light pad, but the wall was blank.

"What do you want?" he called. "Who are you?" The walls soaked up his scared voice and all was silent again.

Then, out of the blackness, a shape rushed him. He ducked, seeing something bright reflect light from the window. He received a heavy blow in the chest and fell backward, clutching at his assailant. Whatever it was smelled foul, but at least it was composed of warm and resilient flesh. They rolled across the floor, grappling. Trevithick caught a glimpse of the tall figures as he rolled. They hadn't moved. They seemed to be watching events coldly.

"Let me go, bugger it!"

It was a female voice. Trevithick slackened his grip automatically. Then he realised the bright object was a knife, and quickly grabbed the hand holding it. The adversaries lay together, both struggling for breath. Now he could see a mane of lank black hair and a bright, venomous eye. He tried to think of something appropriate to say. He didn't have much breath to say it with. The watchers stood mutely by.

"What's all this about?" he asked at last.

"Get off me, will you!" she yelled.

"Not until you tell me who you are and what you're doing here." Trevithick was beginning to feel a little foolish. The other figures still hadn't moved. Maybe they never would.

"None of your bloody business, Mister! Who are you, anyway?"

"I'm a guest in this house," he said. Pompous words, given the circumstances. "You're the intruder. I'll ask the questions."

"You won't get any answers." But she relaxed slightly. "You a friend of that Susanna's?"

"Yes."

"Then to hell with you!"

She seemed very young. Trevithick took the knife from her hand. She didn't resist. "Stay right there," he said. "I'll put the light on. Uh. . . Where's the pad?"

"You don't know much about this place, do you? You sure you're a guest?"

"All right then, you put the light on. Come on." He stood, still keeping hold of her wrist and pulling her to her feet. She was slim; the top of her head barely reached his chin. And he'd been manhandling her. He didn't feel good about it. He let go of her wrist.

She went to the window and pushed something. There was a humming, then the whole wall hinged outward from the top, dropping away until it stopped at an angle of about forty-five degrees. Sudden light blinded him. The wall was a huge mirror, reflecting sunlight into the room.

After a moment he was able to look around. The girl stood watching him cautiously. She wore a ragged dress that had once been yellow, but hadn't seen a laundry for some time. Her feet were bare. Black hair fell below shoulder level and covered most of her face; her eyes were like those of a wary animal, green, slanting and narrowed. Her bare arms and legs were filthy, and he could smell her from halfway across the room.

It was the girl from the aeolus fields. Ralph Greene's daughter, the one who lived in a burrow. Mistral.

"Oh, it's you," she said, recognising him too.

Then her eyes left his and she was looking over his shoulder with expression of disgust. Trevithick followed her gaze.

The room was an artist's studio. The humanlike figures he'd seen in the gloom now proved to be easels with canvasses on them, covered by drapes. More paintings leaned against the wall. Shelves held artists' supplies. A pallet lay on a nearby stool. He removed the drape from an easel, exposing an oil painting. It was a Grecian landscape, idealised, with a temple standing on a bare hillside. It was nicely done.

"Garbage!" came Mistral's venomous comment.

He removed another drape. This time the scene was a small settlement beside a body of water. Little shacks wandered up a hillside and small people were gathered around bowl-shaped boats. It was a Goronwy scene. Orange firepots brightened the middle distance.

Trevithick heard a sharp intake of breath; almost a sob. He turned round. The girl was staring at the painting wide-eyed. "Garbage," she said again in a forced voice. But she was wrong. This painting was beautiful.

"Does Susanna do these?" Trevithick asked.

"You don't know her too well, do you?"

"I hardly know her at all."

"So what are you doing in her house? Don't tell me, I know. She'll take any guy home."

Damn the girl! "Come on. We're going upstairs. You have some explaining to do."

"Not to you I don't!"

But she followed meekly enough as he led her up the stairs and sat her down in the chair Susanna had used the previous night. He'd have it cleaned later. "Would you like a mug of nectar?" he asked, trying to inject a civilised note.

"Mead."

"You're not getting it. It's nectar or nothing." He put the mug in her filthy paw and said, "Okay. I'm Bryn Trevithick. I used to be Director of Ecology. Now it's your turn."

"You used to be Director of Ecology? They kick you out?"

"Yes," he said tiredly. "They kicked me out. Now talk, Mistral."

She was regarding him with something akin to respect. "How do you know my name?"

"You couldn't be anyone else, from what I've heard."

"Why did they kick you out?"

"Why do you live in a burrow?"

"No business of yours." Green eyes stared at him thoughtfully. "You got a woman?"

The sudden question took him by surprise. "I'm not married, no."

"Susanna?"

"I only met her yesterday."

"I don't have a man."

She was young to be talking this way, or was she? It was difficult to see her properly, behind all that black hair. And humans born off-Earth matured differently. "Why were you breaking into this cottage?"

"Didn't break in. The window was open down there."

"Let me rephrase that. What were you doing in the basement?

"Nothing."

"Do you have another name, Mistral?" He was waiting for her to acknowledge her father.

"Why should I? Susanna only has one name. She thinks she's so bloody great she doesn't need another." She hesitated, watching his face. "So why should I have two, huh? Fancy a walk to the caves with me? They're only a step away."

Again she'd caught him off guard. "Why would I want to do that?"

"You'll get bored sitting around this dump all day. You'll be okay at the caves. There's no humans there right now. You'll be a sight safer than here. You trust that Susanna? I don't, I tell you. You watch. Tonight she'll bring a copterload of Security guys. They'll take you away. And that'll be the end of you. Too bad."

"What?" He stared at her. Her assumptions had taken a quantum leap. "Do you think I'm hiding out here?"

"Natch. You were fired by the Organisation. So you hide out if you want to stay alive. You'll find out. Don't find out too late."

"There are hundreds of people living on Goronwy who don't work on the Project."

"Fifty-three." She stood, putting down her mug. "Thanks for the nectar. I'll be going. See you again."

"Hold it!"

"Am I a prisoner or something?"

"Of course not." His attitude had changed. She might be a useful ally. "I'll do a deal. If you'll take a shower, I might walk to the caves with you."

"Stink, do I?"

"I've told you the deal."

"How about my clothes? They stink worse'n me."

"I'll put them through the dry-clean while you're in the shower."

"Okay." Suddenly she smiled. White teeth lit up what he could see of her face. She ran to the window. "Won't be long, Wilfred," she called. "Wilfred's my stoag," she explained. "He loves me. Samaritans don't have pets. Tough on them."

The lake shore was only about two hundred meters away, but getting down there involved some precipitous slopes. Trevithick descended carefully, clinging to fronds of ripplegrass. The fronds clung back hopefully. Mistral simply sat on her backside, hauled the back of her skirt up between her thighs, and slid. Trevithick wondered why he'd bothered to launder her dress. But at least her hair was clean, although more unruly than ever. Wilfred descended sure-footed, and there were moments when Trevithick envied him his six legs.

Reaching the foot of the last slope at a speed that sent her rolling across the beach, Mistral jumped to her feet. Bright green eyes watched Trevithick. "Fun, huh? Don't be such an old fart. Sit down and let yourself go!"

But he still retained some notion of dignity and descended with care, jamming his heels into the soft ground with each step. By the time he reached the sandy beach Mistral was far ahead, splashing through shallow water and yelling with joy. He felt an unexpected surge of pleasure and began to run after her. Wilfred was built for digging rather than running, but he pounded gamely behind, snorting.

Then Trevithick remembered he hadn't taken his anti-pheromone pill that morning. The joy was spurious. He was picking up the emanations of contented gorons at work. He wasn't really happy at all. Mistral probably never took pills. He shouted after her. "Hey, Mistral!"

"What?" She wheeled round, hair flying.

"Come here!"

She stood before him, breathless. "What?"

"We must take our antifero pills."

"Why?"

There was something infectious about her happiness. "Otherwise we won't be in control of our emotions," he explained doggedly.

"So what? I never take them stupid pills. Never did, not even when . . ." A faint shadow crossed her face, then it was gone. "Pills does rotten things to your mind."

"So do goron pheromones."

"Why, do you feel bad?"

"No."

"Okay, then, what's your problem? Catch me if you can!" And she darted off, laughing.

He forced himself to reach for his pills. It was the sensible thing to do. And he'd have taken one, only his pockets were empty. He must have dropped the tube somewhere. With hardly a touch of guilt, he ran after Mistral.

They chased around the shallows like a couple of kids, splashing each other, yelling and laughing, Wilfred catching the mood and galumphing with them. Meanwhile the gorons of Clan Gatherer rowed past, winking at the funny humans as they went and twisting their lips into humanlike smiles. Bridget Booker had taught them that, because there is no use of learning a language if you don't have the right gestures and expressions to go with it. What those gorons really thought of them, Trevithick couldn't imagine; but one thing he did know: there was plenty of mutual happiness about that morning.

It came to an end too suddenly.

He caught Mistral around the waist and they fell to the sand just beyond the waves. She laughed up at him; all white teeth and black hair, the thin dress soaked and clinging to her small breasts. He wasn't sure what he intended. Maybe to kiss her. And maybe she expected that, because her eyes were suddenly grave. But it would have been a stupid thing to do.

Trevithick realised that in time and instead he touched her cheek, lifting the thick hair and brushing it aside. She flinched, and struggled under him. Thinking she was still playing, he pinned her down more tightly and smoothed the hair away from her face. He wanted to see what she looked like.

He saw.

Her brow and one cheek was covered by a livid, disfiguring scar, like an untreated burn.

Otherwise she'd have been very pretty; he still had enough sense left to realize that. But his shock showed. Humans took perfection for granted; there was no reason for ugliness. It offended the observer and it demeaned the sufferer. It was unnecessary, given the cosmetic techniques available at the hospital. So the sight of her face had been horrifyingly unexpected and he'd reacted accordingly.

"Yeah," she said quietly.

They lay there still, as a wave lapped at their legs. There was nothing he could say. He smoothed her hair back over her face the way she wanted it. He thought she might push his hand away, but she didn't. She just lay there looking at him. It was unnerving. The green eyes told him nothing at all.

Then he heard a splash and looked up. A goron was beaching his coracle nearby. Others were approaching, rowing in. They sculled facing forward. It was as though they wanted to keep the humans in view, because they never took their eyes from them. They beached their coracles and drew closer.

And they were all crying.

Bridget Booker hadn't taught them that. It was instinctive, genetic. Tears flowed unchecked from their round little eyes as they began to gather round the couple in a big circle. Mistral had been watching Trevithick's face. Now she saw the gorons and struggled from under him, jumping to her feet.

"It's okay!" she cried. "Everything's fine!"

"Everything's fine," repeated one or two gorons. "Fine."

Mistral laughed and performed a skipping little dance. "Laugh!" she whispered as she danced close to Trevithick. He tried but it didn't convince him or anyone else. "Listen!" she called to the gorons. "I'm happy, you're happy. Us humans, we have these moods but they don't mean nothing. They're soon gone. We don't need no help, really. You get back to your work. This is Bryn. We're taking a look at Ladysmouth. Isn't it a lovely day?"

She took Trevithick's hand and pulled him through the circle of gorons and along the beach. He looked back. The gorons were regarding them without expression. He suddenly felt vulnerable. There were at least twenty of them, and many more just offshore, sitting motionless in their coracles, watching.

"Is there any danger?" he asked.

"No, they'll cheer up soon. They're not into suicide."

She'd misunderstood his question. Clearly he had a lot to learn about the gorons. "I'm sorry," he said.

"Sorry for what?" She was hurrying along; they'd reached the shadow of tall sandstone cliffs. "Come on, it's happier here. This is Clan Gatherer's hive. See all those little caves? That's where they live. Stoags help them dig. There'll be some gorons around. Guardians, and people taking the day off."

"Taking the day off?"

"Oh, sure. They don't work all the time. They don't have no feeling of guilt, see? That's why they're happy most times. If they feel like a day off they just bloody well take it. Nobody blames them. They earn it."

He heard the sound of singing from the caves and saw Mistral's step lighten. "Do you have some kind of affinity to them?"

"All Goronwy brats do. Some other folk do. You might. The pills block it. Come on. We go in here."

A few hours of enchantment followed. Trevithick had never experienced anything remotely like it before. Some fifty gorons were assembled in a large chamber, seated against the curved wall. As they stared into a glowing fire of driftwood, they sang. The songs were long, the melodies wandering, the words beyond human understanding, but the rhythm was universal. It was the rhythm of the heartbeat; a steady pulsing picked out by clicking sticks, skin drums, and a muttering bass chorus. It was a lovely alien beguine. It captured Trevithick's senses and lifted his soul. It brought him a peace he'd never known before.

Once, Mistral whispered, "Like it?"

He was holding her hand. He didn't need to reply. He was holding the slender hand of the goron to his left, too. He glanced at the little man, their eyes met, and he understood a goron for the first time. It was the pheromones. The cavern was full of the emissions of fifty contented gorons. And he hadn't taken a pill.

Mistral whispered, "Don't fight it!"

He relaxed again and let the music take him.

Later the singing was followed by socialising. Jugs of nectar were passed around. Gorons strolled about, speaking their simple tongue and hugging one another. The humans stood. The goron whose hand Trevithick had been holding spoke.

"Stand fast, human. Who are you?"

Mistral replied for him. "He's Bryn Trevithick. He was a Samaritan but they threw him out. I think he's probably okay."

The goron said, "Yes, I think he's okay, but he didn't like you saying that."

"No, I didn't," Trevithick said, mildly irritated. "What do you mean, I'm okay?"

Mistral laughed. "Touchy, aren't you? That's what living with humans does to you. What I meant was, you got an open mind. Don't worry. Nobody's gonna ask you to take sides."

"Take what sides? Who's against whom?"

"It don't matter. Early days, huh?" She changed the subject with suspicious alacrity. "This is Brennan. He's a bargee."

"Oh, yes?" That seemed odd. "I thought it was all Clan Gatherer here."

"Yeah, you been with humans a long time. Notice how every-one stays with their own people, in Samarita? Biologists with biologists, cooks with cooks? Gorons aren't like that."

"We all love music," said Brennan. "We all love talking. We do it together, why not? Come, I'll show you my barge."

As he led the way down a dim passage so low that Trevithick had to duck, Mistral murmured, "He's sure proud of his barge. Get to know him, Bryn. You never know."

"Never know what?"

"Just fifty-three humans on Goronwy who aren't Samaritans. And I'd trust a goron more than any of them. You may need Bren-nan sometime."

At the time it seemed an unduly pessimistic notion and he told Mistral so, but she just shrugged and walked on behind Brennan. Soon he saw light ahead, heard an excited grunting and then Wilfred was stamping heavily around Mistral, nosing her hand. A fresh breeze blew along the beach, and the sun was setting. They'd been in the cavern far longer than Trevithick had realised.

"Some other time, Brennan," he said. "I have to be going."

"What do you mean?" asked Mistral sharply.

"Susanna's expecting me at the cottage."

"What is she, your keeper or something?"

He sensed a dangerous situation brewing. "Listen, it's been a great day, Mistral. Thanks a lot for showing me around and every-thing."

The green eyes were bright. "I didn't just show you around. There was more to it, and you bloody well know it, Mister. And you mess around with that Susanna, you'll be food for Lady. What's so great about her, anyway?"

"I'm her guest," he said weakly.

Brennan was edging away, finding the pheromones not to his liking. "Stand fast." He muttered the goron dual purpose greeting and farewell.

Mistral shouted, "Why can't you be my guest? She's one of them!"

She was losing control, fists clenched as though about to attack him. Brennan was running away down the beach. Trevithick didn't blame him. Wilfred was whining miserably, cowering at her feet.

"Stop behaving like a kid," said Trevithick. He could have been more tactful.

She stared at him with a look of incredulity. Then, quite simply, she began to scream. He glanced around, embarrassed, but Clan Gatherer had beached their boats for the night and melted away into the caves. He caught sight of Brennan ducking into a dark hole in the cliff. It was just Mistral and he, and the stoag. Mistral paused for breath, then screamed again. Wilfred howled. Mistral screamed. Their breath coincided so that the yelling began to sound like a crazy harmonisation.

Mistral stopped screaming and laughed, a horrifying cackle without any mirth but with more than a touch of insanity. "You idiot!" she shouted. She clutched the top of her dress and ripped it downwards, exposing small, conical breasts. "You could have me! What will she ever give you?"

He was trying to think of a reply when, quite suddenly, he heard a wasplike buzzing. He looked up. A copter was dropping directly toward them. They were totally exposed in an expanse of empty beach.

"It's Security!" yelled Mistral. "You're dead, and serve you bloody well right!"

CHAPTER 11

T REVITHICK WATCHED THE COPTER LAND. There was nowhere to go. Cliffs to the south of him, lake to the north. The wide open expanse of the beach east and west. Mistral's last words still echoed in his head.

Then, in huge relief, he saw Susanna jump from the copter to the sand and hurry toward them.

She was not her usual smiling self. Glancing at Mistral she said briefly, "Cover yourself up." Then to Trevithick she said, "Hop in."

As they rose from the beach Mistral's breasts were still bare. Her hands were otherwise occupied, preventing her hair from swirling away from her face as she stood watching Trevithick with cold green eyes. Less than two minutes later Susanna was checking a monitor in the cottage.

"You haven't seen anyone snooping around?" she asked.

"I haven't exactly been around," Trevithick admitted. "Not since I found Mistral in your basement."

"Mistral in the basement?" Her tone was sharp. "When?"

"Just after you left."

She ran down the stairs. A short while later she reappeared, looking pink and relieved. "It's okay."

"What did you expect?"

Without replying, she went into the kitchen and called back, "Fancy a bite to eat? We don't have much time."

"All I've had today is nectar. I'm starved." Why had she avoided his question? And why had Mistral had refused to tell him why she'd been in the basement? He had no idea what was going on around him, but he didn't want to push Susanna too hard. She seemed to be on his side despite Mistral's warnings, but he wasn't totally sure of her yet. He wandered into the kitchen and watched her doing mysterious things with pans and heating gadgets and raw food. She was very good at it. She was much better equipped for survival than he was.

Then he noticed something else. A film-wrapped slab labelled M16 on the counter.

"How did you know?" he asked.

"Oh . . . You're big news these days. People are anxious to gossip about you. It was easy enough to ask, casually, what was the code of that disgusting food you always ate?"

Trevithick was touched. "Well, thanks."

"I had this feeling you didn't like my home cooking."

"It's just that I'm not used to it. I'll take just a spoonful of whatever you're having, to go with my M16. Nothing too exotic, mind."

"Okay." She tossed some green stuff into a pan. It looked the kind of thing stoags might throw up. "So what have you been doing with yourself today?".

He described the events, omitting the more peculiar details of Mistral's behaviour.

She chuckled. "All very healthy and educational, for sure. Odd that when I found you both, there seemed to be a lot of tit on display."

He tried to babble some explanation.

She cut him short. "No, I should have warned you. I just didn't know Mistral was in this neck of the woods. Took a fancy to you, did she? Can't say I blame her. You are something of a hunkish example of ex-Directorhood, if a little prim and proper. But be careful with her, huh?"

"I sure will." It was heartfelt. "What's her problem, anyway?"

Susanna hesitated. "Maybe it all stems from that ghastly scarring. It must be terrible for her. She hates herself for it."

"So why doesn't she have it seen to?"

"Her father's offered to pay, but she won't take his money. She thinks it's dirty."

"Why would anyone have to pay?"

"If you work on the Project, you get free medical treatment. If you don't, you don't."

"The poor kid. That's inhuman!"

She eyed him thoughtfully. "Take today, for example. I was tending to a sick goron near the cottage. I'd spotted him from the copter. He was trying to walk to Ladysmouth and he'd been spiked by a bushtrap. I was cutting out the spines and disinfecting the wound. We were well hidden under an overhang, because if Security had found us I'd have been in big trouble. They call it Interfering with the Course of Nature. It's a crime in the eyes of the Organisation."

"But that's garbage! There's no question of ecological balance. The gorons aren't animals in some reservation. They're intelligent beings!"

She laughed. "My, just listen to the great protector! It wasn't so many hours ago you were quibbling about my giving our little friends a neighbourly lift over the mountains!"

He felt himself flush. "Yeah, well, perhaps I've got to know them better since then."

"Keep up the good work. Truth is, the Project is too cheap to throw open its hospital doors to all and sundry. Anyway, my injured goron suddenly pricked up his ears and began to wail. He'd been a brave little guy up to then, hardly flinching, and I'd just finished the dressing. So I guessed he was picking up bad pheromones from not far off. I asked him. He pointed. I ran for the copter and the rest you know. Interesting tale, huh?"

He considered this while she tipped hot things from a pan onto two plates. They took them into the living room and sat down to eat. Between mouthfuls, he asked, "So what's the story behind Mistral?"

"She was born on Goronwy. She's nineteen, but you wouldn't think so. She's the daughter of the Director of Engineering, an ex-buddy of yours."

"I'd heard. But what about the mother?"

"Wendy, lovely woman. She died two years ago. Mistral took it hard. She'd never got along with her father, and she had the final bust-up with him soon after the death, and moved out. She won't let him help her in any way. Sometimes pride can be another word for stupidity."

"She wouldn't admit to me that her name's Greene."

"She doesn't acknowledge it. And she doesn't qualify to change her name officially. She could give herself an unofficial name, of course. But I think she has her own reasons for not doing that."

It was too bad, thought Trevithick. A potentially nice young woman ruining her life because of some childish principle. They finished their meal in a thoughtful silence. Susanna was different from the carefree woman of the morning. He caught her looking at him speculatively a couple of times. And occasionally she'd glance at the visiphone, as though expecting a call.

"What's happened?" he asked eventually. "You said we don't have much time." He'd have liked to spend an intimate evening skirting the edges of flirtation.

"I'm sorry, Bryn. Events have moved along. I got the word from Rob that Security aren't happy. Rob was one of the guys who came here last night."

"I'm surprised he'll speak to you after you pulled a gun on him."

"Oh, Rob doesn't harbour grudges," she said, then grinned. "Although that would have been a doozy of a grudge to harbour. Another guy would have brooded over it for yonks. Well, anyway, it seems Tillini knows Rob and Porky didn't search too thoroughly. And maybe my excuse for the excess weight didn't convince anyone."

"I've got you in trouble. God, I'm sorry."

"The hell with it, I'm always in trouble. Anyway, they've upped the ante. They've dropped the pretext of wanting you as a witness to attempted murder. It never was a very compelling reason to hunt the victim down. So now they want you for theft of Organisation property."

"What!"

"And they're not talking petty cash, either. They're accusing you of erasing data from the mainframe yesterday and walking off with the back-up disks."

"What data, for God's sake?"

She was watching his face. "Results of biological research on Lady that throws new light on the cause of her sickness."

"Garbage! There was no such data. The research I saw was getting nowhere. Why am I supposed to have done this, anyway?"

"They say you're probably going to try to do a deal. Your passage to Earth for the disks."

Not a bad idea—if he had the disks. "It's ridiculous. I had no way of getting into the data base to erase files. They'd already invalidated my voiceprint." He described how he'd gone back to his office to find Ivor Sabin had been warned against him. "Even my desk had been cleared. There had been some disks there, just summaries of recent research I'd made myself. But they were gone. I assume the back-up disks were locked in the safe. I took nothing away. There was nothing to take! Ivor was there. He'll back me up."

"Unfortunately," she said quietly, "It's Ivor Sabin who says you took the disks."

Ivor? What was going on? "They've got at him," he said. "It's the only answer. They've bribed him, probably with my job. The little creep! But . . ."

"I know what you're thinking. Well, let me tell you this, Bryn Trevithick, it doesn't surprise me one bit. There's been something fishy going on for a few years now. It just happens that you've been sucked into it. And I'll tell you something else. I had Ralph Greene run a check on communications between Ecology and other places. And guess which of your staff came up top of the list for outside calls to a specific person?"

"Ivor, I bet! Who's he been talking to?"

"This won't surprise you. None other than Manning Edlin, our revered Director of Systems and Communications."

Trevithick walked over to the window and stared into the late afternoon. Around the curve of the bay he could see little blobs of darkness in the wall of the cliff; the cave entrances. Contented gorons sat in there, probably singing and drinking, their day's work done. And he was on the run, and he didn't know the real reason why. He saw a human figure standing at the water's edge, tossing pebbles into the waves. A small, heavyset animal stood there too. Mistral and Wilfred. He activated the zoom just as she turned to look up at the window. He moved away, just in case. Just in case what? He didn't know.

He heard Susanna's voice. "As I said before, when they hired you they got the wrong man for the job. So they tried to dispose of you quietly, but you escaped and went into hiding. So now they've gone public. And it's two-pronged, this accusation of theirs. It'll set the gorons against you too, if they choose to believe Tillini."

"What am I going to do?" And what Trevithick did then was not easily explained. Turning from the window he found Susanna standing right behind him. Her eyes were bright, her expression unusually grave. Golden hair spilled over her shoulders. He took one step toward her and took her in his arms, burying his face in her hair and holding her close. Some tiny voice of conscience was telling him this was no way to treat his protector, but he didn't pay too much attention to it. He just wanted to stay like that forever.

She took it well, considering she'd only known him for one day. She gave him probably ten seconds, then disengaged herself gently. "Patients often fancy their nurses." she said softly. "It's kind of an Oedipus thing. It doesn't mean anything."

"Sorry." She was still holding his hands. He was embarrassed at what he'd done. What had happened to the Director of Ecology, that respected and dignified pillar of Operations Division? Had he lost his moral sense with his job?

"I know. You don't know what came over you." She chuckled. "Well, I do. You've had a rough time of it and Ladyjuice stays with you for days, so you don't act quite normally. And it wasn't long ago you were goggling at Mistral pulling her clothes off. It all adds up."

He detached his hands from hers, reluctantly, and sat down opposite. "There's one other factor you didn't mention."

"Oh, yes. You think I'm the greatest. That goes without saying."

Her smile took any sting out of the words. Her tone implied that she simply meant what she said.

"Yeah," he muttered, avoiding her eyes.

"Now we know how we stand," she said brightly, "Let's consider our course of action. Firstly—"

The visiphone buzzed.

"Oh, God," she said. "I think this is it." She pressed the Connect button. A face appeared; an anxious-looking young man wearing a Security cap. "Yes, Rob?" she said.

"They're on their way," he said without preamble. Hurriedly he went on, "Listen, the theft of the disks scares me. I mean, this is big. I mean, it has to do with the whole purpose of the Project. Doesn't it?" He peered worriedly out of the tiny screen.

"If the disks were stolen."

"You think it's all a blind?" he said doubtfully.

"Could be."

"You've talked to Trevithick? Does he deny it?"

"You don't want to know about Trevithick, Rob."

"I guess not. I mean, no, of course I don't." He was talking fast. "I wasn't trying to trick you or anything, honest." Trevithick watched him, keeping out of range of the visual pickup. Mauser was very young, broad-shouldered, good-looking in his way. A stereotypical Security man. Except that he seemed to be a nice guy. "Anyway," he continued, "I called to let you know they're on their way. Covert apprehension. They've sent Griggs and Seldeman. You know what that means. And I'm up before Tillini tomorrow. It . . . It'll go much better for me if they don't find Trevithick at your place. For God's sake don't try to brazen things out. I know what you're like."

"Fear not, we are about to flee," said Susanna gravely.

"Don't flee," he almost shouted. "And for God's sake take this seriously. Just get rid of you-know-who, if he's there, and behave normally when the goons arrive!"

She took pity on him. "Thanks for the warning, Rob, but I was leaving anyway. I owe you one. I'll be lifting off in a couple of minutes so I'll miss Griggs and Seldeman; what a shame. Give them my love. I've decided to close up the cottage for a while and go back to my apartment."

"Your apartment's the next place they'll look!"

"And good luck to them. Don't look so worried. Always remember, any supposed link between Trevithick and me is pure guesswork on the part of Tillini and yourself, based on the dubious evidence of the payload of my copter."

"And a whole mess of goron gossip. The termites—uh, the little guys—they've been talking. They had no reason not to!"

"Goron gossip is notoriously unreliable. It becomes myth by nightfall, then they make it into songs. Tell Tillini that tomorrow. It may appeal to his sense of the poetic, and it's perfectly true." She paused. "My light's blinking. Someone's easing into this frequency. 'Bye."

She broke the connection and replaced the visiphone on the table. They sat watching it. It buzzed.

"It'll be Griggs telling you to stay put until they get here," Trevithick guessed.

"No, he wouldn't want to alert me." She glanced at him mischievously. "It's probably some random lover, dying to grab me. Too bad." She let the visiphone lie and went to the window. "Speaking of which, your girlfriend's out there, I expect you know."

"I did notice."

"Call her."

"What? Why do you want me to do that?"

"Well, she sure as hell wouldn't come if I called her. And she has a starring role in my scenario."

"She does?" he said nervously. He'd already found that questioning Susanna's complex thought-processes consumed a lot of time—of which they were short, with the forces of darkness winging in their direction. He opened the door and yelled. There was a distant answer, and in a couple of minutes Mistral arrived, scowling and well covered up.

"Yeah?" Her glance at Trevithick was neutral; at Susanna, hostile.

"We're taking off for Samarita in a couple of minutes," Susanna told her.

"Bully for you."

"When I say we, I mean all three of us. Plus your stoag."

"What if I refuse?"

"Then it'll go badly for Bryn. You see, he can't stay in my apartment in Samarita because I'm already under suspicion of harbouring him. And he can't stay here. So you'll have to look after him for a while. You have the, uh, facilities, right?"

Mistral regarded Trevithick consideringly. He regarded her worriedly. Was this the only way?

Then she blinked and looked away. "How long for?" she muttered.

"Until it's safe for him."

"When's that gonna be?"

"We don't know."

"Maybe I don't want him around all the time, had you thought of that?"

"It's not exactly all the time. Security have instructions for covert apprehension, so Rob says."

"What's covert apprehension?" Trevithick asked. He wasn't used to the terminology of pursuit.

"It means they have to take you at night or in some remote area. They can't capture you during the day in a crowded street, for example. Your pheromones would panic the gorons. If you tried to escape, or fight Security off, the gorons might join in instinctively. That could result in a mass brawl and release of more aggressive pheromones. That would attract vespas."

"Oh." He digested this information. "But why doesn't all that apply after dark as well?"

"Really, Trevithick, and you an ecologist? After dark there's no sun, so the aeolus flowers all curl up and go beddy-byes. So you don't get those little winds puffing in all directions, spreading people's pheromones. So then the baddies can lay rough hands on you and nobody the wiser."

"Of course. Sorry. Does that mean I'm safe to walk the streets of Samarita in broad daylight?"

"Yes. Just watch out for anaesthetic darts and suchlike. If

you see someone pointing something at you, duck. And after you've finished promenading, make sure you're not followed back to base."

Mistral was watching Susanna. "Why are you trying to help him? What's in it for you?"

"He's one of the good guys."

"Oh, yeah. Sure." She looked from Susanna to Trevithick and back again, suspicion in the green eyes.

Five minutes later they were airborne.

They sat in a row across the front bench seat, Susanna at the controls. Trevithick sat in the middle, representing a buffer zone between two warring parties. Wilfred lay behind in the area intended for stretcher cases. Conversation was not coming easily, and Trevithick was getting increasingly apprehensive about trusting his safety to the unpredictable Mistral. Darkness fell as they hummed southward.

Susanna suddenly said, "By the way, we were talking about Marik Darwin and Clan Active. If you want to know more about that can of worms, they're holding a meeting tomorrow night. Maybe you should attend. You'll be quite safe in a crowd like that."

Mistral suddenly spoke up. "Marik Darwin's crazy. He's twisted a whole bunch of poor silly gorons into thinking his way. It's rotten! It's like kids plotting to kill their mother!"

"True," agreed Susanna. "It stinks. Unless Marik's playing some deep game. It won't do any harm to find out."

Mistral leaned forward, looking around Trevithick at Susanna. "Who the hell are you working for?" she demanded.

"Life and Liberty and the Organisation Way, of course."

"Crap! What's going on, huh?"

"Just accept that we three are on the same side, girl. I know it's not easy. But it's best that you don't know too much."

Mistral was annoyed. "Huh! Well, let me tell you something. I got my own ways of getting at the Organisation. And I'd be dumb to tell you about them. One day you'll see!"

"I hope not," said Susanna seriously. "There are dangerous people out there."

"I know a trick or two!"

The conversation continued in this vein, on and off, until the lights of Samarita appeared below and Susanna put the copter into a steep descent. Soon they touched down beside Lady, close to where Trevithick had been pushed in.

"Happy memories, Trevithick? Okay, you two. Out you get. I can't afford to stay here long." Unexpectedly she kissed him lightly on the cheek. "Look after him, Mistral," she said.

"Huh," the girl grunted, jumping lightly to the ground. The stoag followed her in a clumsy bound.

The copter lifted off and was soon gone. Lady slid beside them, slow and slimy. It was very dark; there was rain in the air, mud underfoot. Strands of ripplegrass caressed Trevithick's ankles.

"Which way?" he asked.

Mistral sighed. "Oh, God, I wish . . ." Then her voice hardened. "Uplady. Round the north end of town. She's made us walk a long way."

Her attitude made him angry. "She's taken all kinds of chances for me. They'll know she landed here. They'll ask her why and she'll have to think up a reason. What reason could she give if she'd dropped us at your front door, eh?"

The was a long silence, then a warm hand stole into his. "Sorry. Let's get going. It's not all that far, really."

They'd gone less than a hundred meters when he heard the hum of a copter again. "She's coming back," he said. "What's happened?"

"No," said Mistral. "Not her. Them!"

And as she spoke, a cone of light descended through the rain and picked out every detail of the riverbank ahead of them as though it were a sunny day. Mistral uttered a little scream. The cone moved toward them. Trevithick looked around desperately.

He couldn't see any available cover. It was too dark, and when the light reached them it would be too late.

CHAPTER 12

"THIS WAY!" CRIED MISTRAL.

She tugged Trevithick's hand and he followed her. He had no alternative. From what he remembered of the area, there was no cover.

There was Lady. There was the Ladyside trail, used as a towpath for barges. There was low ripplegrass and a scattering of firepots. And further west lay a vast tract of bushtrap, which was not a good thing to stumble into in the dark. It was big, thorny and strong. Stoags ate its leaves, but with their six powerful legs and thick fur they were the only creatures that could resist the pull of its vines. It was the origin of the goron greeting 'Stand fast.'

So when Mistral began to drag him in that direction, Trevithick did not go willingly.

"Hurry up, you idiot!" she cried.

Light flooded the surface of Lady. Then the vertical beam swung toward them. Trevithick prepared to throw himself flat, in the hope that the occupants of the copter would see him as a nondescript mound half-covered by ripplegrass.

"In here!" shouted Mistral.

It was a cave in some kind of rock wall. She urged an unwilling Wilfred in first, then she followed and Trevithick brought up the rear. There was room enough to crawl, but not to stand. Wilfred hated it, scrabbling and whining up ahead. The air inside was oddly warm and smelled acrid. The tunnel walls were quite smooth. Trevithick felt trapped in there. "They'll follow us in!" he protested.

"No, they won't. Come on around this bend."

They huddled together in the darkness, watching the play of light against the far wall of the tunnel. The hum of the copter became louder, then died.

"They've landed," Mistral whispered. "Keep still, Wilfred!"

He heard a voice. "Round about here, wasn't it? He can't have gone far. Jack says Susanna's just touched down on her apartment roof."

And another voice in sceptical tones. "A waste of time, if you ask me. She can't have been so dumb as to drop him off here. If he was with her at all. We don't even know that; there's no evidence she's ever met him. The whole thing could be a typical Security screw-up. And I'd arranged to meet Sandy at the Barge tonight."

After a short silence, the first man spoke again. He was so close that his voice reverberated up the tunnel. "Well, he can't have gone in here, that's for sure."

"If he did, he won't have lasted long. We can write him off."

And Wilfred chose that moment to snuffle loudly.

"What's that?"

"Sounded like someone sneezing. He's around here somewhere."

Trevithick felt Mistral shifting position, then Wilfred pushed past with an unhappy whimper. They heard him scramble from the tunnel and drop to the ground.

"It's just a stoag."

"Lucky to be alive, huh? Maybe that's why she landed here, to turn the stoag loose."

"Why would she carry a stoag in the copter?"

"Maybe it was causing problems at that cottage of hers. Like rooting around and begging at the door, the way they do. So she decided to relocate it."

"Why not just shoot the bastard?"

"Not her style. Rob tells me she doesn't like to kill things. He sees her as some kind of angel. You should hear him talk about her."

Trevithick heard Mistral sniff. The voices began to fade. The search party drifted away. He was drenched in sweat. "Why didn't they look in here? They had us cold."

"Take it easy. You don't wanna be spreading no bad pheromones about." She sounded scared herself. "Just lie still for a while, huh? We can't do nothing until they've gone. I hope Wilfred's okay."

So they lay close together, and now the immediate danger had passed his mind began to wander. Why hadn't they searched the tunnel? He can't have gone in there, that's for sure. That's what one of them had said. And the other had said, If he did, he won't have lasted long.

Why not?

"Mistral," he whispered. "What the hell is this place?"

"Just a tunnel, that's all." She was shivering, yet it was warm. He hugged her close and decided not to pursue the matter for the time being. People were making a habit of keeping facts from him: Mistral, Susanna. Ivor Sabin...

He began to wonder about his old colleague Ivor Sabin, who'd been at his side through the two most disastrous episodes of his life. Annecy, when they'd both worked for Outward Ho, and now Goronwy, when they'd both worked for the Samaritan Organisation. You'd think a guy would have some sympathy for another guy, in such circumstances. But Ivor had shown precious little sympathy for him. More like embarrassment at being involved with a loser. There'd been no offers of help when Trevithick was on his uppers after Annecy; in fact Ivor had disappeared from his life with unseemly haste. And he hadn't exactly leaped to Trevithick's defence over the firing here. No, his old colleague Ivor was no friend in a crisis. And now he was mixed up with Manning Edlin in some way.

They'd been at college together in Eurobase, Earth, sharing a room, always short of money. Both Trevithick's parents died in the Sentry Down shuttle disaster during that period. All their possessions had been on the shuttle and insurance companies would not cover events outside the earth's atmosphere. The companies couldn't be blamed for their caution; the cost of the Sentry Down accident would have bankrupted every insurer on Earth.

So there they were, Ivor and Trevithick, sharing a room and sharing a girl—although he hadn't known they shared the girl at first. Mandy. Plump, bright-eyed, brown-haired and unable to make up her mind. He'd dated her first and Ivor—the conniving little Celt—had stepped in one evening when Trevithick had failed to show up for a date through no fault of his own. She'd two-timed them for weeks. Oddly enough, Ivor had dumped her immediately after Trevithick did.

And also oddly enough, Ivor must have left Outward Ho soon after Trevithick had been fired, because he'd joined the Samaritan Organisation almost two years previously. There'd been no need for him to make the change. No blame was attached to him for the Annecy fiasco.

Was the parallel pure chance, or did it have something to do with personalities and outside circumstances? He'd have to get hold of Ivor and find out exactly why he left Outward Ho, and how he came to join Samaritan's Goronwy project. And why he hadn't been appointed Director of Ecology when Marik Darwin quit. It would have been the natural thing, surely? He was well qualified. Why pick Trevithick, a failure from a rival outfit?

Unless, as Susanna said, they wanted a failure.

So what did that make Ivor?

A humming sound shattered his train of thought. "They're going," said Mistral. The hum faded with distance and they crawled backward from the tunnel. The air outside smelled fresh and pleasant. Wilfred bumped heavily against Trevithick's legs, trying to get to Mistral. They indulged in a few seconds reunion. Trevithick could see the tunnel entrance dimly now; it was part of a big edifice, rising several meters and blotting out the stars.

His mouth was dry. "But it's. . ."

"Yeah," said Mistral casually. "Vespa's nest. Best not to tell you. You'd have freaked and sent pheromones up the tube, and woke them all up. Nasty."

They started walking. The eastern sky showed a faint duck-egg blue, giving enough light to avoid bushtraps. They headed north up the Ladyside trail as far as the Passing Barge. The lights were out; the last customers had gone home or fallen asleep in their chairs. Trevithick saw the dark outline of a barge on the far side of Lady, moored for the night. He envied the bargee; not a care in the world, just the simple pleasure of the passage and the simple expectation of company at the Ladyside inns. Nice life.

Perhaps it didn't pay to be a member of an intelligent species.

Not that the gorons weren't intelligent. It was a matter of degree and social structure. An individual goron might not be so bright as a human, but collectively they amounted to something incomparable. Theirs was a near-perfect society: stable population, jobs for all, absence of poverty, no crime, no wars...

But there had been wars, once. Goron oral history told of a time when there were many Ladies, and fierce territorial battles at the lake. So now there was one Lady and no wars—but the threat of extinction instead. You couldn't have it all ways.

They turned inland. The sky was getting lighter; the stars were washing out. "If we see anyone, we separate," he said. If anyone saw them together Security would be at Mistral's door within the hour.

"Natch." She walked on, treading warily like a deer; slender, peering through her curtain of thick back hair.

He glanced at her. "How did it happen?" he asked.

She knew what he was talking about. It must have been on her mind every minute of every day. "Accident. Soon after I . . . left home. A vespa got spooked, stupid thing. Nobody was gonna harm it. It came for me and I ducked. Missed my face with its sting, but . . ." I caught a flash of green eyes in the half light. "What business is it of yours?"

"None. It must have taken a lot of guts to crawl into that nest tonight. Why did you do it?"

"Didn't have no choice, did I?"

"You could have stayed outside with Wilfred. You could have told those guys that Susanna had just dropped you and Wilfred off."

The hair swung, the green eyes flashed contempt. The light was getting better, unfortunately. "You're so stupid. If she'd just been giving me a lift home, she'd have dropped me off at my place. This is all because of you, don't you see? Now they think she dropped off a stoag, so everything's okay."

"Well . . . Thanks anyway."

"That thing happened yonks ago. I know how to handle vespas now. Just don't scare them, that's all."

The sunlight was touching the tips of the domes by the time they arrived at Mistral's home. At first Trevithick didn't recognise it for what it was. They'd passed among the apartment blocks at the edge of town and walked through mounds of sand denoting an extensive stoag warren. Arriving at what looked like an abandoned guardhouse of cracked concrete, Mistral said, "Here we are." Her tone was defensive.

She pushed the door open. Wilfred shoved his way in and they followed. The first thing Trevithick noticed was the smell; a rank combination of stoag and unwashed Mistral.

"Down here," she said.

He saw a pit in the far corner. There wasn't much else to see; the floor was covered with litter and the small window was filthy. Wilfred had already disappeared; presumably into the pit. He followed Mistral and found the pit levelled out into a tunnel. Tunnels seemed to be the order of the day; but at least this one was high enough to stand in. After some five meters it broadened into a chamber. Mistral lit an oil lamp.

The chamber was roughly oval, about four meters by five. Another tunnel led off into darkness at the far end. The uneven floor was partly covered by an old rug; the walls were bare packed sand. The rough concrete ceiling appeared to be the underside of a long-abandoned building. A table held a few scraps of food and a simple oil burner; there were no chairs. A heap of furs lay piled against the wall. Mistral threw herself onto these and stared up at him challengingly.

"Well?"

"Well what?"

"What do you think of this dump?"

A moment of anger. "Why do you enjoy putting me on the spot?

I guess I feel exactly the same as you do about this place. Now stop behaving like a kid!"

"Wanna show you something." She leaped to her feet, took his hand and led him through the far tunnel, past several junctions until the ground sloped up to daylight again. And here was a surprise.

They stood in a large clearing hacked out of bushtrap. The scrub was over two meters high and impenetrable, so they were hidden from view on all sides except for the balconies of the distant domes.

The clearing was a garden, coloured brightly by the morning light. Earth-type vegetables grew in rows, Earth-type flowers grew in bright beds against the bushtrap. The place was a model of neatness; not a weed or a blade of ripplegrass in sight.

"Not bad, huh?" said Mistral proudly. "Susanna's got nothing like this, right?"

"Right," he said.

"Just like Earth?" she asked anxiously. "I never been to Earth. Look," she pointed, "Earth trees."

Ten saplings stood in line to the north. He recognised Pacific Coast conifers: Douglas fir, western hemlock, larch, sequoia and red cedar, two of each. They looked so incongruous, somehow so courageous against the alien bushtrap that he felt his eyes sting. It was years since he'd seen trees like those.

And they were dying.

Each tree was covered with a mass of cones. This gave an impression of fruitfulness, but he knew a distress crop when he saw one. If a conifer is put under severe stress—such as extensive damage, or a potentially fatal climate change—it puts out one last immense crop of cones before it dies. It hopes, if trees can be said to hope, that this will ensure the survival of its species. Other living things behave similarly. Even humans, in their own way.

Trevithick didn't know why the trees were dying. The Goronwy climate was fine; similar to Earth. So it must have been the soil.

"Collect the cones," he told Mistral. "Keep them in a cool place. We should run a test on the soil sometime."

She was watching his face. "Okay. Something's wrong?"

She was so proud of those trees, he couldn't hurt her. "Maybe not, but you have to remember this isn't Earth. Just to be on the safe side, it's better to have a back-up."

"No, it isn't Earth," she repeated quietly. She stared at her trees unhappily, sensing that he'd criticised them in some way but not knowing exactly how or why. This garden was a small outpost of Earth she'd created; a link with the homeland she'd never seen, and maybe never would see. He felt an enormous pity for her. In doing this he forgot to feel pity for himself. Perhaps that moment in Mistral's garden was when he began to snap out of it. He'd been lucky enough to know Earth, and the Organisation could not take that away. "I never said it was Earth," added Mistral defiantly.

"It's beautiful," he said, meaning it. "Where did you get the seeds?"

"Gardens around the domes." He knew she was lying; the vegetables, for example, must have come from the hydroponics plant in the service dome. He didn't pursue the subject. It didn't really matter.

On the way back to her living quarters he heard stoags grunting down a branch tunnel. Mistral had a direct connection to the warren; that was where Wilfred had gone. Near her living quarters two more tunnels branched off; the roofs of these were high enough for a human to stand, unlike the other stoag-sized tunnel. He asked about them.

"That one's the biffy," she said bluntly. "Best take a light when you go in there."

"What about the other?"

"None of your goddamned business." They passed into the main chamber. "If I catch you snooping around in there, I'll kick you out of here so fast you'll swear you had a rocket up your arse, Mister!"

He didn't pursue the matter. She told him to get out of her way while she prepared breakfast. She chopped up various vegetables and fried them on the oil burner. The smell was strange, but had the benefit of overpowering the smell of the furs on which he sat. She shot him curious glances from time to time as she jiggled the pan. She seemed to be reappraising him. In the dim light she was little more than a black shadow, almost witchlike.

Suddenly she burst out, "On the beach. I behaved real bad. Sorry."

Some reply seemed called for. He said, truthfully, "It's okay. I thought you looked very pretty. So forget it and let's start again."

"It's the pheromones." She pronounced it ferry-moans. "I don't have no pills."

"Neither do I. So we'd better watch ourselves, huh?"

"You wasn't born here. Us Goronwy brats, it hits us hard. It can be bad." Suddenly he saw her teeth flash in a grin. "And it can be good. Dome people are zombies, really. You don't know what the real world's like."

So here she was living in a cave and eating wild plants, and she saw it as the real world. There wasn't much he could say. "Isn't it better to have your own emotions," he asked, "instead of getting them second-hand from gorons?"

She said quietly, "I got my own emotions. And the pheromones, they work both ways." She took the pan off the burner. "Okay, let's eat."

She'd carved spoons from bushtrap vines. They spooned the green stuff from the pan and forced it down. At least, he forced it down. She seemed to enjoy it, eating noisily. "Got some taste to it, this has," she observed. "Better than pap out of them machines." Finished, she took his hand and led him to the heap of furs. He sat beside her warily. "So what you gonna do about Lady?" she asked.

"Do?"

"You gonna make her well again?"

"With no laboratory and the Organisation after my blood?"

"You don't need no lab. You got your learning. And you got your commonsense. And you got Lady near. You can talk to the gorons, can't you? I bet you got more chance of curing Lady than anyone." She squeezed his hand; she hadn't let it go since they'd sat down. "You will cure her, won't you? I got to live here the rest of my life."

Suddenly it became a hellish responsibility.

A woman on Annecy had said, the day after the fatal injections,

Russ will be okay, won't he? I mean, you often feel sick after shots, right? And sitting there in Mistral's smelly little cave Trevithick could see that woman's face, thin and anxious and curiously red. It would have been better if she'd cried, like she wanted to. Then maybe he could have felt annoyed at the responsibility she was laying on him.

"I'll do my best," he said.

She seemed to accept that. "Well, let's get started, then."

"Get started?"

"You thought you was going to sit around on your behind all day? No way. So tell me what you know. Maybe I can help. Two heads is better than one."

Why not? He didn't have anything else to do. He wondered what Mistral did with her spare time, stuck there in that hole. Most immigrant humans needed some kind of creative relaxation after a day's work, unlike gorons who were quite happy singing and socialising. Susanna painted; Trevithick liked to develop dictionaries of the local languages, if there were any. A lot of people dug into local history and legends—again, if there were any. Arts and crafts using local materials were popular. They were trying to build up a culture. It was necessary. It was the alternative to Earthsick nostalgia and boredom.

Mistral was not an immigrant, however. She'd been born here.

Wondering about this, he leaned back against the wall and made himself as comfortable as possible. The cave was purely functional; no decoration of any kind. Mistral let go of his hand and sat primly upright, to his relief.

"First maybe," she said, "I should tell you something. You might not like it. You might not believe it."

"Try me."

"I got proof," said Mistral, "the Organization's trying to kill Lady off."

CHAPTER 13

FIVE PEOPLE WHO WOULD HAVE BEEN very interested to see such proof were gathered on the patio of the Passing Barge Inn at that moment. They were all employees of the Samaritan Organisation. Under normal circumstances they would have been at their places of work, but Manning Edlin had deemed the situation so critical that an immediate meeting was needed.

"And we meet outside the domes," he said in answer to a question, "because I don't trust the walls of my office."

"Are you suggesting your office is bugged?" Albert Brassworthy gave a nervous little titter.

"It's the only reason I can think of why confidential communications seem to be common knowledge these days," snarled Edlin, staring at the gigantic Tillini. "Have you ever found it necessary to use listening devices in the course of Security's work, Tillini?"

"Occasionally." The muscan leaned back in one of the chairs specially provided for its species. "I wouldn't be doing my job if I didn't. But I can assure you there are none of my devices in your walls, Manning."

Edlin wasn't so sure. Over this past year he'd become increasingly suspicious. He'd even taken to inventing confidential warpwires to see if the bush telegraph picked them up. "All right, so tell me how there's a rumour going around that the Organisation is pulling out of Goronwy."

Ivor Sabin answered that one. "That rumour's been going around ever since I've been here. You get the same rumour on every project. We used to get it when I worked for Outward Ho."

"It's natural," boomed Tillini. "Don't worry about it, Manning."

"I wondered," said Edlin quietly, "because this warpwire came yesterday. I kept it to Ivor and myself because I saw no reason to unsettle people, and I wanted a chance to take corrective action. However, as the contents seemed to be common knowledge even before the bloody thing arrived, you may as well see it." He handed it to Brassworthy. "Read it to them, Al."

Brassworthy stared at the printout. "My God." He cleared his throat. "'CONFIDENTIAL. FROM: VYRWNY, EARTHAID, EARTH. TO: RUSTON ANTROBUS, PRESIDENT, SAMARITAN ORGANISATION, EARTH. COPY TO: THE BOARD OF DIRECTORS, SAMARITAN PROJECT, GORONWY. RE: FUNDING, GORONWY. TEXT: REGRET WE CANNOT EXTEND FIFTY YEAR GRANT ELIGIBILITY DUE TO LACK OF MEASURABLE PROGRESS IN PROJECT OBJECTIVES. SUGGEST YOU AND GORONWY LIAISE RE WINDING DOWN, EARTHAID WILL FUND PASSAGES OF ALL PERSONNEL BUT NOT EQUIPMENT. WARPWIRE ENDS.'

Brassworthy's voice was shaking toward the end. "You had no right to keep this to yourself, Manning," he said. "It's addressed to the Board."

"And it will go before the Board at the next meeting."

The enormity of what he'd read out was coming home belatedly to Brassworthy. Head in his hands, he was muttering quietly, "Christ. Oh, Christ." The warpwire fluttered to the ground.

Jonathan Cook, Director of Sustenance, said, "Trevithick must have gotten word through to Earth. It was my understanding that the Trevithick situation was under control."

"He didn't get word through," said Edlin positively. "Maybe it was the lack of word that precipitated this. Maybe Earthaid's simply lost patience."

"Well, someone's slipped up somewhere, obviously."

Brassworthy suddenly burst out, "I'll say somebody slipped up! Do you know what I heard yesterday? Somebody tried to kill Trevithick! Somebody pushed him into Lady and a bunch of gorons fished him out just in time. What the hell's going on? When we agreed to silence Trevithick, nothing was said about murder. He was going to be kicked out of the domes and left to fend for himself, that was my understanding. He'd be out of the way, and HQ need never know he'd been fired. And Ivor would run Ecology the way we want it run. Clean and simple. I won't be involved with murder, no way!" He scanned each of them in turn, scared and wary.

"Easy, Al, easy," said Edlin, as though addressing a skittish horse. "Nobody's talking about murder. It must have been an accident. Anyway, all that's water under the bridge. We have bigger things to worry about. There's a whole lot of people here depending on us."

"You said you wanted to take corrective action," said Cook. "Did you?"

"I did what I could. We won't know if I've been successful for a while yet. These things take time."

Brassworthy, still in the throes of an adrenaline rush, burst out, "You'd better be successful, Manning!"

Edlin glanced at him coldly. "Or what?"

"Or... Or there'll be a whole lot of very angry people out for your blood!"

"For pity's sake don't pretend to threaten me, Al. It makes you look pathetic."

"You still haven't told us what corrective action you took," said Tillini gently.

Edlin frowned. "If I tell you four and it gets about, it'll narrow down the source of the leaks quite a lot, won't it?"

"Nevertheless," said Tillini.

"All right. I sent a warpwire to Organisation HQ purporting to come from Trevithick. It said that dramatic progress was now being made, and gave a few details Ivor was kind enough to cook up for me. I don't doubt it'll take time for HQ to make up their minds about it. But soon enough they'll realize it's in their interests to try to persuade Earthaid to continue the grants."

"And if Earthaid refuse?" asked Brassworthy, looking for difficulties.

"Well, there's a hell of a lot of money invested in this place. My guess is, the Organisation will keep us going, all enthusiastic about an upcoming payoff when Lady's cured."

"But Lady's not going to be cured."

"Correct, Al. Correct." Edlin leaned forward and tapped the Director of Finance on the knee. "But we never say so, Al. Remember that. We never say so, not even in the middle of an empty aeolus field. Not even in the privacy of our own bathrooms."

Brassworthy shivered. Sometimes Manning Edlin could be even scarier than the muscans.

Meanwhile another view of the future was being discussed some three kilometres away.

"The Organization's trying to kill Lady off?" repeated Trevithick sceptically. "A dead Lady is the last thing they'd want, by my reckoning. They want to spin things out. I'd like to see your proof."

But now Mistral's lips were compressed in a thin and stubborn line. "You'd tell that Susanna," she said. "And she'll blab it to everyone. Pretty soon I got Security kicking down my door."

"I won't tell Susanna."

"So what will you do?"

A difficult question. "I'll listen to your proof and decide if it really is proof. Then—"

"This isn't proof you listen to. It's proof you look at."

"All right, I'll take a look. If I'm convinced, I'll speak to someone in authority about it. In confidence," he said quickly, as he saw her mouth begin to open. Then he hesitated. Sure, he could speak to, say, Janine Starseeker. But what next? Talk to the Board? He'd have to dispose of Security's trumped up theft charge first. Once he was inside the domes Tillini would be freed from the need for covert apprehension. Talk to Manning Edlin? No, it was beginning to look as though Edlin was leader of the opposition. Appeal to Earth? He'd never get a warpwire past Edlin's department.

"Mistral," he said, "I don't know what the hell I can do."

"Not much help, are you?"

"I'm sorry. But if you'll show me your proof, at least it'll be a step in the right direction."

She uttered a harsh laugh. "Oh, sure. Well, I'm not taking the chance. Not until I'm a helluva lot surer of you. Huh." She stood. "I got work to do even if you don't. Maybe I'll see you later."

She called to Wilfred, who appeared from the shadows. They left by the tunnel that led to the guardhouse and the outside world. Trevithick heard her talking to the stoag as they went. To what extent had she gone native? She'd been living rough for two years. Her speech had become simplified and bastardised. She could already speak the goron language. In due course it might well become her natural tongue.

He sat there for an hour or more, trying to make sense of what she'd said. Susanna's theory had satisfied him. The people of Samarita were getting a free ride on Goronwy and would like it to continue. They didn't want to cure Lady, but they didn't want to kill her either. The status quo, with Lady dying by slow degrees, was very satisfactory.

So why would Mistral think they intended to kill Lady off?

As he was puzzling over this, he began to feel the need to use Mistral's toilet facilities. Not a pleasant prospect. Eventually he got to his feet and took the lamp down the tunnel. The latrine was no worse than he'd expected and the chamber did have a long vertical vent, at the head of which he could see the sky.

Afterwards he paused outside, his curiosity aroused by that other full-height tunnel. If I catch you snooping around in there, I'll kick you out of here so fast you'll swear you had a rocket up your arse! But Mistral was safely out of the way. It seemed foolish not to seize the opportunity.

The tunnel soon opened out into a chamber as big as Mistral's living area. The light from the oil lamp was poor, the shadows prancing.

Two easels stood in the centre of the cavern, complete with paintings.

But here the similarity to Susanna's studio ended. The easels were roughly constructed of local timber and the paintings had been executed on stiff packing material instead of canvas. More paintings leaned against the wall. He saw a stand-alone terminal on a crude table at the far end of the chamber, and wondered where she'd got it from. A cable pierced the roof, presumably leading from a solar unit. The floor and walls were bare soft sandstone, like Mistral's main chamber.

He examined the paintings, wondering.

They were amateurish, showing at best a slight talent. The subjects were all of Goronwy: a barge on Lady, boat builders at work, a stoag in a thicket of bushtrap. One in particular caught his attention: an underground scene in browns and black, showing three stoags clawing at something that glittered, with water flowing nearby. It was muddy, crude, incomprehensible and depressing. The pictures were all the same size; about a meter long by three quarters high. They were executed in oils and bore signs of much corrective overpainting. The use of perspective was good, but the goron figures were ill-shaped and the colours peculiar, with bright daubs of yellow and red predominating. They were, quite simply, primitive without the charm the word implies.

And they explained—at least in part—Mistral's jealousy of Susanna.

He wandered around the room, flipping through the paintings, and eventually found himself at the terminal. Curious, he put on the proximation headset and called up the menu. He found a diverse collection of educational material in there: courses in different aspects of engineering in particular. So this was one of the things Mistral did with her time; quite praiseworthy too. There were also ego-fic travelogues. He called one up. Soon he found himself among the hills of Earth, walking a ridge with rectangular green fields spread out on either side. Nostalgia took him by the hand. Hedgerows, sheep, trees, barns. He was looking at things he might never see again. He made his way toward a small farmhouse, entering the yard and paddling through manure while cattle watched him incuriously. He opened the door into a small and cosy room. Feedback from his own mind furnished the image of Susanna smiling, greeting him. They kissed.

"Had a good day, darling?" she asked.

"Great. Looks like it's been raining back here, though."

"A bit. Here, look." She indicated the plain board table. "I've baked some bread. And the Irish stew's all ready." The table was laid with plates and cutlery; a vase of flowers stood in the middle. Trevithick's super-domesticated Susanna began to spoon stew from an iron cauldron on an old-fashioned range occupying the whole of one wall. Then he lost proximation for a moment and commonsense took over; this was not the Susanna he knew. Was this the Susanna he really wanted? She bent low so that he could see bare breasts beneath the blouse, and placed the bowls of stew on the table. She smiled, so typical a Susanna smile that credibility was restored.

"Let's eat," she said.

He was persuaded that the stew smelled delicious, and took a spoonful. Then he dropped the spoon in horror.

A toad stared up at him.

It crawled from the spoon to the table, wet and steaming. Other toads popped their heads up from the stew, winking at him.

"Let's eat," said Susanna harshly.

But it was not Susanna. A black-haired witch stared at him from the other side of the table. She thrust her spoon into his bowl and held a toad before his face.

"Eat! Eat!"

The toad jumped from the spoon into his mouth.

He sprang up, gagging. He could feel the creature crawling on his tongue but it was too big to spit out. He hooked his finger around it and pulled. It wouldn't come. It was growing, spreading down his throat, forcing his jaw apart, blocking his windpipe. He tried to scream, but couldn't. The witch stood before him, face contorted.

"You bastard! You bastard!"

He tore the headset off. His face was cold with sweat. He swallowed. He could breathe again.

Mistral hit him violently across the face. "You bastard!" She snatched the headset. "I should've left you in that dream. I could've killed you in there, you know that?" She hit a couple of keys and switched the terminal off. "I should've killed you."

The room steadied up. It always took a moment to return from proximation to the real world, particularly when someone had pressed the horror-genre key without one's knowledge. "I'm sorry," he managed to say. His throat still felt sore.

"Sorry, are you? And I trusted you!" She was shaking with temper. He heard thumping and scrabbling sound. "Sorry?" she screeched, her fingers hooked into his collar. Then abruptly she let him go and swung round. "Oh, no!"

Trevithick caught a glimpse of wild eyes and glistening teeth as a herd of stoags burst into the cave. The easels crashed to the floor. The lamplight flickered as the desk lurched. Something warm and heavy hurled itself at him, throwing him against the terminal.

"No!" shouted Mistral. "Back off!"

Claws accustomed to digging in sandstone dug easily into Trevithick's thigh. He yelled. Elsewhere, sharp teeth took hold of him, pulling and worrying. His feet slipped. He fell to the floor, his head smashed into the wall and he lost track of events. The stoags were everywhere, trampling and snapping. He lay stunned and unable to resist.

Mercifully, there came a time when the danger seemed to pass. He became dimly aware of Mistral herding the stoags from the cave, chiding them. In annoyingly gentle tones too, considering they'd been about to eat him alive. She returned, holding the lamp to his face.

"You okay?"

"I think so. A few scratches." Well, maybe a bit more than that.

"You're a bastard, you know that?"

"Don't start that again."

"It was my pheromones. The wind from the shaft carried them down the tunnels. They thought I was being attacked, see? So they came to protect me."

That was her story, for what it was worth. For Trevithick's money, it lacked credibility. Certainly it was her pheromones that brought the stoags. But at the time she was the attacker, not the attacked. The stoags had come to help.

And that was a worrying thought. It would be advisable to stay on the right side of Mistral.

She helped him into the main cave, undressed him without the kind of banter Susanna would have offered, washed his wounds and bound leaves on them. "They'll heal fast," she said confidently. "Serves you right," she added.

The moment for flattery had arrived. "I liked your paintings," he lied.

"You did?" She examined his face, wanting to see honesty there. "Thanks," she muttered. "But you shouldn't of. I told you not to go in there . . . They as good as Susanna's?"

The image of teeth and claws prompted him to say, "Better."

"I sell them. That's how I get money to buy things at the Organisation stores. Otherwise . . ." The green eyes were suddenly bleak.

"Who buys them?"

"That Martha Sunshine. And she sells them to people going home. Going back to . . . Earth. A little bit of Goronwy to take with them. Souvenirs, like."

"Nice."

"I told Martha I'd like to have a show. Artists have shows, you know. That Susanna had one once. Lots of people coming to look at her stuff, telling her how good it was, puffing her up like you wouldn't believe."

"Maybe a show's not a good idea." He could smell disaster. "People would get too used to your stuff. Much better to sell the paintings individually the way you do now."

"Maybe," she said doubtfully. "You know Martha Sunshine?"

Before she could ask him to put a good word in, he asked, "One of those paintings was quite different from the others. It seemed to be stoags at a kind of underground river. What was it?"

As he was speaking, her face set in hard lines. "None of your business, Mister. You got no right to snoop around. Be glad I'm looking after you, and stay out of my things."

"Of course. I'm sorry."

This mollified her and she fired up the tiny oil stove. "I brought something for you," she said. For the first time, he noticed a small slab of M16 on the table.

"Where did you get that?"

"The Organisation store, of course."

"But . . . How did you know I like it?"

"That Susanna got it for you, didn't she? I got eyes, I saw the wrapper on her table. If she can get it for you, so can I."

"Well, thanks a lot." Would some observant and deductive mind tie the purchase to him? Probably not. The store was automated and the supervisor sat in her office most of the time. And Helen Minsky didn't have a deductive mind, or she wouldn't be a supervisor.

Mistral fried his M16 with cabbage and onions, a novel combination. They ate. Afterwards she sat on the furs with Wilfred. He joined her. "Usually I'd be doing my learning right now," she told him. "But you need company. Sit with us, huh?"

Wilfred lay between them as they talked about the gorons. Trevithick was surprised at the depth of her knowledge. She had a different viewpoint from the average Samaritan. She identified with them, and spoke from the inside.

"They do everything for Lady. Years ago, they even had a special clan for construction work on the banks. When it was a river it had all kind of sharp bends, see? They said this hurt Lady. They could tell. So all these little guys were digging along the banks, moving them and smoothing them out until they look like now. They didn't like it when the Project put in those concrete banks at Samarita, I can tell you. But what could they do about it?"

"How do they know how Lady feels?"

"She gives off pheromones just like they do. D'you know, the pheromones are like part of their language? That's why humans can never learn it, not properly."

"How well can you speak goron?"

"Okay, I guess. That's how I know what Lady doesn't like. D'you know, once the Project tried using propellers on her? Really! They had this boat with a big slow propeller cutting into Lady. The gorons said she screamed. One night the boat just disappeared. Nobody knew where it went. The Project took the hint. They didn't build another."

"What really happened to it?"

She laughed, tossing her hair back, showing bright eyes and white teeth in the lamplight. "My guess is, Lady ate it. Like she eats old gorons. She ate that boat and passed it down her gut, then she shat it into the sea in little bits."

"Rather big for eating, surely?"

"Why not? She don't open no mouth when she eats the oldsters. She just dents herself and folds over them. Size don't matter."

"But doesn't that mean Lady must have some kind of intelligence? She'd need to remember the boat as the source of her pain during the day, and deal with it at night."

"She's no fool, Lady."

He looked at her, pretty and happy and smiling, and under that hair, disfigured. Disfigured in a way that might be affecting her mind. It was such a waste. "Why don't you like your father, Mistral?" he asked gently.

Immediately she changed. "Who told you that?" she snapped. Trevithick lied. "He did, of course."

"Huh. He did, did he? And I suppose he said it was all my fault."

"No. I'm sure there are faults on both sides. It seems a pity, that's all."

"There's no bloody fault on my side, Mister! My dad's a traitor. He sold out to the Organisation." Her fists were clenched as though to punch the absent Ralph Greene. Her emotions had a destructive strength.

"Well, what did he do, exactly?"

"All kinds of things. When my Mom was alive I put up with it. Now I don't have to. Sure, I can't stop him building domes and digging holes and laying bloody concrete everywhere, but I don't have to pretend I agree with it any more. He's paid by the Organisation to mess Goronwy up, and that's what he does."

"But the construction work is essential. Humans couldn't live here without it."

"Who says we need humans here?"

Why he felt it necessary to defend the Organisation, he didn't know. The argument dragged along its predictable course. As he spoke his lines, he found himself thinking of the gorons, who didn't need to argue. Any deliberate falsehood or hypocrisy would be immediately detected by the pheromones. In effect, they had built-in lie detectors. "All right," he said at last. "But at least you could let your father pay for cosmetic surgery."

"Take his dirty money? No way!"

"He's just doing his job."

"Sure, but it's the way you do it. It's the rotten things you agree to. Some time maybe I'll show you what I mean. Lady can shiver when she hurts, you know that?" At the time, Trevithick thought this was a rapid change of topic. "She can twist about and try to escape. But she can't do no more than try. She's stuck in her channel, helpless like a big baby. She's an easy target for your Organisation."

"Not my Organisation. They fired me, remember?"

"You could be a plant."

"For God's sake, Mistral!"

"Well, how do I know? I've only got that Susanna's word they tried to kill you."

He could feel anger and frustration building up in himself, and probably in Mistral too. They were not a compatible pair. It was as well Susanna chose that moment to arrive, otherwise the stoags might have done so.

"Hello, everybody," she greeted them cheerfully. She wore a bright yellow dress with a blue sash and a matching blue purse, eye-catching to the point of dazzling, totally non-regulation, and brightening up the whole interior of that wretched cave. Then, wrinkling her nose in distaste, she said, "Honestly, Mistral, you could come and stay at my apartment."

"Huh!" was the only reply she got.

"Find anything out?" Trevithick asked. He didn't remember getting to his feet but he was standing, taking hold of Susanna's hand. He'd asked his question purely for something to say. The only thing that really interested him, was that she was here, lighting up the cave and his soul.

"My word, you're starved for news," she said, "and things. What about the social niceties, like a wee dram?"

"I don't keep no mead here," muttered Mistral. "Scrambles your brains, it does."

"It just so happens . . ." Susanna produced a flat bottle from her purse. "Do you mind drinking straight from the bottle, Doctor Trevithick?"

"I got mugs." Mistral took two mugs from a shelf, pulled up her skirt and gave them a perfunctory wipe. Then, hesitating, she put a third mug on the table. "Why the hell not?" she said defensively.

They sat on the furs with their charged mugs. "All set for Marik Darwin's meeting tonight?" Susanna asked eventually.

"Yes. Are you coming?" Trevithick asked.

"Not with you. I may take my place in the audience to lend a touch of class to the proceedings. You'd better get there unobserved and find some hidey-hole to watch from. Grab Marik afterwards and talk to him before he leaves the building. Don't advertise your presence or Tillini's goons will be waiting for you when you come out. I wouldn't want that to happen."

"Huh! Neither would I!" Mistral interjected.

"I'm glad to hear it. We're both good guys really, you know, Mistral. Anyway, now for some bad news." She hesitated. It wasn't like Susanna to show uncertainty. "Very bad news, I'm afraid."

"Go on."

"It looks like the Project is going to wrap up."

Trevithick felt a small and selfish moment of joy. If the Project pulled out *en masse*, he'd be able to bum a ride. They wouldn't have the gall to maroon a man on Goronwy with no means of support, would they? And for the first time he wondered about those other non-Samaritan residents. The fifty-three, as Mistral kept reminding him. Would they go, or would they stay? Many of them had been born on Goronwy, but they were still very dependent on the Project's presence. They would all have to leave. Including Mistral?

All this flashed through his mind as he heard Mistral say, "Good riddance!"

"How do you know?" he asked Susanna.

She took a folded piece of paper from her purse and smoothed it out. "Copy of a warpwire," she said. "Here, read it."

Trevithick read the words that Albert Brassworthy had read aloud a short time previously. "Looks conclusive," he commented, still looking at those last sentences. Earthaid will fund passages of all personnel. That included him. Brassworthy and his budget didn't matter a damn any more. "How did you get hold of it?"

"I have my methods. Yes, I know it says 'Confidential', but that's just to make the sender feel important. It's all academic. The Board can't keep it to themselves for long; people would notice the evacuation shuttles touching down beside the domes." She took the paper from Trevithick and handed it to Mistral. "So that's it, Bryn old friend. Give it six months, and we'll be off into the wide blue yonder."

"Maybe this blows their charges against me."

"I wouldn't jump to conclusions. Somebody tried to kill you and we don't know why. They may still feel they have good reasons. You should watch your back for a while."

"So . . . you've been with the Organisation longer than I have. What exactly does that warpwire mean? What's the fifty year grant eligibility?"

"It's the standard term for Earthaid grants. They give us fifty years to bring in results, otherwise they cut us off. This is going to be a big loser for the Organisation. They'll have to walk away from a heck of a lot of equipment. To say nothing of the domes and staff accommodation. And there'll be no payback from the gorons either."

There was something wrong here, surely. "If we'd done a better job, maybe the free ride would have lasted longer. Why did we screw Operations up so consistently? Unqualified staff. Firing me wouldn't have looked good. And Marik Darwin walked out. Operations has been a disaster for years."

"Operations has been something of a joke with people," she said thoughtfully. "If Lady's incurable—like we thought yesterday—it might explain why they let Operations Division fall apart. But you'd think they'd make some effort to give a good impression with Earthaid."

"Always on the brink of a major breakthrough, that kind of thing?"

"It could have bought us another twenty years."

"Yeah, that's all fine and dandy." Mistral threw the warpwire to the ground. I saw tears glistening. "But what am I gonna do, huh? When you all climb aboard that shuttle, what do I do, wave to you?"

"You come with us," said Susanna gently.

"Oh, sure, sure. And what about Lady?"

"There's not much anyone can do for Lady, Mistral."

"How do you know, Miss Smartipants? The gorons haven't given up. Why should we?"

Susanna and Trevithick exchanged helpless glances. "You can't stay here alone," he said.

"Why not? Why the bloody hell not, huh? Who cares? I don't need none of you people, I've got the gorons. They're worth a hundred of you." She began to sob uncontrollably. Wilfred whimpered. Low-slung, thickset shapes began to sidle into the chamber, whining.

"The hell with this," said Susanna quietly to Trevithick. "She's not going to listen to reason right now. I'm going." She kissed him lightly on the cheek. "Look out for me in the audience tonight. I'll be the blonde bimbo asking dumb questions. Surprising how much I can find out that way."

He sat there a while longer, giving her time to get clear, then went up to the guardhouse. It was dark outside. Covert apprehension. She'd said they'd take him in the dark if they could. Well, the heck with it.

He called goodbye to Mistral and left, his collar turned up in approved fashion.

CHAPTER 14

HE REACHED LADYSIDE WITHOUT INCIDENT. Nobody stepped out of a darkened doorway to challenge him. No half-glimpsed follower flitted from shadow to shadow. Nothing like that happened.

The meeting was to be held at the Passing Barge, on the patio overlooking Lady recently used by Manning Edlin and his cohorts. The gorons had no large assembly buildings of their own. Possessing no leaders, they didn't normally hold formal gatherings.

As Trevithick approached the inn by a circuitous route he saw signs of activity all along the riverbank. Gorons hurried to and fro; little groups formed and as quickly broke up. Piping voices were raised in discussion. Alarmingly, a number of the little people simply ran silently in small circles. It was weird, it was uncanny, and an uneasy premonition began to build in Trevithick's mind.

He debated walking boldly into the Passing Barge and joining the audience on the patio. He'd have been safe from covert apprehension among that crowd. But he didn't have the nerve. And he wasn't that kind of person. In fact, until the last few days he'd seen himself as the soul of conformity; he was still self-conscious about joining a crowd that consisted entirely of meter-tall men.

But conformity had to be cast aside when his safety was at stake, so he made his way to the back of the building, found a convenient bench, climbed onto it and then onto the low, flat roof. The roof was solid, installed by humans to provide better shelter than the original firepot-leaf roof. Nobody paid any attention. Gorons still milled about aimlessly under the meagre lighting, and some had started wailing on a shrill note that sent shivers down his spine.

He crawled Ladyside of the roof and looked down. The concrete patio measured about twelve meters square, bounded by a low fence. Outside, the Ladyside trail was packed with curious and fearful gorons. Inside, about one hundred members of Clan Active sat cross-legged on the concrete.

They were not a clan in the true goron sense, because they had not been trained from birth for this situation. Clan Active was made up of members of all clans. Because of this the members had experienced even more difficulty than usual in reaching any consensus—except to agree in general terms that things were not good and the human presence didn't help.

But that had been before Marik Darwin.

Darwin had united them. Had he been planted by the Project to destroy Clan Active from within? Or had he drifted away from his masters' intentions, drunk with power? The latter was a worrying possibility. Susanna had said Clan Active had shown no sign of losing impetus since Darwin took over.

He saw Susanna picking her way among the seated gorons. She found a spot and sat down; conspicuous, and not only because of her size. It was a warm night and the gorons were all naked; Susanna looked very much overdressed in a pleated navy skirt and white blouse.

Watching her—and desiring her—Trevithick wondered what the little men would think of her undressed. They were humanoid but their only woman, their mother Lady, their lover, was not. Incredibly enough, they would probably think of Susanna as looking like a big male goron, since they had no external genitalia themselves. Only her breasts and body hair would give them cause for puzzlement.

Time went by. Lath Eagleman weaved his way through the crowd, a mug of mead in one hand, violin and bow in the other, and squatted beside Susanna like a big stick insect. Two elderly women carried chairs out from the bar and took their place in the audience. Trevithick didn't recognise them.

"Why are you lying on the roof?"

It was Mana, goron operator of the inn, regarding Trevithick from a hatchway with wide-eyed surprise.

"I wanted to watch the meeting. Do you mind?"

He waved his hands, presumably meaning that he couldn't do anything about it whether he minded or not. Then, surprisingly, he lay down beside Trevithick. Together they peered over the edge. A human Trevithick took to be Marik Darwin had just arrived and was making his way toward a small platform set up against the fence.

"A strange man," said Mana. "Why can't he leave my people alone? I don't know what he wants. Neither do I know why he wants anything."

Mana had been a bright student at Bridget Booker's Ladysend school. She'd always persuaded her best pupils to join Clan Service as innkeepers, being the gorons who most often dealt with humans on a one-on-one basis. Mana was a good example.

Trevithick said, "Marik is my predecessor. I've never met him."

"Is that important, to have met him?"

"It is with humans. We can't assume that because a man's a ecologist he'll think like all other ecologists."

"I see. That must be difficult for you. Excuse me, but I haven't been in my job long."

"You're doing fine."

He hesitated. "We in Clan Service feel Marik Darwin is very dangerous. If he were a goron we would offer him to Lady. He would recognise his sickness, and would not resist."

"I wish it were that easy. Humans cling to life. After all, it only comes around once."

"That is not true. It comes again and again. I have many memories of gorons whose parts I carry. How can a society progress, if you lose life and knowledge when you die?"

Trevithick had more practical matters on his mind. "You'll get used to us, Mana. Take it from me, we're afraid of dying."

The lamps of coracles glowed like fireflies across the breadth of Lady. Their occupants didn't need to hear what Darwin said. The pheromonic reaction of their fellows would be news enough.

Gorons stood shoulder to shoulder on the trail. Darwin had taken his stand on the platform. He raised a hand, and his audience stilled instantly.

Mana murmured in Trevithick's ear, "You have a word for what Darwin does. You call it crime. We do not know how to handle crime. What can we do with this man, if you do nothing?"

"We can kill him." A different voice spoke in his other ear. It was Mistral. She rested an arm around his waist and snuggled close. "Easy shot from here, huh?"

"We don't have a gun. What are you doing here, anyway?"

"I came to watch the fun."

"Gorons!" The shout came from Marik Darwin, warming up. "Friends!"

"Look here, Mistral, I'm not staying here with you unless you take a pill. I can't have you turning into some kind of animal if things get rough down there."

"Things won't get rough. Those are gorons."

Mana said, "Excuse me, but the air is not good. Our people outside on the trail are angry. I've never felt so much anger."

Mistral chuckled. A whiff of mead reached Trevithick's nostrils. "I'm anes . . . anaesthetised. I feel like I'm flying. That suit you, Bryn?"

"Why are we here?" roared Darwin rhetorically. He had a powerful voice but a less than impressive presence. Medium height, premature balding, hatchet face. Edlin would have looked better down there. "We are here because Lady is sick and the best efforts of the Samaritan Organisation have been fruitless. We are here because Lady is suffering, and we are here because there is a natural course of events that we poor people are helpless to stem. We are here," he paused impressively, "because Lady is dying."

"Can't argue with that," said Mistral cheerfully, giving Trevithick's waist a squeeze. She was in an alarmingly affectionate mood.

Darwin's words had caused an outbreak of shrill keening from his audience. Mistral, her senses dulled by alcohol, remained unmoved. Mana, on the other hand, was wailing.

"After all," Darwin continued once the noise had subsided, "what is sacred about life? A single goron meets his death with dignity and joy. For him it is a time of fulfilment. If it is joyful for one goron, why should it not be so for Lady and all gorons? What would Goronwy lose, if Lady were dead and gorons gone? Nothing! Life would go on. The firepots would still grow, the squitos would still fly.

"So perhaps the time has come to save Lady from further suffering. Perhaps the time has come to ease her gently out of her life and her pain. It is easily done . . ."

He went on for some time in this vein, interrupted from time to time by outbreaks of keening from his audience and, increasingly, from those outside the fence. Trevithick's misgivings at this development were strengthened when Mana suddenly remarked, "There is sense in what he says."

"What!" Mistral exclaimed.

"What is the use? What is the purpose? If we are to die anyway, why allow Lady further suffering?"

"But less than half an hour ago you said Darwin was dangerous and should be offered to Lady!" Trevithick protested.

"That doesn't alter the facts."

Trevithick's earlier premonition had strengthened to a feeling of dread. Despite the darkness and consequent lack of aeolus effect, a light shifting wind blew. The pheromones had gotten to Mana, and probably to every goron for a kilometre around. Mistral didn't improve the situation by saying suddenly, "I'm gonna be sick," and crawling away to vomit noisily. She returned a few minutes later with a mug of mineral water from the bar and an abashed expression.

Darwin's harangue took on a practical note. He advocated withholding nectar from Lady, which put the responsibility for her death squarely on Clan Gatherer's shoulders. "In due course Lady will pass quietly away, freed from pain and suffering."

At this point one of the two elderly ladies levered herself to her feet. "Disgusting! Marik Darwin, you're a disgrace to your profession! You're proposing genocide, no matter how you dress it up!

And who will be left after the gorons are all dead? People like you, I suppose, living off the fat of the land!"

She'd played into Darwin's hand. He waved a piece of paper at his audience. "It is inevitable," he cried, "that some people will attribute base motives to acts of friendship and altruism. To put your minds at rest, I should like to make public the contents of a warpwire from Earthaid, that benevolent organisation on my mother Earth."

He read out the celebrated warpwire.

At first the contents were received in silence. Then, as the significance dawned on the gorons, a babbling of surprised conversation broke out.

"I am so sorry, my friends," shouted Darwin. "We tried to help you, we tried for fifty years, but we failed. It will go down in history that we did our best. So humans and gorons will leave this world, each in their own way, and Goronwy will be left to the wild things." His voice rose to a bellow, his finger stabbed at his audience, and the babbling subsided. "You've heard the warpwire. Now can you doubt the wisdom of what I have said?"

And into the subsequent hush came the clear voice of Susanna. "Yes. I can doubt it."

Darwin frowned. "This is a matter for gorons. I—"

"For instance," Susanna interrupted, "If you already had the warpwire, then you already knew the Organisation is pulling out. So why do you care what happens to Lady? Why do you want her to die? You won't be around to see it. You'll be evacuated with the rest of us."

"I cannot bear to see a living creature suffering. Surely—"

"Bullshit! You call yourself an ecologist and you're talking genocide? I don't know what your game is, Darwin, but there's something here that stinks. Let the gorons make up their own mind what to do with Lady after we've gone, why don't you? It's no bloody business of ours!"

Trevithick glanced at Mana to see how he was taking all this. Had the feelings of the gorons begun to swing in a less suicidal direction? He couldn't read the expression on that tiny face. He turned to Mistral. She was crying. The numbing effect of the mead had worn off.

"He's got them," she said miserably. "I can feel it. It doesn't matter what Susanna says. It's that bloody warpwire did it. They feel that if we've given up, maybe they should."

"Go back to your homes, gorons!" cried Darwin. "Go back to your clans and tell your people. The suffering of Lady will end!"

The little people began to move away, both inside and outside the fence. There was no difference of opinion between the two groups now. Lady had to be put out of their misery and they were going to do it. Susanna stood staring at Darwin while the gorons poured past her. Suddenly she strode forward, pushing little people out of her way.

"Go!" Darwin was shouting. "Do what you must!" The coracles began to move, gliding away.

"They'll do it," cried Mistral, tears glistening on her face. "They listen to him and they believe. They'll pass it on to the others, and all. We gotta stop him!"

Trevithick saw Darwin raise his arms as though to bless their departure. "The end of Lady's suffering is—"

He said no more, because Susanna had hiked up her skirt and climbed nimbly onto his platform. She measured him up and hit him squarely in the mouth.

It was a well-timed blow from an athletic woman. Darwin reeled back and toppled over the fence with flailing arms. Several gorons were knocked to the ground as he fell.

"Stay where you are!" Susanna shouted.

And for an instant all movement ceased. Gorons paused, turning.

"Get her!" yelled Darwin, climbing to his feet. "She's an enemy of Lady!"

The gorons on the patio changed direction, surging toward the platform. Those around Darwin began to climb onto the platform from the other side of the fence. Susanna was surrounded. She went down under a tide of small bodies. Trevithick rolled to the edge of the roof, hung by his hands momentarily, dropped to the ground and fought his way through to her. Pulling her to her feet he began to shove hostile gorons off the platform.

"Good to see a friendly face," she gasped. She was bleeding from a cut on her forehead. "Tough spot, huh?"

Together they teetered on the platform while a multitude of small hands sought to drag them to the ground. The broad face of Edlin watched from the bar; Vorda and Tillini stood beside him, dwarfing even that powerful figure. There would be no help from that direction. On the other side, the way was barred by a horde of gorons and one grimly smiling Darwin.

"You underestimate my little friends," he said, wiping blood from his mouth.

The gorons watched Darwin and awaited his word. He was their leader. A leader was a rare and wonderful thing in goron experience, and they were prepared to obey him implicitly. And Darwin was savouring his moment, smiling.

Susanna whispered, "Sorry, Bryn. My fault."

"Any chance of running for it?"

"Best not to try. It may trigger them off. Leave the responsibility with Darwin. If you were alone up here I wouldn't give much for your chances. But I'm a Samaritan. Officially," she tried to smile, "I represent the might of the Organisation. There are people watching from the bar, too. Darwin may chicken out."

"And if he doesn't?"

"They'll feed us to Lady."

"I thought gorons were supposed to be peace-loving little guys."

"So did I. This kind of thing has never happened before. But then, they've never had a leader before. I guess we didn't think all the angles through."

The gorons waited. Trevithick turned to Darwin. "Call them off, Marik," he said. "This whole thing's got out of hand. You have nothing against Susanna. She acted in the heat of the moment."

There was something unnerving about Darwin's smile. He glanced toward the bar. He nodded, as if in response to a signal.

"These people would cause Lady pain!" he shouted. "Take them!"

Trevithick felt the small hands grasp at him. There was one last rite to be performed, one last truth to be told. "Wish we'd had longer, you and I," he muttered to Susanna.

"Likewise," she said. "Such a short acquaintance, yet so promising. What a waste, huh?"

They waited. The tiny hands held them; nothing more.

Darwin's smile had faded. He was looking slightly puzzled. Edlin watched dispassionately, Tillini and Vorda nearby. Others watched: human customers of the inn, staying out of it when they were most needed, the way humans do.

But the gorons on the patio had all turned around and were looking up at the roof of the bar.

Mistral stood there, arms outstretched. The gorons had started to pick up pheromones from her. Everybody was very quiet. The people in the bar were craning their necks, realising something interesting was happening overhead. Mistral began to speak in a normal voice that carried clearly in the hush.

"You stupid little men, you were all gonna kill your mom, weren't you? Just think about that. All it took was one crook human, and you believed every bloody word he said. You're a bunch of clowns, aren't you? Okay, so now you'll believe me instead. And you got more reason to believe me—" here she paused significantly, "—'cos you can tell I'm speaking the truth, can't you?"

Susanna whispered, "The wind's shifted again. There is a God."

The gorons were picking up her pheromones, murmuring assent. "Mistral speaks the truth." There was a minor commotion as Darwin tried to climb onto the platform but was restrained by gorons.

"Sure, Lady's sick," Mistral continued. "But we can cure her. Don't believe Darwin's piece of paper. You never read it yourselves. It could've said anything. You don't know. But now . . . Some of you have bad stuff in your heads. Stuff Darwin put there. Maybe you can forget it, maybe not. Those who can't, well . . ."

She stopped speaking. The gorons sighed, a vast communal exhalation. Trevithick wondered at the power of the pheromones she was exuding. He felt Susanna's hand squeezing his.

Mistral stood silent.

Then the gorons on the patio began to move. Hands dropped away from the pair on the platform.

"What's she doing to you?" yelled Darwin desperately. "Stay where you are! Listen to me!"

The gorons filed out through the gate in the corner of the fence. Their eyes were blank, as though sleepwalking. Some gorons on the trail moved aside to let them through, others joined them. The coracles drew near until they could be seen in the patio lights. There were far more than Trevithick had thought. The oarsmen waited silently. Gorons began to climb into the coracles, as many as five to a boat. Laboriously, the first few began to move out onto Lady...

Trevithick felt a sudden dread. Was this what his recurrent premonitions had been leading up to?

"Mistral!" he shouted. "Stop them!"

But she stood silent, commanding without words.

"What the hell is she telling them?" said Darwin.

Susanna said, "I guess you've lost your followers, Marik. Fickle little fellows, the gorons. We need to talk about things, the three of us."

"Talk about things?" His eyes were frightened, now. He kept glancing toward the bar. "Talk about what?"

Trevithick said, "That can wait, Susanna. We've got to stop the gorons!" The coracles were sliding away from the lamplight, onto the darkness of Lady. Although overloaded, they still rode high.

"This is the only way, Bryn," said Susanna. "It's Mistral that's going to need help. She's taken one hell of a responsibility on. I don't know if she can handle it. She loves the little guys."

"Listen," said Darwin urgently. "You found a place to hole up, Trevithick? We have to help one another, huh?"

"Weren't you the one who was about to commit us to the tender mercies of Lady?" asked Susanna.

Trevithick watched the receding points of light. There were over a hundred gorons about to commit suicide; surely stopping them was the number one priority? Gorons were entering the patio and calling for nectar. Others were drifting out of sight up and down the trail, going home. Mistral had disappeared. He saw Mana closing the roof hatch as he descended to the bar. Tillini was now seated with Murdo and Vorda; the three muscans were deep in conversation. Edlin had been joined by his deputy, Carstairs. The rest of the spectators had dispersed. Out on Lady, gorons were about to capsize their coracles.

And nobody cared.

"For Christ's sake!" he shouted.

Susanna and Darwin had been disputing some point; they looked at him in surprise. They were alone and conspicuous; by now Darwin had climbed onto the platform and if anyone had a gun handy, they could have burned the three of them down with ease and anonymity. But that was not the point.

Susanna pressed his hand. "You've got to understand, Bryn. There's absolutely nothing we can do. We have no power over the gorons. Only Mistral can do anything."

"Well, let's find her, then!"

She saw something in his face. "For your sake. It's probably too late, but we can try the bar." She jumped down from the platform. Darwin tagged along, staying close.

There were over fifty humans in the bar, as many gorons, and a handful of muscans. Mistral was nowhere to be seen. A feeling of futility took hold of Trevithick; the evening was like some weird nightmare. Gorons were dying out there and people weren't even talking about it. "But they don't mind dying," Susanna said. "You know that, Bryn." He looked into her eyes and saw honesty there. She was right, of course. When she led him to a table, he didn't resist. At least he was safe among all those people.

A tiny waiter scurried up, bringing mead. He experienced a sudden nostalgia for Earth, beer and sanity.

"So . . ." said Susanna, regarding Darwin who seemed to be almost cowering in his seat. "Maybe if you tell us what this is all about, we'll be able to help. Why do you want Lady killed, and who put you up to this? So talk, Marik old son."

He remained silent, shivering, staring at his hands on the table.

"Whoever put you up to it, you're no use to them now. It's time for a few answers, if you want any help from us. Speak up, Marik," she said kindly. "We're good guys, Trevithick and I. I'll lead you into this gently. First, tell us about you quitting the Organisation. That was just a blind, wasn't it?"

"Listen, you're helping Trevithick, is that right?" Darwin began to talk fast as though knowing his time was running out, glancing across at the table where the three muscans sat. "I know they're after him, covert apprehension. But there are places, you know, outside Samarita, where a fellow can stay out of sight. I can pay, no problem there. I'm only talking about a few months until the evacuation shuttles arrive." He was almost weeping, peering at Susanna pathetically, totally transformed from the ranting leader on the platform. "There's no time to go into it all now. I'll tell you everything you want to know, once you've got me somewhere safe."

"Before we do that, just tell us why you were persuading the gorons to destroy Lady."

"Well, it's the best way, you see," he gabbled, anxious to please. "Nobody could blame anybody if the gorons killed Lady themselves."

"You're avoiding the issue, Marik. Lady dying is the last thing anyone wants, surely? And now Earthaid's cut us off and we've got to leave in any case. So why bother?"

His eyes widened. He was staring beyond them. "Hold on. Gotta go to the toilet. Won't be a minute."

He jumped to his feet and scurried away, leaving the other two looking at each other. Susanna said, "Do you get the impression we've let him slip through our fingers?"

"Something's scared him badly. Maybe it's like you said—he's no use to them any more." He swivelled in his chair and looked around. Tillini was on his feet, vast and stooping under the low roof. "We'd better split up. I'm bad company. You deal with Darwin when he gets back and I'll go and find Mistral."

She grinned. "Stay right where you are, Trevithick." He felt her knee push against his under the table. "Us being together is innocence itself. I'm merely thanking you for a gallant rescue. Any girl would do the same."

"All right. Just for a minute. As soon as Darwin gets back I'll—" He broke off. The room seemed to have become suddenly darker. He looked up.

The huge figure of Tillini loomed over them.

CHAPTER 15

"WHERE DID MARIK DARWIN GO?" asked the muscan. Pot-bellied, a mountain of naked grey flesh, it stared at Trevithick with cold eyes. At least, he assumed its eyes were cold. Who could tell, with muscans? They hadn't the advantage of a Bridget Booker education in human facial expressions.

"What's it to you?" asked Susanna.

"My dear woman," said Tillini slowly and insultingly, crowding the table so that it tilted and the mugs began to slide, "I had credited you with a greater intelligence. You yourself witnessed an attempt by Darwin to incite the gorons to matricide. The attempt almost succeeded. And you ask me why I wish to know where he went? Security is here to protect gorons as well as humans and muscans."

"Go away, Tillini," said Trevithick. "This is a private conversation."

"The Manager of Health Services in private conversation with a known fugitive?" The amber eyes swivelled back to Susanna. "You keep dangerous company, my dear woman."

"My God, if I thought I was your dear woman I'd shoot myself. You heard what Bryn said. Go away right now, before I create an embarrassing scene for you. I'm good at that."

Tillini ignored her, regarding Trevithick again. "You're already accused of having stolen data vital to the current research on Lady. Now you are seeking to protect a man whose stated objective is to kill Lady. You're an intelligent man, Trevithick. Surely you must see how this all adds up? Obviously you wish to hasten Lady's death. I can see only one reason for that. Having been fired by the Organisation, you now want the Project wrapped up as soon as possible so that you can be included in the general evacuation."

"Makes sense," said Susanna lightly. "What a logical fellow you are, Tillini. My respect for the muscans grows by the minute. Trevithick, you're a swine."

"You will not find this so funny when Trevithick is in our hands, my dear woman." With a fine sense of drama, the muscan turned its back on them, presenting huge and sagging buttocks as it began to amble away.

The temptation was too much for Susanna. Snatching up a fork, she stabbed Tillini in its gigantic rump.

She might as well have stabbed a mattress. Showing no sign of pain, the muscan plodded back toward its table. In a perverse way it looked almost humanoid, like a big hairless cartoon bear. Bipedal, short-legged, sloping shoulders. People moved aside to let it pass. It could have killed anyone of them with one swat, and it wouldn't have been charged with murder. Muscans were not subject to the laws of humans, who recognised the logic of their culture. They never killed without good reason—as they saw it—and they had no concept of guilt. They had no need of the concept. In their own eyes, they were well-meaning creatures.

"An unsavoury episode," said Susanna. "That creature made me quite lose my temper . . . You're in demand tonight, Bryn. Manning Edlin's beckoning to you."

"To hell with Manning Edlin."

"No, I'm curious. Pop over and see what he wants, there's a good fellow. I'll wait here for Marik." Raising her voice for the benefit of Tillini who was still lumbering steadily in the direction of the muscan table, she said, "And thanks for coming to my aid out there, Bryn. It's good to know chivalry is not dead!"

Reluctantly, Trevithick followed in the muscan's wake, then branched off to the table where Edlin and Carstairs sat. "Yes?" he said coldly. "What do you want?"

"Sit down, Bryn. Well, now." He smiled pleasantly as Trevithick seated himself. "A lot has happened in the past few days."

Trevithick was in no mood for small talk. Tillini, with its talk of Marik, had diverted him from a more important concern. What had happened to Mistral? Was she hiding in a corner somewhere, shattered by events and her responsibility for them? He wanted to go to her, and tell her she'd done the right thing and, if she hadn't done it, Susanna and he might well be Ladyfood by now.

Instead he said impatiently, "Yes. I've been fired, an attempt has been made on my life, and a charge has been trumped up against me. I suspect you and your friends are responsible."

He looked surprised. "You were fired by Personnel on instructions from Earth. I know nothing about the attempt on your life, and obviously I know nothing about the charge against you either. I'm the Director of Systems and Communications, Bryn. Anyway, these may well be minor matters in the overall scheme. Murdo and Security might well find themselves apologising to you. Mistakes happen."

Carstairs spoke suddenly. "Listen to him, Bryn."

"Why the hell should I?"

"For your own good."

He felt anger flush his face. "For my own good, huh? Is that some kind of a threat? Well, you sure as hell can't kill me here and now, in front of all these people!"

"Kill you?" repeated Edlin. "We have no desire to kill you, Bryn. You could be very useful to us."

An odd thought popped into his head. "As a replacement for Marik Darwin?"

"But Marik was trying to persuade the gorons to kill Lady, remember? Why would we want him to do that?"

"You tell me."

"Well, it was the last thing we wanted, obviously. So why did Marik do it? Simply to spite the Organisation? Hardly. I find his motivation very difficult to assess, but I think he became overwhelmed by his inability to effect a cure for Lady. He was Director of Ecology before you came. He knew Earthaid would not

156

last for ever, and he began to feel personally responsible for the failure of the Project. He became irrational. In his sickness, he came to believe the best solution was to put Lady out of her suffering, as he phrased it tonight. He couldn't do it alone, so he enlisted the help of the gorons." The grey eyes regarded Trevithick steadily. "Does that have the ring of truth?"

He thought about it. It certainly explained the facts as he knew them. But he reserved his judgement. Tillini, Vorda, Murdo, Edlin, Carstairs . . . and others. Ivor Sabin? Who else belonged to this group of conspirators, and what exactly were their objectives?

And what had they got against him? Why the firing, the attempted murder, the fake charge? Again accepting Susanna's theory, was it all to get him out of the way in case he informed Earthaid that the Project had been marking time for fifty years?

Didn't they know that would be the last thing he would do? Didn't they realise his reaction would be to try to get the Project on track?

But they wouldn't have wanted that, either. Whichever way you looked at it, he was a thorn in their side.

Then came the surprise.

"Let's not beat about the bush," said Edlin. "How would you like your job back? I'm sure I could fix it with Murdo."

Trevithick stared. "What? It was Earth HQ that fired me, not Murdo."

"I believe Murdo may have made the recommendation that HQ acted on. For reasons of local morale, you understand. People can feel very vulnerable, far from Earth."

"Oh, yes? And what do you expect me to achieve in the few months before we pull out?"

"Window-dressing." Edlin smiled at him blandly. "We're appealing Earthaid's decision. We need a Director of Ecology to formulate grounds for our appeal. Who better than you? All is forgiven, as they say."

Slowly-mounting anger was becoming a familiar emotion. "So you'd like me to lie to Earthaid about progress here, is that it?"

"An optimistic report detailing current developments and future plans," said Edlin smoothly. "You must have written plenty of them in the past. Think about it, Bryn. It'll please a lot of people who look on Goronwy as their home. And it'll restore your reputation. Once you leave Goronwy you'll be a marketable commodity again instead of a fired and burned out ecologist."

"HQ fired me because of the Annecy affair, remember? That kind of disaster doesn't happen to marketable commodities, not if they want to stay marketable."

"The Board will give you an excellent recommendation. Annecy is history. You'll be seen to have redeemed yourself."

And for a moment he was tempted; the shame of Annecy went that deep. Then he remembered: they wanted him to lie. They wanted the handouts from Earthaid to continue on the basis of a deceptive report signed by him, Bryn Trevithick, Director of Ecology. So the Goronwy bureaucracy could trundle on. And what would happen five, ten, twenty years down the road, when Lady died and the fact couldn't be hidden? Earthaid—that all-powerful body—would ask the Samaritan Organisation what had gone wrong. And the Organisation would say: perhaps Trevithick's report was overoptimistic. We trusted him; after all, he is the expert, is he not? Too bad.

"Manning," he said quietly, "You can stuff your job up your rectum."

The big man's expression hardly changed. "What a pity. I guess that means you're still unemployed. And on the run. I'm sure we could have persuaded Tillini to drop the charges, but it's hardly worth the bother in the circumstances, is it?"

There was nothing further to discuss. He stood. He walked away. He could feel their eyes on his back all the way to Susanna's table.

Or what had been Susanna's table. She was not there. Neither was Darwin. Empty mugs testified mutely to thirsts quenched. It was something of an anticlimax, after his grand exit.

At least—he thought unhappily—it gave the impression Susanna and he were comparative strangers. Walking past the table as though he'd never intended to sit there in the first place, he made his way out into the warm night air to look for Mistral.

"Well, if it isn't our local fugitive!"

A familiar voice hailed him from the far side of the unpaved street. It was Martha Sunshine, Director of Entertainments.

"What are you doing here?" he called, crossing toward her. She was standing before the low doorway of a goron dwelling, big and buxom in the shadows.

"It's this idiot Lath, darling. He seems to have passed out. I can't just leave him lying here."

Trevithick could see the long figure slumped against the door, bony legs outstretched, pale ankles exposed. The violin and bow lay beside him. "Do you know where he lives?"

"No idea. He could live behind this door, for all I know."

"A goron hut?"

"He spends most of his time on all fours, anyway. He'd fit in there okay. What are we going to do with him? He doesn't exactly give a good impression of the human race."

Trevithick took hold of Lath Eagleman's wrists. They were very thin, almost skeletal. He hauled, lifted and shrugged him onto his back. Eagleman was frighteningly light and smelled of vomit. "I'll take him."

"Where?"

A voice of caution warned Trevithick at the last moment. "Better that you don't know, Martha."

"The heat's off you now, surely, darling? Hell, nothing matters now we're pulling out, does it?"

"I've been told otherwise."

"Too bad. Still, you've found someone to mother you, huh?" She sighed and laid a plump hand on his arm, a big sexy lady. "Lost chances, lost chances. Speaking of which, I was on the brink of getting *Barker Sam* here from Deganwy. Everything was agreed, Brassworthy was going to spring for the costs, and Outward Ho hadn't got a leg to stand on because their nearest colony's in another system. Now I've got to cancel out. Too bad."

He found himself regretting it with her. Martha had a knack of transporting him to a different world, probably because she lived in a different world herself. A world of big shows, big stars and big money. A world of glamour. Bright lights, special effects, colourful costumes and great music.

He jerked himself back to the here and now; the squalid doorway and the drunken half-wit on his back. "I'd better get going. I don't want to hang around in the dark too long."

"Covert apprehension, huh? Well, watch yourself, darling. Here, take his fiddle." Then she stood on tiptoe, kissed him on the cheek, observed the lolling head of Eagleman with a moue of distaste, and trotted off toward the nearest dome.

Mistral was not in her burrow. Within half an hour Eagleman was stretched out on her pile of furs while Trevithick fed him a hot stimulant. He groaned and vomited. Trevithick was ready for that with a bowl. Eagleman kept the next mouthful down, and the one afterward. His eyes opened, red-rimmed in the lamplight. Mistral would have had scant sympathy for this situation. But where was she? The lamp on the table had been alight when he'd carried Lath in.

She was probably hiding in a nearby cave, trying to come to terms with her responsibility for the death of a hundred-odd gorons. That was going to take some doing. Best to leave her alone for a while, he decided, then offer sympathy and rationalisations when she'd calmed down.

Eagleman groaned. "Oh, my bright eyes. What have I done to myself? Where am I? Is this Earth?"

"Wake up, Lath. I'm Bryn Trevithick. You remember, we met at the Barge the other day."

"Bryn Trevithick . . ." Dull eyes flickered. He was sixty-five years old but looked ninety. Susanna had said he might have some answers concerning happenings on Goronwy, but Trevithick was reluctant to question him too closely in his present condition. Did it matter any more, now they were pulling out? In the end, curiosity got the better of him.

"Tell me about your dad, Lath."

The eyes brightened. "My dad was the first senior biologist, you know that? Very important position. Clever man, my dad."

"Yes, I know. What happened to him?"

Now the pale eyes were sad. "Mom was clever too. She knew when to stay out of the way. She's on Earth. She stayed behind and she stayed alive. I get warpwires, you know."

"Your dad, Lath. He brought you here. You'd have been about fifteen. Do you remember much about those days?"

"Dad's gone. Mom's on Earth. Tell me about Earth." His voice was wistful. "They still have trees and such?"

"Where did your dad go?"

"Dunno. One day he wasn't there."

This was heavy going. Eagleman lay back on the furs, his head propped on a pillow, grey-faced, wispy grey hair showing grey scalp underneath. But at least he was talking.

Trevithick said, "After your dad left the Organisation you and he lived alone for a while. Did he say anything about why he left?"

A sudden look of alarm came over the tired face. "My violin. Where's my violin?"

Trevithick laid it in his lap. He placed a hand on it and began to stroke it, the way one might stroke a cat. The strings murmured.

"Did your dad tell you anything about the Project?" Trevithick asked.

Eagleman looked troubled, brows knitted. Trevithick wet a cloth and began gently to wipe the muck and sweat from his face. He brushed the thin hair back; Lath looked different that way; more intelligent. He had quite a high forehead.

And a pale circular scar at the hairline.

A lobotomy.

CHAPTER 16

THAT WAS TREVITHICK'S FIRST THOUGHT. But he was wrong, surely? Lobotomies were a barbaric treatment of bygone days. Nowadays mental rebuilding was a fine art. Nobody used the trepan any more, did they? Lath must have suffered an accident causing a depressed fracture of the skull, and this was the result of subsequent surgery.

Perhaps Susanna would be able to dig something out of the records about this.

He found himself shuddering, and quickly smoothed Eagleman's hair back over his forehead. The thin man smiled back the way a child might, and took hold of the bow. Soon, the slow tune of Mendelssohn's violin concerto began to fill the cave.

Trevithick left him there. The tunnel split into four others a short distance further on. First on the right was the studio. Second on the right was the latrine. Straight on led up to the garden. This left the third tunnel on the right, the low one. He got down on all fours and began to crawl, sliding the lamp before him.

It was tough going. The tunnel walls were dry sandstone, fairly smooth and obviously part of a stoag warren. Some twenty meters further on he came to an extensive junction of tunnels; six at least. It was difficult to tell exactly how many because several of them forked again near the limit of the lamplight. Which way to go? He examined the ground for signs that Mistral had passed by, but could only see the claw-marks of stoags.

He could hear the characteristic grunting of the animals in the distance, and the squeal of youngsters. Best to steer clear of nurseries; stoags were very protective of their young. An enraged six-legged animal with forepaws adapted for digging would be more than he could handle in this confined space. Mistral could be down any one of those tunnels, probably cuddled up to Wilfred and confiding her problems to him. But which one?

In the end he chose a tunnel at random. He'd crawled about ten meters and his knees were becoming sore when he came to a dead end at an odd-looking wall. It was grey and sprouted what looked like fine roots. Had he been crawling uphill without noticing, and was approaching the surface? The lamp showed a narrow crevice beside the wall. He crawled into it. At first he thought he'd gotten himself into a blind alley, but the crevice proved wider than he'd thought. There was a peculiar smell; a warm organic smell almost like human sweat. Then he noticed something else.

The walls of the crevice were moving apart as he crawled forward.

There was no doubt about it. The sandstone wall to his left stayed in place but the grey wall to his right shifted, as though to allow him room to get through. What was going on? It was unnerving. He had to get out of here. He tried to back up, but the crevice had closed behind him. There was no way to go except forward. His heart began to pound. He was perilously close to panic. The grey wall shifted behind him, squeezing his feet.

He jerked them free and slid the lamp forward. The wall moved away. He crawled a meter or so and pushed the lamp forward again. The wall moved again.

It was reacting to the lamplight.

He held the lamp closer to the wall. It retreated, forming a dent near the lamp. He struck it with his fist. It was hard, but not rocklike. Again he felt pressure on his legs as it closed behind him. Another moment of claustrophobic panic. He dropped the lamp.

It went out.

He was not familiar with the workings of the lamp. It was one of a consignment of virtual museum pieces given to the gorons in the early days of the Project. He knew it had to be filled with oil; the gorons had an ample supply of this from bushtrap pods and other vegetable sources. The lamp might be empty, but more likely the impact had extinguished the flame. It had to be relit.

The wall advanced, squeezing him against the sandstone.

He managed to get his hands into his pockets, feverishly searching for some form of light before he was crushed to death. He carried no miniflashlight; he'd forgotten to pick one up. He had no lighter or matches. He was ill-equipped for life on the run and he was going to pay the penalty. He tried to think. It wasn't easy, given the circumstances.

This was Goronwy. He didn't expect technological sophistication on Goronwy. So a light-sensitive moving wall was unlikely to be mechanical. What else could it be? Organic. Some kind of giant earthworm, perhaps. But why should the skin of an earthworm be light-sensitive?

By now his shoulders were immobilised by the pressure. The situation was desperate. He felt about on the ground and burned his fingers on the glass surround of the lamp. He didn't know what he intended to do with it, but he managed to pick it up.

The pressure eased.

He held the lamp against the wall. The pressure eased further, convulsively. He hadn't been thinking clearly. The creature—if it was a creature—was sensitive to the heat of the lamp, not the light. He began to crawl again, blindly this time, pushing the lamp into the crevice before him. The walls parted.

The air had become increasingly foul and he was close to suffocation when he saw a glow ahead. Suddenly he was clear of the grey wall and could breathe easily. Strange sounds echoed around, giving the impression of a large cavern filled with activity and endeavour. Clicks, snapping noises, and whistles overlaid the grunting of what sounded like a large number of stoags. The smell became identifiable: stoag and rotting vegetation. The glow firmed up into a small light illuminating a recess within the cavern. A tiny hand reached out and took hold of Trevithick's.

"Samaritan, come here out of harm's way," said a goron voice.

It sounded like friendly advice. Overwhelmingly pleased at hearing an intelligent voice, Trevithick crawled into the recess. A goron sat on a ledge, a lamp on the ground before him.

"Stand fast," Trevithick greeted him shakily. "I am Bryn Trevithick."

"Stand fast. Mistral calls me Caball. What brings you here? This is dangerous ground for a human."

"I was looking for Mistral."

"She hasn't been here for seventeen days," said the goron precisely.

"Yes, but have you seen her? Or heard of her? Today, I mean?"

He smiled, pleased to be of assistance. "She is at the new place where the waters run, I believe." He went on to give directions. Due to the warren-like nature of the tunnels, these were difficult to follow. Meanwhile the sounds continued unabated, and finally the goron fell silent, still smiling.

Trevithick said, "Thank you for your help."

"I am of Clan Service. When you leave, take care to keep by the walls. There's a lot of activity in the middle of the cavern."

It was an understatement. A bellowing had now started up, accompanied by a heavy thudding as though a powerful creature was swinging a sack of cement about.

"What is this place, anyway?"

"This is the chamber of the mother stoag. She occupies many meters of tunnel, and her head is nearby. The male stoags have been out in the fields all day, and now they're feeding her, just as we feed Lady." He smiled again. "It's a wonderful time, full of significance."

"It sounds violent."

"Occasionally the mother stoag will take a male if he is not quick enough. It is meant to be that way, because the slow males are the old ones. Unlike us, they don't have the intelligence to go willingly."

The bellowing rose to a squeal, then suddenly stopped.

"It's done," said Caball. "She will be replete for a while. It's safe for you to go."

"What are you doing here, anyway?" Trevithick asked.

"I told you. I am of Clan Service." His face was twisted with thought, as he tried to frame his explanation in a way a human would understand. "Life is precious. We are lucky, we gorons, to be members of an intelligent species. Stoags are not so lucky. So we watch over them, to make sure they come to no harm." His tiny, smooth face became devoid of expression. "Ironic, is it not, that we gorons are the ones who will become extinct?"

Trevithick lit his lamp from Caball's and left. Stoags lumbered to and fro, brushing past him in the gloom. He tried not to think about his recent contact with the flank of that vast female. Male stoags weighed up to two hundred kilograms. The female had been slinging a doomed male around like a puppy. Supposing she'd turned to deal with the itch in her side? He crept nervously through the tunnels and was hugely relieved to find himself back at the main junction.

He needed a different approach. Caball had said Mistral was at the place where the waters ran. Now, perhaps, he should try to use evidence at hand.

He'd felt a light breeze in his face during his original journey from Mistral's quarters and he could feel it now. Stoags were diurnal creatures, grazing in the ripplegrass fields during the day and sleeping in their warrens at night after feeding their mother. Obviously they couldn't pass through Mistral's living quarters every time they wanted to go up top. So somewhere down here there would be a way to the surface.

He crawled to the mouth of each tunnel in turn, gauging the strength of the breeze by the flickering of the lamp, and sniffing. Mostly he smelled stoag. But two tunnels were obviously open at the other end, to judge by the breeze coming from them. The one smelled neutral; a fresh air, Goronwy kind of smell. The other was different; a stale damp smell. Without wishing to criticise his own species he had to admit there was something human about that smell. And he could hear distant sounds down there too: water trickling, a rhythmic scraping.

And Mistral's voice.

There was no doubt about it. She was down there, shouting at something. He crawled in that direction.

The sounds became louder. "Come on, Wilfred! Now you, you bugger! Get a move on, you two!" She was exhorting stoags to some kind of effort.

He rounded a corner into a large chamber lit by two lanterns at the far end. At first he couldn't make out what was happening. At least ten stoags milled around, and sand was flying in all directions. The dank smell had intensified, as had the sound of water trickling. Mistral knelt at the far end of the cavern, naked apart from a pair of brief and very sandy underpants, directing operations.

"What's going on?" he called.

She whirled round, hair swirling, firm breasts shivering. "Get out, Mister!" She raised a forearm to cover herself. "It's none of your bloody business!"

He crawled forward. "Take it easy."

"I'll set the stoags on you!"

"You wouldn't do that. You saved my life earlier on."

She appeared to reassess her values. "Yeah. You'd gotten yourself into a real bind, hadn't you? Galloping off after that Susanna like a bloody knight in armour. Serve you right if I'd let the gorons take you."

"But you didn't."

"Well, don't put too much store by that. What you doing here, anyway?"

"I came to see how you were. And to thank you. Are you feeling all right now?"

She looked puzzled. "All right?"

"Well . . ." He began to feel they were at cross purposes somewhere. "All those gorons dying, and so on."

She shrugged. "So what? Maybe a hundred gorons died. They'd have died in any case, sooner or later."

"That's a very callous way of looking at it. I thought you were fond of the gorons."

Her eyes flashed, but she spoke calmly. "You're talking like a human. Gorons aren't scared of dying, because they know there's thousands of other gorons still alive. They think: What's a hundred here or there? If Lady dies, that's different. That's final."

"So what happened tonight doesn't bother you."

"It'd have bothered me more if you'd been the one fed to Lady." She bit her lip. "And stop looking at my tits. You're always doing that. I didn't expect visitors."

He approached her on hands and knees. Together they knelt at the edge of a low sandstone bank. Below us, dark water rushed by. To his right, the twisted remains of a corrugated metal culvert wall projected from the sandstone.

He recognised the location. "You did a painting of this place. I saw it in your studio. So what's it all about?"

"It wasn't no easy picture to paint." She sounded pleased, and leaned her body against him the way a cat might. "It was all so dark, see?"

"Yes, but what is this place?"

Now her voice was triumphant. "I told you I had proof they were trying to kill Lady and you wouldn't believe me. Well, here's the proof. This is the sewer pipe from the domes. It flows into Lady. What do you think of that, huh?"

"Where does it come out?"

"Just above the Passing Barge. And just below that Susanna's apartment. You remember I said I seen Lady tremble? That's where."

He regarded the rushing stream. There was a treatment plant in the service dome. In theory, this water should be pure enough to drink. It wouldn't cause Lady any harm; in fact it might even have a nutrient content.

He told Mistral so.

She snorted derisively. "Oh, sure. I'll go and get a mug for you, if you're so bloody keen on the stuff."

It was dank and claustrophobic in that tunnel, and Trevithick disliked confined spaces almost as much as heights. A million tonnes of sandstone were pressing on him from all sides. Large and potentially dangerous animals were exercising their powerful claws a few meters away. In a situation like this, a man begins to think the worst.

Suppose—he wondered—someone did want to kill Lady, for reasons yet unrevealed.

What simpler way, than to release poison down this sewer?

There would be an inquiry, and the tragedy would be attributed to human error, and a scapegoat would be found. Trevithick knew all about the finding of scapegoats. The whole thing would be written off as an unfortunate accident, one in a million.

And Lady would be dead.

But why?

"Dunno," said Mistral, when he asked her. "All I know is what I see here."

There was no good reason for the sewage to flow into Lady. It could have been channelled the other way, out into the western desert where it could do no harm. Mistral's father Ralph was in charge of Engineering. Although this sewer must have been laid when the domes were built, he might be able to explain why this route was chosen. He decided to talk to Susanna about it.

The stoags dug on busily. "All right, Mistral," he said. "It doesn't look good, the sewage flowing into Lady. But it doesn't matter too much now we're pulling out."

"Don't make it right, though, do it?"

"No. So what are you doing here right now? What are the stoags doing?"

"Blocking it off."

"What! But it'll all back up in the service dome!"

"Yeah." Black hair hung past her face as she knelt there gazing at the water. He couldn't see her expression. "Yeah, won't it?"

"You can't do this!"

"And you can't stop me." Suddenly she rolled over onto her back and stretched her arms over her head, catlike. Small breasts rose in the lamplight. Green eyes stared into his. "So whatcha gonna do about it, huh?"

It seemed to be an invitation. Uncomfortably aware that he'd had a powerful erection for the past few minutes, he pretended to ignore it. "Sooner or later they'll notice the damage on their sensors. They'll send men and machines down here to find out what's going on, if they're not already on their way," he said as calmly as he could. "And they'll find this tunnel. They'll trace it back to your place."

"No, they'll think it's just stoags, digging like they do." But the eyes showed a flicker of alarm. She hadn't thought it through.

"They're not fools, Mistral. Stoags don't go tearing metal culverts apart; they dig round them. They'll guess the stoags were commanded by someone. And your place isn't far away."

"I'll get the stoags to backfill," she said. "They can fill all this in, right back to the big junction. They'll pack it tight. They'll—"

A stoag screamed.

It was an unearthly sound in the confined space; a shrill echoing almost-human sound, and it went on and on. The ground trembled as the other stoags began to panic, milling about. Then Trevithick saw the flash of tracers, and heard men shouting.

An armed force was coming down the sewer.

CHAPTER 17

"Come on!" he shouted. "Let's get out of here!"

Mistral rolled over. Kneeling, she peered up the sewer. She seemed to have no idea of personal safety. Trevithick grabbed her around the waist and hauled her back. A tracer lanced past, chips of sandstone exploding nearby. Mistral squeaked. The stoags were milling around now, heavy paws stamping, claws slashing aimlessly. The lamp fell over; he let go of Mistral and righted it. The injured stoag continued to squeal.

"Get them," he heard Mistral whisper. "Get them, get them, get them!"

The stoags quietened. Big, dim shapes, coarse black hair thick with sand, they wavered between fear of the agonising threads of light and obedience to Mistral. For a long moment there was silence.

Then they heard a shout. "There's a whole herd of them down there! They've broken through the culvert wall!"

"They don't know we're here," Trevithick told Mistral. He took hold of her arm. "Let's get out while we can. We'll be okay if we stay quiet."

"Let me go!" She tried to jerk away. "We're not going nowhere. I'm gonna give those bastards something to think about!"

"They've got lasers. We have nothing. Use some sense, girl." He blew out the oil lamp.

"Did you see some kind of light down there?" somebody said. "It's gone now. I could swear I saw something."

"Just a reflection. Jesus Christ, look at that! Get the floodlight on, quick!"

Instantly the tunnel walls sprang into brilliant light, reflecting from the bright metal corrugations and illuminating the chamber. A packed mass of stoags was surging down the bank and into the water, clawing their way upstream toward the floodlight, all tiny eyes and bared teeth. For the first time Trevithick realised the full extent of the chamber. A circular section of the culvert had been torn away and the stoags' excavations had produced a vast, almost flat roof above it. Obviously Mistral intended to collapse this into the sewer in a single, huge subsidence. It was probably the only way to achieve her objective. Anything smaller would be swept away by the current, like the sand they'd excavated up to now.

"Burn the bastards down!" came the cry. The task force was still several meters up the tunnel.

Later, looking back on those last moments in the cavern, one image burned in Trevithick's brain. Above the backs of the stoags surging upstream, a single stoag reared up, agonised. Its jaws were stretched so far open that the flesh between upper and lower jaw was white. It screamed as the hair on its chest, and the flesh under that hair, smoked. In terminal agony it gave a convulsive leap, broke clear of the ruck and, scrabbling for a foothold, was carried on the backs of its fellows out of sight, still screaming, to its death.

The din was deafening. The herd hesitated. Those on the bank stared anxiously up the sewer, heads weaving to and fro like captive bears. Others joined them, scrambling terrified out of the water, eyes narrowed against the light.

"Bring them back!" Trevithick whispered. "They'll all be killed! Is that what you want?"

But Mistral had already seen sense. The stoags were backing up now with six-legged clumsiness, treading on the forepaws of those behind. Those on the bank were retreating toward Trevithick and Mistral. There was a stifling stink of excrement. Trevithick couldn't see the tracer beams any more; they were lost in the general glare. But the lasers were hitting home, and the squealing of injured stoags drowned out all other sounds.

"Please, Bryn," Mistral muttered unsteadily, "tell me what to do."

The situation was already hopeless, the battle lost. "We have to get back down the tunnel before the stoags do," he said. "It's the only way. Come on!"

The stoags were all around them, shoving and stamping. The task force had almost reached the chamber; soon they'd turn the corner with their floodlight. Trevithick took Mistral's hand and began to pull her out, away from the noise and turmoil. She checked once, and he heard her throwing up. Then she came on.

They were soon back in the small tunnel. He pushed Mistral in first and followed close behind, butting her rump with his head to keep her moving. They were probably safe, but for all the wrong reasons. The stoags would follow them, driven back by the lasers of the task force. The tunnel was only big enough for one animal at a time. They would die in there and choke the passage with their bodies. It would take time to clear them out.

Only a few would make it back to the warren. Trevithick felt an overwhelming pity for Mistral. She'd shrugged off the death of the gorons at the Passing Barge, but this would break her heart.

"Wilfred," she whispered.

There was a stoag close behind Trevithick; it kept stepping on his legs as he crawled. He hoped it was Wilfred. Gradually the sounds of suffering became muffled, then finally died away. The tunnel was blocked behind them. They were safe, at a great cost.

When they reached the main junction a shuddering reaction set in and they huddled against the wall, Trevithick's arms around Mistral and her face buried in his chest. He could feel her sobbing, but she made no sound. Something big and hairy joined them; it had to be Wilfred.

A long time later Trevithick awakened to the slow melody from Mendelssohn's violin concerto, inexpertly played.

"Oh, here you are." Susanna and Lath were sitting on the pile of furs. Susanna's smile died as they emerged into the lamplight and she saw their condition. "What happened?" she asked. Lath played on, unheeding.

Mistral stood above her, tears flowing down her cheeks, her hair plastered back with sweat and sand, the big scar livid. "You know bloody well what happened! Me and the stoags, we been digging that tunnel for ages and no problem. And just when we're finished the bastards are ready for us, and you know why!"

"What the hell are you talking about?" Trevithick had never seen Susanna really angry before, but now her face was pale. She got slowly to her feet and faced Mistral. "I don't know what you've been up to, but don't blame me if it went wrong. And for Pete's sake get some clothes on, will you?"

Trevithick caught Mistral's hand from behind as she began to swing it clawlike at Susanna's face. He slapped his other hand across her mouth and held it there, cutting short a stream of invective. Holding her firmly while she squirmed and kicked, he explained the situation. Lath fiddled on regardless. Wilfred retired to a corner to lick his wounds. Finally, Susanna said more calmly:

"It was a stupid thing to do, Mistral. They'll have all kinds of sensors in that sewer. You'd never have got away with it. You're lucky they didn't find out days ago and come up your tunnel after you."

Trevithick uncovered Mistral's mouth long enough to discover that the reply was going to be unsatisfactory, and covered it up again. Susanna dug a tiny transdermic out of her purse and held it to Mistral's arm. There was a quick hiss. "The pheromones from the injured stoags have done this to her," she said. "She feels almost as bad as they feel, poor kid. She'll be all right in a minute or two."

"She won't take the pills," he said. "I've tried. She says they make her feel only half alive." Mistral was relaxing, slumping in his arms.

"That's probably true, for her. Personally I don't like to borrow emotions; I've got quite enough of my own. Uh, by the way. Why is it whenever I find you two together, she's only half dressed? Pure coincidence, I hope?"

"Absolutely." Why did he feel so guilty? Probably because

Mistral did have an exceptionally beautiful body. But that was no fault of his, he told himself firmly. He removed his hands from her slowly, ready to clamp down on any further outbreak of unpleasantness. "She was like this when I found her. I guess it's more comfortable for her that way, in the tunnels. She wasn't expecting me."

Susanna regarded him with a half-smile. "You're babbling, Trevithick. You're guilty as charged."

"Listen," said Mistral sullenly, "it's none of your bloody business what I wear or don't wear. You don't have to look." Nevertheless she took a grimy dress from a heap of clothing against the wall and pulled it on. As her head appeared tortoise-like from the folds, green eyes stared coolly at Susanna. "Reckon I owe you an apology. Sorry. It's just that I was depending on plugging that sewer. That's what's killing Lady, all that muck."

"Perhaps. Perhaps not. They do have a purification plant, you know."

Mistral, now in full possession of her senses, said, "Okay, now maybe you'll tell me whose side you're on, huh? It'd be easy for me to do the wrong thing if I don't know where you stand. Maybe I already did the wrong thing last night at the Barge, for all I know. Huh! You two'd be in Lady's belly now if it hadn't been for me."

"Yes," said Susanna thoughtfully. "Thanks for helping us out. I guess I owe you an explanation. But keep this to yourself, Mistral. Bryn knows most of it already. You see, there's been so much going on lately that I don't know who I can trust. Things have been happening that I don't understand."

"What kind of things?" asked Mistral.

Susanna sat down beside Lath again, smoothing her skirt over her knees, and recounted to Mistral the discussion she'd had with Trevithick. Meanwhile Lath Eagleman sawed away at his violin as an accompaniment to her voice. "Anyway, we're all relieved the Project's wrapping up," she concluded. We feel things have gone kind of rotten here. We just hope we can get out of here quietly, without some kind of disaster. All we're after, really, is a quiet life. But it has to be an honest life."

"So who are these crooks you're talking about?"

Trevithick answered, "You remember Edlin wanted to talk to me? He tried to offer me my job back." He told them about the conversation in the Passing Barge.

"My God," said Susanna quietly. "That about clinches it. All the same . . . Yes, a whole lot of people look on Goronwy as their home and don't want to leave. But . . . Somehow I keep sensing something else. Something I don't understand. Something not so innocent as a simple desire not to lose one's home."

"Is my dad in on this?" asked Mistral resignedly.

"Your dad is one of the good guys. It's about time you realised that."

"Huh!"

"Anyway," said Susanna briskly, "we haven't pulled out yet. It's still business as usual, and now we've got to worry about you as well as Bryn. Security's going to investigate that tunnel and trace it back to your cave here."

"My dwelling," Mistral corrected her stiffly. "And anyway they'll think it was just stoags, burrowing like they do. Sure, there's a way through to my quarters. But there's tunnels everywhere."

A thought hit Trevithick like a blow. "We left the lamps behind."

"That'll do it," said Susanna. "You've got to move out. Both of you."

"I'm not moving for anyone," snapped Mistral. "I'm gonna get the stoags to backfill the tunnel and pack it tight. Security'll need digging equipment to get through that lot. And the stoags can dig a few more tunnels to put them off the scent, like a maze."

"Mistral," said Susanna patiently, "yours is the only dwelling in the area. Security aren't fools. Once they find the lamps they won't need to dig through any tunnels. They'll know humans are involved and they'll come right to your front door."

"I . . . I been living here for ages. This is my home."

"Yes, I know that. It's too bad. But Security's going to be after you, now." Susanna regarded Trevithick. "I'm surprised Tillini isn't dropping those charges now everyone's pulling out. It's such a waste of time, chasing you. I mean, does it matter any more?"

"How about you?" he asked. "They may connect you with Mistral and me, after that business at the Passing Barge."

"Maybe they will," she said. "But I can watch my back. And I have friends in high places."

For the first time he noticed a pale glow of daylight at the end of the exit tunnel. It must be morning, at least. Suddenly he felt exhausted. Susanna noticed. "Sit down here before you fall down, Bryn. When did you last eat?"

"Some time yesterday, I guess."

She seemed quite at home with Mistral's primitive utensils and even went out to the garden and picked unidentifiable vegetables. By now Mistral was crouched beside Wilfred in his dark corner, tending to his wounds. Susanna saw the remains of the packet of M16, glanced from Trevithick to Mistral with a faint smile, said, "We've got to wean you off this muck," and within minutes had produced a meal that, although peculiar, was acceptable.

After eating he was feeling a shade more human. "What happened to you at the Barge last night?" he asked. "I looked for you, but you were gone."

"I went home. It seemed best not to let them think we were together."

"I missed you."

They heard a "Huh!" from the corner. Green eyes watched them catlike. "Why did you give me that shot? I can't tell how Wilfred feels. It's rotten, this is."

Susanna glanced at Trevithick and said quietly, "Is there somewhere we can talk?"

Mistral was preoccupied with Wilfred and showed no reaction when Trevithick took the only remaining lamp and led Susanna into the back of the cave. They entered the studio. The sun was shining almost directly down the vent. It was another day.

"Have you been to work yet?" Trevithick asked.

"Good grief, yes. It's afternoon, didn't you know? Time flies when you're having fun with half-naked nymphets, Trevithick. Anyway, we'll have to get you and Mistral out of here by nightfall. And we'll have to find somewhere for you to stay."

"There's the cottage."

She hesitated. "I'm not happy about turning Mistral loose at the cottage. You remember when you found her in my studio, with a knife? Did you ever wonder why she was there?"

He regarded Mistral's crude daubs on their easels, and thought back to Susanna's exquisite work at the cottage. And he considered the depth of Mistral's jealousy of Susanna. "Oh, no. She wouldn't."

"I'm not sure I want to take the chance. Really, Bryn, I don't want her to come to any harm, but there are limits. She may have been a nice enough girl in any other circumstances, but here on Goronwy, picking up whatever pheromones happen to be passing, her face all scarred and her mind scarred too, and too stubborn to do anything about it . . . She goes out of kilter from time to time, and I'd rather she didn't do it in my studio. No, don't worry about it. You can go to the cottage, and I'll find something around Samarita for her." Unexpectedly, she flashed him a mischievous grin. "Maybe not a bad idea to keep her away from you, anyway."

"I can handle her."

"Oh, sure you can."

Wilting under the amused gaze of those big eyes, he muttered, "You're much prettier than she is."

"You're absolutely right, Trevithick. I cling to that thought. But give Mistral a little surgical treatment and a damned good shower, and she'd be devastating. Believe me. It's easy for a guy like you to be shocked by those scars because you're used to seeing nothing but beautiful people. But I'm a doctor. I've seen sad cases. And I've seen them leave their hospital beds looking like angels. Anyway, thanks for the compliment. It's nice to be reassured from time to time."

This gave him enough courage to take hold of her hand. She didn't object. It was odd how his attitude had changed. When he'd first met her—such a short while ago, too—he'd felt that fine careless lust that a guy feels for a beautiful, lively and intelligent woman. He'd even made a crude grab for her; he felt his face flush at the memory. Now things had changed. Now he knew her better, and she had become very precious to him. He didn't want to screw up. He wanted to take this thing slowly, to let it grow further. He hoped she'd forgotten the grabbing incident, which was unlikely, or at least written it off as a momentary aberration brought on by mead. "So what about this sewer?" he asked, to make the hand-holding into a thing a guy might do naturally while talking about something else.

"I'll speak to Mistral's dad about it. There's got to be a good reason for having that stuff flow into Lady. Or at least a convincing excuse."

They wandered around the cave, examining the paintings and seeing little of merit. "Do you think a few lessons might help?" he asked.

"It might help, but it wouldn't make her into an artist. You've either got it or you haven't. Mistral hasn't. It's too bad. She tries hard, you can tell. There's a hell of a lot of work gone into this stuff, but it's not art."

"Huh! Shows how much you know!"

Mistral stood in the entrance to the cave, her face pale in the lamplight.

"I'm so sorry," said Susanna quickly. "I didn't know you were there."

"Yeah, just as well I was, huh? Best to know the kind of people you're dealing with. So you don't think my pictures are art, huh? How come I can sell them and you can't, Miss Smartipants?"

Susanna looked at Trevithick helplessly.

"It was a private conversation," he said. "Let's forget it, shall we?"

"Forget it, huh?" Mistral took a couple of steps into the cave and stood before Susanna, fists clenched. "Let me tell you something. You know as much about art as—" She searched for an appropriate Philistine "—as my dad. And why? Because Martha Sunshine's having a show for me, that's why!"

After an instant of stupefaction, Trevithick managed to say, "A show? Martha Sunshine?"

Triumph was gleaming in her eyes. "Yeah, a show, like with my paintings hanging on walls and everybody coming to look at them and buy them. That kind of a show. Okay?"

"When . . . when was this arranged, Mistral?"

"Martha and me had a big talk last night."

"After the Marik Darwin thing was all over?" Susanna asked.

"Yeah, but anyway that made no difference. It's my paintings they want on the wall. And that Martha, she's nice. Nicer than some I could mention. So what do you say about that, huh?"

"I'm very pleased for you," Trevithick said.

Mistral's gaze snapped to Susanna.

"I'm pleased too, Mistral," she said. "Really. But don't expect too much. Art shows can be tricky things."

"Yeah, sure. Now you two get out of my place and take that Lath with you."

"You'd better come, hadn't you?" said Susanna.

"I'll take my chances. I got work to do. And don't you two come back, huh? I reckon I found out who my friends are."

CHAPTER 18

MARIK DARWIN SAT ON THE DIRT FLOOR with his back against the wall, cold, hungry and desperate. It seemed he'd been cooped up there for ever, only knowing day from night by the slender thread of light along the cracks in the rough timber. The place stank; he'd had to use the opposite corner as a latrine. Sooner or later the inhabitants of the apartment above would investigate. Every morning and evening he heard their footsteps overhead, and their voices too, although he couldn't distinguish individual words.

Before he'd holed up here, the place had been a storage area for Clan Boatbuilder materials; a rude warehouse built by stretching woven walls between posts supporting the apartment above. Flooding by excess surface water on Lady a few days ago had forced him to perch on a woodpile for a full day and night. At least it had flushed his latrine for him.

The gorons came and went, carrying wood, pegs, nets and other materials in and out, ignoring the human who crouched in the corner like an animal. All except the one he called Tich, a survivor of Clan Active; possibly the only survivor. Tich brought him nectar, and news.

The door cracked open. Darwin felt his customary surge of fear. But it was the faithful Tich once more, bringing sustenance.

"Thanks." He drank from the gourd. It was firepot nectar as usual; he wished the little fellow would bring mead for a change. He'd asked for it once, but Tich hadn't seemed to understand. Mead was a human invention and he'd never known a goron to drink it. Tich squatted beside him, head cocked, eyeing him devotedly.

Was he was beginning to replace Lady in the little guy's mind? Some kind of imprinting was going on. Maybe in the glory days of Clan Active he'd been a surrogate mother, rather than a leader.

"Why do you help me?" he asked.

"You need food," Tich replied, logically enough. "But why don't you rejoin the humans?"

Darwin felt a quick irritation. If the little fool had asked that once, he'd asked it a hundred times. He simply couldn't grasp the idea that Darwin was a fugitive.

His mind went back to that fateful evening at the Passing Barge. Everything had been fine up to that point. Then it had all fallen apart. Who'd have thought that crazy girl Mistral would have had such an influence on the termites? And that dumb blonde with her right cross; good grief, it was like being kicked by a horse. She'd been sympathetic afterward, though. Then the frightful Tillini had reared up from his table and headed in his direction, and he'd known the game was up. He'd outlived his usefulness. They'd always made it quite clear they wouldn't accept failure. He'd escaped through the door at the back of the washroom.

It was almost a relief to hole up here away from the plotting and scheming, and to have it clearly in mind who his enemies were. At least, it had been a relief at first. Now, in his present condition, he wasn't so sure. Walls could close in on a man.

"Jesus Christ, how I hate this goddamned world!" he burst out, startling Tich who'd seemed to be dozing.

"We've always understood that," said a voice that was not goron.

His heart gave a great thump and he uttered a little scream of fear. He peered into the gloom, and saw an indistinct shape standing beside a woodpile. They'd found him.

"Who the hell is that?" he quavered.

"You failed us, Marik." The voice was human, smooth and low, almost musical. "And you hid from us. We had a deal, remember?"

"Listen," he said desperately, "I did my best."

"You failed to carry Clan Active through to the end. You allowed that fool of a girl to defeat you."

"How was I to know—"

"You should have known, Marik," said the voice softly. "The whole thing was your idea, if you remember. You detested life in Samarita and the job was nothing like you'd been led to believe. We agreed to ship you back to Earth with a generous severance package in return for a small favour. It was a simple deal and a fair one. So we assumed you were being honest with us when you said you could destroy Lady from within. We assumed you had allowed for the girl. It was a reasonable assumption. But now," the voice sighed, "you've failed and we've been forced to take alternative measures. There is no place for you in the scheme of things now."

"I can help! I know more about Lady than any human on Goronwy!"

"Well, to tell the truth, Marik, you're a loose end. We don't like to have loose ends lying around. Trevithick, for example. He's a loose end as well. Right now he's heading for a cottage up by the Great Lake, and we'll be waiting there to tidy matters up. That's the way we operate, you see. The secret of our success."

"Listen, I've got all kinds of knowledge." He tried to snap his fingers. "I could poison Lady for you just like that!"

A chuckle. "Really, do you think we could do anything so crude with all of Samarita looking on? Good heavens, Marik! Lady must die of natural causes, or as near to natural as raises no eyebrows. Where's your finesse?"

Something snapped in Darwin. He felt weak, filthy, degraded, light-headed with hunger and suddenly nothing mattered any more. He struggled to his feet, leaning heavily against the wall. "The hell with you and your people!" he spat out. "I can screw everything up for you any time I like, don't you know that? "

"Oh, and how do you propose to do that?"

"By telling a few people the answer to the Lady problem, that's how!"

"You know the answer, Marik?"

"Of course I know the goddamned answer! I'm a biologist, remember? And in case you were thinking of trying anything, I have insurance. Disks. I have everything on disk, and I sent the disks somewhere you'll never find them."

Again the chuckle. "Oh, but we have found them." A scattering of small disks landed in the dirt at Marik's feet. "You sent them to the wrong person, Marik."

He stared into the darkness. "You? Oh, my God."

"Yes. Me."

He had time to see the thread of light bridge the gap between the dark figure and his own chest. "You won't be talking any more, Marik," said the voice, and the agony began and ended almost simultaneously.

Bridget Booker had never pretended to relate well to humans, but she thought she knew her gorons. The little men were friendly, they were peace loving, and they were intelligent if a little rigid in their thinking. They appreciated her work and she got along well with them. Such were the gorons as she knew them. Then came the announcement that the Project was being wound down, and everything changed.

For a few days it had shown itself as an indefinable unrest. Members of Clan Birthcare moved more slowly over the surface of Lady, and seemed almost reluctant to remove ripe foetuses to safety. The nurses worked well, but the school was a disaster. The students had become inattentive, and as for her four teachers . . . Well, it was almost as though they'd begun to forget the human language!

Finally she confronted Gaston, the senior teacher. She found him on the beach basking in the afternoon sun while his tiny pupils frolicked in the nearby waves instead of sitting at their lessons.

"What on earth is going on?" she cried.

"But this is not Earth," he replied, deliberately misunderstanding her.

"Gaston," she said grimly, "take those children into the classroom and get on with the lessons, at once!"

"There is no need. This afternoon I would have instructed a class in the human language. But they do not need the human language any more, now you are leaving us. It is pointless to teach them something they do not need." He stood, his face twisting slowly into a worried expression. "Far better that the time should be given over to practical clan studies."

"I don't see much in the way of practical clan studies going on right now."

"This is the old way. We let them play, and we observe their capabilities. Their preferences. Their leanings. Then we assign them."

"Yes, yes, I'm sure you do. But it's just as important for them to know the human language. When we're gone, you'll still need to communicate with us."

"I doubt it."

She felt a tired frustration bring her dangerously close to tears. She'd have to check her blood pressure after work; perhaps the old problem was recurring. "The human language is universal, Gaston. I've taught you well. Don't throw it all away."

He laid a reassuring hand on her buttock. She didn't flinch; she was accustomed to this friendly gesture that unthinking humans called the Goron Goose. If he'd been taller, he'd have put an arm around her shoulders. "We are grateful to you, Bridget. But we don't want the language any more. We shall all be dead in less than a hundred of our years, and in the meantime our duty is to Lady, not you. We must ease her final years."

"But the children! Learning the language is a fine mental exercise!"

He just laughed, squeezing her buttock. "You're a good human, Bridget, and you try very hard. I shall remember you until I die. Now let me watch the children, please."

There was nothing she could do. Eyes brimming with tears, she made her way to the nursery, expecting the worst. To her surprise she found everything in order. The nurses were busy, the handful of babies well cared for. She left them and climbed the steps to her apartment.

Ladysend had been built almost a hundred years ago out of local materials but to human design. Three boxy buildings stood beside an ancient settlement of goron huts. One housed three classrooms, another the nursery, and the third had a small research laboratory on the ground floor, with outside stairs to Bridget's apartment above. The apartment was standard Organisation issue with windows in two opposite walls. One window looked out over the ocean, the other commanded a view directly upLady. She made her way to the latter, and received an unpleasant shock.

Ten gorons were strolling along the Ladyside trail in her direction, about half a kilometre away. They were the members of Clan Birthcare she'd detailed to work on Lady. What was going on? They were supposed to be checking on the foetuses and bringing in any hatchlings. They couldn't have finished work for the day; not yet. She tried to zoom in on them without success. The window hadn't been working properly lately and all attempts to get a technician out of Samarita had failed. The Organisation seemed to have no idea of the importance of her work at Ladysend. She hurried down the stairs and ran to meet the gorons.

By the time she reached them she was completely out of breath and could only stand gasping while they patted her sympathetically. They murmured wordlessly but were unable to select a spokesman.

Eventually she recovered enough to address Morgan, their designated leader. "Finished for the day?" she said as calmly as she could, having learned her lesson with Gaston.

"For ever," said Morgan. Clearly this had been rehearsed, because the others echoed his words, smiling happily. "For ever."

"So what happens to the babies?"

If anything, Morgan's smile widened. "Some die, some crawl ashore. The strongest survive. It is the way of the Universe, so you have taught us."

"But not with intelligent species! And anyway, they'll drown in those pools of decay. You can't just leave the babies, Morgan!"

"We talked it over, and we believe it is better this way. If there are less babies born, there will be less adults to grieve when Lady dies."

To her horror, the gorons dissolved into a mist and she found she was crying uncontrollably. "I will not have you abandon those poor little creatures out there! I won't have it, you hear!" She felt solid flesh under her fists and realised dimly she was hitting somebody. "You're horrible, ungrateful little men and you will get back to work this instant, you hear?"

There was no reply.

She knuckled the tears from her eyes. The gorons were running away, along the trail to the settlement. They seemed to be helping one of their number who was staggering a little. Whatever had possessed her? She began to run after them. One of them glanced over his shoulder, said something to the others and they began to run faster, practically dragging their injured member.

"Come back! Please! I'm sorry!"

This was the end. She'd have to hand in her resignation. She wasn't fit to have charge of gorons. She'd call Manning Edlin from her apartment and confess, right now, before rumours began to spread up Lady. She'd plead a nervous breakdown, which was probably the truth. But why was she thinking of Manning Edlin? He wasn't her boss. She must speak to the Director of Personnel, Murdo. But Murdo was a muscan; she couldn't possibly confide in that creature.

Mind racing, she climbed the steps, re-entered her apartment and poured herself a stiff jolt from the jar of mead she normally kept for visitors. What if she'd killed that little man? Just for a moment she'd completely lost control; become violent, murderous. It was a good job the Project was wrapping up.

Manning Edlin. Edlin was capable and sensible. She poured herself another shot and sat at her terminal. She called Edlin's office but the screen remained blank. A brief display said he'd gone home for the day. What would happen to the babies if nobody was there to save them? She tried Janine Starseeker; Janine was a sympathetic soul. Maybe a chat with Janine would help get things in perspective. If they weren't already in perspective.

Janine had gone home for the day, too. She went to the side table and topped up her mug. The babies would drown in those horrid pools of pus. There was that Manager of Health Services, Susanna. She had her head screwed on the right way. And she'd know all about nervous breakdowns.

She sat down again, called Health. Susanna had left for her cottage a minute ago. Probably just as well, she might be just too practical and matter-of-fact. What she needed was a shoulder to cry on for an hour or two. Bryn Trevithick! Nice man. No, he'd been fired, what could they have been thinking of? Nobody to help, and the little babies no bigger than her hand, gulping pus. It was still light outside. At least a couple of hours before nightfall. She'd go and check Lady herself, and to hell with Clan Birthcare.

She ran down the steps and strode along the Ladyside trail. The coracles were kept on the bank, quite a way upLady. If she resigned it would be the end of the gorons. Not one baby would ever make it to the shore, the way Lady's sickness took her in these reaches. And with her gone . . . What would the gorons do when the Organisation pulled out?

More to the point, what would she do?

She was getting too old for another posting, yet she had no friends on Earth. She'd been so happy here with the gorons, but in a few months it would be all over . . . A long time later she saw the coracles up ahead, all piled up. She'd eke out her last years in loneliness, dreaming of her friends the gorons and boring the neighbours with tales of them. And the neighbours would nod their heads and say to each other, What a pity she never had any children of her own . . .

Here were the coracles, but there was something wrong. Usually they were laid out in a neat row, all ready to launch. But now they were piled in a heap, as though someone was intending a bonfire. The gorons wouldn't do anything like that, surely? She took hold of the rim of the nearest craft and slid it off the heap.

The bottom was smashed in.

She scrambled over the shifting pile, bruising her shins, frantically seeking an undamaged coracle. There were none. Every single boat had been wrecked, and there was no way she could get out onto Lady this evening.

She stood still, collecting her thoughts while a cold anger began to take hold. So the gorons had turned against her, for no good reason. So to hell with them. She'd wallowed in enough self-pity for one day; she would not cry again. She'd go home and get a good night's rest, and in the morning she'd call Manning Edlin in a sound and rational manner and simply report the facts. A plain recitation of events, no blame attached, and together they'd sort things out. Lucky she hadn't been able to get through tonight; she'd have made a complete fool of herself.

She'd take over the school herself, and ask them to send a human team to handle the birthcare on Lady. She needn't worry about the nursery; everything was under control there. And that was because the nursery was necessary to the gorons with or without the Organization's presence.

The short Goronwy evening was closing in. She took a deep breath preparatory to starting back. And at that moment something caught her eye.

There was a lump on the surface of Lady quite close to the bank.

It was moving. It was close to birth. She felt the familiar stirring in her chest and belly. A goron was about to be born, and at least she could help this one to safety and take him back to Ladysend.

He lay about four meters from the bank. Lady was decaying closer to the bank, so she couldn't slide out on the remains of a coracle. And the baby wouldn't be able to crawl ashore; he'd drown in all that yellow stuff. The dead trunk of an ancient tree leaned almost horizontally out, just downLady from the baby. She could crawl along that tree, couldn't she? Of course she could, for the sake of a baby.

She sat astride the trunk, placed her palms on it, and began to lever herself along, a couple of centimetres at a time. The trunk swayed, but seemed solid enough so far. She reached a fork, managed to swing her right leg over it and continued along the left branch. Now the tree felt much less secure, bouncing, and her feet touched Lady's surface which was healthy at this point, fortunately.

Finally she reached a point level with the baby. The cocoon was little more than a membrane, and there would be no danger to Lady if she simply tore that skin with her bare hands and lifted the baby out.

Except that the baby was just too far away.

She lay along the branch, twisted so that she could get both arms over the same side, and reached out. The membrane was just within her reach and she could see movement underneath, but she knew she wouldn't be able to reach the baby. Not yet.

But Lady flowed slowly, and in another hour she'd be able to break the membrane and lift the baby out, carefully, two-handed.

Then she'd carry it back to Ladysend and roust Morgan out of his bed and confront him. Look at this, Morgan. This baby would have died if it had been left out there. Is that what you want? What has Clan Birthcare come to, Morgan? Yes, there were a lot of things that would have to be said.

Evening deepened into night. A single light winked upLady; a barge moored for the night. The bargee would be sleeping on the afterdeck, his stoags grazing on the bank. The insides of her thighs ached terribly from sitting astride the narrow branch, but she couldn't go ashore, not now. She might not have the strength to get back again.

Once or twice she caught herself swaying as she dozed. This would never do. If she fell into Lady she'd never be able to pull herself out, not at her age. These days her mirror showed a stick figure of skin and bone; no muscle at all. She began to sing, a nursery song that she sang to the goron children when they couldn't sleep. Rock-a-bye baby, on the treetop . . .

Good grief, she must have been dozing again! She could just make out the oval of the membrane, almost beneath her now. She wriggled into position and prodded it with a bony forefinger. It split with an audible pop! Carefully, slowly, she manoeuvred herself until her hands hung down on either side of the baby.

Then, with an almost painful rush of love, she lifted him from Lady, twisted herself upright and took him onto her lap. There, there . . . she crooned, rocking to and fro.

The baby moved. She felt him shift in her lap and she heard the tiny gasp of his breath. He was all right. In a minute she'd start backing off this branch. Then a short walk home, a brief confrontation with Morgan, and bed. But maybe she shouldn't be too hard on Morgan, after all. He probably thought he was acting for the best, according to the ancient goron custom. She'd take the baby straight to the nursery and see Morgan in the morning . . . She adjusted the baby on her lap, preparatory to backing toward the bank.

And immediately knew something was wrong.

The baby sat oddly.

Fear struck her like a blow in the chest. She ran quick hands over the tiny head, the little chest, the arms, the . . .

A shuddering took hold of her, then she began to retch violently. She didn't hear the small splash as the creature slipped from her lap into the pool of decaying matter. She retched, again and again until her stomach was a pit of pain.

Then she laid her head on the rough bark of the ancient branch and sobbed until morning.

CHAPTER 19

On her way to Ralph Green's office Susanna came across Martha Sunshine regarding a poster taped to the wall. "Too bad about *Barker Sam*," she said.

The big woman chuckled ruefully. "You work your guts out, and just when you figure you've got it made, this is what happens. In my line of business you have to learn to put it behind you. And that would have been easier if I'd relied on terminal advertising instead of sticking these bloody posters all over the place."

"Leave them up. They're fine art."

"Yeah, because you designed them." Martha stepped back and admired the colourful print. "Speaking of talent, I'm producing a homespun show in about thirty days as a kind of consolation. There's a vacancy for a leading lady. Some singing, some comedy."

"I'll think about it. By the way, I hear you're putting on an exhibition of Mistral Greene's paintings."

"That's right. They're kind of primitive, but I sell them for her from time to time." A flicker of some indefinable emotion crossed Martha's face. Susanna's antennae tingled for an instant.

"But are they good enough for an exhibition?"

"It's worth a try." The big woman laughed. "I don't imagine you're jealous, not for a moment."

She left Martha considering the poster and entered Ralph Greene's office.

192

The Director of Engineering looked more worried that usual. "Have you seen Mistral?" he asked.

"She's fine. She made it through Ladycanyon without problems and I brought her back to her, uh, dwelling a few days ago. Maybe you should drop by and see her sometime, Ralph."

"She'd set the stoags on me. I tried, once. My God, what a dump that cave of hers is. I . . . It makes me ashamed, you know? I need to talk to people about her, but I don't want to."

"You can talk to me. I'm trained to listen. And by the way, thanks for that data on visiphone calls."

He regarded her suspiciously. "Yeah. Kind of odd, the people some people keep talking to. Makes a guy wonder what's going on around him, or did I say that last time we talked? I'm getting old. Sit down, will you, and tell me what little job you need doing this time."

She laughed. "No little job. Just an honest exchange of information. Last time I was here, I noticed you were looking at a culvert hologram. You probably don't think I'm all that interested in culverts, but you couldn't be more wrong. I'm fascinated."

"You're kidding." He keyed in a command and the hologram reappeared, revolving. "Personally I can take them or leave them."

"It's all in the line of duty. I'm filling out a report on public health with particular reference to sewage treatment. You know how big we health people are on sewage. The treatment plant is in the service dome, I believe?"

He regarded her thoughtfully. The perfect face was all innocence, the blue eyes wide and guileless. She was up to something. "The service dome, that's right. More or less where you'd expect to find it."

"Where does it discharge?"

"Eastward."

"Eastward is Lady."

"This isn't some kind of environmental witch hunt, is it?" he asked suspiciously. "The stuff's pure enough to drink."

"I must try a glass sometime. But does Lady like it? I'd have thought the obvious thing would be to discharge westward onto the plains."

He sighed. "Okay, here's the story. The culvert was built at the same time as the domes, and it has a dual purpose. Like I said, the effluent is harmless—for all I know it may even be nutritious from Lady's point of view. But there was another reason for the culvert. It can be used as a kind of giant hypodermic for introducing other substances into Lady subcutaneously. In the early days we tried various drugs on her, so I'm told. Antibiotics, antigerone, that kind of thing. Apparently nothing worked."

"Anything recently?"

"Nothing so far as I know. Ecology would have the records. If they haven't been accidentally deleted," he said cynically. "Funny you should be so interested in the culvert. We've had an incident there, I don't know if you've heard. I'd noticed the load factors were changing, and I didn't know why, and a few days ago it got so bad I sent a team down there. Guess what?" He eyed her closely. "A herd of stoags had broken in."

"Would you believe it? They must have smelled the water."

"I guess so. Maybe I'm getting paranoid these days."

"What kind of team did you send?"

"Well, actually I reported it to Tillini and he sent armed Security people down. Just as well. The stoags rushed them and they had difficulty driving them back. Apparently it was one hell of a battle. Stoags don't usually behave like that. Good thing I didn't send an ordinary maintenance crew down. They'd have been slaughtered."

"So that was it, was it? Just stoags looking for water? Nothing sinister?"

"Not according to Tillini's report. We're in there repairing the damage right now." He clicked off the hologram. "Have I satisfied your idle curiosity, or are you going to tell me what this is all about?"

"Yes, you are getting paranoid, Ralph."

He said slowly, "If you plot the line of that culvert you'll find it passes quite close to my daughter's hovel. She's good with stoags, they say. I haven't pointed this out to anyone else. I don't want to get her in trouble, you see. If I'd thought of it before, I wouldn't have sent in Tillini. What the hell is she up to, Susanna?" His face was grey with worry and lack of sleep.

She regarded him, considering, sympathising. "If she was up to anything, it's all okay now, Ralph. You have nothing to worry about. I give you my word."

"I accept it. Look after her, will you?" He made an obvious effort to dismiss the painful subject. "So. How are you getting along with the fugitive? Has he fallen for your fatal charms yet?"

She laughed. "He doesn't stand a chance."

She left soon after, and he started to think about Wendy.

Susanna's apartment was standard Samaritan issue with the same floor plan as Trevithick's old place. A living room overlooked Lady to the west—the equivalent of the ocean view so prized on Earth—and a small area on the opposite wall held the essentials: the food store, the dispenser, the countertop, the terminal. A door in the north wall led to the bedroom and bathroom. The windows were sealed and the front entrance valve had a small anteroom, all in the interests of minimising pheromones. One never knew when a Samaritan might forget to take the pills and go emotionally berserk.

Susanna and Trevithick had discussed the matter of his accommodation at some length. It was a risk for her, letting him stay in the apartment. But as she'd pointed out, Security would be keeping a close watch on copter use. There was little point in taking him to the lake cottage, only to find Tillini and a copterful of goons arriving on the next flight.

Nevertheless he was worried for her. "What the hell alternative is there?" she'd asked, pink with frustration as he raised one objection after another. "You can't sleep rough; if Security doesn't find you the vespas will, or the squitos. And Goronwy has its full complement of smaller insects too, nasty little brutes. No, you'll stay on my chesterfield and I'll lock my bedroom door if you're scared you might get all ungentlemanly. Good grief, what a prude."

He'd settled in well. His only problem was boredom while Susanna was away at work. Occasionally he'd take a stroll down to the Passing Barge in the safety of daylight and on one occasion he saw Edlin in there. Edlin nodded briskly the way he always did, but he didn't join Trevithick. Lath Eagleman was there too, scraping away at his fiddle, ignoring everyone as usual.

Trevithick spent some time on Susanna's terminal, but most of the historical data was protected. He didn't know exactly what he hoped to find, anyway. Possibly an old report establishing that nothing could be done about Lady; that her sickness was simply terminal old age. But if there ever had been such a report, doubtless all traces of it would have been erased long ago.

Anyway, he didn't want it on record that any old reports had been accessed with Susanna's voiceprint and code. So he frigged around, as Susanna would have expressed it, using the terminal as a stand-alone and playing with the ideas he'd had since first arriving on Goronwy. And getting nowhere.

And not really caring, because he was only killing time before the evacuation shuttles arrived.

One day as he made my way down the Ladyside trail to the inn, he fell into conversation with a member of Clan Boatbuilder. The little man was working on a barge drive belt, repairing the rents torn in the woven material by the foreclaws of stoags. As they stood at the entrance to the small workshop other gorons trudged slowly by, towing empty Ladybarges back to the lake, each with the help of a pair of barge stoags in harness.

Ladybarges were big vessels by goron standards, each being about fifteen meters long, although only three meters wide. Unlike coracles they did not skid over the surface of Lady, but instead rolled on a continuous woven fibre belt the width of the hull. This belt was mounted on three long rollers; the bottom two at the ends of the hull, the top one above the deck, mounted on an A-frame.

So the belt formed an approximately equilateral triangle. When the barge was loaded and travelling south two stoags climbed the sloping part of the belt continuously, side by side, digging their claws into the fibre. Their weight caused the belt to roll around the rollers, and the weight of the boat kept the bottom of the belt in firm contact with Lady. So the Ladybarge rolled south like a giant triangular treadmill.

Watching a team hauling an empty barge north, Trevithick asked, "Why not tow loaded barges downLady with stoags and ropes? The barges would hold twice as much nectar without all that machinery, wouldn't they?"

It was the wrong question to ask. The goron stared at him. Trevithick hadn't taken a pill that day, and he could sense a deep resentment. "What would be the purpose of my life then?" the goron asked.

"I'm sorry."

He sensed Trevithick's remorse, and added, "There is an answer that humans like, too. Long ago we used tow ropes. We towed loaded barges down the eastern bank, and empty ones up the western bank. But most settlements are on the western bank, and they need supplies. The barges had no means of crossing Lady, so the nectar urns had to be loaded into coracles and rowed across. It took time, and while it was being done, another barge might want to pass. There were many problems. It is better that loaded barges should be free to navigate away from the bank and cross Lady if necessary. The belt drive barge is a great invention."

"But they must have had to cross at Ladysend in the days before the belt drive."

The goron worked on with remarkable dexterity, using a wooden needle to draw the ragged splits in the belt together, weaving patches into holed areas. He barely glanced at Trevithick as he talked. "Ropes were strung across Lady permanently," he said briefly. He was embarrassed to talk about the primitive nature of times past. Trevithick would have liked to ask him why they didn't use drive belts on the empty run north, but thought it best to get onto more important topics.

"What do you think about the Organisation leaving?" he asked.

"It doesn't matter. Lady is dying. We will die too. The other animals and the plants will live on."

Trevithick regarded him, a busy little man slaving away at his life's work in perfect contentment. "How about you personally?" he asked curiously. "How do you feel about it?"

"I feel I've done my best. How else can I feel? I am at peace. Are you?"

"You don't need me to tell you that."

"There's a world of difference between humans and gorons. We all die sooner or later, and when the last male goron dies that event is no more tragic than when I die. Our sorrow is for Lady, our mother. We feel we should have saved her, but we couldn't."

"Does she know she's dying?"

He glanced up. "You've never met her?"

It was an odd question. How do you meet an organic river? "I guess so." He gestured at the glistening surface a few meters away.

His expression was one Trevithick hadn't seen before; a goron look not taught by Bridget Booker. Then he concentrated on the belt again, weaving away without speaking.

As the silence lengthened, Trevithick asked, "Does Clan Active still exist?"

"Mistral did the right thing," he said. "Clan Active were misguided gorons."

"Have you seen Mistral lately?"

"I hear she stays in her quarters. Mistral is the best of the humans, with no disrespect to yourself. Mistral is like one of us. She feels what we feel. We will be sorry when she leaves. As for the rest of you . . . It will be good to have the world to ourselves again, free of turmoil and false hope."

As Trevithick walked away he realised he didn't even know the little man's name. Mistral, in his place, would have found it out or given him one. He looked back guiltily. The goron was looking for the next worn patch in the belt, which ran over rollers similar to those on the barges. Trevithick walked on. One goron looked very much like another. He couldn't be expected to know every one personally.

But as he let himself into Susanna's apartment he had the uncomfortable feeling he didn't know any of them.

Rain fell steadily and darkness was falling early. From the window he could make out a barge moored on the far side of Lady. Bargees didn't like to work in wet weather; the moisture softened the belts and wore them out too quickly. It had been raining heavily in the mountains for some days and Lady looked like a real river with flood water from the lake flowing over her surface. The ripplegrass on the bank was a misty blur as the tiny blades whipped to and fro, flicking raindrops toward the central root systems. The gorons didn't mind the wet. There was a festive atmosphere in Samarita as coracles paddled about, aglow with lanterns, casting nets to trap the unaccustomed run of fish. Gorons looked on Ladyfishing as recreation, not restricted to any specific clan.

Susanna arrived home from work and the apartment brightened up as though the sun itself had strolled through the door valve. She kissed him briefly, took off her raincoat and hung it up, then handed him a mug of mead. She sat down opposite, crossing her legs provocatively. He liked the way she wore a skirt. Sometimes it came to just above the knee, sometimes just below; but she hardly ever wore the uniform pants that were a more usual feature of Samaritan women's wear. He wondered how much longer he'd be able to live under her roof without making a grab.

"Let me tell you about the sewer," she said. "This is interesting, so it's best you take your eyes off my legs and concentrate." She went on to relate the conversation with Ralph Greene.

"A huge hypodermic?" he said. "I guess it's feasible."

"It's convenient, too. I don't see how else you could inject large quantities of beneficial drugs into Lady without all kinds of equipment. But maybe it's too convenient. It can be used for pumping in something not so beneficial." She gazed at him thoughtfully. "Potassium cyanide comes to mind, I can't think why."

It was an odd thought. "Why would anyone want to do that?"

"I don't know. Maybe they don't. I'm just saying they could."

The notion began to build up some validity in his mind. "Who would want to?"

She hesitated. "Someone who wanted to wrap up the Project quickly and get everyone the hell off Goronwy. Somebody with a grudge against the Samaritan Organisation." She grinned suddenly. "Someone like you."

"Oh, sure. Well, it's all academic now, anyway. They have their wish, whoever they are. If they exist."

"Too bad. That rules you out." She glanced at the clock. "Better put the 3-V on. There's going to be an announcement in a couple of minutes. You never know; it might be important. Or then again, it could be a Board member telling us what wonderful people we are and how much they appreciate our efforts over the past fifty years, and how they intend to give us tangible recognition in the form of a fat bonus."

"And stoags might fly." He switched on the 3-V and took the opportunity to sit beside her on the chesterfield, facing the alcove. He held her hand. She shifted position, cuddling up against him. It was nice.

The alcove glowed and a familiar scene appeared: the boardroom. The Board members sat in their accustomed places, although the chairs had been shifted around the table to fill the vacuum created by Trevithick's departure. It was as though he'd never been there.

Susanna must have noticed this because she gave his hand a squeeze. His heart began to thump in adolescent fashion as his concentration wandered from the figures in the alcove.

"Watch it," she said gently.

"This has been a most difficult decision," came a small voice.

Janine Starseeker, amiable old Janine, was on her feet. She faced them out of the alcove, a small grey-haired figure thrust into an unaccustomed limelight. If the announcement was so important, why wasn't one of the big guns making it? Edlin, for instance?

Janine's voice quavered nervously. "The decision was not reached without considerable discussion among Board members and, I might add, some disagreement. In fact our decision—" She waved vaguely at the members of the Board "—was reached a few days ago, but confirmation from Earth Headquarters was only received today. And I'm happy to say that Earth Headquarters is fully in agreement with the unprecedented step we are taking."

"Get on with it, you old windbag," whispered Susanna.

"We have laboured long and hard on Goronwy and we have had our share of disappointments. We have been blessed, however, with a loyal and able staff and it is this more than anything else that has lightened our burden over the years. We, the members of the Board, see you as friends rather than employees of the Samaritan Organisation, and we hope you feel the same way about us . . . "

"You were right," Trevithick said. "It's a fat bonus for all except yours truly."

". . . and I shared your regret on hearing that our Project was at an end, and that this great team of ours would inevitably be dispersed among different worlds.

"So it is with great pleasure that I inform you that our work here on Goronwy is not ended after all. We cannot in all conscience run out on this troubled world. Despite the withdrawal of funds from Earthaid, the Samaritan Organisation has decided that the Goronwy Project will continue."

Trevithick heard himself shout "What!"

"I don't believe it," muttered Susanna.

". . . so much effort," the small voice continued, "that it would be a pity to throw it all away when we are so close to success. So we shall be shipping in the latest analytical equipment, and we shall increase the staffing of the Operations Division . . . "

Janine Starseeker spoke on, occasionally taking sips of water when her weak voice dried up altogether, but there was nothing else of significance to be said. Trevithick could imagine the population of Samarita sitting stunned in their living rooms, staring at their alcoves. The Project would continue. They would be staying on Goronwy after all.

He said to Susanna, "What does it mean?"

"My first thought is, they can't bring themselves to write off the chance of a future payback."

"Cynical, aren't you?"

Her hand still rested in his. She was looking very thoughtful. "I'm not fooled so easily. Assuming there's something crooked going on—and it's much more fun to assume that—then let's ask ourselves what's behind this."

"I'm asking myself. And I just don't get it."

"Well, we haven't gone all soft and sorry for the gorons, that's for sure. And Edlin's people would have had to tell HQ some pretty convincing lies for them to agree to keep the funds coming."

"Maybe we were wrong when we thought Lady was incurable."

"Which leaves us with an interesting possibility, Dr. Watson. Perhaps we found out Lady was not incurable, long ago. Perhaps we've always had a cure waiting in the wings."

It began to make sense. "So even though Earthaid's run out of patience, the Organisation itself can look benevolent for a while until we suddenly announce that lo! we've found a cure."

"Everyone's to stay on for another ten years or more to oversee Lady's convalescence, and the Organisation can collect its payback from the gorons over the next century or so. The Organisation doesn't have to repay Earthaid, you know. It's a gift to encourage projects like this."

"Janine did say they were close to success," said Trevithick thoughtfully. "They wouldn't have had time for a breakthrough since I was fired, would they?"

"It is as I say, Trevithick. They knew all along. You wait and see. I'll give it a month, maybe two, then they'll make the dramatic announcement before they have to go to the expense of shipping in all the extra people and equipment they're talking about. Lady's cured and we will now watch devotedly over her convalescence."

It made sense. But then everything Susanna said made sense. He wondered how the gorons would take the announcement. With mixed feelings and some scepticism, if the discussion with the belt repairer was anything to go by. And the humans? Most of them would be overjoyed. Then he wondered again why Janine had made the announcement instead of one of the heavies. He asked Susanna.

"To demonstrate the emphasis on Operations, of course. Janine's got your job as well as your own now. She's Director of Ecology and Earth Sciences."

This was a surprise. "But she knows nothing about ecology!"

"She doesn't need to, if we already have the cure for Lady tucked away somewhere. In fact her ignorance is a positive bonus for the forces of darkness. She won't be suspicious when one of her assistants conveniently comes up with the answer. I wonder who this genius will be?" She regarded him quizzically. "Your old friend and colleague Ivor Sabin is at the centre of things these days."

"He never was much of a friend." The implications of the announcement began to sink in. "This could mean I'll be stuck around Goronwy with nothing to do for years to come."

"Is this Bryn Trevithick talking? The man who was unjustly fired and swore vengeance on his oppressors? Or is this some pathetic clone who holds my hand?"

"Well, there's not much I can do now, is there? It seems somebody already knows all the answers."

"Oh, what a trusting man you are. It's flattering you hold my views in such esteem, Trevithick, but I've been known to be wrong. I misdiagnose, a worrisome thing for a doctor to do. I could tell you some horror stories. But instead, I'll tell you something I'm sure about. You were fired because you were getting close to the truth. The cure for Lady was at your fingertips, as you sat at your terminal with analytical eyes and dancing fingers. And somebody thought you were looking in the right places, and reported it to his bosses. *Trevithick is on to something*, he said. *He's not such a fool as he looks!* Doesn't that arouse a little pricking of curiosity in your tired old brain?"

He was about to protest when a change of scenery in the alcove caught his attention.

Mistral appeared in there.

She stood beside a desk in the centre of a large room, dressed in a dark businesslike suit and looking very uncomfortable in it, but very clean. Standing with her, dwarfing her, was Martha Sunshine. All around the walls were Mistral's daubs, hung with little sense of presentation, some of them even hanging crooked. Mistral looked like a trapped animal, green eyes more shifting here and there, seeking a way of escape. A handful of people wandered among the pictures, glancing, raising eyebrows, moving on.

"Welcome to the Samarita Gallery, and another in our series Alien Art," said Martha, smiling hugely, all teeth and cleavage. "Firstly, I'd like to take this opportunity to share some great news with you. As a result of the Board's recent decision, which I'm sure you've all been watching, I shall be able to bring that wonderful galactic show, *Barker Sam*, to Goronwy after all!" Scattered applause from around the gallery. "So on with tonight's show. Our feature artist is Mistral Greene, daughter of our esteemed Director of Engineering, Ralph Greene. Tell me, Mistral, what inspired this landscape?" She picked up a framed water-colour from the desk. It was horrible. "This is Ladysmouth, is it? Is that what it is?"

But Mistral had been thrown so far off balance by the reference to her father that she couldn't reply. She grunted, staring at the floor.

"What the hell is Martha thinking of?" Susanna said.

Something rotten had come home to Trevithick. "It's revenge. They've linked Mistral to the sewer business. They're teaching her a lesson, hitting her where it hurts most."

"Oh, no, Bryn. Not Martha. This is too dirty for her."

"Someone's put her up to it. Forced her into it, I wouldn't be surprised. Probably written the whole goddamned script for her."

"I can't believe it." Susanna's eyes were unnaturally bright.

Martha, holding Mistral firmly by the elbow, led her across to a group of people around a painting of something unrecognisable. "Good evening," she said. "I hope you people are enjoying yourselves. You'll find the price of each item on a little tag on the edge of the frame."

"We won't be bothering, thanks," said a tall man.

"Did you, uh, paint these?" a plump woman asked Mistral, who nodded wordlessly. "The artist is a little prettier than the pictures, Aldo," she said to someone. "But not much."

More people were coming in. Ralph Greene stood just outside the entrance, out of Mistral's line of sight. His expression was anguished. People walked from picture to picture, shrugging, passing audible and uncomplimentary comments, moving on. Mistral was back in the middle of the room now, leaning forward with her palms on the desk, black hair falling past her face, eyes closed as though trying to escape into a private and happier world. Martha moved among the visitors with a tray of drinks. Before long everyone had gathered around Martha and an impromptu party was developing, the paintings ignored.

And suddenly Mistral wasn't there.

The figures disappeared as the alcove darkened. Susanna had switched it off. She stood before Trevithick, tears glistening below her eyes. "It's too cruel!" she burst out. "And those people were paid to say those things, I'll bet. It's part of the script. Oh, God, poor Mistral!" She blinked, and the tears rolled down.

"What can we do?" he asked. This was a woman thing and Susanna might have an answer. On the other hand, maybe it was a human thing and he was passing the buck.

Susanna's fists were clenched. She made no attempt to wipe the tears away. Probably she hadn't noticed them. "I'm going to talk to Martha Bloody Sunshine and find out who put her up to this. We all know Mistral's paintings aren't the greatest, but she does sell a few as curiosities to people leaving Goronwy. After this she'll never sell another. She'll be a laughingstock. Well, tomorrow Martha's going to come up with a few answers!"

"But what about now?" The image of the small, tense figure at the desk was still with him. "What can we do about Mistral, right now?"

Susanna sat down beside him, suddenly and heavily as though her knees had given out. "I guess we both know that."

"What?"

"Well, I can't go over to her place. She'd kill me, or do her best to. It has to be you, obviously." She put a cool hand against his cheek and turned his head to face her directly. Her eyes were very blue, still bright with tears. "She's fond of you," she said. "You'll have to do whatever you can."

Then she pulled his head toward her and kissed him, long and soft.

"Watch out for the forces of darkness," she whispered.

CHAPTER 20

MISTRAL'S MAIN CAVE WAS EMPTY but Trevithick could see a glow from the tunnel beyond. He found her still in her new suit, sitting on the dirt floor of a studio empty of paintings. The three easels had been folded up and leaned against the wall. The cave was otherwise bare apart from the terminal at the far end. He noticed all this during the time it took him to drop to his knees beside Mistral. It was one of those vivid times when every detail stands out clearly, as at the scene of a fatal accident.

She sat cross-legged with the lamp before her, staring down at the flame. The narrow suit skirt was rucked up around her thighs. She didn't look at him. She knew who it was. "Come to gloat, have you?" she said in flat tones. He couldn't see her face because her hair hung past it.

"I'm not gloating."

"You should. You said my pictures weren't no good, and you were right. You saw the show, I guess. That's why you're here."

"Yes, that's why I'm here."

"Well, you can just go right back to that Susanna."

"In time. When I'm sure you're all right."

Her head snapped around, hair flying. There were no tears in her eyes, only anger and despair. "All right? How can I ever be all right? I never have been and I never will be. I'm weird, that's what people say. Maybe they're right!"

"Only if you want them to be."

"What's that supposed to mean?"

"You could make the effort to get along with people better." His pity was turning to irritation, and he hated himself for it. For the first time he noticed an empty mug on the floor. She'd been at the mead, but he couldn't blame her.

"I don't need no people. I don't need you."

"I think you do."

"Okay, if you're so bloody necessary, you can tell me this. What do I do now? I can't paint. I'm no good for any bloody thing. So what shall I do with the rest of my life, huh?"

It was a difficult and disturbing question; the kind Trevithick might have asked of himself. "If you think you can paint, then you can. It doesn't matter what other people say. What matters is the enjoyment you get from it."

"Oh, sure."

"And there's more to your life than painting. The gorons need you. There's a lot of work for you to do there. You're the only human who understands them, and the only one they really trust. You should be acting as a go-between."

He was wasting his time; she didn't really want answers. What she wanted was a target for unanswerable questions. "The hell with the gorons!" she shouted. "I'm not their bloody nurse!"

"So that rules that one out. What else wouldn't you like to do?"

"Huh?"

He got a grip on his rising anger. "Would you go to Earth if you had the chance?'

She calmed down too. She was very easily influenced by his pheromones. "Nope. I was born here. It's my world. Mind you," she added with some slight animation, "I wouldn't mind seeing Earth." Then she shrugged. "Maybe not. I'd get lonely right away, without the gorons."

"There'd be plenty of humans."

"Humans? Huh! You can't know humans. They don't have hardly no pheromones, with all the stuff they put on and the pills they take. 'Cept maybe you. They're like strangers, almost. Half alive."

"So you must be pretty happy about the Organisation staying on. You wouldn't have wanted to be shipped back to Earth."

She stared at him. "I'd stay here anyway. Nobody ships me off nowhere. So . . ." She picked up the lamp and the mug, and stood. "Thanks for coming, anyway. You meant well. But we're different, you and me. See, I don't need no humans and all their stuff. You do. So you get off back to that Susanna, huh? I'll see you around."

They went back into the main cavern. There was little more he could say. She waited for him to go, her face expressionless. He'd been wasting his time. "Stand fast, Mistral," he muttered awkwardly. He reached out to touch her hand, but she moved away. So he turned and left.

He never knew for sure what made him go back. Certainly he saw lights on the road to Lady, and the notion of covert apprehension occurred to him. But he didn't think it was that. More likely it was sad pheromones, as he stood in the doorway of the old guardhouse above Mistral's cave with a light breeze blowing from inside.

So, very quietly, he descended the tunnel back into the cavern.

And he found Mistral lying face-down on her pile of furs, her whole body shaking with the intensity of her sobbing.

It happened as Susanna had known it would.

His heart went out to her and he fell to the soft pile of furs and took her in his arms. She stiffened for a second, then relaxed and huddled against him, wailing softly and wordlessly like an injured animal against his chest. They stayed like that for a long time. Then, sniffing, she detached herself, sat up and took off the jacket, followed by the white blouse. She wore nothing underneath. Small and perfect breasts gleamed in the lamplight, infinitely vulnerable. He reached out and cupped one in his hand, protectively.

She stared at him for a long moment, then raised both arms and lifted her hair back, exposing the scar. It covered half her forehead and one temple, extending down past her ear. It didn't seem to matter so much. She continued to stare at him.

"You sure you know what you're doing?" she asked quietly.

Maybe his mind didn't, but his body did. His desire was an agony. He tipped her backwards and rolled toward her, taking one hard nipple between his lips. He heard her gasp and her arms came down and held him against her, hard. Then she released him and he looked into her face. She'd stopped crying. Her eyes looked sleepy, her lips were swollen. He kissed her face softly, in different places.

"I don't know nothing about this," she whispered. "Tell me if I'm doing it wrong, won't you?"

Pity dimmed his desire, but only for a moment. She'd raised her hips and was sliding off the skirt. She wore nothing underneath. Of course she wouldn't; the suit was just a shell to appease society and she needed the small rebellion. Her thighs were strong and perfect, her body hair jet-black. She glanced into his face, then bent to unzip him with an almost violent haste, as though she feared he might change his mind. He tried to help, but she wanted to do it all herself. When his erection sprang into view she became suddenly motionless; then she touched it experimentally. It jerked in her hand. He tried to think of something else before it was too late. Anything. Clan Boatbuilder, working away with their crude saws and hammers. Anything but this soft body next to him. But he couldn't sustain the image.

"Careful," he said.

"I'm hurting you?" she asked anxiously.

"No. It's just . . ." He slipped his hand between her thighs. They parted. She was hot and very wet. A spasm went through his penis. "Sometimes it can be too quick," he said. "Sometimes a man can want a woman too much. You wouldn't like that. Not this time."

"I see." She let him go and took hold of his hand instead, moving it gently against her. A semblance of control was restored. They kissed, long and thoughtfully, as though signing a contract, then he moved on top of her and she guided him in. For a beginner, she did very well. The next time she cried out, it was not through sorrow. Simultaneously he knew a long hot joy, the like of which he'd never experienced before. It was endless, almost frightening. In some way she'd bewitched him.

Later she asked, "Was that okay?"

"It was great. You were wonderful." He hoped he sounded convincing. Those moments pass for a man, and now he was thinking of Susanna. Perhaps part of him had been thinking of her all along.

"I suppose I love you," she said. For once she looked totally happy, lying back with all bitterness gone. Bryn Trevithick had replaced the dreams of art with something more tangible. "I didn't know what this kind of love was," she continued, "but I guess this is it. Wow. A girl doesn't need much else."

He didn't know what to say or do, except possibly cry, but that would have given the game away. She was looking at him mischievously. "Better than that Susanna, huh?"

"I've never made love to Susanna," he said. At least he could say it truthfully, if regretfully.

"You won't be needing her any more," she said contentedly. "Not now you've got me."

The sudden muffled crash came almost as a relief.

"What's that?"

"Susanna at the door." She lay back, smiling. "Too late."

"It's not. I can hear men shouting."

She was on her feet, dragging her clothes on. "You bolted it, did you?"

Mistral usually left the heavy guardhouse door open during the day, pulling it closed at night but no more. Why he'd bolted it, he didn't know. Possibly because he'd foreseen the outcome of his visit. But it had been a good thing to do. There came another heavy crash, and faint shouting. "You in there! Open up!"

"It's Security," he said with a sudden certainty.

"They've come to get you!" cried Mistral. "Well, I'm not going to let them." She put her fingers in her mouth and whistled for Wilfred. By now Trevithick was standing too. "Get dressed, quick!" she urged.

The shouting continued, and now the crashes had taken on a splintering sound. They had an axe. The door was heavy, but it was not impregnable. There wasn't much time. He pulled on pants and shirt, found his socks with some difficulty and stepped into his shoes. Mistral had stuffed some possessions into a hempen bag and was already tugging at his arm. "This way!"

They ran into the tunnel, past the empty studio and up the slope to the vegetable garden. Surprisingly, it was light out there, the morning sun just lifting over the horizon beyond Lady and brushing the northern mountains with pink. Two stoags followed them from the tunnel mouth. The vegetables lay in neat rows, the bushtrap loomed impenetrably beyond, shoulder-high and waiting.

"Your stoag is called Monty," said Mistral. "Get on him." She climbed onto Wilfred, lying along his elongated back, one hand dug into his neck fur, the other carrying the bag of possessions. "Hurry up!"

"I'll be too heavy for him, won't I?" Although big and powerful, Monty barely reached his chest.

"He's got six legs. Stop arguing and get on, unless you'd rather talk to Security!"

He did as he was told. She seemed to know best. She shouted to Wilfred and he began to lumber across the garden. Monty followed. It was an odd sensation, riding a stoag. The six-legged gait had an almost snakelike smoothness compared to a horse.

Wilfred entered the bushtrap, thrusting the thick vinelike branches aside with his snout. Monty followed. The bushtrap waved slender twigs toward Trevithick but without any real conviction. One grasped his arm but let go quite readily when he levered it away. They forced their way onward. Bushtraps knew adult stoags were too strong for them. Like most of the vegetation on Goronwy, they were not stupid.

"Stop!"

The shout came from behind. Trevithick turned his head, careful to retain balance, and saw three men in Security uniforms standing at the edge of the bushtrap fifty meters away. They had pistols. They didn't really expect anyone to stop; the shout was just a formal preliminary to the main business of opening fire.

Mistral said something to Wilfred, who turned sharp right.

A red tracer lanced past Trevithick. A bushtrap branch smoked and fell. He cringed, pressing his face into Monty's dank fur. From the corner of his eye he saw the tracer swing wildly, cutting a swathe off to the left. He turned and saw the Security man struggling with a vine wrapped around his arm. The others trained their weapons on the plant, trying to cut him free before other vines took hold. One curled around his thigh. He yelled.

Then Monty followed Wilfred into his right turn, and they were out of sight.

Much later they emerged from the bush onto the Ladyside trail, almost ten kilometres north of Samarita. Thankfully Trevithick slid from Monty to the ground and rolled over onto his back, looking at the sky. It was almost cloudless. It was going to be a fine day.

"Where to now?" he asked.

Mistral lay beside him. "Reckon we need to get to the lake. I got friends there. And Organisation people hardly ever go there, except Susanna." For once she didn't call her 'that' Susanna. "Then after a while we'll go downLady."

"How?"

"On a barge, silly." She watched him, bright-eyed. He got the uncomfortable feeling she was looking on their flight as a kind of honeymoon. "There's lots happening down at Ladysend, and I haven't been there for ages. Bridget Booker'll be able to help us. I like her. She's nice."

That was a surprise. But it was no surprise when she suddenly made a lunge at him and fixed her mouth firmly on his. He put his arms around her and wondered about the situation. Eventually he saw, through the curtain of her hair, a pair of stoags plodding toward them accompanied by three gorons and drawing an empty barge. He disengaged himself. "Gorons coming," he warned.

She chuckled, sliding her hand down his stomach. "It means nothing to them. Come on, let's teach them how humans do it. This is much more fun than jumping into Lady."

She'd changed. Her voice had changed, her face had changed, and she'd even started using the language a little more correctly. Despite the panic back at her quarters she'd had time to put on a clean dress. What had he done to her? How was he going to get out of this? She'd taken his hand and was pushing it under her skirt. Against all his better judgement he found himself rising to the occasion.

He must have groaned with despair, because she said, "What's the matter? You got a pain or something?"

He said as firmly as he could, "We've got to decide what to do. They'll be sending a helicopter to look for us soon."

"Not in daylight. Not with gorons around. We're always safe if we stay with gorons. You haven't been taking any pills, I hope?"

"No."

She stared searchingly into his face. "It's best you don't. You're on the run, see? Like a hunted animal." She grinned suddenly, and he was reminded of Susanna. "Hunted animals need all their senses. You can hardly read human pheromones, and you can't read goron pheromones like I can because you weren't born here. But you can read them some. They're strong. You never know when they might warn you of something. So stay off the pills."

"Yes, doctor. Can you read my pheromones?"

"Uh-huh."

"Well?" He might as well know the worst.

"You want me. And you're scared of me, I don't know why."

"Is that all?" He felt his heart thump.

"I can't read your mind, silly. All I know is how you feel. And you want me," she said, smugly. "There's no doubt about that. It's nice to be wanted. I've never been wanted before. But what are you scared of?"

"Forget it. Maybe I'm just scared of Security. They seem to think I know something I shouldn't know." He hesitated, looking into rapt green eyes. "I want to find out what that is. Will you help me?"

"Natch. It's my job, now we're together. Whatever you want, darling." The last word sounded awkward, as though she was experimenting with it. "But let's be careful, huh? I don't want to lose you."

The gorons drew level. Mistral immediately named two of them Calder and Cameron. "I'm working my way through the alphabet," she told him. The third goron, who turned out to be the bargee, had already been named Tresco, he told them proudly. Glad of the break, they sat down. Tresco produced a jug of nectar and passed it round. The stoags pushed into the bushtrap and began to browse on immature shoots.

Tresco told them there was an inn some five kilometres up-Lady where he intended to spend the night. He was a jolly goron, smiling often and proud of his clan. Bargees were the gorons who saw the world. The others, he implied, were mere workers. Calder and Cameron took all this without expression or comment.

"What clan are you two from?" Trevithick asked.

"I am Clan Service," said Calder.

"I am Clan Birthcare," said Cameron. "We are both from Ladysend."

"So why are you going upLady?"

They sat silent, puffing themselves up in a peculiar way, shoulders hunched as though trying to make themselves look bigger.

Mistral laughed. "They can't see why you're asking something so easy," she said. "They're on their way to screw Lady and they're trying to look proud about it. Once they get to Ladysmouth, they're going to jump in."

"Why can't they jump in here?"

"They can. But it's best they go as far upLady as they can, to give the baby longer to grow. And the lower part of Lady isn't too healthy these days." She put an arm around him. "Think I might be pregnant?"

That was something else to worry about, but as he began to do so, Tresco spoke.

"The mountains and the long canyon lie between the inn and Ladysmouth. The way is very difficult and weaker gorons die on it." He puffed himself up in a similar manner to the others. "When I was younger I took that trail and fertilised Lady. It is a . . ." He hesitated, searching for the words.

"It's a churchy thing," explained Mistral. "Like, religious. They got to do it once in their life, at least. To keep the population up, see? And the weak ones don't make it. It's real rough for them in Ladycanyon."

"A kind of natural selection."

"I guess so. But it'll be okay for us, being bigger and stronger than them. I done it before, lots of times. I'll look after you, my love. You remember when we first met in Susanna's basement at Ladysmouth?" She made it sound years ago. "I'd come up the trail that time."

They heard a distant hum. A copter was moving slowly above the bushtrap to the west. "They're looking for us."

The copter kept its distance, however. It was methodically quartering the ground to the north of Samarita. Meanwhile they made good time on the trail. Mistral, Trevithick and their two stoags helped with the towrope, and they reached the inn in the sultry heat of mid-afternoon. Lady lay flat and steaming, yesterday's surface rain almost gone. Mountains rose behind the long low wooden building. The back wall of the inn was built into a slope of the foothills. Squitos swooped and hovered everywhere, picking dead fish from Lady's warm surface. The still air was thick with the stink of decay.

Mistral knew the innkeeper and addressed him as Cakeman. Disappointingly, he stocked no mead. Mistral explained that humans were rarely seen in these parts. So they settled for two mugs of a juice squeezed from a local fruit and, crouching under the low roof, crossed the room to the window and sat on the floor.

This inn was in sharp contrast to the humanised Passing Barge. The ceiling was well under two meters high, and the timber walls were bare. The benches and tables were designed for very small customers. Tresco, Calder and Cameron joined a small group of gorons at the far end of the room. They all sat in total silence, eyeing the humans.

Trevithick found this eerie. After a while he asked Mistral, "Why don't they say something, for God's sake?"

"They don't need to. Most of them probably know me already, so they're making sure they'll know you again. They're talking by pheromones. Telling one another you're not dangerous." She sat on the floor with total abandon, knees apart, raised and bent, the skirt of the thin dress rucked up around her waist and exposing strong thighs and female anatomy to the whole room. Trevithick could not get used to the idea that it meant nothing to the gorons present.

He heard Mistral laughing softly and caught her looking at him. "Embarrassing you, am I?"

"Not in the least. Might be an idea if you put some underpants on, though."

"I don't have none in my bag. What you see is almost all the clothes I got. Never mind, darling. We'll raid Susanna's place when we get to Ladysmouth. I bet she has nice things. Until then you'll just have to put up with me the way I am. Is that so hard?"

"It's of no consequence." He knew he sounded pompous and that she was laughing at him. Her sexuality had caused an alarming shift in the balance of power between them. He stared determinedly out of the window. Two gorons sat in a coracle on Lady, one rowing, one standing in the bow. Soon the standing goron tumbled over the side. The oarsman stayed beside him, beating off squitos with an oar for a long time before his companion finally disappeared below the surface.

"That's religious as well," said Mistral. "That's why they don't have space travel, or even explore their own world properly. They need to stay close to Lady so they can return to her when they're ready to die."

"Suppose they die by accident?"

"Then someone else brings them to Lady and chucks them in."

The nectar they drank for supper was undoubtedly nourishing, but it seemed to leave a void in the stomach. The notion of raiding Susanna's cottage when they reached Ladysmouth began to look increasingly attractive; Trevithick didn't know how long he could last without solid food. Later Cakeman showed them to their room. They had to crawl through the entrance, but the room was just long enough for them to stretch out on the deep carpeting of soft fibres covering the floor. There was no light. Trevithick could hear Mistral's breathing, fast and shallow.

He took her in his arms and tried to think of Susanna.

CHAPTER 21

THE INN LAY SOME FORTY KILOMETRES from the lake, which might not have seemed far to the average human. Given difficult terrain, maybe two days hike. But the thought of that canyon awakened Trevithick early the next morning, and kept him awake and worrying while Mistral slept the sleep of the innocent.

There was no accounting for his vertigo problem. Normally he was as brave or foolhardy as the next man, if a little hidebound by conventions. But on the edge of a hundred-meter cliff—the brink, as he tended to think of it—he became unhinged, a gibbering wreck. He'd tried to minimise it by concentrating on the solid nature of the ground beneath him, and the unlikelihood of a sudden gust of wind lifting him off his feet. But it never worked. He even had problems in near-zero gravity situations.

The truth was, he didn't trust himself. He had the fear that something in the complex mess of his brain would malfunction, as it had done often enough before, and his leg muscles would convulse and hurl him into the invitingly yawning abyss.

And he suspected the abyss known as Ladycanyon would, if it did nothing else, yawn invitingly.

"Can't you sleep, darling?" Mistral was watching him, propped on one elbow, body glowing in the sunlight that filtered through the loosely-woven roof.

"I'm fine, thanks. I was just trying to work things out. How long will it take us to reach the lake?"

"We'll make it by the day after tomorrow. There's another inn in the canyon."

"About this canyon. I've seen it from the air, and the walls looked kind of vertical. What's the trail like?"

She smiled, sensing his apprehension. "Nothing to it. A bit of a scramble here and there. A fairly wide ledge, though. It's tough on the gorons, they're not used to heights. Or climbing at all, really. They get totally out of breath and dizzy. But it's no problem for us."

There was one way to rid his mind of the demons, and he took it, reaching out and stroking her breasts. She said quietly, "It's been ages since we made love."

The opposing senses of peace and guilt that he got from the act kept him occupied for an hour afterward, by which time they'd thrown cold water from a nearby stream over one another, dried off and got dressed. It was a fine, warm morning, not yet humid. They joined Tresco, Calder and Cameron for a mug of fruit juice while their stoags grazed contentedly outside.

Afterwards Cameron took Trevithick aside and said, "I'm older than Calder and not so strong. I may not live through the day. Ladycanyon is rugged and I may tumble. You must not grieve if that happens."

His words sent a shiver through Trevithick. "You'll be fine," he said unhappily. "It's only a canyon. Thousands have passed through it and lived. Don't worry about it."

"I'm not worried," the goron said. "Whether I die in falling or whether I live to breed, I still serve Lady. It's you I'm worried about. You may find yourself distressed by my death. I wouldn't want to think myself impolite by dying in your presence."

It was alarmingly defeatist talk which did nothing for Trevithick's confidence. "I'll try to accept it," he said. "If it happens."

The other three had walked on ahead with the stoags, leaving him alone with the earnest little goron who seemed to have a lot on his mind. "You and Mistral," he said. "You are what you call lovers?"

"In a sense," Trevithick replied cautiously.

"We hold Mistral in high esteem. I have often seen her from a distance but never been named by her until yesterday. It is a great honour." His round brown eyes were watchful and his big nose was twitching. He was trying to read Trevithick's pheromones. "You must feel honoured too, to be her lover. You will stay beside her for the rest of your life, just as we stay beside Lady."

"Humans don't always do that, Cameron."

"I am aware of that, but this is a special case. You see, I know how Mistral feels about you, and to leave her would be to destroy her. And I know how you feel too. It is not as she feels. Or as I feel toward Lady. This puzzles me."

Guilt washed over Trevithick. He watched Mistral walking ahead, black hair hanging below her shoulders, slim and erect, the grace of her body making every step look like part of a measured dance. He swallowed and looked away; the whole thing was too painful.

"I can't pretend to understand fully," Cameron went on, "but I know that certain things are right. We gorons will always do what is right, even though it may not be what we want. To do otherwise is what humans call a crime."

"But you gorons are genetically incapable of committing crimes against your own society," Trevithick said defensively. "Everything you do is right, by definition."

"It makes for a satisfying existence." He smiled. "Once, many years ago, I had the opportunity to speak to Lady Herself. I will carry the memory with me for the rest of my life. You will stay beside Mistral for the rest of yours."

"Sometimes our women die first." Why he said that he didn't know. It was a stupid excuse for not committing himself.

"The sorrow must be unbearable," Cameron said.

Later, as we towed Tresco's barge north, Trevithick said quietly to Calder, "Cameron will get through, won't he?"

"I doubt it. He is much older than I, almost past the age for breeding. It's possible Lady would have taken him to herself anyway, instead of accepting his pollen."

"Does that happen often?"

"At Cameron's age, one never knows if one will emerge again."

"That's rather an unsettling thing."

"It's an honoured thing." Although Trevithick had started the conversation by whispering, Calder was talking in normal tones and Cameron was obviously listening.

"I stumble a lot, these days," confided the latter. "Ladycanyon is not a place for stumblers."

By the time they reached the point where the trail began to climb above Lady, Trevithick was thoroughly demoralised. They halted for a drink from gourds supplied by the inn, and to say goodbye to Tresco. His stoags climbed ponderously aboard the barge and took their places on the belt. Trevithick drew Mistral aside.

"I've had an idea. Why don't we simply get Tresco to give us a ride to Ladysmouth on the barge?"

"You scared of the trail?"

"I'm not the greatest at dealing with heights."

"I wondered what the problem was." She squeezed his hand reassuringly. "You'll be fine with me. I'll never let anything happen to you. And we can't go on the barge. It'll take Tresco ages to get through just by himself. The current, see? The canyon's narrow so Lady flows fast through it. With our weight he'd hardly move at all. As it is we'll reach Ladysmouth long before him. If it gets too bad you can ride Monty. Six legs are safer than two."

"You know how I see that? It's six chances of losing your footing instead of two. I'll trust to my own feet, thanks."

She licked her finger and held it up. "Wind's from the north. Calder and Cameron can go first so they won't sniff your fear. No point in panicking them, huh? We'll follow a bit behind."

"But supposing I pick up a sudden suicidal urge from Cameron?" His worst nightmares were coming to pass. "I might throw myself off."

"Listen, darling. Cameron is not suicidal. There's no such thing as a suicidal goron."

"Well, put it another way. I might pick up an irresistible urge to pay homage to Lady."

"You won't." She was regarding him gravely, but he saw a twitching at the corners of her lips. She was struggling not to laugh. "I gotta explain this to them," she said. "So they'll be ready, in case. They won't think you're a coward, 'cos they won't understand it." She sniggered unbecomingly. "What I think is another matter."

"Copter!" said Calder sharply.

They'd been so engrossed in discussing his fears that they hadn't heard the approaching hum. Calder had seen the source; a copter skimming low over Lady, still some distance away, scattering squitos in its path.

"Into the barge!" called Tresco.

His stoags were already at work on the belt, and the barge was pulling away from the bank. Trevithick took a run, leaped the gap and landed on deck. The thin planks sagged under his weight. He turned to help Mistral, but needn't have bothered. She cleared the gunwale easily, her bag of possessions in one hand.

"Down here!" she gasped. He followed her and found himself on an open platform about ten meters long by two wide, beneath the upturned V of the belt. The upper roller revolved slowly overhead, and he could see the shadow of the stoags through the loose weave. Their claws dug in as they climbed, and a thin dust of hemp drifted to the platform. He could see why belts didn't last long. "This is the cargo space," she explained.

"They can see straight into here from the bank. It'll be the first place they look."

"I was just telling you, that's all. I wasn't saying we hide here, stupid. Come on." She led him forward. A wide roller revolved there, leading the belt beneath the platform to the aft roller. "Down you go."

He lowered himself onto the moving belt. It was wet from residual surface water on Lady. Light entered from cracks in the woodwork but they were well hidden by the thick side frames. Goron barges were lightly built; basically little more than frames to carry the structural assembly of the rollers.

There was less than a meter of clearance between the belt and the underside of the platform. Side by side, Mistral and Trevithick crawled forward on hands and knees while the belt rolled away beneath them. "Just keep going," she advised him. "You wouldn't want that aft roller to catch up with you."

Before long they heard the hum of the helicopter above the creaking of the rollers; then it stopped. It had landed. They heard voices. Security were questioning Calder and Cameron.

One of the gorons said, "No, not on this trail."

They missed some of the conversation, then there was a shout. "Hey, you on the barge!"

"Yes?" Tresco called back.

"Pull in to the bank."

They heard Tresco shout orders to the stoags. The barge tilted and the creaking became shrill. After a moment the belt stopped moving.

"Nobody on deck," a human voice said.

"Jeez, what a stink." This voice was very close. "These stoags just let go whenever they feel like it. If this is the cargo area, I'll stay clear of nectar from now on. Nobody there, anyway."

"Told you there wouldn't be. Why would gorons want to help a couple of humans, huh?"

"Yeah, okay. But we have to go through the motions. Where to now?"

"We'll go as far as the canyon, then head west. I always knew we'd be wasting our time. They wouldn't take the canyon trail; Records say Trevithick has a vertigo problem. They'll take the mountain passes inland. Poor bastards, they'll freeze up there. They may as well give up; we'll get them in the end. At least it's stopped raining."

"Don't start feeling too sorry for them . . ." The voices faded. The copter hummed, the hum deepened then gradually faded. They were gone.

The two humans climbed onto the bank. Trevithick said to Calder, awkwardly, "Thanks for covering for us."

"Cameron lied," said Calder. "Not I."

Cameron said, "I was able to justify it in my mind."

"Could you have justified it?" Mistral asked Calder.

"I didn't have to."

"We live and learn, don't we?" said Mistral. "And we reckoned all gorons think alike. Just shows you, huh?"

"I didn't say I'd have betrayed you," said Calder, hurt. "Cameron spoke first, that's all. And when I said he lied, I was using a human word. Lying can't happen in our language. So we can't consider it wrong."

Cameron was smiling. "All the same, I deemed it wise to speak first, in case Calder was not so quick-witted as I."

By now Tresco was forging steadily upstream again, the stoags stolidly climbing their endless belt. The small party began to climb the trail through the foothills. Calder grasped Trevithick's arm sympathetically at one point.

"You are fearful of the trail ahead, I believe. It is certainly treacherous. I must reassure you that Lady will be honoured by your arrival and will likely make full use of you." Then he raised his head, sniffing.

"There is a human on the trail behind us," he said.

Calder led, followed by Cameron. Trevithick came next, then Mistral and finally the two stoags.

By noon the trail had turned east and rejoined Lady, but at a much higher level. The foothills of ripplegrass had petered out to bare sedimentary rock, jagged and crumbly. The last of the wild stoags watched the party pass, grazing impassively. They were quite different in appearance from the domesticated Wilfred and Monty, being long, lean and lighter in colour. The trail steepened and the drop to the right became unpleasantly sheer. They'd left all vegetation behind. Soon they were using hands as well as feet, climbing outcrops of rock obstructing the trail.

Trevithick kept his eyes on the narrow path. Occasionally he heard scufflings up front, and the clatter of dislodged pebbles. The path became steadily more narrow, and the rock degenerated into loose gravel.

"Calder seems to think someone's following us. Who would that be?" he asked Mistral.

"No idea." She sniffed. "He's too far away. Or she," she added suddenly. "It better not be that Susanna. Anyway, it doesn't matter. They're a long way off. What we don't want," she said, with a heartless amusement in her voice, "is to meet someone coming the other way on this ledge. A runaway stoag would be worst," she added.

Cameron replied seriously, "There is no need for anyone to travel south on the trail. It has never happened in all the times I've been through Ladycanyon."

That was reassuring. "How much further to the inn?" Trevithick asked, a few centuries later.

"Good grief, we've hardly started," said Mistral. "We'll take a break in a minute. The trail gets wider."

Possibly it did, but she'd have needed a measure to prove it. They stood with their backs to the vertical face, passing a gourd along the line. Mistral held Trevithick's hand. He made an effort to take in his surroundings, yet still retain his sanity. Squitos swarmed far below, just above the surface of Lady. He remarked on this casually.

"They wait for falling travellers," explained Calder. "The pickings are good."

Both he and Cameron were breathing fast. The altitude was affecting them, although they couldn't have been more than five hundred meters above sea level. The wind was getting up, funnelling down the canyon into their faces. Clouds scudded across the sky. A vespa hovered at their level. This unnerved Trevithick further as he looked across the void at the huge wasp. It seemed to be watching him.

"I don't like the look of that," he remarked.

"Try not to show fear," said Mistral. "They only attack if you're scared."

"But I am scared."

"Think of me. Think of making love."

"I'm thinking."

She chuckled. "Let's get going!" she said to Calder. She tossed the empty gourd over the edge. Trevithick heard it hit once quite soon, then nothing more. He visualised it tumbling endlessly, and noticed the vespa still eyeing him. Determinedly he turned his thoughts to Susanna. Maybe when they reached the cottage he'd be able to get in touch with her. She'd be wondering what had happened to them. Security was a closed and mysterious arm of the Organisation, and Tillini seemed to see itself as independent of the local Board of Directors. Given that, it would be quite easy for a person apprehended by Security to disappear without trace ...

On one of the rare occasions when he'd lifted his eyes from the trail he'd noticed an unpleasant overhang up ahead. It had been preying on his mind for some minutes: a huge breast of rock sticking out above the trail. Headroom was barely one meter. The trail disappeared abruptly around a corner immediately afterwards. As if all this were not terrifying enough, just before the overhang the trail degenerated into a narrow shelf about half a meter wide and over five meters long. This shelf was not flat. It sloped outwards, covered with gravelly debris fallen from the cliff above. He looked up again. They were almost there. He hesitated, felt Mistral bump into him, tottered and uttered a startled yell.

She threw an arm around him. "What's the matter?"

"Look at that up ahead. I'm not sure I can make it. We'll have to go back."

"You'll be fine. I'm here, remember? And I went through here not long ago. Just tread carefully."

They shuffled on. Calder and Cameron drew ahead. All too soon they reached the bad part. Calder hesitated for a moment, gauging the distance, then made a quick scurrying run. Gravel spurted from under his feet and cascaded down the cliff. He reached the overhang and threw himself to the ground beneath it, exhausted by the effort.

Cameron, already spent, took it more slowly. He'd hardly started when the gravel began to slide. He fell to his knees, weakly scrabbling at the shifting dirt, breath coming hard and harsh. He was trying to get back to where the others stood. Trevithick found himself lying along the shelf, extending his right hand. Cameron grasped it.

Trevithick's hips were pressed into solid ground, his shoulders were on loose stuff. Cameron still scrabbled, then suddenly he slipped further, pivoting Trevithick toward the edge.

He heard Mistral scream. "Let him go!"

It was not in Trevithick to do that. The little man slipped further and finally lost his footing altogether. A shower of gravel clattered down the cliff face toward Lady far below. Cameron swung vertically from Trevithick's right hand. The ground shifted under his chest. He felt Mistral throw her weight upon his legs. If only he could have got his left hand to Cameron he might have been able to lift him to safety. But in order to do that he'd have to pivot further, and the trail simply wasn't wide enough.

Cameron's eyes stared up into Trevithick's. He looked calm; but who knew what expression a goron used in the face of imminent death? He said quietly, "Let me go."

"I can't do that. Hold on. We'll think of something."

Mistral said, "You've got to let him go, darling."

"There has to be a way."

Trevithick felt himself slip a fraction nearer the brink. He heard Mistral give a small scream. And still he looked into Cameron's eyes; the eyes of this little goron whom he'd come to look on as a friend. He felt tears in his own eyes.

"Let me go," said Cameron.

CHAPTER 22

TREVITHICK FELT MISTRAL'S HAND SLIDE DOWN beside his arm. She held a knife.

"I'm so sorry, Bryn," she said. "But if you don't let Cameron go I'm gonna have to cut his hand off. See, nobody minds Cameron dying except you. Everyone else understands. Cameron will go to his mother, and she'll take him. You're stopping him doing what he wants. Now are you gonna let go, or do I have to hurt him?"

Cameron said, "She's right."

So Trevithick let go. He felt as though he was using their arguments as an excuse for his own cowardice. Cameron fell quietly, keeping his eyes on Trevithick's until he was out of sight. It was only a matter of seconds, but they were seconds Trevithick dreamed about for long afterwards.

Demoralized, he struggled to his feet and examined the route ahead. One down and two to go. He could probably get across the crumbling gap by taking a run like Calder. But he no longer had the nerve. And there was that blind corner beyond the overhang. Supposing he couldn't stop? Supposing he was still moving too fast when he flung himself under the overhang? He visualized tobogganing out over nothingness, and his stomach heaved.

"I've been thinking," said Mistral.

"We're going back?"

"No way! I got a plan. Okay, our problem's that stretch of loose stuff? You're scared it'll roll away under your feet. And tell the truth," she admitted, "so am I. So we'll send Wilfred and Monty first, and get them to stand there, spaced out a bit with their paws dug well in. They're not gonna fall, not with six legs each and claws and all. Then we'll crawl over their backs."

"Oh, God." He glanced back at the stoags. They were watching Mistral impassively. Two companions had joined the hovering vespa; they hummed in vee formation, motionless apart from the blur of their wings, staring at him with compound eyes.

"Stand back," Mistral told him. "We're coming through."

Was she as confident as she sounded, or did she regard Wilfred and Monty as disposable? She edged past him, her feet on the brink, giving him a quick kiss on the way. The stoags followed, sure-footed and stinking, brushing past him and Mistral and heading out onto the loose scree. They showed no hesitation. Wilfred went first, digging his claws into firmer ground beneath the gravel. He stopped at Mistral's command, a meter short of the overhang, and waited. Monty followed and positioned himself behind Wilfred.

"Nothing to it," said Mistral. "I'll go first. Maybe you'll feel obligated to follow, that way." She leaned forward, took a hand-ful of Monty's fur, and climbed carefully onto his shaggy rump. Then she inched her way along his back. The stoag stood still, head down. She slid down his neck and in the same movement seized Wilfred's furry hindquarters. A few pebbles trickled over the edge. It would have been easier if stoags had tails. She clambered over Wilfred's back and a moment later crouched beside Calder under the overhang.

"Nothing to it," she said again, but he detected a tremor in her voice. "Your turn now."

He knew he'd done it, because an eon or two later he found him-self lying under the overhang. But he never knew how he did it.

The horror wasn't quite finished. He lay face down, eyes closed, fingers gripping rock to reassure himself the trail was still there. After a moment he felt Mistral's arm around him. When he opened his eyes he was looking straight down; his head hung over the edge. Far below on the glistening ribbon of Lady, Tresco's barge struggled along.

And off the port bow, as they say, was a tiny imperfection in Lady's smoothness. Cameron. Trevithick watched for the stoags, beetle-like forms far below, to shift their weight to the left side of the barge. That was how barges turned. The belt dug in further on the side where the stoags placed their weight, so the craft tended to swivel a little. It was slow, but it worked.

But the stoags climbed on, scaling their belt without pause.

"Isn't he going to pick Cameron up?" Trevithick whispered, still in shock.

"You're thinking like a human, darling," said Mistral. "Sit up and have a shot of mead."

He rolled away and sat with his back against solid rock. Mistral took a small bottle from her bag. He drank. "I could have done with this a while back," he told her.

She took the bottle from him, firmly. "There's times when a shot of mead's needed," she said reprovingly, "and times when it's the worst thing. The trail gets easy from now on."

She told the truth. The trail widened as they approached the halfway point in the canyon, and by mid-afternoon the inn was in sight. Perhaps Mistral had exaggerated for Trevithick's sake when she'd persistently described it as an inn. In fact it was little more than a wooden shack, and his hope of getting a meal, or at least a mug of mead, began to fade. Although nectar was nourishing, it didn't have the ability to fill his stomach the way good old M16 did. It had been some time since he'd eaten, and he'd have welcomed even Mistral's cooked vegetation. As they started down the hill to the inn he found himself wondering what a slice of Lady would taste like, barbecued. She wouldn't miss a kilogram or two. Her jelly-like consistency might be unpleasant, though.

The trail descended and the view opened up. The inn was situated at the confluence of two canyons. One of these carried Lady; the other, coming in from their left, was little more than a pre-cipitous gash in the mountainside, narrow and rugged. During the forthcoming rainy season there would be huge waterfalls, but now the rocks were dry, just a trickle of silver threading through the cracks and hurrying past the inn to flow onto the surface of Lady. There was a welcome profusion of bright greenery down there.

The proximity of the inn to Lady gave him some hope. There would be deliveries by barge. "This inn," he said to Mistral. "What's it like?"

"Okay. It has nectar, if that's what you mean." Her tone was abrupt. Her mood had undergone a change for the worse over the past hour or so. He couldn't begin to understand what was troubling her, and he knew better than to ask.

They reached the floor of the narrow valley and crossed the stream by stepping stones. Far above, a rope bridge swayed in the breeze. Even looking up at it made his stomach churn. Calder was watching him.

"We use it in the rainy season," he explained.

"Designed to carry the weight of a goron, huh?"

Calder glanced from Trevithick to the bridge: three strands of rope linked with cross-ropes to form a long, sagging vee. "I think it would support you possibly one-third of the way across."

There was something cold-hearted about Calder. They left the stepping stones behind, climbed the low bank and hurried along the trail to the inn through unusually lush vegetation. Wilfred and Monty began to browse happily. The closer they got to the inn, the smaller it looked. When finally they reached the door, Trevithick found he stood taller than the roof ridge.

"I'll have to crawl to get through that doorway," he said.

Mistral shot him an unfriendly glance. "Beggars can't be choosers."

Calder was already entering. Mistral followed and Trevithick brought up the rear. The inn was empty: a low rectangular room with no furniture, no gorons, and no doors leading off. Dry brown vegetation lay thickly on the floor. Trevithick assumed that was the bedding. He would have to be careful with his questions or Mistral would be at his throat, in her present mood.

"Cozy spot," he observed cheerfully.

Calder was inspecting a row of gourds against one wall. "There's nectar here," he said. "Good."

"No mead?"

He stared at Trevithick reprovingly. "This is the sacred trail of Ladybound gorons. There would not be mead."

"Gorons don't drink mead," said Mistral. "You know that. And the only human who's ever been on this trail before is me."

"And now me."

"Yes. You'll put up with what's available, like I do."

"For God's sake, I only asked!"

It was a bad start to their stay at that place, which Calder said was called Ftando. This, he said, meant The-Place-Where-Lady-Bathes. It seemed a long human equivalent for such a short name, but Trevithick didn't challenge him. The atmosphere between the three of them was tense enough already.

He left the other two after they'd drunk their fill of nectar and went outside to stretch his legs. It was oppressive in the ravine, despite the wealth of vegetation. A variety of firepot grew beside the trail, orange and shaped like giant tulips, well over a meter tall. Avoiding a struggling insect, Trevithick dipped his finger into one and licked it. It tasted good, though watery. This was the nectar the members of Clan Gatherer fed to Lady. The nectar people drank was disgorged by the clan into evaporation ponds near the lake and shipped south after being reduced to about half its volume. Humans distilled mead from this nectar, and tried not to think about the disgorging process.

Trevithick heard light footsteps. Calder was approaching.

"I thought firepots only grew at Ladysmouth," he said, trying to make conversation with this taciturn goron.

"Mostly they grow there. But they will readily grow elsewhere."

"So why don't you plant them all the way downLady? You could dig evaporation ponds at intervals, then you wouldn't need to ship nectar all the way from Ladysmouth."

Calder stared at Trevithick uncomprehendingly. "We don't need to do that. We have barges."

"You wouldn't need barges any more."

"But . . ." Now his expression was amazed. "What are you suggesting Clan Boatbuilder should do, if they don't build boats? It is a very numerous clan, with many different tasks all connected with barges and coracles."

Trevithick was suddenly on dangerous ground, yet all he'd intended was a friendly suggestion. Now he made another mistake, possibly out of a mild annoyance. "Lady would be pleased to accept the redundant members of the clan."

"Few members of Clan Boatbuilder are of acceptable age," snapped Calder. "Which means Lady would breed with them rather than absorbing them. Which, in turn, means our population would increase by a considerable amount. How would we find jobs for the newcomers?"

"No, you're right. It was a stupid suggestion. Forgive me. I was thinking like a human again."

Calder shot Trevithick an unfriendly glance. He was disappointed this insensitive human had backed off so easily. "Speaking of humans, Mistral is crying," he said. "Rather than try to revolutionize our culture, you should go to her side."

It would been a more pleasant journey if Calder, rather than Cameron, had fallen into Lady. But Trevithick managed not to say so, and hurried back to the inn. Mistral was huddled in a corner. He tried to put an arm around her. She flung it off.

"Go away!"

"What the hell's the matter now?" He was rapidly losing patience with his traveling companions.

"You know!"

"No, I don't."

"So you say. Well, you don't fool me!" She snatched up an empty gourd and hurled it at his head without warning. It missed, but he felt the wind of it.

He backed away. "That's enough. Pull yourself together or I'm continuing on the trail, right now. By myself. The choice is yours. So what's it to be?"

"Yes, you'd want to get onto the trail, wouldn't you! With that Susanna all ready and waiting for you at her bloody cottage! Unless it's her following us on the trail. One way or another, you two can't seem to stay apart!'"

He decided on honesty. "My guess is, Susanna will be at the cottage. She's probably guessed we'd head up through the canyon. She'll be pleased to see us both. And she'll tell us the news. And soon she'll have to go back to work, and you and I will be alone again. Probably still on the run. Together."

There was a long silence while she considered the prospect, eyes downcast. Eventually a small hand stole across the floor toward him. "Maybe I got jealous. She's so beautiful, Susanna is. All that blonde hair and blue eyes, and she can do anything."

He took the hand. "We've got better things to do than fight about Susanna."

She pulled him closer, and after a while matters improved. But not much. As he went to sleep that night, he was thinking that Mistral would not be an easy person to live with. She was scarred in more than one way, and some of the wounds might never heal.

He awakened the following morning to find everything curiously dark and damp. It took him a moment to realize that the sun wouldn't clear the cliffs for another hour or two, and in any case, it was raining. The roof, like all goron roofs, was not intended to keep rain out; merely to provide a degree of shelter from sun and wind. The goron metabolism slowed down at night and their body temperature dropped considerably, so they didn't feel the cold as humans did. In winter they deserted their buildings and went into virtual hibernation in caves lined with dried vegetation.

But Trevithick was cold and miserable. He crawled outside and began to jump up and down, flapping his arms. It served only to circulate more cold air inside his wet clothing. He crawled back to find an unhappy Mistral.

"I'm f-frozen. Cuddle me."

They lay close together for a while but it didn't seem to do much good, so they set about the difficult business of awakening Calder. He slept as though dead, his skin icy cold.

"Maybe he's hibernating already," Trevithick suggested hopefully.

"We'll lie either side of him and warm him up between us."

"I'm not lying down with that little creep! We'll bring in the stoags. They can lie with him."

It was midmorning before a groggy Calder was finally ready for the trail. They slung two gourds of nectar across Wilfred's back and started up the steep trail out of the valley and into Ladycanyon again. Mistral led and Calder stumbled along between them. By this time even Mistral was finding the pessimistic little goron irritating.

Trevithick noticed him eyeing the three vespas, which had resumed formation off to the right as though they'd been waiting all night. By noon, their numbers had been augmented by others arriving from the north and they began to look restless, breaking formation and buzzing in circles. There was another noise too. It took Trevithick a moment to realize it was Calder whimpering with fear. Gorons didn't mind dying, but the thought of pain was terrifying to them.

The party arrived at a recess in the cliff face and stopped, weighing up the situation. "I think it's the nectar," said Mistral. "They can sniff it out a mile off. We'd better get rid of it."

"Toss it down the cliff, you mean?"

"No, drink it." She was untying the vines that held the gourds to Wilfred. Seeing this, the vespas' buzzing became frenzied. "We've got a long way to go yet. We'll be needing the energy. Here, Wilfred!" The stoags were shuffling about uneasily. Mistral positioned both animals at the entrance to the recess, providing cover.

"Do vespas attack stoags?"

"I've never seen them. They have no reason to, unless a stoag starts digging into one of their nests."

They unstoppered the gourds and began to drink, hurriedly. The buzzing became louder. Calder set up a thin scream, piercing in the confined space. Mistral offered him some nectar, but he was too busy screaming and pushed her hand away. Nectar slopped over her arm. The thick sickly smell filled the recess. The stoags panicked and began to lumber away. Mistral's eyes widened.

"Bryn . . ."

A vespa was perched on the edge of the trail, staring at them with compound eyes the size of dinner plates. It was at least three meters long. Its mandibles were clicking hungrily and digestive juices dripped from a long hypopharynx. As Trevithick watched, paralyzed with fear, its legs straightened and it thrust its abdomen forward between them. A stinger pointed at Mistral. It must have measured fifty centimeters, vibrating between chitinous plates.

Mistral was frantically trying to wipe the nectar from her arm. They had no weapons; nothing with which to fight the monster off. And now others arrived until they were perched in a row, six of them watching from the lip of the ledge while others circled behind. Trevithick dragged his shirt off and made what he hoped was a threatening flapping gesture with it. The nearest vespa hesitated, then moved forward.

"Get behind me," he said to Mistral. Her hair, wet with rain, was plastered back and the scar showed big and angry. Calder was already cowering into the furthermost corner of the recess. Trevithick felt a moment of fury, born of helpless fear. This was Calder's world. Surely he knew a way to deal with these brutes? Surely an intelligent race would have developed a defense by now?

Mistral blinked and shook her head, as though clearing her mind. "Okay," she said quietly. She was talking to herself. Surprisingly, she didn't seem to be afraid any more.

Something had distracted the vespas on the trail. A fight had broken out between rival factions and they were lifting off to join in. For a while some twenty vespas whirled and swooped above the canyon, occasionally grasping each other, stingers curling forward as they fell from view. Suddenly they turned as one and dived out of sight.

Trevithick and Mistral crawled to the edge of the trail. Far below, a barge headed south. Within seconds the vespas were swarming around it. They could make out the figure of the bargee, doing something at the side of the A-frame while his stoags plodded on. The vespas continued to swarm, but showed no inclination to land on the barge.

"Let's get going," said Mistral shakily.

"What happened?"

"I guess a rival group arrived. The first vespas were from the south. The others came from the north. They were fighting over us, then they saw the barge." She looked slightly puzzled.

"Tough luck on the bargee."

"They're used to it. They have their defenses."

They hauled Calder from his crack in the rock. His legs were too weak to carry him so they slung him across Wilfred's back. Then they resumed the trek along a trail which, as Mistral had promised, was much wider than the terrifying ledge of yesterday.

Trevithick wondered about the vespas. There was something about their behavior that didn't make sense. For one thing, only the original three had come from the south, but he'd counted at least six on the ledge and almost twenty altogether. Seventeen northern vespas and three southern ones. Poor odds for the south; why had they bothered to fight at all? And assuming the six on the ledge were all northern vespas, why had they backed off?

Was he wrong in trying to apply Earth logic to Goronwy animal behavior?

"Not much further," said Mistral a couple of hours later as the trail began to descend steeply.

They rounded a corner to see the lake below, and a blonde woman standing on the beach.

"Oh, thank God." Susanna was staring at Trevithick hungrily. After a quick glance at Mistral she hugged him tight, then backed off to arm's length. "Had a good hike, have you?" she inquired with studied casualness. "Weather nice for you?"

"I've got a lot to tell you."

"I'll bet you have." She watched Mistral, who was walking slowly away with her fingers entwined in Wilfred's hair. "How is she?"

"Okay. Blows hot and cold."

"The truth please, Trevithick."

"I have a problem there." Mistral sat on the beach out of earshot, with Wilfred lying beside her. She was watching them with a faint scowl. Calder was on his feet, heading for a group of gorons gathered around a cluster of beached coracles. No good-byes.

"It was unavoidable," said Susanna. "Don't blame yourself for anything."

He gave her an edited version of the events of the past three days. "Did you speak to Martha about the art show?" he asked finally, before she could ask him anything more.

"I did, but she wasn't very forthcoming. She admitted she didn't like Mistral's work personally, in which she is not alone. But she insisted it must have some merit because people buy it."

"As last-minute souvenirs."

"True. Listen, Bryn, I'd rather not talk about it, when we have so little time. I feel really rotten about the whole thing. It wouldn't be so bad if I wasn't an artist myself. Then I wouldn't feel I was partly responsible."

There was a hollow feeling in his chest. "What do you mean: When we have so little time?"

They were still standing apart, gripping one another's forearms like reunited brothers in a 3-V show. He was trying to memorize every detail of her: the golden hair, the wide set blue eyes, the plump lips, the chubby cheeks. He wanted to make love to her forever, or more practically until he passed out from exhaustion and dehydration. He wanted to do it right now. But Mistral was a few meters away. Just for an unfair moment, he hated Mistral.

"Okay," Susanna said. "I think they may have finally made the connection between us. They're not fools. They've had a couple of Security men here at the cottage for the past two days, guzzling my mead. They think that's where you'll go. They say it's because mine's the only human residence outside Samarita, but I think it's probably because someone saw you leaving my apartment one day. And then there was Marik Darwin's meeting and your knight in shining armor impersonation."

"I'm so sorry."

"So am I, because I wanted us to, uh, further our relationship when you arrived here. If you get my meaning." She smiled a rather sad smile and he wanted to hug her again. "But instead you'll just have to go on the run with Mistral again, and I'll be lying awake nights wondering what you're doing."

"Are you under house arrest?" It was something else for him to feel bad about.

"Nothing like that. They're very polite about the whole thing. All the same, I'm glad you came along today. They don't expect you until tomorrow. They thought you'd taken the route through the mountain passes."

"So we can't stay here. Why don't you come with us?" he asked stupidly. He couldn't bear the thought of saying good-bye so soon.

"The three of us?" She smiled faintly. "It wouldn't work out. Besides, you need me in their camp."

"We could leave Mistral behind. She helped me out by showing me the trail through the canyon, but that's all. For all Security know, I forced her into it. There's no reason for her to be on the run too."

"Darwin's meeting. They're after you both, Bryn."

He regarded the cliffs, and the caves of Clan Gatherer. Security would be searching those caves pretty soon. The beach ran for many kilometers west, but it was exposed with little cover among the grassy foothills. The lake? It was vast, and there were no boats big enough to withstand the offshore storms. The coracles were inshore vessels, and the barges weren't designed to float on water. Finally he regarded Susanna, loving and beautiful, whom he would soon be leaving.

"Where the hell can we go now?" he asked.

CHAPTER 23

THEY BROUGHT MISTRAL INTO THE DISCUSSION. She took the news that she was now rated a criminal very well.

"I'm not scared of Security," she said. "Piss on them, that's what I say. I know the country better than they do. I can keep clear of them for the rest of my life. I'm not so sure about Bryn. But I can look after him."

"You've done fine so far," said Susanna, rather sadly. "So the question is, where can you hide out?"

"Ladysend," said Mistral promptly.

"Ladysend? How will you get there?"

"We'll go by barge."

"But—"

"Listen," said Mistral. "We can't stay here, right? And we can't head off into the bush; we wouldn't last two days. But at Ladysend, that Bridget Booker will take care of us for as long as we need. She's nice. And they'll never think of looking for us downLady, not if we leave some kind of clue behind to show we've been around here. Susanna could even pretend to find the clue herself," she said grudgingly. "That might get her off the hook."

"A bit risky, isn't it?" Susanna was doubtful. "A barge would take you right past Samarita."

"No problem. We've hidden on a barge before and we can do it again. And like I said, they'll never expect it." She loosened the drawstring on her small sack of possessions, pulled out a man's shirt and handed it to Susanna. Trevithick recognised it, and wondered when she'd got hold of it. She saw him staring and flushed. "Here, this is Bryn's. And here's that bloody skirt I wore at . . ." She frowned. "You find them in the lake, right? Then they'll think we've taken off in a coracle and maybe drowned."

Susanna said, "Good thinking, Mistral. We'll give it a try." She turned to Trevithick. "Bridget Booker's terminal is hooked into the Samarita mainframe. You might find it useful." She hesitated. "I just wonder if it's fair to impose on her like this."

"Bridget is anti-Organisation these days," he assured her. "My guess is, she'll be glad to see us. I expect she'll put me to work right away on the problems of Clan Birthcare. And the journey will give me a chance to observe Lady firsthand, all the way downstream. Maybe I'll come up with something useful."

Mistral said scornfully, "You're wasting your bloody time. Lady's dying and that's it. She's old and she's dying, like anything else that gets old. There's nothing nobody can do."

He regarded her thoughtfully. For some reason he'd never discussed Lady's sickness with her before. She wasn't a scientist, so why should he? Yet she had an empathy with the gorons that no other human had. Did this extend to Lady as well as the males?

"How do you know?" asked Susanna.

"I just do. I can feel it. And further on downLady, she stinks of death. And—" She hesitated, glancing sidelong at Susanna.

"And what?"

"And I reckon she's gone mad," she muttered. "Senile. You know."

Susanna and Trevithick exchanged mystified glances. "How can Lady go mad?" asked the latter. "She's just a mass of jelly."

"Well, anyway, think about it." Clearly Mistral didn't want to pursue the subject. "Maybe I'll show you what I mean. Maybe not. But there's nothing nobody can do. I give her another ten years."

"So you think the Organization's wasting its time, staying on?"

"Yeah. Pointless, it is. They'll never do no good here. They might as well clear out right now, save their money."

"But they don't know that," said Susanna.

"No, because they're stupid. They should've asked me, shouldn't they? I mean, even Bryn didn't ask me. That's because he thinks I don't know nothing." Her glance was distinctly hostile. "But one day I'll show him. You'd better go now," she said to Susanna. "No point making Security suspicious, is there? Don't forget to throw that stuff in the lake. Maybe rip it up a bit. Then find it tomorrow, maybe have one of the Security people with you. Okay?"

"Okay," said Susanna, smiling. She touched Trevithick's hand briefly, ever tactful in front of Mistral. "See you both. Look after yourselves."

Mistral swung away and missed the look Susanna gave Trevithick, fortunately. He watched his girl walking away for a moment, golden hair swinging, strong legs taking her up the slope toward her cottage, and wondered if he'd ever see her again.

Then, strolling casually along the beach toward them, came a stick-like figure carrying a violin.

"Lath!" exclaimed Trevithick. "What the hell are you doing here?"

The lean face was grey with exhaustion. "They—" he mumbled, then his knees folded and he sank to the sand. He remained kneeling, muttering.

"He's been following us," said Mistral. "Poor old bugger."

Now Eagleman was weeping quietly. "Don't leave me," he mumbled. "There's nobody else. Nobody. All alone, all alone."

"Something's frightened him," said Trevithick. "Something back there in Samarita. You don't suppose they're after him as well, are they?" He regarded the unhappy figure helplessly. "What are we going to do about him?"

Mistral knelt beside Eagleman. "Listen to me, Lath," she said gently. "I want you to tell us just what the matter is. We can't help unless we know what's wrong. We're your friends."

He raised his face, tear-streaked. "I saw . . . I saw them do it," he mumbled. "Poor Marik." Suddenly a crazy grin spread over his face. "Alas, poor Marik!" he shouted. "I knew him well." He began to laugh wildly. The mad sounds echoed from the cliffs.

"For God's sake shut him up!" urged Trevithick. "Security are up at the cottage."

Mistral put her arms around Lath, and her smooth cheek against his bearded one. "There, there," she crooned. "It's all right, Lath. Like I said, we're your friends."

He stopped laughing. He turned and looked into her eyes with mild amazement. He nodded vigorously. "You're my friends. You won't leave me."

Mistral regarded Trevithick questioningly. He nodded. They couldn't leave him here. They'd have to take him with them. There was no humane alternative. Gently they pulled him to his feet.

Trevithick would have liked to talk Tresco into taking them, but the bargee was still downLady somewhere struggling through the canyon. The thought of entrusting Mistral, Lath and himself to a strange goron bothered him. Mistral, however, had no such fears.

"Over there," she pointed. A row of barges lay beached under the cliffs to the east. A few members of Clan Boatbuilder worked on them, making simple repairs, greasing wooden bearings, patching belts. The bargees, she told Trevithick, would be somewhere nearby.

They found six of them asleep in the shade of the cliff.

"Stand fast," said Mistral.

They jerked awake. "Stand fast, Mistral," one of them said. "What are you doing here?"

"We need a ride to Ladysend soon as possible. Three of us, on a barge. We'll leave you to talk about it." She drew Trevithick aside, around a rocky outcrop. "They've never had this happen before, so they won't know how to handle it," she said quietly. "They have to mull it over. It might have religious significance, see?"

"Religious significance?"

"Everything they do is kind of locked together in this big thing of serving Lady. Maybe taking us to Ladysend is wrong somehow. Maybe we're meddling in their ritual."

This was worrying. "Go and tell them it's a matter of life and death."

"Good grief, Bryn! That cuts no ice with them."

He thought guiltily about the time he suggested to Calder that they do away with the barges. Fortunately when Calder had left them, he'd walked off in a westerly direction. Right now he'd be spreading the story of heresy around the evaporation ponds and firepot fields.

"Well, they seem to like you," he said. "Appeal to them in some other way. Say Security will torture you if they catch you. Gorons don't like pain."

"They won't understand people torturing people. Leave it alone, huh? They'll get back to us soon."

The sun was dropping behind the low foothills by the time the gorons approached and stood shuffling and looking at one another uncertainly. It wasn't necessarily bad news, Trevithick told himself as the seconds lengthened. It was the usual goron problem of finding a spokesman.

"You, Brennan," said Mistral, pointing.

Relieved at having the decision made for them, the gorons smiled broadly. "I will take you," said Brennan, "because I trust you, Mistral. And I met your companion before, in the caves. You told me he was good. And you say the thin man is good also. I will take you myself."

"And Wilfred," said Mistral. "I have to take Wilfred. He can work his passage on the belt. And I'll leave my other stoag here for you. He's well trained and works hard. I call him Monty."

"You are generous," said Brennan.

"No, you're the generous one. Which is your barge?"

Brennan pointed to the third barge in line. It faced inshore, a pair of stoags already standing on the aft slope of the belt ready to back it off the beach. The central platform was loaded with jars. The foredeck held an upturned coracle and a pile of fodder for the stoags. Mistral coaxed Wilfred aboard—he was not accustomed to barges—and persuaded him to take up station on the belt below the other two animals. Then she and Trevithick climbed aboard. Lath followed, smiling happily. Brennan commanded the stoags to start climbing.

As the barge rolled out onto Lady, Trevithick took a last look around. To the west, a swell sent long waves rolling and breaking up the beach. To the east lay Lady, where there were no waves and the sand was dry. The barges stood right at the demarcation, probably to minimise the distance for transporting loaded jugs. Then Susanna's cottage came slowly into view. He was about to wave when Mistral said, "Get down!"

He hadn't been thinking straight. There were Security people in the cottage. He dropped behind the low gunwale surrounding the afterdeck. The barge rolled on until Brennan gave another command. Then the stoags accelerated, climbing over the top roller and taking their place on the other side. Wilfred was taken by surprise. As the belt checked and began to turn the opposite way he lost his footing and fell clumsily to the afterdeck.

Mistral shouted at him angrily. He gathered himself together and fixed his claws into the belt, now ascending. Soon he was carried over the top roller. The barge shook as he fell on top of the other two animals. The belt stopped. It took a while, but eventually they sorted themselves out and the belt began to move again. Soon they saw the snouts of Brennan's two stoags silhouetted against the darkening sky.

"Sorry," said Mistral.

"I'm sure Wilfred will become an asset when he gets used to us," said Brennan kindly. "We will let the stoags rest during the hours of darkness. The current will carry us along quite quickly, in Ladycanyon. But first," he gave Mistral a searching look, "this Bryn Trevithick here. You know him well, Mistral?"

"Oh, very well. I love him, like you love Lady."

"And the thin man too?"

"No, I don't love the thin man. But he's usually reliable."

"Good. I asked because I have a duty to perform before nightfall. Bryn Trevithick and the thin man will meet someone whose existence we do not talk about in front of humans, except you, Mistral."

"You have to do this?" asked Mistral anxiously. "I trust Bryn, but the less people who know, the better. Lath may not be, uh, the soul of discretion."

"That is true, but we are forced into an exceptional case. I agreed with the other bargees that I would ask permission before we take you downLady. You see, we don't know if such a journey is acceptable. It has never been done before."

"I don't think you'll get much of an answer."

"We will take that as permission granted."

The suspense was killing Trevithick. "Who the hell are you going to talk to?" he asked sharply.

"Lady Herself," said Brennan.

So they rolled on in the deepening twilight. Soon the beach ended and they found themselves hard under the western cliff of Lady-canyon.

It showed up first as a faint luminescence in the distance. As they closed the gap, Trevithick realised the luminous patch was actually a mound on Lady, a little higher than the surrounding dark surface. And there was something in the middle of that mound; something that moved. Something that waved stunted arms in a curiously helpless fashion, as though drowning.

It was Lady Herself.

She glowed a dull blue. The glow started faintly at the rim of her mound, gradually becoming more intense toward the middle where her torso rose upright. Her shoulders were narrow, her head fairly large when compared to male gorons. One thing about her was peculiarly unnerving.

She had no bones. Her head flopped about, her arms waved like tentacles.

She was composed of the same flesh as the abdomen they called Lady, but her translucency showed no underlying structure, no skull. Her brain was clearly visible, as were her internal organs: heart, lungs and various other organs peculiar to the goron species. A throat ran uninterrupted from the mouth past the larynx, through the trachea to her lungs. There was no gullet, no stomach.

She was terrifying.

Trevithick couldn't help it; he bent double and retched, again and again. He'd seen alien species in his time, the weird and the wonderful, but he'd never seen anything so gut-wrenchingly awful as that pallid monstrosity waving limp and luminous arms in the Goronwy twilight. It was fortunate he didn't have a gun with him. He might not have been able to control his revulsion. No wonder they'd kept the existence of Lady Herself from humans.

"You okay, Bryn?" he heard Mistral whisper anxiously. "It takes a moment."

In many ways, he told himself, this creature made sense. The mound she sat on; it kept her mouth clear of any surface waters. The lack of epiglottis and gullet; she didn't need them, she absorbed her nourishment directly into her abdomen. No bones? Bones are for structural strength and protection, but Lady had an army of suitors to take care of her. So yes, she was a logical creature. But that didn't make her any easier on the eye.

Trevithick had always detested the derogatory human term for gorons: termites. Yet the sight of that tiny thorax attached to the vast reproductive abdomen they called Lady reminded him irresistibly of queen termites he'd examined on Earth.

The barge stopped. The squeaking of bearings ceased and the young night was still. Lady Herself glowed in the darkness alongside. He found he was able to look at her. Her eyes were empty blue sockets and her mouth a round O.

Brennan spoke in the goron tongue; it sounded like a short greeting. There was no reply. Trevithick was dreading the moment when Lady spoke. Brennan continued talking.

"What's he saying?" Trevithick whispered to Mistral.

"He said, 'Beloved mother, we have a request.' Now he's talking about the trip downLady. He's saying we are good humans trying to help. Our voyage is for the benefit of all gorons." She reached out and squeezed his hand. "I sure hope that last bit's right." She was in an improved frame of mind, with the threat of Susanna removed.

Brennan talked on, pausing occasionally.

Suddenly, shockingly, the round mouth twisted and sounds emerged; a continuous shrill piping that rose and fell almost musically, quite unlike the short sentences of Brennan. He listened with his head inclined respectfully. Then he appeared to reply.

"He's being polite," said Mistral. "She didn't make sense."

But suddenly Lady Herself said, quite distinctly, "When stops the killing?"

The shock hit Trevithick hard. It was almost obscene, human words emerging from those misshapen lips. Brennan glanced at him anxiously. "She knows there are humans here."

"Yeah. You've already told her that," said Mistral.

"I didn't think she'd understood," Brennan admitted. He was as shaken as Trevithick.

Mistral whispered. "She's smart in her own way. She's identified our pheromones, not what Brennan said."

Trevithick was still in shock. "She spoke human."

"The gorons tried to teach her, ages ago. Some of it must have stuck."

As Brennan addressed Lady Herself again Trevithick found himself watching her heart, almost absentmindedly. It was pumping much like a human heart. But it was too small to pump blood four hundred kilometres down to the ocean and back. Somewhere in the depths of the canyon there had to be another heart; a huge and powerful one. Or maybe there were several at intervals down-Lady. He knew nothing about her. Nothing at all. After fifty years of human research, that was a disgrace.

Brennan was still talking. The dreadful mouth of Lady Herself made sounds too, but they seemed to be random and bore no relation to the pauses in Brennan's speech. That must have been what Mistral had meant earlier, when she'd said she didn't think Brennan would get much of an answer. It was all a waste of time. The fishy stink was beginning to get the better of Trevithick and he wanted desperately to be away from there.

Nevertheless he forced himself to observe Lady Herself. There might be a clue here to her sickness. Was she, as Mistral had said, simply dying of old age? The appalling creature certainly looked old, but how could he be sure? It was very difficult to assess age in an unfamiliar species. Orangutans look elderly from Day One, to the uninitiated.

Now Lady Herself began to cough. He could see a pocket of

liquid wobbling in her lung. She lurched forward like a striking cobra, and coughed violently. A wad of fluid splashed against Brennan's chest and trickled down his belly. He affected not to notice. His self-control was matched only by his respect for this creature.

She was his mother. Not only that, but she was his lover too, in the reproductive sense. Trevithick kept telling himself that, to explain the goron's remarkable tolerance. He hardly knew his own mother, having been put forward for Space work at an early age to allow time for physical adaptation and psychological preparation. He had a vague recollection of a tall, calm figure with a warm voice, but that was all. And as for lovers, he'd never really loved anyone until he met Susanna, the perfect creature. So his background had hardly prepared him for Brennan's travesty of a relationship. All he could feel was an overwhelming pity.

"How long is this going on?" he whispered to Mistral.

"Pretty much finished, I guess."

Brennan was bowing and murmuring, saying goodbye and pledging eternal allegiance. Lady Herself was waving her arms and coughing; the effort of speech had been too much for her.

Then an astonishing thing happened.

First there was a thready scraping sound, then the melody from Mendelssohn's violin concerto sounded boldly from the foredeck, echoing around the walls of the canyon.

"Stop him, for God's sake!" whispered Trevithick urgently.

"No—look!"

Lady Herself had gone quite still, head cocked as though listening. Lath played on, gaining confidence. Lady Herself began to make sounds again, a piping that seemed almost to compliment Lath's music. Her arms waved rhythmically. Trevithick felt a sense of peace steal over him; the creature was emitting powerful pheromones. He heard Brennan murmuring contentedly. Mistral squeezed his hand. The music played on. Lady herself swayed and piped, and the canyon was alive with the music and beauty.

How long it lasted, Trevithick didn't know. The barge drifted slowly away from Lady Herself. The music stopped at last and he heard a faint clatter as Lath laid down his instrument. Mistral kissed Trevithick on the cheek.

"Who'd have thought it," she whispered.

Brennan shook himself visibly, uttered a command and the barge lurched. The stoags were climbing again.

Trevithick watched Lady herself slip astern. Her face was turned directly toward him and he had the feeling she could see him. She raised her nose and sniffed. Her mouth was slack on one side, as though she'd suffered a stroke. Then the lips twisted, laboriously forming words.

She said, "Don't let them kill my children."

CHAPTER 24

BRENNAN LIT A LAMP AND CARRIED IT FORWARD, swinging expertly around the outer edge of the belt. The stoags ceased their endless climb. They thumped around on the foredeck, composing themselves for sleep. Mistral sat with Trevithick on the afterdeck. She was just a dark shape beside him, but he could tell she was looking his way, and in a moment he felt her breath on his cheek.

"Sorry I've been such a bitch," she said.

"That's all right."

"It's that Susanna, see? I know you'll always love me, but she's so bloody pretty and so bloody clever, it makes me sick. All the time we were on the trail, it seemed she was just waiting at Ladysmouth to take you away. And I know you like her, you can't hide that from me. I guess any man would."

"She's a very nice lady," he said, as though talking about a favourite aunt.

"Oh, sure." Mistral snorted derisively. "Anyway, I don't want to talk about her any more. What did you think of Lady Herself?"

"Weird."

"And crazy. I told you she was. All the time Brennan and her was talking goron, she wasn't making no sense. She's senile. Did you want to put her out of her misery? I felt like that. Just to kill her, quietly. Isn't that a terrible thing to say? And if she died, all of Lady would die and there'd be no more goron babies born." She

251

shifted her position so that she was leaning against him. "And she sure doesn't like us culling her babies. That was the only thing that came across sensible."

"Culling's the only way. If we didn't do it, the gorons would have to look after all kinds of . . . things, that couldn't look after themselves."

Mistral slipped an arm around his waist. "Lady Herself don't know that, see? She lives up here, and her kids are born at the other end. All she knows is what the gorons tell her, and maybe they don't explain it too good. Or maybe she just don't understand. I seen the culling." She shivered. "Some of those little things is too weird. When we have a baby, I hope it'll be okay."

It was a warm night like all Goronwy summer nights, but Trevithick felt suddenly cold . . .

He awakened to the creak of the rollers, and opened his eyes to find Mistral looking down at him in amusement. "Sure slept well, you did," she said. "Reckon I'm good for you."

True up to a point. But a nightmare had jerked him awake some hours previously, and afterwards he'd been staring into the darkness for a long time, sweating and trembling. All he could recall now was a tree, ancient and crooked on an endless plain, with little goron babies hanging from the branches by their umbilicals. Something terrible had happened next, something to do with Bridget Booker and a knife, but fortunately it was lost in the mists of sleep.

He shook his head and looked up into the bright green eyes. Lath was presumably still asleep on the foredeck. The air was warm and a breeze blew steadily up the canyon from the south. The canyon was one of the few places on Goronwy free of the fitful winds of the aeolus. They were passing Ftando, the inn where they'd spent the night before last. He could see the trail clinging to the cliff; and further on he could make out the place where Cameron had fallen to his death. It was difficult to believe they'd actually walked along that tiny scratch on the cliff face.

He stood and stretched. Various parts ached from lying on the hard deck. The surface of Lady looked greasy that day and they seemed to be moving very slowly. He wasn't used to this kind of inaction. "How long will it take to get to Ladysend?" he asked.

Mistral put her head on one side, considering. "Less than two reaches to Samarita," she said. "After that, it's eleven reaches to Ladysend." She used the goron measurement for both time and distance: a reach was the distance travelled in a day; usually around thirty kilometres in eight standard hours, but it varied according to the terrain. Each reach-end on Lady was marked by an inn.

"Further downLady we'll be able to stay at inns, will we?"

Thirteen more nights of sleeping on deck and he'd be crippled for life.

"Oh, you poor old thing." She was in high spirits that morning. "Sure we can."

The day in the canyon passed without incident, and the next day too. Lath was very little trouble and spent most of his time dozing, occasionally chatting without making much sense, sometimes strumming his violin like a guitar. The wind continued to blow against them, but not strongly enough to hinder progress. They saw the occasional barge heading in the opposite direction but Brennan didn't stop. The goron bargees raised hands to each other gravely, but nothing more. They did not exchange news.

"They don't need to," Mistral said. "The only news that matters to them is the kind that makes them happy or sad. They don't gossip like we do. And Brennan can tell from pheromones blowing upLady whether there's anything he should know."

Nights, they slept aboard under the ribbon of stars between the canyon walls. By now he'd begun to fret about the notion of staying at Ladyside inns. "Won't word get back to Samarita? I'm sure they hardly ever get humans staying overnight," he said. "We'll stick out like sore thumbs."

"No problem. You just don't realize, Bryn. Gorons and humans simply don't communicate. And gorons don't even talk to one another about that kind of thing. It don't interest them."

On the morning of Day Three they sat on the afterdeck and discussed the situation. Lath lay asleep on the foredeck, one arm hanging over the side and sliding along the surface. They were emerging from the oppressive canyon walls. Patchwork fields of aeolus and ripplegrass spread from Lady's banks into the foothills. A light wind puffed from all directions, influenced by the aeolus. Trevithick had run out of pills and soon became aware of minor mood shifts.

"We pass Samarita late this afternoon," Mistral told him, "so you and me have got to stay below. We can't risk someone zooming in their windows on us."

"Crawl on the belt, you mean?" A nasty thought. They'd be on hands and knees on that slime-sodden belt for three or four hours. "Can't we go ashore and dodge through the bush?"

"There isn't no bush. Unless you want to try dodging through bushtrap. And I'd rather you didn't do that 'cos I got a future planned for you. No, it's got to be the belt."

"Oh, God. With Lath as well?"

Long before noon they could see the five domes of Samarita shining like half-moons on the sunlit plain. Ladyside human dwellings began to come into view. They swung around the outside of the hull, lowered themselves onto the belt and began to crawl, after impressing on Lath the importance of not getting crushed between the belt and the aft roller. Mistral had taken her clothes off, possibly for comfort, possibly to encourage him. Last night they'd made love yet again and he hadn't thought of Susanna during the act. In fact he'd initiated the lovemaking, hungrily. Was he becoming obsessed with Mistral's body? It was an easy body to become obsessed with. Now, crawling on the belt, he kept wanting to reach out and stroke it.

Such thoughts didn't last long. It was hot and smelly down there. The belt was impregnated with stoag dung and urine. Little fountains of slime from Lady squirted up through holes. The thought of that roller behind them, driven by three heavy animals and just waiting to crush him flat, became a more pervasive obsession than even the hanging breasts beside him. They crawled on, endlessly. His knees ached abominably. Afternoon darkened into evening.

Then suddenly the barge lurched. There was a heavy crash, followed by a confused thumping from above decks and a yell from

Brennan. The barge stopped. Trevithick collapsed full-length, glad of the rest, hardly caring what had happened.

Mistral shouted. "What's going on up there?"

"Belt's broken!" came the answer.

"Bugger it!"

"What happens now?" Trevithick asked, hoisting himself onto the bottom of the portside A-frame, the opposite side from Samarita. The belt lay in an untidy heap across the cargo. The stoags shuffled uneasily on the foredeck. The top roller was motionless, silhouetted against the first stars. At least it was almost dark, but the street lights brightened the intervening stretch of Lady and made him feel exposed and vulnerable.

Mistral and Brennan joined him. They sat in a row on the heavy balk, looking at the mess on the platform. There was a clean diagonal tear in the belt. Probably Wilfred's extra weight had caused it.

"We wait," said Brennan, belatedly answering the question. He looked relaxed, resting his forearms on the platform. A trickle of nectar flowed from jars broken when the stoags fell through the belt. "We are lucky. If this had happened in daylight the vespas would be after the nectar."

"Yes, but what do we wait for? You don't intend to drift all the way to Ladysend, do you?"

"That is not a practical idea, Bryn. It would take two hundred fifty long reaches, at least."

"It's not my idea. I thought it might be yours." The inaction was making Trevithick irritable. Coracles were slipping about on the surface not far off. Probably gorons committing themselves to Lady, but one never knew. A couple from Security might be on a romantic row in the twilight. "Why don't we simply stitch the belt up?"

A sharp intake of breath. "That is a job for Clan Boatbuilder."

"So you don't carry a fid and twine?"

"I don't need them."

"Go easy on him, Bryn." Mistral spoke for the first time. "He feels bad about this."

"So do I. We're sitting ducks. Is he going to row ashore for help or what?"

"There's no point. I told you he feels bad. So the gorons on shore'll pick up his pheromones. Somebody'll be here in the morning, don't worry."

"In the morning? You mean in broad daylight, opposite Samarita? Good grief, Mistral!"

"Gorons don't work at night. You know that." A small hand stole toward him and fastened on his thigh. "So quit complaining and let's make the most of it. It'd be nice and soft on the belt down there."

"Cold and slimy, you mean." Nevertheless the idea began to have its merits. He tried not to think about it. Mistral laughed softly as she discovered his involuntary response to her advances. Brennan watched them curiously. The sex drive of humans was an insoluble mystery to gorons.

Then suddenly Lath's head poked out from under the deck and he saw the lights of Samarita close by. His eyes widened with terror. He began to scream and thrash, confined between the deck and the belt.

Trevithick hauled him out. "Brennan, for Pete's sake get his bloody violin from the foredeck, will you? Maybe that'll calm him. Lath, keep your head down!"

It worked. With the violin in his lap and his fingers brushing the strings, the trembling ceased. "Bryn Trevithick. I remember you."

"Yes. We're going downLady together. Mistral too, and Brennan."

His eyes were wide and glittering as he stared across Lady at Samarita. "They're devils, Trevithick. Murderous devils! But you knew that. Oh, my bright eyes." Suddenly he seemed to collapse. He buried his face in his hands and began to weep.

"I guess Security are after him," said Mistral. "Nothing else'd scare him like this."

"But why? He's harmless. I can't see him being a danger to Security."

"Well, something's happened. Maybe he saw something he shouldn't have. You remember what he was saying about Marik."

Trevithick turned to Lath. "Who are after you?" he asked, slowly and distinctly.

"I never saw anything!" he wailed into his hands. "I was drunk, I didn't know what was going on! I swear I didn't see anything. No shooting, nothing!" He seized Trevithick's wrist in a bony grip. "You believe me, don't you?"

"I believe you."

Mistral said, "Just don't play your violin, okay? That would be a dead give-away."

Half a standard hour later it was fully dark and they'd calmed Eagleman down. He lay on the afterdeck, quiet apart from the occasional racking sob. Brennan had retreated forward to sleep with the stoags. The barge was close by the east bank, moving at Lady's natural rate, about one-tenth of a kilometre per hour. By dawn they'd be past the centre of Samarita, although still in full view of Ladyside apartments, some of which were the homes of Security people.

Mistral and Trevithick lay down, side by side. "We haven't lost much time, anyway," she said. "Brennan wouldn't have worked the stoags in the dark."

"It's being in full view of Samarita that bothers me. We'd have made it past the town if the belt hadn't broken. And having to wait for a member of Clan Boatbuilder just to sew up a belt? That's taking the goron philosophy a bit far, isn't it? Doesn't Brennan worry about losing time on the voyage?"

She chuckled softly and took his hand. "You'll never understand gorons, will you? Never mind, my love."

Heavy clouds hung low the next morning, and Trevithick was awakened by rain on his face. And there was something missing; he felt incomplete within himself. Then he realised; the aeolus meadows were all black, all motionless with no sunlight to activate them. What little breeze there was, blew from the east. There were no gorons out there, no alien pheromones to nudge his emotions this way and that.

But the message had reached the shore on the east wind, and shortly after dawn three members of Clan Boatbuilder were sitting on deck, working at the belt with tapering wooden fids and strong brown twine. In less than an hour the belt was positioned over the top roller once more and they were rowing ashore. Trevithick could hardly see the join.

Brennan went forward to roust the stoags out of their slumber. Mistral was lying on her stomach on the afterdeck, peering over the gunwale. Eagleman was still asleep and Mistral wondered if they should leave him that way.

"Suppose he wakes up screaming?" Trevithick said. "Suppose he starts prancing around the barge waving his arms the way he does? They'll see him from Samarita, and they'll send people out to investigate. Then they'll find us. No, let's wake him gently, now. I'll get ready to clap my hand over his mouth."

Despite their precautions Eagleman, thrashing like a hooked fish, slipped from their grasp. "They've got me!" he yelled into the still morning air. "Oh, my bright eyes, the bastards have got me!"

Between them, they wrestled him to the deck. Trevithick peered over the gunwale. A few gorons strolled along Ladybank. A few humans jogged, scorning the facilities in Samarita. Nobody was looking their way. But apartment blocks rose behind the trail and they could easily be seen from the upper windows, or from the balconies on Dome Four further away.

"Let's get him below," he said.

Eagleman fought them all the way, eyes rolling, mouth twisted with fear; but at least he was quiet about it. They got him onto the belt and held him there. Mistral reminded him of the perils.

"You gotta crawl, Lath. Crawl. Like a baby. Otherwise the back roller will get you." The fearful glance he shot over his shoulder indicated he'd understood her so far. "And you gotta keep quiet. Just crawl and keep your mouth shut, that's all."

They felt the familiar lurch as the stoags climbed, then the belt began to roll away beneath them. Lath crawled between Mistral and Trevithick. They were both ready to grab him if he began to lose ground. It was quite difficult for him because the unusual length of his thighs meant his rump kept hitting the underside of the platform. But he seemed to understand what was expected of him, and an hour later they'd passed the last of the Samaritan residences and were in the clear. Thankfully, they joined Brennan on the afterdeck.

Things had changed since they'd been below. The sun was breaking through the clouds, the aeolus fields were flexing their leaves and, more ominously, a flight of three vespas had positioned themselves off the starboard beam.

"All those broken pots," said Brennan. "They can smell the nectar."

Eagleman eyed the vespas fearfully. "Bastards. Bastards."

"Maybe we should throw the junk overboard and wash the platform off," Trevithick suggested.

"We're not at sea," Mistral said tersely. "We can't throw broken pots onto Lady. And where do we get the water to wash the deck?"

Annoyed, he snapped back, "You're the one who knows this world. Maybe you should have thought of scrubbing the platform while it was raining earlier on."

"In full view of Samarita? Do me a favour."

"All right, there are plenty of little creeks. We can pull ashore at the next one, throw the debris onto the bank and scrub off there."

While Mistral was looking for an error in this suggestion, Brennan found one. "We pull into the bank only at night, so the stoags can browse."

The vespas broke formation and began to buzz them hungrily. The sun was warming up the spilled nectar and the air was heavy with the scent. "Is that a religious objection?" Trevithick asked. He was getting pretty tired of obstructive goron customs.

"It is our duty to carry our cargo swiftly to its destination. That is what I have always done." Brennan sat on the gunwale, eyeing him stolidly.

"Brennan's the captain," Mistral pointed out unnecessarily. "He's in charge."

He ignored her. "These are special circumstances," he said, trying to keep calm. "We must adapt to them. What happens if we're attacked?"

"We may die, but others will come," answered Brennan philosophically. "Already news of our plight is being carried on the winds of the aeolus. We will be replaced before any more harm comes to the cargo."

Trevithick had to appeal to Mistral. "I can't talk to this guy. You try."

Her lower lip was thrust forward like a sulky child's. She opened her mouth to say something stupid to him, then thought better of it and addressed Brennan instead. "You gotta defend the barge."

His mouth opened in an O of surprise. He'd been so wrapped up in philosophical negativism that he'd lost sight of his alternatives. "Defend the barge," he repeated wonderingly. "Yes, it's my duty to defend the barge." He began to rummage about in a locker under the deck.

The vespas buzzed them again. One flew slowly through the triangle formed by the belt, head tilted as it examined the syrupy wreckage on the platform. It looked the size of a small helicopter. The other two hovered above the gunwale, weighing up the defences. The noise of their wings was like a battery of bandsaws, hurtful to the ears. One of them placed a tentative claw on the gunwale.

"We don't stand a chance!" came a shrill yell. It was Eagleman, pressed against the after rail. They'd forgotten about him.

Trevithick looked around for some kind of weapon. There was nothing; the afterdeck was empty of everything except themselves. The bank was too far away for a jump. Brennan backed out of the tiny locker clutching a hempen bag. In the emergency he'd forgotten his human lessons and his face was screwed up in a goron expression, alien and disturbing.

As Trevithick was trying to edge around the belt to reach the coracle on the foredeck, Mistral grabbed his arm and pulled him back to the port gunwale. "It's okay," she said. "Brennan's setting out the crabs."

"Crabs?"

"Vespas won't go near crabs. They're a parasite. They cling on and pry their way in and eat the vespas alive."

A commendable lifestyle. So this was what Tresco had been doing when they'd watched him from the ledge in Ladycanyon: placing crabs around his barge. Brennan pulled open the drawstring and upended the bag. A dozen or more black creatures fell to the deck, each about the size of a tarantula. They lay there, some with their legs curled around themselves, some with their legs in the air. They looked suspiciously dead.

"Bugger it!" whispered Mistral.

Brennan poked one of the crabs with a wary forefinger. It didn't move. The three vespas, which had been backing off, closed in again. One after another they perched on the starboard gunwale. Their wings stilled and suddenly all was quiet except for an occasional scrabbling from their claws. The two groups eyed each other across the width of the afterdeck.

"What now?" Trevithick murmured to Mistral.

He found out almost immediately. A vespa hopped to the deck, reared up and thrust its abdomen forward between its legs. Awkwardly it began to advance toward them, foreclaws snapping like huge hooked scissors. Brennan made a quick decision, jumped over the side and committed himself to Lady. It was an option the humans didn't have. The other two vespas hopped to the deck. It was three against three.

Eagleman screamed and jumped overboard. That left two humans.

"Just piss off and leave us alone!" Mistral shouted at the vespas. She sounded furious rather than frightened.

And amazingly, the creatures hesitated.

"Go on, you heard what I said! Get off this boat!"

Each vespa swivelled its head toward Trevithick. It seemed Mistral had assured her own immunity. He prepared to follow Eagleman and take his chances with Lady. Or would the vespas come after him? Probably not; they had other priorities. Nothing against humans personally; they just wanted to neutralise them so they could feast on the nectar in peace.

The middle vespa advanced, foreclaws clicking and reaching for Trevithick, stinger slipping in and out of the tip of its abdomen. He began to hoist himself onto the gunwale, ready to drop over the side. Unfortunately he was so busy watching the stinger that he slipped and fell back to the deck, striking his head on something hard. There was a bright flash in his brain, then everything went foggy for a moment. He felt something grab him. Possibly he screamed.

He could only have been unconscious for a couple of seconds, because he heard Mistral shouting almost immediately.

"Get away from him, you bastards!"

The fog lifted from his mind. Mistral was crouching over him, facing the vespas. They'd withdrawn their abdomens to a less hostile position and seemed to have lost the urge to kill. Trevithick got the oddest impression they thought the next move was Mistral's. They watched her attentively, like troops awaiting instructions.

"Just go away," she whispered.

The bandsaw buzz commenced and their wings became blurs of motion. They lifted off, veered away and took up station off the starboard beam and about level with the top roller. They were no longer a threat. If anything, they were guarding the barge. This became apparent almost immediately as a big squito drifted toward the stern. One of the vespas peeled off, chased the flimsy creature away, then resumed station.

"What did you do?" Trevithick asked Mistral, shakily.

"I . . . I don't know, really. But I know how I did it. It was like . . . you remember, up on the canyon trail?"

"Well . . . Thanks a lot, Mistral. You saved my life."

She flushed and stared at the deck. Suddenly they remembered Eagleman and leaned over the gunwale. He lay face up on Lady with closed eyes, as though asleep in bed. Trevithick grabbed one hand, Mistral took the other and together they hauled him on deck. He weighed very little. Slime oozed from his clothing.

"Will he be okay?" Trevithick asked.

"I guess so. He wasn't in there long. Sometimes Ladyjuice wears off straight away. Might take longer with Lath. He isn't all that strong."

They were too late for Brennan, though. He lay a couple of meters astern. Lady had covered him with a thin film of herself, and already signs of the thicker cocoon were developing around him.

"Best leave him," said Mistral. "It wouldn't be right to pull him out now. He'll be okay. He'll show up at Ladysend some time."

In a hundred days or so. It was a strange mating that the little goron was committed to. Trevithick felt sad. He should have tried to understand him better. He'd been a pleasant shipboard companion within his limitations, and he'd always forgiven Trevithick's ignorance of goron customs. And now . . .

"What are we going to do?" he asked. "Do we get hold of another bargee or what?"

"There aren't any spare bargees, not here. They all have their own barges, see?" They could see one to the south, just coming into sight around a bend. The stoags plodded along at the end of the towrope and the bargee relaxed on the foredeck with his back against an upturned coracle. By now Trevithick knew enough of goron thinking to guess what would happen if they asked him for help. He would tell them, regretfully, that his duty was to guide his empty barge up to Ladysmouth, load it with jars of nectar, and pilot it downLady for unloading, and so on until he died. He told Mistral this.

She smiled briefly, the first smile he'd seen for some time. "Yeah, and if you asked what would happen to the barge if he died unexpectedly, he'd say it wouldn't matter, Lady would take it down to Ladysend in her own good time. And a new bargee would get it then."

"They have spare bargees at Ladysend?"

"Sure they do. Young gorons from Bridget Booker's school. That's how bargees get started. They take over abandoned barges when they arrive at Ladysend."

"So what shall we do now? We can't drift all the way down."

"I'm gonna get the stoags working."

"Can you do that?"

"Well, I can get Wilfred working, and the others might follow." The smile of a moment ago was gone. Her tone was impatient, as though he was a nuisance on the boat. He wondered what was troubling her this time. It wasn't simple reaction from the narrow escape; there was something else, dating back to when they'd emerged from the canyon. And it wasn't just Susanna; she seemed to have come to terms with that particular problem better than he had. Had he offended her? Probably, but she usually recovered from such episodes quickly enough. It was almost a relief when she disappeared from view on the foredeck and he heard her shouting ill-temperedly at the stoags.

Then Eagleman started screaming.

He'd recovered consciousness and crawled across the deck. A trail of slime marked his route. He was lying face down, his chest propped on the starboard gunwale, staring at Lady beneath him. He continued to scream, a high-pitched almost-animal note of terror. Trevithick crossed the deck in three steps and dropped to his knees beside him. Eagleman's right arm hung down, pointing.

Just below the surface of Lady, a human face stared up at them.

CHAPTER 25

I T HAD STARTED OFF BADLY, but over the course of a few days Bridget had brought matters under control. The initial response to news of the Organization's departure had worn off and she'd been able to sit down with Gaston to discuss the educational needs of the students in a society free from humans. The breakthrough came when Gaston admitted that math was not a human invention, but had universal applications. They decided to retain math in the curriculum.

Morgan's attitude had softened too. Bridget had persuaded him that the old tradition of allowing babies to make their own way ashore did not apply in present-day circumstances, with the pools of decay making their journey unusually perilous. A shamefaced team of gorons repaired the coracles and Clan Birthcare resumed its duties on the surface of Lady ten days after the strike. If strike was the right word. Bridget relaxed.

Then came the news that the Organisation was staying, after all.

Amazed and delighted, she'd passed on the news to Gaston and Morgan. They were too startled to react with any learned facial expression, and departed in silence to inform the local clans. Suddenly nervous, she'd spent most of the day in her apartment, walking from one window to the other, observing the workaday scene. Everything had looked almost suspiciously normal. During the late afternoon she'd checked on the schoolrooms to find classes going on as usual, although nobody was speaking the human language any more. She mentioned this to Gaston. If there was to be a human presence on Goronwy after all, they'd need the language, wouldn't they? Gaston received her arguments in silence and with a total lack of expression.

She'd walked upLady in time to meet the birthcare team carefully stacking their coracles. They'd had a good day. There were no births, but there would be one or two soon. There were no malformed foetuses in sight, and very few normal ones.

She'd have been pleased but for one thing. Like Gaston, Morgan's face showed no expression whatever.

It was as though they'd forgotten all the human facial expressions she'd taught them so carefully. Not only that, but they were restricting the use of human speech to the barest essentials. The students acted the same way. Suddenly she had no idea what they were thinking. She felt isolated.

Which she was, of course. But she'd never felt like that before . . .

On the same night that found Trevithick and Mistral stranded in full view of Samarita, Bridget awakened with a start. Was it morning already? It was certainly bright enough. She was suddenly afraid; there was something wrong here. The light flickered strangely, and it shone on the dimmed south window only.

The school was on fire!

She undimmed the window. The flames carried a fountain of sparks into the night sky, brightening the faces of a crowd of gorons standing at a safe distance. Each face wore a peculiarly alien expression. They scared her. She backed away from the window, pulled on her uniform and ran down the steps. The heat from the flames was hot on her face.

There was little that could be done. The school, on which she'd lavished so much love and care was already consumed. The timber framing stood but the thin walls had gone. She could see items of tiny furniture blazing inside. Screens were popping, terminals subsiding in a mess of molten matter. Now the framing itself began to collapse, sparks exploding. It was all ruined, all her work.

"You stupid little men!" she shouted. "Why did you do it?" She saw Gaston watching impassively, ran to him and seized his shoulders, shaking him. "Why did you do it?" she shouted again.

"Perhaps it was an accident," he said. "You teach us to consider the options."

"Well . . . Was it accident?"

"No. It is my doing. I have decided that we will go our own way," he said astonishingly.

"You've decided? How can you decide anything?"

"I'm a goron. This is my world. Let me go, Bridget. You're hurting me."

She dropped her hands. The roof ridge collapsed into the main body of the fire. Burning embers flew. They backed away. Belatedly, Bridget asked, "Is everyone all right?"

"Nobody is hurt." He watched the flames. "Only the school. And we won't need that any more. The nursery is unharmed. So is your dwelling. So there is no loss. Why are you crying, Bridget?"

She took his hand. It felt cold and tiny. "You'd better come up to my apartment, Gaston. We have some talking to do." She felt empty and Gaston felt alien. Everything around her looked alien; the leafy goron huts, the incongruous rectangular nursery, the strange little faces made rosy by firelight. She was very frightened. She ran back up the steps, dragging Gaston behind, and slammed the door behind her, shutting out Goronwy and everything that was weird.

Except she couldn't shut out Gaston. She needed a link with the world outside, otherwise she'd dim the windows, go to bed and never get up again. She pushed Gaston into a chair and sat down opposite, shutting her eyes and trying to sort her thoughts out. She was the representative of a large and powerful organisation. An act of vandalism had taken place within her area of responsibility. She must deal with it. That was all. After a couple of minutes rationalisation she was able to look at Gaston. He still sat there, tiny and inoffensive, dwarfed by the human scale of his surroundings. What had she been frightened of?

"All right, Gaston. Do I take it you're responsible for burning down the school?"

"In the human sense, I am responsible."

She struggled to understand. In over twenty years on Goronwy she'd never come across a situation like this. It was ... It was a human situation, an act of humanlike vandalism. It was not something she'd have expected from the gorons. In fact it was the kind of thing she'd come to Ladysend to get away from. Humans could be vicious and untrustworthy and barbaric, but not gorons.

Not until now.

"Gaston, my people are staying. Don't you understand that?"

He shook his head carefully, as though remembering the gesture. "Your own code prevents you from imposing your will on us. We asked you for help in curing Lady of her sickness, and you've failed. There's no reason for you to stay except your own love of empire. We want you to leave as soon as possible and leave us to handle our grief with dignity."

The pompous little man! "I'll stay for your own good. You can't speak for all gorons."

"Yes, I can."

"How can you? Gorons don't have leaders. Your society is based entirely on tradition."

He regarded her very directly, and his eyes had somehow changed. She felt a little thrill of dread. "I am a leader, Bridget. You taught me long and well. You put me in charge of the students, and you put me in charge of two other teachers. For a long time now I've been forced to make decisions on behalf of other gorons. I'm probably the only goron who has ever done that. Now I've become accustomed to leading. I can see how it can be used for the common good. So I burned down the school. It's my first act as leader of the goron race."

"Oh, my God."

"Your pheromones tell me the notion of a goron leader horrifies you. Why is that? Human leaders don't horrify you."

She had to speak carefully. "Human leaders have a lot of training and experience. And they still make mistakes. You're just a teacher."

"I will learn as I go along. My first duty as leader will be to tell the Samaritan Organisation to go home, on behalf of all gorons. And under universal law you will be compelled to obey me. That's right, isn't it?"

She went to bed, but she didn't sleep. She lay on her back until daybreak, wondering what to do. She couldn't call Samarita for advice, not until she was sure the situation was completely out of control. She'd only spoken to Gaston so far. She couldn't let Samarita think she'd been panicked by a single misguided little goron. It was her responsibility to sort things out. She was in charge.

But was she in charge?

Of course she was! Gaston had no right to set himself up as some kind of ruler. Not that she objected to the idea of goron leaders, but at least they should be democratically elected. Gaston couldn't announce that he was in charge of the whole planet, just like that. It was ridiculous, almost laughable. And that's just what they'd do in Samarita if she went bleating to them for advice; laugh.

Perhaps the most shocking aspect of the whole affair had been a sudden thought she'd had, just before dawn. She'd thought: Everything would be all right if Gaston were dead.

She was ashamed of the thought. It seemed to flit around in the darker part of her mind like an evil bat seeking somewhere to settle. She kept pushing it aside, but it kept fluttering back. Then morning came, and she showered and dressed, and looked south toward the sparkling sea where young gorons played, and the thought finally shuffled off and hid, disappointed.

She descended the steps. The air smelled fresh and clean. A few wisps of smoke arose from the blackened wreckage of the school, but even that failed to dampen her resolve to take command. There was rebuilding to be done. She called a nearby goron.

"Magnus! We need a temporary school. Something about the size of the old one, but built like one of your dwellings. Can you discuss it with suitable clan members, please?"

"I will talk to Gaston first."

She held herself in check. It was a beautiful morning and she was not going to allow this conversation to blow out of proportion. "There's no need to talk to Gaston."

The little man stared at her. "But Gaston burned down the old school for a purpose. If we build a new school it defeats that purpose."

"Exactly. I'm glad you understand me."

He wandered away with a curious gait, almost staggering, and disappeared behind a dwelling. The first stage was accomplished. Perhaps now she should talk to Gaston and find if the new morning had brought some commonsense to his attitude.

She found Gaston in a group of gorons on the upLady trail. A discussion was in progress. No, she corrected herself in surprise. A heated discussion. She'd never heard gorons arguing before. They were squealing animatedly in their own tongue.

"What's going on?" she asked Gaston.

"Morgan is refusing to obey my orders," he said, clearly aggrieved. "How can I be leader if he will not obey me?"

Morgan said sullenly, "He says there is no work for Clan Birthcare today."

"Of course there's work for Clan Birthcare! You told me only yesterday there were foetuses ripening. Now get on your way, Morgan, and let's hear no more of this. Gaston, a word please."

"Don't go, Morgan," said Gaston. "I am our new leader. I am accustomed to making decisions."

"I make decisions too," objected Morgan. "Bridget put me in charge of this team and it's my job to lead them."

"There are degrees of leadership." To Bridget's horror, Gaston hit Morgan violently across the face. "Leadership is power," he informed the reeling little man. "Power will rid us of the humans. I have more power than you, Morgan, so I will do the better job. Obey me. Take your team home. We will restructure the Ladysend clans."

Morgan wiped the blood from his mouth and regarded Gaston without animosity. "You're right. You will be the best one to deal with the humans. You have the leadership attitude."

The group began to walk back toward Ladysend, talking excitedly in their own tongue and ignoring Bridget. She followed unhappily in their wake. There was no doubt in her mind now; things were out of control. And with ripe foetuses about to pop, they must have coracles out on Lady.

There was nothing else for it. She'd have to call for help.

"What!" exclaimed Ivor Sabin.

"I said they've burned the school down, and they refuse . . . they refuse to . . ." She couldn't finish. The image of Sabin disappeared in a haze of tears. Damn it! This was exactly the kind of weakness she'd intended to avoid. She stood and moved out of range of the video pickup.

Sabin's gaze was darting this way and that, trying to locate her. "What's going on? Are you in any kind of danger, Bridget? Sit where I can see you, for God's sake!"

She wiped her eyes and sat down. "I don't think they'd hurt me," she managed to say, "but they're different. They're not like gorons any more. Gaston's taken charge of them."

"Taken charge? A goron? That's a first. I'd need to see it for myself. Okay, so pull yourself together and tell me exactly what's happened."

She described the events since yesterday and Sabin listened without comment, expressionlessly, until she came to the dispute between Gaston and Morgan.

"So there's nobody out there on Lady?" he said, clearly alarmed. "We can't have that. You must get them back to work, Bridget. Have you told Security about this?"

"T-tillini? No, I thought I'd better tell you first, you being in Ecology, and human. I needed to talk to a human, Ivor. I guess I should have spoken to Janine Starseeker, since she's in charge of Ecology now. But she's so . . . So . . ."

"Ineffective. Yes. Well, you're going to have to throw your weight about, Bridget. I know how you feel about those little guys, but this has gone far enough. My advice to you is to immobilise Gaston and get Morgan and Clan Birthcare back on the job. Good God, there could be babies drowning out there right now!"

"Immobilise Gaston? I don't think I can do that. How can I immobilise him?"

Impatience showed on Sabin's face. "You just grab the little bastard and put a rope around him, and throw him in some corner where he can't do any harm! It's simple enough. He's only a meter tall, for God's sake. Are you scared of the guy or something?"

"I wouldn't want to hurt him. How long would he have to stay tied up?"

"Until he comes to his senses, obviously." Sabin paused, thinking. "Listen, Bridget, I don't want you to take this the wrong way. But perhaps you're not the right person to deal with Gaston. These gorons can be slippery little devils when they want to be. Maybe we should send someone down there to help you out. In a low-key way. It sounds like a sensitive situation, and we've already got one of those here in Samarita. It took a lot of persuading to get HQ to continue funding, and something like this could really bugger us if it got about. So I'll talk to Tillini and Janine, and we'll have a couple of experts down there to help out in a few hours. And I'll talk to Brassworthy about your budget. We can't afford to skimp on the work at Ladysend. How's that?" He smiled reassuringly.

She felt such a rush of relief that she almost started crying again. "Th-thank you, Ivor. Oh, what a pity Bryn Trevithick isn't still with the Organisation! He'd be the man for this job."

A faint frown crossed Sabin's brow. "I'm afraid we won't be seeing any more of Doctor Trevithick. Hadn't you heard? He was involved in a boating accident with Mistral Greene up at Ladysmouth. Both of them are missing."

Shocked, she disconnected. Bryn and Mistral dead? She'd only met Bryn Trevithick briefly, but she'd formed a high opinion of him. He'd struck her as competent, sensible and understanding. And as for Mistral: she'd visited Ladysend on several occasions; a delightful girl, down-to-earth and lively, and great with the gorons.

Why did it have to happen to the good humans? There were few enough of them about.

CHAPTER 26

I T WAS LIKE LOOKING THROUGH RIPPLED GLASS. There was a face a few centimetres below the surface, a human face—but it could not be seen clearly enough for identification. Trevithick knew it was human only because of its size and the length of the body. It lay on its back, calm, embalmed, and terrifying. Lath continued to scream, a thin high sound, almost a whistle, fraying Trevithick's nerves.

"Will you shut up!"

He did, instantly, as though he'd been waiting for instructions all this time. Mistral arrived to see what the noise was about. She knelt beside Trevithick.

"Oh, Bryn. Who is it?"

"I can't tell. It looks like a man; it's quite tall. Seems to be wearing Organisation uniform." They stared into Lady, willing her to clear and reveal her secret. "We'll have to get him aboard."

"How?"

"Well, I don't know," he said irritably. This macabre situation, coming on top of the battle with the vespas, was too much for him. "We can't leave him for Lady to eat."

"Usually she don't eat humans. When she finds out what they are she spits them out again."

"You mean he'll come out onto the surface?" It made sense. Lady would prefer genes compatible with her own.

"He's on the way up now."

"How do you know?"

"Well, we've been stuck here for hours, see? He must have been dumped in Lady before we arrived, or we'd have seen it happen. She'd take him down right away. Then she'd find she didn't want him. So now he's coming up."

"Dead, I suppose." He remembered his own experience: the anaesthetic fluids and the subsequent recovery. Could Lady place humans into a kind of suspended animation?

"'Course he's dead. Anyone'd be dead if they hadn't breathed all night."

"All the same, we'd better cut him out of there and get him aboard."

"You're not gonna cut Lady!" She was angry.

"We can't wait here forever."

"You'll have to wait till Lady gives him up proper." She glanced up. The vespas still hovered out there. One of them had moved a little closer. Could Mistral order them to attack? It was a scary thought. Earlier she'd commanded them to back off. Given the unpleasant temper of the brutes, it was probably easier to make them attack than not attack. Trevithick didn't want to find out.

"Right, we wait. How long will it take?"

"How should I know?"

"Look, what the hell's got into you this time?" he demanded.

She jumped to her feet. He did the same, suspecting she might intend to kick him in the backside as he knelt there. She stared up at him, face flushed and blotchy, the edges of the scar angry behind her hair. She wore a faded blue dress she'd pulled out of her bag that morning, and she needed a shower. They all did, Eagleman most of all. Her mouth opened and shut, then unexpectedly her face crumpled. Her hands flew up and covered her eyes. "Leave me alone," she muttered unsteadily.

"Not until you tell me what's the matter."

She removed her hands. Her eyes shone with tears and her lips trembled. He felt like a rat. "Something's wrong," she said. "That's what's the matter."

"What, exactly?"

"Dunno. I can feel it. Two days now. People are real unhappy."

"What people?"

She moved away from him and slowly turned in a full circle, breathing deeply. She winced. "I think it's at Ladysend."

"What is?"

"Told you before, I can't read minds. But there's something real wrong down there." Trevithick had been affected too; he'd been feeling depressed for a couple of days, and not just because he was on the run. He put his arms around her and held her close. After a moment, she hugged him back. "Sorry," she muttered. "Maybe there's times it's best not to feel everything."

"I hope Bridget's all right."

"She'll be okay. It's gorons that feel all pissed off."

"There's a dead man in Lady." Eagleman interrupted them. Now he was sprawled against the stern gunwale, legs splayed across the deck. He regarded them cunningly.

"Don't worry about it," Trevithick told him.

"I know something you don't." His expression was that of a child bursting to reveal a secret. "You want to know who that dead man is?"

"Do you know?"

"Sure I know. I'll tell you on one con . . . condition."

"What's that?"

"Don't let them get me." His eyes were wide.

"We won't let them get you, Lath," said Mistral.

"Then . . ." He hugged his secret a moment longer. "It's Marik Darwin," he said.

Trevithick strode to the rail and stared down at the body. Marik Darwin. The size was about right. He'd last seen him after the meeting of Clan Action, running scared following the ill-fated attempt to destroy Lady. And his words: there are places, you know, outside Samarita, where a guy can stay out of sight.

Well, Marik Darwin may have found his place, but they'd hunted him down just the same. It wasn't easy, hiding on Goronwy.

"Is it Marik?" asked Mistral. "I don't wanna look again."

"I think so."

"Oh, shit. That meeting. Bryn . . . Is this my fault?"

"He was playing a dangerous game. He must have thought the rewards were worth the risk. Anyway, he might have just fallen in."

"Oh, sure, right over this side of Lady?" She forced herself to regard the body, face screwed up in horror. "Look. See that? That's a laser burn, I bet."

Through the translucency of Lady, Trevithick could make out a dark slash across the chest of the gold uniform. Yes, it looked like a laser burn. Marik had been murdered, executed, however you wanted to put it.

He asked Lath, "How do you know who it is?"

In a sane voice, eyes clear and intelligent, the thin man said, "I was nearby when they did it." Then his face changed subtly and he'd regressed again. He picked up his violin, and when Mistral took it away from him he wept tears of anger and frustration.

The ensuing hours were not happy ones. Eagleman kept calling for his violin but they couldn't chance giving it to him because they were within earshot of the opposite bank. Mistral and Trevithick were at loggerheads most of the time; it was one thing to blame bad pheromones, but quite another to resist them.

Mistral kept repeating her theme, with some justification. "Why the hell do you want to sit around here in full view of Samarita? It's asking for trouble. Leave Marik be and let's get rolling, huh? I never liked the bugger anyway. And what we gonna do with him when we get him on deck? Let him rot in the sun? Answer me that, Bryn. What we gonna do with him?"

Truth was, Trevithick didn't know. "It's not right to just leave him. He's a human being."

"He was a human being. Now he's a lump of meat, for God's sake! Ask a goron about dead bodies, why don't you? They'll put you straight. No, before we sit here one moment longer, I wanna know exactly what you're gonna do with him. 'Cos if you're thinking of taking him back to Samarita for a decent burial—" here she mimicked his accents insultingly "—you can count me out. So what's it to be?"

"We can't leave him there," he said stubbornly. Of course the sensible thing would be to leave him. Of course it wasn't safe to sit around just outside Samarita, inviting investigation. But he was not about to give in to Mistral. "We'll drop him off at the next inn."

"And give the gorons the problem of explaining how he got there? No way!"

"Well, whatever. The only way you'll get me to abandon Marik is to have one of your vespas attack me."

And this was unanswerable too. After all, Mistral had been illogical enough in the past. Why shouldn't Trevithick have his turn? The fact that they were behaving like a couple of kids didn't escape him.

The ensuing silence lasted several hours. They sulked at either end of the barge; Trevithick on the afterdeck with Eagleman for company, Mistral on the foredeck with the stoags. As the sun dropped toward the flat horizon he heard her shout, "Look at that, over the domes! I told you so! Now you gone and buggered us proper!"

A copter had risen above Samarita and was heading their way. They watched helplessly as it flitted toward them, a big red star in the reflected sunlight. He remained sitting beside Eagleman at the port gunwale. There was no point in panic, no point in anything but resignation.

Then the copter began to behave oddly. It turned half right shortly before it reached them and, still some two hundred meters above ground level, began to follow the curve of Lady on a southerly course. It receded into the distance. Surely they'd been seen? Surely the sight of three humans on a goron barge was interesting enough to warrant further investigation?

The hum of the copter had died away, but now Trevithick heard it again. A crimson reflection glowed downstream, although at a much lower altitude, and soon the copter swept back upLady. This time there was no doubt. They were the target.

Trevithick swung his way around the belt and joined Mistral on the foredeck. He felt sick with apprehension. The copter, skimming Lady, headed directly toward them.

Mistral said dully. "It's that Susanna."

His spirits rose instantly. Of course it was Susanna. She'd headed downLady at high altitude to give the impression she was making for Ladysend, then sneaked back below the aerial monitors. The copter hovered over the bank nearby, then touched down lightly.

"I'll take the coracle," he said. "Coming?"

"Nope."

He tipped the coracle over the side, and five minutes later he was hugging the beautiful woman under the copter's helix. She felt wonderful; clean and fresh and bouncy; not so slim as Mistral, but then he'd always liked his women well constructed.

Eventually they separated and she said, "Okay, so tell me. Why have you two been sitting out here in the sun all day instead of getting the hell away from Samarita like any sensible fugitives would do?"

"Were we that obvious?"

"From roughly half the dome balconies. Luckily Samaritans aren't the least bit interested in gorons, basically, so what's one stranded barge more or less? Only I knew better, you see, and thought to zoom a window. What's over the starboard side that's so interesting?"

"We think it's Marik Darwin's body."

She drew a quick breath. "Is it, now? I guess he was surplus to their requirements." She regarded him thoughtfully. "All the same, I'd have got bored with looking at his body after about ten seconds, more or less. What kept you all day? Sheer ghoulishness?"

Sheepishly, he explained his ethical dilemma.

"Oh, what a noble fellow you are, to be sure. Didn't Mistral put you straight?"

Even more sheepishly he admitted that yes, she had, but he'd outvoted her.

"I can just imagine her reaction to that. You must have had quite a day." She was grinning broadly. "Something of a setback to your

278

budding relationship, eh? Well, your troubles are over now. You can get rolling in the full knowledge that Marik is in good hands. Mine, that is. I will ensure that his remains are respectfully dealt with, as you would wish."

"For Christ's sake, Susanna, it wasn't funny. Have you ever seen a human body in Lady?"

She stopped smiling. "Yes. Yours. And no, it isn't funny. Sorry." She glanced over at the barge, where Mistral had joined Eagleman on the afterdeck. "I notice you have a thin male passenger."

He related events since he'd last seen her. She gazed at him so attentively with wide blue eyes that occasionally he lost the thread. From time to time she chuckled, nodding as he described the arrival of Lath.

"Poor guy. You remember you asked me to check his medical records? Well, there's no mention of a lobotomy, if that's what it was."

"Nothing at all?"

"Zilch. Just the usual check-ups until he and his father left the Organisation. Then the records end. They would, of course. As I told you, we don't treat exiles."

"So that means . . ."

"Precisely, Dr. Watson. At some time after his exile, he was dragged kicking and screaming back into the domes and illegal surgery was performed."

"My God. Who by?"

"Who knows? Medical Services is big. Staff come and go. Bribery and corruption are everywhere. Face it, Bryn, it's a dead end. All we know is, surgery was performed. We can guess why. Somebody was scared that Paul Eagleman may have passed useful data on to his son."

"Whatever it was, he can't tell us now."

They thought about it for a while, then Susanna asked with studied casualness, "And how is the delectable Mistral?"

"We've both been kind of irrational. Do you have some pills?"

"Sure. I'm not surprised you've been getting bad pheromones. Things have been happening down south. You're out of touch."

"Fill me in."

"Okay. First of all I should tell you Security swallowed the notion of your tragic drowning in the lake. Hook, line and sinker. I rather think the lower orders just needed an excuse to stop combing the countryside; it can get boring quite quickly, grappling with bushtrap. What Tillini thinks, I don't know. Probably biding his time. Anyway, things are happening at Ladysend and I thought I'd better warn you before you got there."

"What's happening?"

"Exciting stuff, like fear, loathing, arson and rebellion."

"Rebellion? Who rebelled?" He had a mental picture of Bridget Booker marching on Samarita at the head of a column of juvenile gorons.

"Perhaps rebellion is a bit strong, but it sounded good. And there's plenty of fear and loathing. Still is." She went on to relate the latest news. "You know, we talk a lot about non-interference, but there's one place where we impose ourselves mightily on goron culture. In fact we rule them. And that's at Ladysend."

"I wouldn't say we rule them. I don't see Bridget Booker ruling anyone."

"She's in charge of birthcare and teaching. That covers the most impressionable years of goron life. She uses guidelines from Samarita. The gorons have no option but to work under her direction. That's what I call ruling. Sure, she does it for their own good. But the gorons have learned enough of human history to know that's what empire-builders always say."

For a moment they stood in silence, busy with their thoughts. Trevithick held Susanna's hand lightly; now she gave his hand a small squeeze. She glanced at the barge, not for the first time. Suddenly she seemed uncertain; unusual for her. "It'll be dark in ten minutes," she said.

He felt a pulse beating in his throat. "Yes. Thanks for the warning. I guess I should be getting back to the barge."

"You know, I never do rotten things to people. That's how I've climbed to dizzy heights on the corporate ladder; that, and being bloody good at my job. I try to be Miss Nice Girl. It's not so hard when you're easy on the eye because people aren't so likely to try to needle you. They like to see you smiling. But now . . . Just for once in my life, I'm going to hurt someone. I hate for it to happen. But there's something I want badly, and if I don't take it now I may never get the chance again."

She indicated the copter's casualty compartment. "Remember that cosy little cubby-hole, Trevithick? You've slept in there before, and history is going to repeat itself. Not immediately, because actual sleep is toward the bottom of tonight's agenda. But in the fullness of time. Hop aboard. Just this once, we're both going to behave like heels."

Ten minutes later, they landed in an aeolus field several kilometres to the east and some distance from civilisation. They climbed through to the casualty compartment.

For Trevithick, a natural-born pessimist, it was all much easier than it should have been. By rights, everything should have gone wrong from that moment on, because he didn't deserve it. There was a bed in there, designed for a single casualty but more than adequate for love. It was quite dark, but not so dark that he couldn't see the beauty of Susanna's breasts as she pulled her white sweater over her head, or watch the expression of anguished joy on her face the first time they reached the pinnacle of lovemaking. There were other pinnacles; and some quiet hours of simple stroking and murmuring. There was laughter too, jokes shared and ribs tickled.

And a few kilometres outside the world of love a lonely girl sat on a barge, maybe looking their way, maybe not. At least there was no east wind; it would have been too cruel if their pheromones had reached her. Once Trevithick awakened and, about to reach for Susanna, found she was sitting up. It was first light and he saw her eyes glistening as she looked out of the window. He heard her whisper, "May God forgive me," which was odd because she'd never mentioned God before, except as a happy blasphemy. He took her in his arms and made love to her yet again. The Goronwy night was too short for sadness.

It was full daylight the next time he awakened. Susanna's face was close to his and her eyes were open. He thought how easy it would be, simply to take off right then and fly to some remote corner of Goronwy where there were no humans or gorons, and set down in a forest glade, and make love forever and to hell with everything else.

"But it wouldn't be right," she said when he mentioned it. "We're the good guys, remember?" As they touched down the bank near the barge, she took his hand casually. She spoke in a rush, uncharacteristically awkward, without looking at him. "Before you go I want you to know that just because I'm kind of smart and capable and I don't have scars on my face and, okay, so guys seem to like me—I want you to know that I love you just as much as anyone could. I may not need you as much as Mistral does, but I love you just as much. So somebody's going to get hurt one day, and I think it might be me. You're a lucky bastard, Trevithick, being loved the way you are. There's just too much love coming your way for you to return it all, but do your best, eh? Spread it among the ones who are worth it. 'Bye."

They brushed lips. Then he climbed into the coracle and slid over Lady to the barge where Mistral sat waiting.

CHAPTER 27

H E TOLD HER THEY'D PAID A QUICK VISIT to Ladysend to make sure there were no unpleasant surprises in store, but it didn't wash.

Justifiably, there was a period of sulky silence on the barge. He knew he deserved it—but how could he have resisted Susanna, whom he loved so deeply? Answer: he couldn't. He would betray the whole of Goronwy for her. So Mistral sat silently on the foredeck lamenting his perfidy, and he sat with Lath Eagleman on the afterdeck, lamenting the departure of Susanna. They were extremely vulnerable, in full view of the domes in clear morning sunlight. But there was nothing he could do until Mistral consented to get the stoags moving. If she could get them moving. Meanwhile Marik Darwin would soon be freed from Lady's clutches and open to the warmth of day. They had to leave, and soon.

"Stand fast!"

The greeting took him by surprise. He swung around to see a barge coming up astern. A goron stood in the bows. Tresco.

"You are delayed?" he asked, small face wrinkled in anxiety.

"We lost Brennan." Trevithick told him about the vespas' attack.

"So . . . Who is this thin human with you, and what happened to Mistral?"

"The thin man is Lath Eagleman." Here Lath uncoiled himself, stood and performed a comic bow. "And Mistral is on the foredeck."

Tresco craned his neck, trying to see around the stationary belt. "You don't need Brennan, with Mistral on board. I am sure she can control your stoags. Why doesn't she?" As his barge drew level he was able to see her. His face assumed a respectful expression. The accident of evolution that caused gorons to venerate all females could be irritating, thought Trevithick.

"You ask her," he said.

He heard Mistral shout, "Okay! Okay!" The barge lurched as she tried to arouse the stoags from their slumber. "You realize they haven't been fed since Ladysmouth," she yelled, as though it was his fault. "That's why they don't want to wake up!"

"There was a pile of bushtrap leaves on the foredeck when we started," he shouted back.

"Yes, well that was for the canyon, how long do you expect it to last? Stoags go ashore every night for a good browse, once a barge is out of the canyon. Instead you're the only one who's been ashore."

Clearly she intended to remind him of his night of joy at every opportunity. "Why don't we get out of sight of the domes," he suggested in reasonable tones, "and then pull in to the bank. The stoags can work for an hour or two until then, can't they?"

Tresco put in his bit. "We do not moor during the day." He'd stopped his stoags and lay alongside, eyeing them reprovingly. "It delays the following barges."

"The following barges can pass, surely?"

"One barge does not overtake another."

Trevithick did some quick thinking. "That was in the days of towropes. It would have been difficult then. But now you have belts and you can do whatever you like. It was a goron who told me what a wonderful invention the belts are."

"That is very true. But we must not allow the old ways to be swept aside by technological progress. We have many customs, and they all add up to the best way to serve Lady. Question one and you question them all, and in the end you will question the purpose of our existence."

"Let it go, Bryn!" shouted Mistral from the foredeck. "I'll get us moving. The stoags can go hungry for another day. And it won't do any harm, having Tresco keep us company."

With much shouting and swearing she got the stoags onto the

belt. They began to move. She swung her way back to the after-deck. Tears had washed clean rivulets down the dirt on her face and her green eyes were very bright. She wore a short, crumpled red dress. Trevithick knew it was her favourite and guessed she'd put it on for him.

"Nice to see you," he said awkwardly.

"I thought you wouldn't need Susanna any more," she muttered. "I guess I was wrong. I've got a lot to learn." She swallowed. "Please help me."

"I'm sorry," he said. What else could he say? The alibi had failed, the domes of Samarita were still in view and they depended on her.

In fact her affinity to the stoags was needed within ten minutes. A fight broke out between Wilfred and one of the original beasts. The barge shook, the belt flapped, Mistral went forward and suddenly a stoag appeared on the top roller, the whites of his eyes showing. He took a bite from behind, yelped with pain, over-balanced, and tumbled down the belt onto the afterdeck, knocking Eagleman into a heap.

"Easy there, boy!" Trevithick shouted, backing off as the animal thrashed about on his back. Six paws, four of them equipped with digging claws, could be a fearsome sight in a confined space. Soon the stoag quietened, rolled to his feet and stood trembling, head low. By this time the barge had stopped and the head of Wilfred appeared over the top roller, staring angrily down at his adversary. Then Mistral's face appeared. She had her arm around Wilfred's neck, trying to drag him back.

"Down, you bugger!" she yelled, smacking Wilfred on the nose with her spare hand.

Wilfred shook his head, and the savage look left his eyes. Almost immediately the stoag on the afterdeck stopped trembling, yawned, and lay down. Mistral slid down the belt. "Don't let him go to sleep, for God's sake! It took me forever to wake him up in the first place!" She drove her foot into the stoag's hairy flank. He heaved himself to his feet. "Up there, you!" she shouted, hauling his head around to face the belt, then getting behind and push-ing. "Lend a hand, you two!" she shouted at the men.

Between them they got the stoag up and over the belt. Mistral returned to the foredeck to organise things, and soon they were moving again. Tresco rafted the two barges together with heavy rope and stepped aboard their vessel.

"Mistral is a remarkable human," he informed Trevithick. "She has a knack with our animal species. My people have the greatest respect for her, second only to our respect for Lady."

Trevithick was saved the need to reply by three personnel copters rising above Samarita and buzzing toward them in formation. He grabbed Lath and got him below, meeting Mistral under the platform.

"They're not after us," he said quickly, before Mistral and Lath could work each other into a panic. "Too strong a force. Each of those copters holds at least ten people. They must be on their way to Ladysend to help Bridget out."

"Help Bridget out?" Mistral repeated. "What for?"

Trevithick passed on Susanna's latest news while they crawled on the belt. Within minutes the hum of copters had died into the distance and they reassembled on the afterdeck. Mistral asked Tresco if he knew anything about the Ladysend situation.

"You are my friends," he said. "I find this very difficult, being friends with two humans yet knowing my people are turning against humans as a species. The bad feeling started at Ladysend but it has now spread on the winds to Samarita. You may find unpleasantness at the Ladyside inns. I am sorry."

Trevithick said, "Those copters. That's rather a lot of help for Bridget. Does it mean there's more trouble?"

"I think so. You see," he said apologetically, "we older gorons are accustomed to living with humans and respecting your great knowledge. But our younger people, the ones at Ladysend . . . They act instinctively, you understand? They do not have the advantage of our years of experience and co-operation. And their instincts tell them it is wrong to kill embryos, even though the deformities may be threatening the species. In vain we tell them that malformed breeds malformed. In vain we predict futures where many gorons lack arms and legs and have to be cared for by the few remaining whole people. They simply say yes, they understand that, but nevertheless it is wrong to kill embryos. They say it was never done before the humans came—which is true. But malformed embryos hardly ever occurred in those days. I am glad my clan is not involved in such a dilemma."

"Are there any older gorons at Ladysend?" Trevithick asked.

"Less than a hundred, apart from transient members of other clans, but there are about four hundred students of educable age. Full grown," he added significantly. "We attain full size within three years of birth, remember."

The thought of four hundred young gorons, united against humans in that unanimous way that only gorons can unite, filled Trevithick with misgivings. Maybe it hadn't been such a good idea after all, making for Ladysend. It began to sound as though Bridget Booker was under siege. And there had been a warlike look about that flight of copters. The Project was treading very close to the line between protection and aggression.

As Tresco had predicted, they found scant hospitality at the Ladyside inns. Night after night they were received with veiled hostility, to the extent that Trevithick began to wonder if they should stand watches. Nectar was offered only grudgingly. They drank what was available, but by now Trevithick was reaching a condition close to starvation. He'd lost several kilograms, his stomach was flatter than it had been for years, he was suffering from attacks of dizziness, and only the thought of Bridget Booker's freezer kept him going. Mistral, on the other hand, seemed to thrive on nectar. Even Lath appeared to have no problems, which was fortunate because he could ill afford to lose weight.

"You just don't fit in here, my love," said Mistral one day, as Trevithick stumbled while boarding the barge and fell full-length on the afterdeck. She was concerned for his health, but comforted herself with the thought that they were within two days of Ladysend. Friendly relations between them had been resumed.

Meanwhile the appearance of Lady had changed. The air

smelled of fishy decay and the surface was pocked with little pools of yellowish fluid. Trevithick hoped they wouldn't need to crawl on the belt, with that stuff oozing through.

"Lady's just rotting away," said Mistral. "It's like gangrene spreading up her. Horrible."

"Her time is near," said Tresco heavily.

The next day they sighted coracles, the first since Samarita. Eight tiny craft sat motionless on Lady. Humans sat in them, looking much too big for their boats.

"It's bad," said Tresco. "Clan Birthcare has withdrawn its services."

"I thought you said the older gorons respected our knowledge," Trevithick said. "Why aren't they working out there? Why leave it all to us?"

"I think Clan Birthcare has given up. Lady is beyond saving, so why save new babies? What will they do with their lives? Much better to say: our time has come. Let us meet the end with dignity."

Suddenly the barge lurched, then listed heavily to port. The lines securing them to Tresco's barge snapped; first one, then the other.

"We're sinking!" shouted Mistral.

The barge had rolled into a dying patch of Lady, yellow and stinking. There was no support for the belt. Fluid was rising up past the lower rollers and the platform was already awash. Goron barges had a high centre of gravity due to the A-frame construction and heavy upper roller. Their craft was in danger of capsizing.

Tresco jumped the widening gap between the two barges. "Bring your animals onto my barge, Mistral!" he shouted. Mistral was already on the foredeck, wrestling with the panicking stoags. Then Wilfred stepped onto Tresco's craft with six-legged smoothness. The transfer of his weight caused Trevithick's barge to list further. He and Eagleman jumped across to join Tresco, then Trevithick went forward to help Mistral. She was already persuading the next stoag across the gap. Once the final stoag was safely aboard he held out his hand to her and she jumped. Safe on Tresco's foredeck, they watched the last moments of their barge.

"It's a shame," she said. Slowly the barge capsized, the top roller slid into the ooze, and the underside of the belt came uppermost. It didn't sink any farther. The top of the A-Frame was resting on the bottom, or possibly on a more solid area of Lady. "It was a good old barge," said Mistral unhappily as they went aft to join Eagleman and Tresco.

"You should have watched the surface ahead," said the goron.

"Maybe you should," snapped Mistral.

"I did. My barge was not in danger, but yours was."

"You knew, and you didn't warn us?"

"It was not my place."

"Oh, for God's sake!" For once Mistral was angered by goron philosophy. "Would you have warned us if we'd been goron?"

"I wouldn't have needed to."

"The pheromones," Mistral said to the others. "If I hadn't taken those bloody pills Susanna gave us, this would never have happened. I'd have picked a warning up from him." Furious, she stared at the underside of the barge, just breaking the surface. "That's taught me a lesson. From now on I'm gonna stay clean. You can take the rotten pills if you want."

"So what shall we do now?" asked Trevithick.

"Well, Tresco can't take us all, that's for sure. He can put us and the stoags ashore at the next stretch of healthy Lady, and we'll walk the rest of the way. It's not far."

"Having problems?" The shout came across the water; Bridget Booker rowed toward them with easy sweeps. "Is that Bryn Trevithick there?" Her coracle bumped lightly against the barge and she climbed aboard. "And Mistral too?" She stared at them in delighted surprise. "Ivor Sabin told me you were dead."

"He always was an optimist," said Trevithick dryly.

"Oh." She thought about this for a moment, then said, "And Lath Eagleman, I haven't seen you for years. Quite a human enclave here. What brings you people to Ladysend on a goron barge?"

Mistral explained the situation. Bridget nodded from time to time, dark eyes hooded.

"We saw copters coming and going," Trevithick said. "Susanna said something about a rebellion."

"Not exactly. Oh, no, not a rebellion as such." Clearly Bridget didn't want them to think badly of the gorons. "Just a withdrawal of assistance. A strike, you might say. All my teachers, catering staff, Clan Birthcare and so on. All the working gorons at Ladysend, except the nurses. But the Organisation has been very good. It wasn't Security people in those copters—that would have been too horrible. No, they were just ordinary folk come to help out. Some of your old people, Bryn. Others from other departments. They've been feeding us and helping with the little foetuses. All those things that need doing, that the clans have refused to do any more. Ladysend would have closed down, if it hadn't been for my new staff." She smiled briefly, proudly. "I'm still in charge. Nobody blames me for what's happened. They've upped my budget, you know."

Trevithick said, "But if the gorons don't want us here any longer, why are we staying on? Doesn't this nullify their original request for assistance?"

"Good grief, I can't be bothered with all that political stuff. My job's to make sure the young gorons are healthy and well educated. It's for their own good. And besides . . ." She hesitated. "It's not as though the gorons have said, officially, that they want us out of here. All we have is the word of Gaston. And Gaston's in the hands of my new staff. They're trying to talk some sense into him. And I really believe that deep down the gorons appreciate what we're trying to do for them. But they're so hidebound by their own customs, they find it hard to understand there may be better ways of doing things. And if they really need someone to speak up on their behalf, the obvious person is Lady Herself."

"She's mad," Trevithick said bluntly.

"Oh, I don't think so. She hasn't been well taught, that's all. She's learned all her Earth tongue second hand, and she's had no other teaching at all. No, you can't expect much from Lady Herself. But she could act as a simple mouthpiece for all gorons. All she'd have to do, is to say: Humans, go."

Tresco suddenly spoke. "Lady is not mad. Her mind is very clear. She is different from the rest of us, but that is not madness. It would not be right to ask her to speak on our behalf for that reason. Her issues are very different from male goron issues."

"Possibly," Bridget Booker's mind was clearly elsewhere, "but as I said, I'm not interested in politics. My work is here and I do it well, and the Organisation is pleased with it. Now, Bryn. Since you're here too, I'd like you to take a firsthand look at the kind of problems we're facing with the foetuses."

Trevithick was about to ask whether there was any point, considering; but then he realised there was a point. Quite simply, he was interested. He wanted a closer look at the foetuse problem as a matter of professional curiosity. And—who knew?—he might spot something that others had missed. And if the malformed foetuses were just another symptom of Lady's sickness, well, at least he'd given it his best shot.

Tresco ferried them to the west bank. A number of gorons there were demonstrating against Bridget's work, although Trevithick didn't realize at first what they were doing. There were no placards or slogans. They simply lined the bank and stared at the coracles with oddly exaggerated versions of a human scowl. This, and the fact that they were not working, was enough to register their disapproval. There were about twenty of them, and it didn't occur to them that the humans in the coracles would have taken their pills, and so be immune from hostile pheromones.

"The whole question of whether we get help from Clan Birthcare or not may be academic within a few days," said Bridget, bringing her coracle to a halt. Trevithick stopped rowing his. Less than a meter below the surface lay a silvery cocoon with a small figure lying curled up in it. He was about three-quarters the size of a fully-grown goron, and perfectly formed. His arms were pressed into his side, his legs were drawn up toward his stomach. He lay on his side, his limbs moving slowly, experimentally. It was probably incorrect to refer to him as a foetuse at this point. He was a child goron, all ready to be born, and detached from the umbilicus which lay beside him. Trevithick wondered how he breathed in there.

Maybe he didn't need to. Maybe he went into a kind of hibernation until the cocoon reached the surface and split open.

"He will be born soon. Three days, maybe," said Bridget. But strangely enough there was no joy in her voice.

"What's the average birth-rate?"

"We used to get one a day, sometimes two. That's about two percent more than is needed to sustain a stable population. Now it's much less because of the deformities. The population is shrinking. More than shrinking. This last couple of days, I'm very much afraid . . ." Her voice trailed away. She seemed to be trying to see far below the surface.

"Two percent per year? That was quite a growth rate."

"It was, even allowing for accidents. If only we knew the history of the gorons; but we don't. Just legends of a time when there were numerous Ladys, and territorial battles. Almost as though we're seeing a kind of devolution now the competitive edge isn't needed."

"That growth rate." He was thinking aloud. "I think it's linked to Lady's ability to increase in size. She has no natural enemies apart from other Ladys. In the old days, the bigger Lady got, the more males she could produce, and the more effectively she could compete against other Ladys. It was survival of the fittest by individual instead of by species, and our Lady here is the final result. The dead end."

"Theories are all very well," said Bridget unhappily, "but they don't get the job done. Come over here." She slid her coracle to a point ten meters away and he zigzagged after her, clumsy with the oars. "Look at that."

She indicated a foetuse that must have been within hours of birth. The cocoon formed a low dome on Lady's surface. He drew close and peered inside, and felt the hairs rise on the back of his head. Despite all his training and practical experience, despite all the strange creatures he'd seen in his travels, he'd never been able to accept fettle deformity easily. It didn't matter what species he was looking at, there was normal and there was abnormal, and that abnormal goron foetuse aroused in him the same horror, pity and regret as an abnormal human foetuse would. Abnormal was wrong; it was wasteful and pathetic and disastrous for the species. When one got down to basics, it was evil.

And an evil little creature dwelt in that cocoon.

The lines of its face were in constant motion, successive expressions of rage, glee, sorrow and cunning displaying a moving mirror of its thoughts. It was no good Trevithick telling himself these were goron expressions unrelated to the human equivalents that Bridget taught; it was no good telling himself this creature might be thinking beautiful thoughts, for all he knew. To him, that unnaturally plastic face looked sly and calculating and crazy. Yes, it looked evil.

Its shoulders were narrow, its chest shallow, its arms mere stumps. And lower down its body deteriorated, if that were possible. It had an unfinished look. It degenerated into a formless mess still partly attached to the wall of the cocoon. Appalled, he looked up at Bridget. She was crying.

"You shouldn't be doing this job," he said without thinking.

She shrugged and grimaced as though squeezing her tear-ducts shut. "But now you understand why I do it."

Oh, God, yes, he understood why. Or did he? He forced himself to look at the creature again. That little thing would never have lived in the open air, unprotected. It would have flopped on the surface with those flipper-like little arms until a squito decided to use it as an egg repository. It was doomed from the start, wasn't it?

Trevithick voiced his thoughts. "Why not let it die naturally?"

Her face was still twisted. "It might not die. Don't you feel it? There's an immortal evil about it, as though ... As though it's waiting to take over the world. Look at that face. Look at it! That's not right. That has to be destroyed. There have been a lot of them ... until just recently. Die, you little bastard!"

And she snatched up a pistol, and cut a steaming, smoking gash across the cocoon, slicing the fetes in half. Trevithick stared at her in astonished outrage. There was a hatred there, a violence he hadn't thought her capable of.

She said, "I love them, you see. I can't bear to see them go so wrong."

"What would happen if you left them all alone, the good and the bad?" he asked, sliding his coracle away. He didn't like the way she was waving the pistol about.

"They'd all drown. The good little guys used to crawl ashore, you see, but now with all these rotten patches..."

"How about the bad ones."

"Oh, they can swim, I'm sure. They'd be at home in all that pus, and in the ocean too. Sometimes I wonder if they were intended to be the next evolutionary step. God, they'd probably burrow into Lady and eat her alive."

"But you don't know that."

For a long time she stared at the surface with hooded eyes. "Perhaps it doesn't matter. Did you know, we're a long way upLady from where we usually work. In the past there have always been foetuses making their way downLady at this point. But the two you've seen, the good foetuses and that . . . thing, were the last. There may be more travelling deep, out of sight. I hope so. But I'm very much afraid Lady has stopped producing."

Deeply disturbed, Trevithick rowed toward the shore.

CHAPTER 28

BY NOW TEN HUMANS WERE GATHERED on the bank outside the inn, laughing and drinking mead, ignoring the goron demonstrators. As Trevithick drew his coracle onto the bank Mistral was there to help him.

"Bryn, I don't like it here. There's something wrong about these people. Can we start on the trail to Ladysend, please?"

He looked at her in surprise. Her manner had undergone another change. She'd found some water and washed her arms and face; he could see where the clean skin of her face met her rather grimy neck. He was oddly touched.

He helped Bridget with her coracle. "You two carry on if you like," said the teacher. "You can use my apartment. I'll be staying here for a couple of days." She looked strained. Trevithick guessed she intended to search for foetuses.

"Bryn, I thought you were dead." Ivor Sabin stood before him, short and saturnine, mug of mead in hand. "The jungle drums must have lied. It's good to see you. Does Samarita know where you are?"

"No, and I'd rather you didn't tell them, huh? I'm not too sure of my status these days." It was bad luck, Sabin being here.

Mistral chose that moment to take his hand and pull it like an impatient child. Sabin observed this with a saturnine grin. "You seem to be doing fine. This is Mistral Greene, I take it?"

"Just Mistral," she corrected him sharply.

"So you've risen from the dead, too. And what's your status these days, my dear?"

Trevithick could have warned him that Mistral reacted violently to any hint of patronising. "I'm Bryn Trevithick's lover, not that it's any bloody business of yours!"

Sabin took it in his stride. "Well, congratulations and all that stuff, but what I really meant was: Now you're alive, will Security be after you?"

"I have no bloody idea, and I don't care!"

Sensing conflict, the rest of the human birthcare team had begun to gather around, interested. Trevithick said quickly, "We'll be getting on our way. It's a long walk to Ladysend and we'd like to be there before dark."

"Fine. We'll be staying here for the night. We've provisioned the inn for human customers; the termites have no idea of creature comforts. Eagleman and Bridget will go with you, okay?"

"I'll be staying," said the teacher quickly.

"I really don't think that's a good idea, Bridget."

"I've had more experience in birthcare than anyone here."

"Your place is at Ladysend," said Sabin firmly. "I can handle things here. We're going to set out a grid and search every inch of Lady for cocoons. Hell, we're going to organise this thing. Up to now, the termites have been wandering around Lady at random. No wonder we have a problem."

"I'll help you," said Bridget, voice unsteady.

Trevithick decided it was time to step in. "Ivor, I really think it's Bridget's choice. She's in charge, after all." He didn't notice any overt movement, but suddenly the small crowd around them seemed oppressive, hostile. Was he was becoming sensitive to pheromones himself?

"Certainly Bridget has an overriding advisory role in what happens here," said Sabin smoothly. "But operationally I think you'll find I have the authority. It's not a thing to quarrel over, Bridget. We're all in a difficult situation here and we understand the need to cooperate. You're more useful supervising the school rebuilding at present. Okay?"

Bridget seemed to crumple. "I suppose so."

As they started on their way down the Ladysend trail, Trevithick said, "You seem worried about the kind of job those people are going to do, Bridget."

She replied acidly, "With good reason. It's all very well for Ivor Sabin to talk about grid patterns, but the truth is his helpers have a slaphappy attitude and they drink too much. They seem to regard the whole thing as a holiday, and I don't trust them."

Mistral had other thoughts on her mind. She held Trevithick's hand tightly as they walked. "I guess you still have that shower in your apartment, Bridget," she said wistfully.

"The apartment didn't burn, no thanks to Gaston," she replied. "You're very welcome to the shower, and the laundry too."

"I've never been properly civilised since Bryn's known me," said Mistral. "I want him to see what I can look like when I really try."

The following morning Bridget activated her terminal for Trevithick. Meanwhile Mistral took her second sonic shower in an hour, then began carefully to launder the contents of her bag of possessions. Bridget supervised the team of gorons reluctantly rebuilding the school while the rebellious Gaston languished in a shack guarded by two of Ivor Sabin's men.

Trevithick picked his way through a maze of directories at the terminal, and within an hour was becoming disheartened. True, Bridget's terminal was capable of accessing research data in Samarita, but most of that data was password-protected. He had no way of knowing whether the protection was because the information was genuinely important and secret, or whether it was the whim of some minor research assistant. It was infuriating, particularly as he'd encouraged the use of password protection during his brief spell as Director of Ecology.

It was time for a break. He stood, opened the door and called down to Bridget. "Can you spare a moment?"

They met on the tiny deck at the top of the steps. Bridget was frustrated too. "I wish they'd move Gaston to Samarita. He's causing real problems this morning."

"I thought he was all locked away and guarded."

"Goron dwellings have woven walls. His pheromones can pass through. He's making things very difficult for my construction people." Absently, her eyes followed Mistral, walking by in a bright green dress, clean and transformed, lustrous black hair swinging, leered at by the guards outside Gaston's prison. "We're going to have a lot of trouble with that young lady. By the way, she said something yesterday about, you know, you and her." She was slightly pink. "Was that just Mistral mouthing off the way she does?"

"Not this time, I'm afraid."

"Oh." She was silent for a moment, then changed the subject. "You wanted to talk to me?"

"Yes." He tore his gaze away from Mistral's hypnotic figure. "I wondered. Have you had any difficulty accessing Ecology data in the Samarita mainframe?"

"Difficulty? I've given up trying. What I don't understand is, what's the use of research data if nobody can get at it?"

"Exactly. I wish I'd thought of that when I was Director. But it wasn't a problem then, because they all worked for me. Now I've forgotten most of their passwords."

Bridget said thoughtfully, "You know everyone has to register their passwords with Personnel? They're all on file there, with the rest of the personal data. But Murdo's in charge of Personnel," she added significantly.

"Maybe we can bypass him."

"How? Those muscans are so efficient."

"We may have a way." He called up Susanna.

As soon as she saw him her eyes brightened. "If it isn't the fugitive! And with access to a terminal too. So I take it you reached Ladysend in good health, Bryn? Eating well? Bowels moving regularly? And how is Mistral?"

"Very clean these days. Listen, I'm not sure how long I've got before they close me down. Ivor Sabin's in charge of a task force here, and it's only a matter of time before he lets slip that he's seen me."

"Lets slip? My God, Bryn, he's one of the forces of darkness himself! He and Edlin, they're inseparable these days. If Ivor's seen you, then he's told Edlin. And if Edlin knows, then he's told Tillini. And if Tillini knows . . . It's rather like one of those tedious Mother Goose stories. So before they drag you away from that terminal kicking and screaming, let me tell you I love you devotedly."

"Likewise," he muttered, embarrassed by Bridget's presence at his shoulder. He stared hungrily at Susanna's face. God, how he wished she was with him, right now. It took an effort to pull himself together and explain his need for access to the personnel records. "And maybe some of the older ones too, going right back. Can you help?"

"My good man, do you imagine Health Services are in the business of prying into personal histories? Shame on you. But it so happens you're right. We have a blanket access to help us in medical emergencies. Just tell me what you want, and I'll bring it up on your screen. It will be a poor substitute for my face, but you can't have everything."

"I need the passwords all my ex-staff use, including Ivor Sabin. And the passwords used by all the past Directors of Ecology. That should do for a start."

"Stay there," she said. "This won't take long. I'll bring up the records, you jot down the passwords you need." She blew him a kiss, then froze the screen. Her face gazed out at him, motionless, pouting.

Beside him, Bridget laughed. "In all my life I've never come across anyone with such an incredible ego as that woman. How does she get away with it?"

"She's very talented," he said weakly.

"And she really does love you. You're a lucky man. Or perhaps you're a man with problems you can't solve."

In a rare lucid moment, gazing at Susanna's face, he said, "She's too good to be true." And as he said it he heard his destiny behind the words, and felt an overwhelming sadness.

"It'll work itself out," said Bridget awkwardly. "She'll make sure it does."

Then the personnel records began to scroll up the screen. First came the present members of Ecology, several screensful to each person. Trevithick noted down each password as it appeared, and inside fifteen minutes he had a complete listing. Next came the past Directors of Ecology. Suddenly Susanna's face appeared again, looking concerned.

"No passwords for a couple of these," she said briefly. "Marik Darwin, for one. Do your best."

Finally the file of Paul Eagleman, father of Lath and the first Director of Ecology, appeared. Trevithick held his breath as it scrolled up the screen. Eagleman had died five years after his arrival. Accident, it said. Maybe killed because he'd discovered Lady's decay was irreversible and was about to go public? Were the forces of darkness already in operation at that time? The screen scrolled on. Eagleman, Paul, one wife, one son and one daughter. His professional credentials were impeccable. His research data would be invaluable.

But there was no password.

Susanna's face appeared. "Okay?"

"There's no password for Eagleman."

"Someone must have deleted it. That should tell you something, my dear Watson."

"It sure does. Someone doesn't want people to see Eagleman's research. But if that's the case, why didn't they wipe out the research itself?"

"Because they might need it in the future. Anyway, I'd better sign off, much as I enjoy looking at your ugly mug. I'll snoop around at this end, see if I can find anything useful. Print out Eagleman and Darwin, huh? You never know; there might be a clue there. 'Bye!"

The screen went blank. The printer spat out the condensed life stories of Eagleman and Darwin. Trevithick scanned them again, then heard footsteps on the stairs outside. Mistral appeared in the doorway, sunlight shining through her worn dress and silhouetting strong thighs. Frantically Trevithick tried to chase a thought, something important, something about Paul Eagleman, what was it?

"You'd better come, both of you," said Mistral. "Something awful's happened."

Heavy rain had fallen upLady. Water flowed several centimetres deep over her surface. A group of gorons gathered at the bank. Morgan held a baby goron in his hands. It couldn't have been more than ten centimetres long. It was dead.

"What happened?" asked Trevithick.

Morgan said, "There was nobody to help him when his cocoon burst. He drowned in the flood waters and washed up here. This is my fault. I should never have listened to Gaston. I should have been out there with Clan Birthcare, doing the job I was born for. I shall commit myself to Lady tonight."

"It's not your fault. Ivor Sabin has men up there. He must have missed this birth."

Bridget said, "I don't understand how he could. We had all the cocoons charted. There were only three ripe ones."

"I knew it!" said Mistral. "I bloody well knew it! That shifty bastard is murdering the babies! The proof's in Morgan's hands. Now, what are we going to do about it, Bryn?"

"It's not exactly proof. This baby drowned; there isn't a mark on it. It could have been a genuine oversight by Ivor's team. Sloppy organisation. We can't go accusing the man of murder because of one dead baby."

"How many dead babies do you want, for Christ's sake?"

Bridget said, "It's just poor organisation and inexperience, Mistral, but there's no excuse for that either. Ivor had all the lower reaches charted. With the flooding, there should have been a coracle attending that cocoon at all times. Whatever the reason for this, I must relieve Ivor and his men of their duties immediately, and get Clan Birthcare back to work."

"I don't think they'll want to be relieved, Bridget," said Trevithick gently. He'd been thinking, and his views had shifted. "Not if Mistral's right."

She stared at him. "But what possible reason could Ivor have for wanting these poor little babies to die?"

"Perhaps it's the same reason some people don't seem to want Lady cured. There's no answer to xenophobia. And there may be other reasons too. Political reasons. Listen, this isn't the time or place to discuss it." Belatedly, he realised he was talking rather loosely in front of the gorons. "I think you should speak to Janine Starseeker about it right away."

Leaving the gorons crouched unhappily around the baby, they hurried back to the apartment. Bridget, skinny legs pumping with resolve, drew ahead. Mistral said quietly to Trevithick, "No, maybe it's not murder. I can't see the reason for . . ." Her eyes widened.

"I think Ivor's crowd just don't give a damn," said Trevithick bitterly. "They're probably lying drunk on the bank."

"Shut up. Let me think this through."

She sat in silence while Bridget called Janine. Trevithick took up one of the printouts and glanced through it idly. Eagleman, Paul. b. 03.01.31 Europe, arr Goronwy 38.05. W dec'd, 2 children, Frank (q.v.) aka Lath b. 23.06, Melanie aka Brighteyes b. 31.15 d. 38.21 . . .

Brighteyes . . . Lath's sister, six years old when she died on the voyage, by the look of the dates. It was her name Lath called out in times of stress, not just some odd expression he'd picked up. He'd been fifteen when she died. Brighteyes . . .

It was worth a try. He waited until Bridget had finished what appeared to be a frustrating conversation with Janine Starseeker, then sat at the terminal himself. The directories began to appear on the screen. He calendarised them. They shuffled about, funny little pictures of old fashioned books.

He heard Bridget say, "She says I'm in charge here. Well, I know that. But it's one thing being in charge of a handful of gorons, and another to send ten humans packing on grounds of inefficiency. You know what I'm going to do? I'm going to call Security and have them arrested!"

Eagleman, Paul. Methodically, now . . . He keyed in FRANK. Not recognised. LATH. Not recognised. MELANIE. Not recognised. BRIGHTEYES.

And the files opened up.

It was all there, the summarised results of five years of research by Paul Eagleman and his assistants. It had been there for almost fifty years. It was impossible that nobody in Samarita knew of it, surely?

The creature known as Lady can best be described a hive-mother, as is the case with the females of all species of large life-forms on Goronwy. The goron males were originally all providers, bringing food to the hive mother and doing little else. It is possible there were guard males during an early period when the lake was occupied by several hives, but physically distinctive groupings of males according to task never evolved. The present clan system must therefore be of relatively recent origin, and arose because the increasing size of Lady gave rise to the need for differing specialised tasks. Membership in clans is determined by preferences of the individual infant, and may be partly genetic. Since all gorons have the same mother and the identity of an infant's father is never known, the existence of a genetic drive toward specific clan membership cannot be proved.

Intelligence must have evolved at some point before the inception of the clan system. Clearly the primitive males were aquatic like the female, and gathered food from the lake to feed their Lady. Competition from other Ladys' males and the limited area of the lake forced them onto land and into contact with predatory species such as the vespas; these factors could have accelerated the development of intelligence. Another factor could have been the increasing size of Lady and the need for diversification of tasks already mentioned . . .

And so it went on, the conclusions of the first five years of research, orderly, methodical, with tables and charts. Trevithick was impressed. In those days the research was directed toward specific goals: learning about Lady with a view to understanding her sickness. Unlike the present day when the purpose had been lost, either accidentally or deliberately.

He scrolled through the files and picked one at random. It wandered a little further from the main issues; well documented, developing a theory explaining the males' transition from lake to land hinging on their discovery of the firepots; but not relevant to his present concerns. He wasn't even sure whether the answer would be found in Eagleman's research. He returned to the core file.

The growing population made it necessary for Lady herself to evolve, a rare capability in a single living organism. But at some time in the past her reproductive system must have developed beyond the single point of entry for sperm to the present system, whereby sperm can be injected anywhere in her upper reaches. Each foetus then develops in its individual cocoon and there is no centralised reproductive system as such. The obvious disadvantages of such a method may be the cause of the malformed foetuses occasionally encountered in the lower reaches. But in this connection, see Wolf's paper concerning goron sexuality, 43.05.23., same directory.

Trevithick felt a tingling in his chest. Research itself was a plodding thing, but the conclusions often required an intuitive leap. He'd known such leaps in his time, and he recognised the symptoms: the adrenaline rush, the accelerated heartbeat, the unnatural clarity of mind, the triumphant silent shout of Eureka! He hardly needed to read Wolf's paper. But he did so.

And everything fell into place.

The only question remaining was: who else in Samarita had read these files? It was obvious somebody had.

Shakily, he arose from the terminal. He found Mistral standing behind him; she'd been reading over his shoulder. Bridget sat opposite staring into space, no doubt wondering how to exercise her supposed authority over Ivor Sabin.

He walked over to the window. Lady gleamed patchily in the noon sun, pools of pus disfiguring her face like Mistral's scars . . . It all held together. In a roundabout way it all came back to Mistral and her sad little garden surrounded by encroaching bushtrap. Even now, the tentacles would be reaching out for her cabbages, and pulling them bodily from the ground, and transferring them to the central root system to rot and fertilise.

And that row of sickly Earth trees with their distress crop of cones; the bushtrap would get them in the end too. But it didn't matter, now.

Mistral said into the silence, "I've thought of something. I'm not a child, you know. You could have told me about my trees."

She was looking up at him, brushing the hair from her face. The green eyes were wide, almost frightened. He glanced at Bridget, then said quickly, "Come for a walk."

They went out into the afternoon sunshine, leaving the sad, fated figure of Bridget sitting in her chair, her life's work a terrible lie.

CHAPTER 29

"TREVITHICK'S HERE. With the girl Mistral."

Susanna made a few adjustments and the voices came in more clearly. The message originated from Ladysend via radio. The speaker had to be Ivor Sabin. The little bastard certainly hadn't wasted any time.

"Trevithick and the girl? Rob told me they were drowned."

"Maybe Rob just wanted to think they were drowned. Easier that way."

The voice was cold and metallic. "You're talking about my staff."

"We all make mistakes. You'd better send a task force down here."

"Can't you handle it?"

"No way. Most of my people worked for Trevithick. They like him, in spite of the Confessional. I'd have a mutiny on my hands if I told them to take him prisoner, for God's sake."

"I understand. I'll have a crew down there right away. You stand by and remember to—"

"Susanna, I need your advice." Janine Starseeker stood diffidently in the doorway. "Who's that talking?"

"Oh, nobody . . ." Susanna switched her device off hastily. "Just a crossed line, I guess. What can I do for you?"

"I couldn't help hearing, really. What are you up to?"

Susanna regarded the elderly woman thoughtfully. There were times when she really needed to take someone into her confidence, and this was one of them. But it would be a mistake. Far better to let this fluttery old lady go with the flow, instead of pitching her into something she couldn't handle. "It's best you don't know," she said firmly. "Believe me. Now, how can I help you?"

"Secrets, secrets." Janine sighed. "I wish I knew what was going on around here. And now I think I've made a silly mistake."

"Join the club and tell me about it."

"First tell me what you think of Ivor Sabin. You have a reputation for honesty."

"He's a poisonous little creep."

"Fair enough. Now, Bridget Booker called me a little while back. I am responsible for Bridget, aren't I? There've been so many changes I hardly know where I am."

"I imagine so. She has to be a member of Ecology, surely? She's been on her own for so long, she's kind of disappeared off the organisation chart. Murdo would know."

"I don't want to discuss this with a muscan. They're so . . . inhuman, if you know what I mean. Anyway, Bridget's having problems with Ivor Sabin, and it's pretty obvious he should be recalled. Apparently Clan Birthcare is willing to go back to work, so really he isn't needed down there. Well, I told Bridget it was her job to handle Ivor." She regarded Susanna anxiously.

"And now you realize she's not up to it."

"Exactly. The truth is, I should have handled him myself but I actually forgot I'm in charge of Ivor too, since Bryn Trevithick, uh . . . I think it was despicable what they did to Bryn, don't you? Such a nice man."

Susanna said automatically, "He can take care of himself." But he couldn't. The forces of darkness knew he hadn't drowned. They were coming to get him, and somehow she had to warn him.

"So I've put poor Bridget on the spot. What on earth can I do?"

"Simple. Contact Ivor direct and tell him to come home."

"Could I do that? Wouldn't that be undermining Bridget?"

"It's the only way," she said briskly. The woman would stand here vacillating all night, given the chance. "Tell him to get his arse out of there. Now I hate to hurry you up, but I'm really busy right now."

She shepherded the reluctant Janine from the room, then sat down again and tried to contact the Ladysend terminal. Busy signal. Bryn must still be viewing the personnel files. She used the emergency interrupter, without success.

Possibly Edlin had disconnected the Ladysend terminal from the mainframe, now he knew Trevithick was down there.

She got onto Engineering. "Ralph? I'd like my ambulopter standing by for a trip to Ladysend . . ." Belatedly she remembered a news item far more important to Ralph. Christ, she'd been a heel not to take the poor guy into her confidence, but who could you trust these days? "By the way, it seems Mistral's all right. She's at Ladysend with Trevithick."

His face was transformed. "Thank God! Oh, thank God!" The poor bastard was crying openly, not even bothering to dim the video.

"But the point is, a task force is being organised to round them up. Lucky it takes forever to get anything organised anything around here. I figured I'd get down there first and spirit them away."

"Is that Tillini's task force you're talking about?"

"I guess so."

He wiped away the tears and pulled himself together. "Sorry, Susanna. They've already commandeered all copters. Just a minute ago. They've scrambled the pilots and the copters are warming up right now. They're only waiting for the troops."

"Good grief, that's fast work. Anyway, they wouldn't be taking my ambulopter."

"It's out on an emergency call. Back in half an hour."

She disconnected, leaving Greene to gloat over the news of Mistral. What now? The task force would arrive at Ladysend before her. There was nothing she could do about it. Too bad. Still, it would be dark soon. She'd leave as soon as she could, park out of earshot of Ladysend, walk in and play it by ear.

She enjoyed playing things by ear. Events could be so predictable when you planned them in advance.

"My trees are dying, aren't they? I kinda felt there was something wrong with them." said Mistral. "That's why they have so many cones on them. I just didn't know how many cones they were supposed to have, normally I mean. You'd know that, having been on Earth." She was talking around the real subject; they both knew it. This was a thing that had to be led up to carefully.

"It's called a distress crop. The trees sense they're in trouble and they put out a bigger than normal crop to maximise the chance of their species surviving. You can make them do it artificially, by putting them under stress. A lot of species act the same way."

"What was it put Lady under stress?"

Yes, she'd guessed. She was clever, and she had an affinity for Lady. "It could have been anything. One thing's for certain—it wasn't us. The problem started before humans arrived. My guess is, it was when Lady's lower end reached the sea and she couldn't grow any more. She has no skeleton to limit her size, you see. So it's natural for her to keep growing, and when she couldn't her only alternative was to start to die."

"Couldn't she have just stayed the way she was?"

"Life doesn't do that. Life is based on growing and dying and reproduction."

She was looking up at the apartment, hair hanging down her back, the scar exposed. Trevithick caught sight of Bridget passing the window. Mistral said, "Yeah, I guess so. And for a long time now, Bridget's been killing the female babies. The distress crop."

"I'm afraid she has. She wasn't to know. They looked so different from the males. So weird, she couldn't recognise them for what they are. With Lady in poor health, it was natural for Bridget to think in terms of malformations. Monsters."

Mistral's face was pink. "Poor Bridget!" she burst out. "Why didn't the gorons stop her? They must have known, the stupid little buggers!"

"They didn't recognise them either. No living goron male has ever seen the process of female development, you see. They didn't like Bridget killing them, but it was an instinctive reaction and they couldn't explain why. So Bridget overruled them."

"And now there are no more females coming. Lady's all birthed out."

"Seems like it. It's too late to save the species now."

"What are we going to say to Bridget?" She slipped an arm around his waist as they regarded the apartment window. "How can we tell her, Bryn? Is there any way she needn't know?"

He put his arm around her shoulders and led her away, past the apartment and down to the beach where a couple of goron youngsters were playing with a coracle in the shallows, learning to be gatherers. He wondered if they would ever need their skill. They strolled west, where the beach ended in a small cove bounded by rocks. Fishy things abounded here like everywhere else in the Goronwy sea, with no fishermen to net them. Were the fish social males with hive mothers, like the land-based Goronwy life-forms?

They lay down in a sandy hollow between rocks and made love, quick and violent and desperate, as though trying to compensate for what Bridget had done to Lady. There was no peace afterward; all the problems came surging back at them. Mistral lay looking up at Trevithick, hands behind her head. They hadn't undressed; there hadn't been time.

She said, "I don't have the guts to tell Bridget. Do you?"

"No. They knew in Samarita, you know. Someone else has always known. They found out almost fifty years ago; the situation was obvious enough to a biologist. But they made sure ongoing research stayed away from Lady herself. I expect the problem's been solved several times in the last fifty years, but the answer's been suppressed . . . one way or another. So they let Bridget go on killing the females. They even encouraged it. It wasn't in their interests for those females to survive. They might have made their way back to the lake and started new Ladys up there, and then the Organisation would have to pull out, its job done. That's why they were so quick to send in a team when Clan Birthcare went on strike."

"Who are they, Bryn?"

"Well, really it's a huge conspiracy. Most humans born on Goronwy want to stay here for the rest of their lives. This is their home.

Over the years they may have had their suspicions that everything isn't straight here, but they'll have shut it out of their minds. They'll have left everything to a few leaders. And they wouldn't even acknowledge that those people are the leaders."

"So who are these leaders?"

"I'm guessing. Manning Edlin, my old friend Ivor Sabin of course, a couple of Board members, maybe Brassworthy. Jonathan Cook. Tillini probably. They're the ones who are actively doing the dirty work for everyone else."

"What about the Organisation itself?"

"I think they've been hoodwinked by Edlin and his team."

"So you're going to tell them the truth." She hesitated. "If they pull out, will you stay here with me?"

"What would I do here? My job's disappeared now Lady's finished."

"Answer my bloody question, Mister!"

He regarded her, propped up on his elbow. Her hands were still behind her head, raising ripe young breasts against the worn fabric of the green dress. The skirt was rucked up around the slender waist, exposing neat hips, dark body hair, strong thighs. She'd have been beautiful but for the scars. Did the scars matter, really? Probably not. All right, so why was he hesitating?

Because he didn't love her.

What a stupid, old-fashioned reason, he told himself.

"It's Susanna, isn't it," she said quietly.

He closed his eyes and laid his head on her breast. He couldn't bear to see the accusation in her eyes. He felt a hard nipple against his cheek and began to desire her again. It was hell, being a human male. The gorons never had this problem.

As they made their way back toward the apartment, she said, "I'm not worrying about you and me any more. I'm gonna make the most of what we've got. There's plenty happening soon and who the hell knows how things'll be in a few days time?" She laughed, shakily. "There, how's that for maturity, huh? Just tell me you wanted me again back there, when you had your face on my tit."

"You know I did."

"That'll do for now. So, what do we do about poor old Bridget?"

"Nothing." He'd been thinking about it. "I can't face telling her. You never know, we might all go back to Earth without her ever finding out. We'll call Susanna, get her to give us a ride back to Samarita, and warpwire the Organisation about everything that's been happening. Then we'll tackle Manning Edlin."

"And get ourselves fried? Remember Marik Darwin?"

She had a point. But then there was no need to assume Darwin had been killed to silence him. There were several thousand humans on Goronwy. Any number of those might have a motive for murder totally unconnected with Edlin or Lady. "We'll be okay if we handle it right."

"And how are we gonna get word through to Earth? Edlin's in charge of communications, remember?"

"Susanna will figure a way."

"She's not bloody perfect, you know!"

She'd had one of her violent mood swings. He didn't know whether to be glad or sorry when the copters appeared over Lady. They flew in formation, three of them, and they had a purposeful air. "I guess Ivor's talked," he said, resignedly. "Here come the forces of darkness."

The copters landed in a wide triangle; one beside Lady and close to the Ladysend dwellings; another almost directly to the north, and the third on the beach nearby. It was from this last copter that they saw a dozen men in Security uniforms emerge. Mistral said nervously, "What are they gonna do to us?"

"I tell you one thing. They won't let us get through to Earth." The men arrived at a run and, pistols drawn, surrounded them as though they were armed and dangerous. "Easy, boys," murmured Trevithick. "We're coming quietly."

"I'll say you are." It was a young, fresh faced man whom he recognised vaguely; Rob something. "You've no idea the trouble you caused me."

312

"You people have caused us plenty, too. What's it all about?"

"No good asking me, I'm just a pawn, for God's sake. My orders were to take you both, and that's what I've done. Easier than I expected. I can't think why we had to bring a bloody army for this. Still, that's Tillini for you. Okay, come along."

One of the guards tried to take Mistral officiously by the arm and she shook him off violently. "You heard we were coming quietly!" she snapped. "Now keep your bloody hands off me!"

"Gently does it, Jack," said Rob. "We've got nothing personal against these people."

They were taken to a goron dwelling. As they entered, Trevithick saw Gaston sitting in the far corner, tied to a chair. The little man took in the situation at a glance. "So the humans have turned against their own kind, have they?"

Mistral said, "You hit Morgan. He's a goron. So just shut up, huh?"

A guard was posted to watch them from the doorway; a slab-faced unimaginative-looking man, probably bred for the job, thought Trevithick cynically. He wore his laser pistol ostentatiously, hand close to the butt. A long and unhappy silence followed, finally broken by voices outside.

"I reckon we should take them back right now." It was Rob's voice. "I'm in deep enough shit already over these two. I'd like to hand them in personally."

"Yes, well, I want to talk to them." That was Ivor Sabin. "I've got a dozen men here, for God's sake. They're not going to get away. And it'll be dark in another hour. Leave them with me and I'll ship them back tomorrow."

"I was told to bring them in," said Rob stubbornly. "Tillini's orders."

"And you will bring them in. You can stay here overnight if you like. Just remember I'm responsible for everything at Ladysend, right? And I want to question them now—it could be important."

They heard Rob mutter an grudging assent, then Ivor Sabin breezed into the dwelling, smiling.

"Well, Bryn, what have you been up to this time? You seem to have upset Tillini. Too bad. He can get quite nasty." He turned to the guard. "You can go now, Jamie. Just leave me your pistol." With the guard out of the way he motioned them to sit on the floor and he did the same, leaning back against the woven door with the pistol in his lap.

"You didn't have to tell Samarita we were still alive," said Trevithick bitterly.

"It just slipped out," said Sabin airily. "But no matter. It gives us the chance for a little chat. Uh, I had Janine Starseeker on the blower earlier on, trying to fire me and my birthcare boys on the grounds of incompetence. And I hear through the grapevine that you were responsible. That's not very friendly, Bryn."

"Why are you killing the babies, Sabin?"

The other man eyed him for a moment. "It doesn't matter now, does it? She's not producing any more. Not a one, we've used infrared all the way up to Samarita. Anyway, you already know the answer, so why don't you accept it? There must be no quick cure for Lady, and that means no babies. Face it, Bryn you're in the minority on Goronwy. Pretty well everyone wants to spin this tour out for the rest of their natural lives."

"I know about the females, too." He wasn't sure why he said that. Probably it was to wipe the smug look of Sabin's face, and in this he succeeded.

"Thanks for telling me," said Sabin grimly. "We wondered how much you knew. Why do you think we've been looking for you all this time? Jesus, you're a hard man to catch up with. So now you've signed your own death warrant. And Mistral's too. What a waste." His eyes dwelt on the girl for a moment. She regarded him uncertainly. A cold triumph shone in Sabin's eyes. "Come and sit with me, girl," he said.

"For God's sake leave her alone."

"It's her choice. You see, she's like all women. She gravitates to where the power lies." Mistral settled beside him and he put an arm around her, cupping a breast, stroking it casually. He rested the pistol on the dirt floor on the far side from her, keeping his fingers around it. "And she thinks maybe if she sucks up to me, she won't die. And maybe she won't, who knows? Oh, yes, Trevithick, the power lies here with me. That's twice you thought you had power over me, you bastard, and twice I've got the better of you."

"Twice? There's now. When was the other time?" Keep him talking. If he's talking, he won't be shooting.

"Annecy, when the hell do you think?"

Annecy. All those people dead. Trevithick's mouth was dry. "What in God's name did you do on Annecy?"

"You're not bad, girl, you know that? What was that you said, Bryn? Annecy? Yes, I made a little mistake on Annecy. Could happen to the best of us. I mistook a test batch of Annecy 8 for the vaccine that had been stored in the freezer, and vaccinated a few people with it. Too bad."

"You vaccinated them with live virus?"

"Yeah, and by then it had mutated into Annecy 9. Well, it was too late to do anything about it, wasn't it? I had to switch a few vials to make the numbers add up. It would never have happened if we'd used different coloured vials and a better indexing system. Still, that was your responsibility."

"Over a hundred people died because of your stupid mistake!"

"You were the Director. They'd have nailed you to the wall whatever."

"Yes, but it would have gone a lot better for me if you'd come clean."

"Ask yourself. Why in hell would I do that?" He shrugged. "Anyway, I put in a good word for you with Murdo when I came here."

"Only because you knew they wanted some kind of deadbeat figurehead for Ecology. Well, you were wrong, weren't you!"

"Not really, Bryn. I mean, consider the here and now. You're a loser. Always have been, always will be."

Trevithick shifted, tensing himself. Sabin's fingers curled around the pistol and he lifted it slightly. Trevithick forced himself to relax. Sabin was right. The power lay with him. Nothing could be done. Except to keep him talking.

"I don't understand why it's so important that Lady dies. I understand that some people want to stay here as long as possible, but the Organisation will pull everyone out in a few years anyway. The extended funding's only temporary. Why kill off intelligent life on Goronwy before we go?"

Sabin grinned. "You think real simple, like a termite. You—"

There was a splintering crash. Trevithick caught a brief glimpse of a huge paw as it smashed through the weave of the door.

It seized Sabin around the waist and dragged him bodily outside.

CHAPTER 30

ISTRAL HAD ROLLED OUT OF THE WAY. Sabin was screaming outside. Trevithick jumped to his feet and picked up the pistol. He jerked open the flimsy remains of the door. Sabin was on the ground, struggling with a huge stoag. The light from the nursery windows showed a crimson wound in Sabin's belly. The uniform had been ripped from his chest and arms. Trevithick raised the pistol, trying to get a clear shot at the stoag. His chance came when Sabin kicked free and rolled clear.

"No!" Mistral threw herself at him, dragging at his wrist. Taken by surprise, he allowed her to twist the pistol from his hand. "You're not gonna shoot Wilfred!" she shouted. "You stupid or something?"

And she took deliberate aim, and burned a hole in Sabin's chest. He jerked convulsively, then lay still.

"Now let's get out of here!" she cried. "Come on."

Shocked, he hesitated. "What the hell did you do that for?" He found himself kneeling beside the body, feeling the neck, trying to detect signs of life.

"What's the matter with you? He was gonna kill us!" Her hand was in his hair, tugging. "Now let's get going before the others come!"

He stood, looking around dazedly. "What about Gaston?"

"Bugger Gaston! He's not a real goron any more!" She began to run toward the Ladyside trail. "Hurry up!" she shouted over her shoulder.

Ladysend was coming alive. There were shouts of inquiry from around them. Flashlights began to jerk about, silhouetting running figures.

Trevithick quickly freed Gaston and caught up with Mistral. "Sabin said they've got infrared on one of the copters," he gasped out.

"Let's hope he was lying."

Soon Trevithick found himself running through open aeolus fields, the fleshy leaves squelching under his feet. He could hear something heavy pounding along behind. He hoped it was Wilfred and not some unknown Goronwy predator. More lights were coming on to the south, illuminating the way before them. They ran on. Before long he was gulping for breath, but Mistral seemed tireless. Soon the darkness closed around them and he could only hear her. The ground became firmer; they'd left the aeolus and were on the Ladyside trail. He plunged onward in the unhappy knowledge that Lady was immediately to his right.

"You okay?" he heard her call.

"Can you . . . see where you're . . . going?" he jerked out.

"No. Can you?"

"But we're right next to Lady!"

"Better not fall in, then."

He summoned up a desperate sprint, caught up with her, threw an arm around her waist and dragged her to a halt. "Listen, we've got to think about this."

"No time! They'll have copters up in a minute!"

"I know. So how are we going to avoid their infrared?"

"There's an inn not far off." She jerked herself free and began to run again.

He followed, wishing he'd kept himself in better shape and wondering how an inn would help. The infrared would penetrate the leafy roof very easily.

It seemed they ran for hours. After a while he ceased to worry about the nearness of Lady; the burning pain in his lungs occupied his thoughts. How much longer would this go on? How much longer could it go on, before he collapsed? He snatched a quick glance over his shoulder. One helicopter was in the air; a bright star winking over Ladysend. They'd recall the guards, then start spiralling outward, scanning, until they'd covered the immediate area. Then they'd take a run along the beach. Finally, satisfied that there was only one route their quarry could have taken, they'd head north.

Maybe they should have struck off to the north-west, across the aeolus fields. They might have gained an extra hour of freedom that way. He tried to shout to Mistral, to put this idea to her, but could do no more than croak.

Then, ages later, she said, "Here we are."

He collapsed full-length, unable to speak.

"Here, you poor old thing." There was scant sympathy in her voice. "Take my hand and crawl." She led him through the tiny doorway and into the darkness of the inn, warm with gorons. "It's Mistral and Bryn Trevithick," she announced.

"Stand fast." A chorus of piping voices.

She showed little signs of breathlessness. "Bad humans are after us in a copter," she explained. "They'll be coming this way and they'll detect the heat of you all with their machine. So they'll land and take a look. We'll need to hide. And we'll want you to lie to the humans, to protect us."

"I will lie for you, Mistral."

"Is that Morgan?" she sounded surprised. "I thought you and your clan weren't working."

"Gaston was a bad goron. He is discredited. Our duty is to Lady, not Gaston. I don't know why we ever thought otherwise. But . . ." he hesitated. "We may be unnecessary here. We've seen no babies today. Tomorrow we go upLady to the next inn. We hope to find babies there . . ." Again he paused. "You feel very sad, Mistral. Is there something you know about Lady?"

"I can hear a copter. Come on, Bryn." She took his hand. They made their way to the far end of the inn, gorons moving sleepily aside to let them pass. "Wilfred!" she called.

Trevithick lay along the angle of floor and wall, Mistral close beside him. He was aware of the bulk of Wilfred next to her, and then other stoags arrived, grunting and shuffling about, until a heap of the animals separated humans from gorons.

The search party arrived a few minutes later. He heard the copter approach, then the dying hiss as it landed. Soon, human voices spoke.

"They wouldn't be in here, would they?"

"Could be. The girl's gone native."

The interior of the inn was flooded with light. Trevithick felt Mistral burrow herself tightly into the stoags. He shut his eyes and waited.

"Jesus, what a stink!"

"They all sleep together, termites and animals, see? Hey, you! Yes, you I'm talking to!"

"Can I help you?" It was Morgan.

"Sure you can. Have you seen two humans tonight? Mistral Greene and Bryn Trevithick? You know them?"

"I know them, yes. But I haven't seen them."

"Okay. If you do, send a runner down to Ladysend, right? They're bad humans. They killed a whole lot of gorons down there tonight."

Another human voice spoke. "That was a dumb thing to say, Porky. They'd know if any of their people had been killed. You know how they sniff these things out."

"Garbage. Anyway, there's nobody in here." The light snapped off and the voices began to retreat. "Think we can trust them?"

"I reckon so. They never lie. They don't know how to. You know what I think? There's a whole lot of caves past the west end of the beach. The termites used to live there before they built shacks around Bridget's complex. That's where we should be looking. The infrared wouldn't have picked them up if they were in a cave."

The copter lifted off, the hum faded into the distance.

"Thanks, Morgan," said Mistral.

"Deceit opens up whole new fields of behaviour," came the reply. "I must try not to dwell on the possibilities."

Trevithick relaxed while Mistral and Morgan delved into the aspects of lying. He found he was smiling to himself. So they were still on the run, but he couldn't help feeling a pervasive joy.

The ghost of Annecy had been laid.

He'd hardly had time to think about it since Ivor Sabin's confession, but now, in the warm darkness, he could allow his mind to play with it like a wonderful new toy. Annecy had not been his fault. There had been a criminal mistake, a skilful cover-up, and he'd been the scapegoat for something for which he could in no way be blamed. Certainly he'd been in charge. But he'd been entitled to assume that his assistant—hired as a competent professional by the Organisation itself—would take reasonable precautions when administering drugs. And Ivor had screwed up. He'd been thinking of something else—maybe some job he'd applied for, maybe some woman he was after—and he'd screwed up.

And now he was dead.

The memory came back to him, of Mistral with the laser pistol, ruthlessly drilling a smoking hole into Sabin's chest.

He felt her shift beside him. She'd stopped talking to Morgan. "Make love to me," she whispered. "I need to be made love to, real bad."

Another memory, of her nipples rock-hard with desire, her hand in Sabin's lap.

"Not right now," he said.

There was a pause, then she said angrily, "What do you mean, not right now? When, then? In ten minutes time? Tomorrow afternoon? When you're good and ready? You don't play games with me, Mister!"

"Take it easy. You'll upset the gorons."

"Bugger the gorons! What's the matter with you? If I tell you I need screwing I bloody well mean I need screwing, you hear? It was you got me started on this thing, remember?"

He said nothing, feeling her tense with anger beside him. He tried to ignore her, to recover some of the euphoria he'd felt over Annecy. A long silence followed. Without warning she rolled toward him, seized his hand and pressed it against her breast. He let it lie for an instant; he couldn't take it away without an undignified and ill-tempered struggle. And that instant was enough. His body began to respond to her.

321

She found out almost immediately, and chuckled softly. "You can't resist it, can you?" she murmured. "I can make you do it any time, whether you want or not."

A Goronwy brat, born with irresistible pheromones . . .

As he resigned himself to the inevitable, he wondered at the almost frightening power she had. Not just over men, not just sex; it seemed she could also control the stoags, the vespas, the gorons . . .

She'd used it all on Ivor Sabin, and he'd died horribly. She'd tasted her power. Until Sabin, she'd used that power for good, and her definition of good had coincided with Trevithick's. But now, it seemed, she'd started to go her own way.

As the slim body bucked under him, enslaving his senses, he wondered how far she could go in bending Goronwy to her will. What would be the end of it all? In that moment he had a horrifying vision of the possibilities.

And she was physically so vulnerable. Just a soft, small human female. How many tragedies could he avert by putting his hands around that slender neck, and squeezing, and squeezing . . . ?

Wilfred snarled softly.

Trevithick put the thought away and recalled himself to his duty.

"Anybody at home?"

Trevithick awakened with a start. Sunlight filtered through the leafy roof. A stoag grunted but Mistral slept on, one arm thrown across her face. He tried to gather his thoughts. Had he just heard a voice? Were Security back, making another search?

"Anybody at home?" It was Susanna's voice.

"In here!" he called. He rolled into a crawling position and made his way past Wilfred to the sunlit square of the low door. He could see bare calves and a yellow skirt out there. The gorons had all gone out onto Lady. He poked his head out, blinking at the strong sunlight.

"Well, mercy me, it's a gigantic goron! Oh, no, my mistake, it's

Bryn Trevithick, late of the Samaritan Organisation. What brings you to this lowly inn, Trevithick?"

He stood guiltily, all too aware of Mistral lying naked a few meters away. "It's nice to see you," he said feebly.

"Oh, sure. You can tell her to put her clothes on and come out. It's nice to see you, too. I thought you'd been taken by the forces of darkness. I . . ." She hesitated and swallowed suddenly. "I've been looking for you all night."

Suddenly they were in each other's arms.

"I was so scared," she murmured. "There were Security people everywhere. I joined up with them, so if they did find you I could make sure nothing . . . happened. The search starts again in—" she raised her arm behind him, stood on tiptoe and looked at her watch over his shoulder "—about half an hour. We have to get you out of here. The ambulopter's about a kilometre upLady."

"You can take me to Samarita, can you?"

They moved apart. She was staring at him. "Unwise, Trevithick. Certainly it's the last place they'd expect you to be, but they're sure to notice you around the place."

"We've found out what's happening here."

She listened in silence while he told her about the systematic destruction of the female embryos, their recent imprisonment and the death of Sabin.

"So that explains why they've been so kind to poor old Bridget," she said. "She's been doing their dirty work for them. Does she know?"

"I couldn't tell her. Somebody will. All of Sabin's human birthcare team must have known, obviously. And there must be twenty Security humans at Ladysend as well, now. By now they'll all know. So pretty soon the whole of Samarita will know."

"My God. And seventy-five percent will see the bad guys as heroes, and the other twenty-five will want to string them up. It's going to be rough. Friend will be at the throat of friend. Civil war."

"I'd like to get word through to Earth, but can I trust the Organisation itself? They may be in on this. I've begun to wonder if maybe they're going into the colonisation business."

She took his hand, suddenly tentative. "They're . . . they're not, Bryn. Uh, brace yourself. I haven't been entirely honest with you. About myself, I mean."

"Oh?" There had been so much deceit, so much treachery. Susanna too? He felt a knot of apprehension in his chest.

"I suppose you'd call me an Organisation plant," she said. "The Organization's been unhappy about Goronwy for years. They had a right to expect a bit more action, don't you think? Instead all they got was optimistic reports and pleas for more money. So four years ago they sent me here to find out what was going on. With a suitable cover, of course. That's about all there is to it. I'll answer your questions as they occur to you, but first answer one of mine. Do you still love me now you know I'm a dirty spy?"

Trevithick was not sure love was on the agenda. His whole life—the whole of Goronwy—was in a state of flux. He would shortly be facing powerful enemies in Samarita, and he still wasn't entirely sure who they were. He was a sexual prisoner of Mistral. Susanna had suddenly become an enigma. What could he say? He managed to look into the wide blue eyes, and was captured by them, as ever. "I'll always love you," he muttered unhappily.

"But you don't see a lot of hope in the future? That's all right, my good man. Let's take life as it comes. We can solve your first problem quickly enough. I'll take you back to Samarita and we'll get a message off to Earth HQ. Just roust your toy girl out of there, will you?"

Suddenly apprehensive, he said, "I'm not sure she's much of a toy. I think she's just about the most dangerous thing on Goronwy."

"Is she, now?" said Susanna thoughtfully. "You know, I'd wondered about that. She can control all the local life-forms, right? So we must hope she uses her power sensibly. And we'll have to try to control her."

"She shot Ivor Sabin in cold blood. It kind of took me aback."

"And he bloody well deserved it!" Mistral crawled out of the inn and stood, brushing muck from her dress. She eyed them suspiciously. "Heard a couple things in there. What do you mean, control me?"

"All right," snapped Susanna with uncharacteristic impatience, "This is what we mean. You've been out of touch with humans for a couple of years, but you should still remember how to behave. And if you don't, it'll be the worse for you. Clear enough?"

Trevithick waited for a thunderbolt to strike, or Wilfred to spring, or whatever. Nothing like that happened.

Mistral blustered, "You threatening me?"

"You betcha. Now get your bag of things and come along, unless you want Security to get you. We don't have much time."

Meekly, Mistral dropped to her knees and crawled back into the inn. They heard her shouting ill-temperedly at Wilfred. Susanna raised her eyebrows at Trevithick, but said nothing. Presently the girl emerged, followed by the stoag. They set off northward in an unhappy silence, soon joined by a mud-stained goron.

"Gaston!" exclaimed Mistral. "How did you get here."

He said flatly. "I've been here all the time. I followed you from Ladysend. I heard what Morgan said about me. He said I am a bad goron. He would not lie, but he is mistaken. And I heard what you said earlier, Mistral. You said I'm not a real goron any more. You were mistaken too. I may be changed from what I was, but I'm as good and as real as any goron on Goronwy. I represent what we're capable of, given training and opportunity. I owe a lot to Bridget Booker, and I'd like the chance to prove my worth."

Mistral was regarding him thoughtfully. "I'll give you your chance," she said at last.

"I tried an interesting experiment a few days ago," said Susanna as the ambulopter hummed along above Lady. "Totally unprofessional of course, but then I never was one for conformity. I substituted placebos for the last issue of antifero pills. Interesting, huh? People will start finding out what real life is like on Goronwy pretty soon."

"But . . . !" Trevithick was almost speechless. "It could have all kinds of repercussions. People could get totally irrational!"

"Most certainly they could, my dear Doctor."

"You did the right thing." It was the first time Mistral joined in their conversation. For almost an hour she and Gaston had been talking quietly together.

Susanna said thoughtfully, "Most people want to stay here. It's only natural, not to want to leave your home. They were pretending there was a project going on, but it wasn't really happening, was it? Other things were happening, funny things, and most of them added up to the project lingering on indefinitely. So the other day I had a bright idea. If these people are so in love with this bloody world, I thought, let them find out what it's really like."

Trevithick tried to come to terms with this. It seemed a hell of a step to take, unauthorised. But who would have authorised it anyway? He tried to file the situation away in his tidy mind, and failed.

"Face it, Trevithick," chuckled Susanna, guessing his thoughts. "It's a *fait accompli*. I see my act as a privilege of office—I am Manager of Health Services, am I not? It's healthier this way. I should mention that I contaminated the rest of our antifero stock, too. There's no way back. If people can't take it, they'll have to ship out. Organisation HQ won't be sending any emergency pills after they get our inflammatory warpwire, that's for sure."

"There's Bridget, look," said Mistral suddenly.

A lone coracle slid slowly over Lady. Susanna held the copter stationary nearby. "Poor old girl. Maybe she doesn't know after all. So she goes on doing her job."

Trevithick said slowly, "Maybe she does know."

"Oh, God," said Susanna. "I suppose she's trying to find some last survivors to raise, now."

"I don't reckon she is," said Mistral quietly.

"You mean she can't accept it?" said Susanna.

"No." Mistral's eyes were sombre. "I reckon she feels the way I'd feel, if I'd just found out I'd wiped out a whole intelligent race all by myself."

The ambulopter lurched. "Jesus Christ," muttered Susanna.

They watched Bridget lay aside the oars and hoist herself to her feet. The coracle wobbled. For a moment she stood tall and angular, wispy hair blowing in the wind, composing herself.

"Stop her!" cried Trevithick.

"You are a very conventional fellow, aren't you, Trevithick?" said Susanna sadly. "You really wouldn't condemn that woman to live with it for the rest of her normal life, would you?"

Mistral said, "Bryn, if you have to go, that's absolutely the nicest way."

Then Bridget leaned forward and tumbled over the side in the manner of an old goron committing himself to Lady. The coracle skidded away. She lay face down, spread-eagled as though greeting her fate with open arms.

"She always meant to be a good human," said Gaston. "We bear her no ill-will."

CHAPTER 31

THEY LEFT GASTON OUTSIDE AND ENTERED the main dome. Nobody paid much attention to them as they walked the corridors. In point of fact, people weren't paying much attention to anything. They wandered about in a preoccupied, rather sad manner as though all the cares of Goronwy were weighing them down. Which in fact they were, as their resistance to outside pheromones dwindled away.

"Neat, huh?" said Susanna quietly. "It all works out really well. After a while the gorons' hostility will get the better of people and they'll want to ship out. Anything will be better than feeling depressed all the time. But the few who might want to stay—" She glanced at Mistral "—will be fine if the gorons like them. So there's a built-in incentive to be nice to the little guys."

"Just keep us supplied with genuine pills while all this is going on." Trevithick was still having trouble coming to terms with the situation. "This isn't the way to your office," he said suddenly. "Where are we going?"

"Use your head, Bryn. There's not much use me trying to send out a warpwire, is there? Not with the forces of darkness in full control of Communications. Correction. Not quite full control. There is a loophole, which we are about to exploit." She paused at a door valve.

"Martha Sunshine?" Trevithick was surprised.

"Who else but our Entertainments lady is in the business of sending warpwires all over the Galaxy? Or at least, this arm of the Galaxy.

328

Booking a show here, signing a contract there, cheating a playwright somewhere else. It's become accepted that Martha's warpwires go out direct. There is another possibility, actually. Murdo of Personnel also sends direct wires. But we don't exactly trust Murdo, do we?"

The big woman was surprised to see them. "Good grief! I thought Bryn and Mistral were *personae non grata* around here, if not dead. Has the political climate changed so quickly? Or are you living even more dangerously than usual, Susanna?"

"We've come to ask a favour." Susanna gave a quick summary of the situation to date.

Martha whistled. "I'm way behind the times. Well, this blows my chances of bringing in *Barker Sam*. Or maybe not; it takes time to evacuate a planet. You mentioned a favour, darling?"

"I'd like you to send off a warpwire to Earth, telling all."

"With pleasure." The big woman smiled broadly. "There are a few creeps around here I'd like to see get theirs."

It took over two hours to construct the warpwire; the four of them huddled over the terminal making suggestions, corrections, trying to get the whole mess into a reasonable chronological order. "The last thing we want," said Susanna, "is for them to think I've gone off the rails. I'm asking for a big decision here, and it has to sound convincing. The Organization's made all kinds of political capital out of their benevolence in staying on. And now I'm telling them we should pull out right away because we're all a bunch of layabouts with our snouts in the trough. If layabouts have snouts."

Martha was in high spirits. "Don't pull your punches." As they reached the end of the final draft she laughed. "At the current cost of warpwires that blows my budget for the next five years. But what the hell, it's in a good cause."

She hit a key and the warpwire went on its way.

Trevithick heaved a sigh of relief. He'd never really believed they'd be allowed to alert Earth to the true situation. He'd half expected Martha's terminal to suffer a power failure, or Tillini to burst in, or Edlin to have blacked out all transmissions, or . . . But it was done. And now . . . ?

"And now we stick our stupid necks out," said Susanna, "and beard Manning Edlin in his den. "You still have that pistol, Mistral?"

Mistral rummaged through her bag and produced the gun they'd taken from Sabin. She waved it about, drawing experimental beads on Martha's furniture.

"Careful with that thing," warned Trevithick. "Keep it in your bag and hope we don't need it. Now, let's work out our approach to Edlin."

Ten minutes later they were on their way to the office of the Director of Communications.

As they stepped through the door valve into Edlin's office, four people rose to their feet and not one of them appeared surprised. Edlin was smiling smoothly. Also in the office were Ian Carstairs, Edlin's deputy; Albert Brassworthy; and Jonathan Cook, Director of Sustenance. They were ready and waiting. Something had gone wrong.

"A lot of water's passed under the bridge since we last met, Bryn," said Edlin easily. "Good to hear the report of your death was exaggerated, too. I was sorry to hear about Ivor, by the way. A good man. He'll be missed."

"He was going to kill us," said Trevithick shortly.

Edlin looked surprised. "Kill you? That's a bit, uh, excessive, isn't it?"

"I understood killing was part of your game."

"Game? I assure you we're not in the business of killing for fun. Or for any other reason."

"What about Marik Darwin?"

"Oh, dear me, no." Edlin chuckled, and for the first time Trevithick noticed he held a pistol loosely at his side. "You don't pin that one on me, Bryn. You three had the dispute with Marik, not me. I distinctly remember your right cross, Susanna. And the struggle on the platform. And Mistral's impassioned speech. Now you say I killed Marik? That stretches the credulity."

"I'm willing to believe it," said Trevithick.

"If it suits your purpose. Your staff brought the body in, didn't they, Susanna? He'd been found in Lady. Now who reported him, I wonder?"

"I did," snapped Trevithick, beginning to lose his temper. What kind of game was Edlin playing? "Mistral and I found him just downLady from here, and reported it to Susanna. So you deny having anything to do with his death?"

"Well, really, Bryn. You're the one that has to convince us."

"That's easy enough. There were four of us present on a barge when Marik was found. Myself, Mistral, Lath Eagleman, and Brennan, the goron bargee."

Mistral said, "No, Bryn. Brennan jumped overboard just before Lath spotted the body."

"That's too bad," said Edlin sympathetically, "because gorons make reliable witnesses. So it was just you two and—" he paused "—Lath Eagleman. Let me see, Lath's the guy we see drooling into his mead at the Passing Barge, isn't he?"

The discussion was not going well. "Forget it, Edlin," said Trevithick. "You know quite well we didn't kill Marik. And we admit we killed Ivor in self defence. More to the point is your systematic slaughter of goron females."

Edlin sighed and sat on his desk, crossing his legs and laying his pistol within easy reach. "I doubt if you'll find Tillini so easy to satisfy. But have it your way. Our slaughter of goron females, you say? It sounds as though someone's gotten their wires crossed. Bridget Booker is on your staff, and she's as straight as a die."

"We all know that. She didn't know what the females were. She thought they were deformed males."

"Yes, we've heard what's been happening at Ladysend. It's too bad. Obviously Bridget's been under a misapprehension all these years. It was your department's job to lay down her procedures, wasn't it? I mean, I'm just Director of Systems and Communications."

"My department's been staffed with deadbeats for nearly fifty years!"

"Blame Personnel for that, not me."

Edlin was a slippery customer; there was no doubt about that. Trevithick's mind was racing. Surely there was some way he could be pinned down? He looked at Susanna. She raised her eyebrows and shrugged. Mistral had gone out onto the balcony and was taking no further part in the proceedings. Or was she? She still had the pistol in her bag. She had a look of extreme ill-temper on her face. Cook, Brassworthy and Carstairs had taken their cue from Edlin and resumed their seats.

"You can't deny that Ivor was your man," said Trevithick.

It was a weak enough accusation but it struck home, after a fashion. "Ivor's supplied us with data, yes. He was our eyes in your department, you might say. You see, it was important that we kept up to date on developments in research."

"To spy, in other words."

"Why? Did you have secrets?"

"Yes, I think we did. I think we'd discovered years ago that Lady was giving birth to a distress crop of females. But due to pressure from various sources the news was hushed up. People were just settling in. They didn't want to uproot again, not just yet. So time went by and they settled in too thoroughly, and children were born here, and grew up. Now we have all the makings of a colony, except that the Organisation isn't in the colony business and there's intelligent life already here. Somebody has to co-ordinate all this deception and send optimistic reports to Samaritan HQ, and make sure Lady lingers on, but without a permanent cure."

"You're absolutely right," said Edlin.

"What?"

"I thought it had been obvious for some time. That is exactly the situation. Except that we didn't know about the goron females. You see before you—" he waved a hand at Brassworthy, Carstairs and Cook, "—the core committee, minus Ivor Sabin. Unofficial, of course. I mean, the average resident would rather keep his head in the sand, wouldn't he? So long as someone else does the dirty work for him."

"And you people have been doing the dirty work?"

"I shouldn't have said dirty; it gives the wrong impression. We've done the greatest good for the greatest number. We've made sure Lady lingers on, we've jollied Earthaid along so far as we could, and when they lost patience we persuaded the Organisation to keep us going. All that to keep several thousand people happy and secure. Is that so bad?"

Susanna spoke suddenly. "God, you're a smooth bastard, Manning. So where does Tillini fit into all this?"

"Tillini?" Edlin looked puzzled.

"Isn't he on your core committee?"

"No. Tillini's a muscan, in case you hadn't noticed. They don't think like humans. Tillini wouldn't fit into our plans."

"So why have Security been after Bryn and Mistral all this time?"

"That's clear enough, isn't it? Ivor's reported missing data, Mistral's suspected of sabotage, then there was Marik's body, all kinds of stuff. Nothing to do with us. Security moves in its mysterious way. Anyway, Trevithick and Mistral have been good enough to turn themselves in now, so we shall be pleased to hand them over." He laid his hand on the pistol, ostentatiously.

Susanna said, "You're hoping Tillini will do your dirty work for you this time?"

"These two do represent a potential embarrassment, yes."

She smiled. "Well, I'm afraid you're too late, Manning. The embarrassment has become grim reality. We've sent a warpwire from Martha's office to Earth HQ, revealing all."

For the first time, his calm deserted him. "Do you have to talk melodrama, woman? What the hell do you mean, revealing all?"

"All the reasons why Lady can't be saved, naming names. All the scheming and unexplained deaths. More than enough to jerk the Organisation into wakefulness. I reckon they'll be fuelling up the evacuation ship right now."

Edlin stared at her. "Why in God's name did you do that? It's thousands of people's lives you're playing with!"

"I did it because it's my job. I work directly for Organisation HQ, Manning."

"You? But ..."

"But you couldn't take me seriously, could you? A blonde bimbo. It's a good cover."

Edlin's shoulders slumped. "You stupid bastards. You've screwed everything up. Why couldn't you let well alone? Nobody was being hurt, and the Organisation wasn't exactly going broke. We could have had another twenty, thirty years here." He crossed the room to his terminal and hit a key. A man in Security uniform appeared on the screen. "Hal, we have Trevithick and Mistral Greene here in my office. Come and take them away, will you." He turned to the others. "The law as we know it still applies, Trevithick. I don't fancy your chances with Tillini, but you deserve everything you get."

Behind him, the screen suddenly fizzed and died.

Simultaneously the hum of air conditioning ceased and the door valve sighed and sagged.

"Power outage," said Carstairs. "It'll be back in a minute."

Mistral stepped through from the balcony. The green eyes were hard and bright. "All this talking and nobody getting anywhere. You really piss me off, you people. No, the power won't be back in a minute. The gorons have taken over the power station. Amazing what the little guys can do, once they have a trained leader."

"Who are you kidding?" said Brassworthy sceptically. "A trained leader?"

"Gaston's his name, if you want to deal with him. Trained by Bridget Booker."

"There's armed guards outside the service dome. And the gorons don't have guns or anything. Even if they did, they wouldn't know how to use them."

"There's other ways into that dome," said Mistral. "There's a sewer, for one. And there's a way into that sewer from outside, remember?"

"I'd heard about vandalism in the sewer," said Edlin grimly. "I understood that tunnel of yours had been filled in."

"It don't take stoags a minute to dig through loose dirt. And gorons don't need guns when they've got stoags along with them. Rough on the humans inside the service dome. They won't be armed. They'll be easy meat."

"We'll get Security to handle that problem," snapped Edlin. He was holding his pistol in a businesslike manner. "Albert, check them for weapons."

Looking embarrassed, the financial man ran his hands briefly over Susanna and Mistral, checked Trevithick more thoroughly, then reluctantly dug into Mistral's bag of possessions. He brought out Ivor Sabin's gun.

"You can keep that as a souvenir," said Mistral. "It won't do you any good. See, I knew from the start we'd be wasting our time talking to you people. Talking is playing into your hands—it's what you're good at. Talking, and wasting time. You'd talk and talk and in the end nothing'd happen except Bryn and me would be locked up by Security. And then you'd get onto Earth and tell them our warpwire was somebody's joke. And instead of shipping you out, Earth would set up an enquiry. And by then me and Bryn and Susanna would have gone the same way as Marik Darwin. See what I mean, Bryn?"

His mouth was dry. "What have you done?" he asked.

"I've short-cut things a bit, my love."

And for the first time he noticed the row of vespas perched on the balcony rail.

Mistral had known right from the start that Susanna and Bryn would foul it up between them. They'd got the message through to Earth all right, but that was all they'd done. From that moment on, things went steadily downhill as she'd known they would. They got together with the bad guys and talked endlessly about who was to blame for what, and in the end—surprise!—Bryn was going to submit himself meekly to that great hippo Tillini, and would expect her to do the same. And he'd also expect fair treatment.

Well, she wasn't born yesterday.

The important thing was the gorons, and everyone was too ready to forget that. The gorons had been screwed by the Samaritans for fifty years and finally set on the road to extinction. It was too late to save them, but it wasn't too late for revenge. The gorons didn't know about revenge. But Gaston had grasped the idea quickly enough, once she'd explained it.

"You see, Gaston," she'd told him, "we could have saved you all, but we haven't done it. In the end we'll have killed you all. But here we humans are, all ready to blast off and do the same thing to somebody else. Now, does that sound right to you? Shouldn't something be done about it?"

Yes, he'd grasped it. And when she'd left him to round up a team of gorons and stoags, she'd been confident he'd do his part.

Now it was her turn.

The vespas acted like well-trained animals, zooming in through the door and going for Edlin and his men in fine style. Edlin got one of them, cutting it half, but then the pistol was knocked out of his hand. Which was just as well, because you can do a lot of damage with a laser pistol in a confined space. Edlin tumbled over backward with a vespa on top of him. He screamed once, which was quite enough.

"Stand over here!" she shouted to Bryn. The poor guy didn't know which way to turn, vespas all around and worried about her and Susanna at the same time.

In the end he dodged through the mess and arrived at her side. "Stop them, Mistral," he said.

"No way." There was an awkward moment when it looked as though one of the vespas was going to get Susanna. Bryn would never have forgiven her for that. So she called it off, and Susanna joined the two of them. It was good to see that bloody woman caught off balance for once.

When Edlin's men were all dead she sent the vespas through the door into the corridor. There'd been six of them at first, but now others were scenting the fun and coming to join in. A parade of vespas flowed in from the balcony, through the office and into the body of the dome. That, she thought, should keep people busy for a while.

On the other hand, she realised belatedly, it might have been a bit of a mistake. Once they were out of reach of her voice and her pheromones, they were essentially out of control.

"Stop them!" Bryn said again. And this time it was a sensible suggestion.

"I can't," she admitted. "It's too late."

"At least we'll close this bloody door!" And he pushed past her and operated the balcony door manually. That left about fifty vespas at large in the dome. So far the operation was quite a success. By now Gaston and his gorons should be well settled into the service dome, in control of the generators. Which left three smaller domes still intact, but a girl couldn't have everything.

What she really wanted, was for Bryn to make love to her right now, here on this thick carpet with Susanna watching. In fact she got so far as to take his hand and press it against her thigh, but he was preoccupied.

"For Christ's sake!" he shouted. "How are we going to get those things out of this place?" He was a wonderful guy, but his thinking was sometimes off base.

Susanna spoke for the first time for ages, sounding nicely shaken up. "We've got to go through the dome and burn them down, one by one. We have two pistols now. One for me and one for you, and Mistral will have to use her influence. Right?"

"Suppose I don't want to use my influence," she said. Didn't they realize everything was going according to plan?

"If you don't, Bryn might get killed. Do you want that to happen?"

"Don't be stupid."

Then Bryn said, "What about your father? His office is in this dome."

Dad, in this dome. Dad, who'd sold out to the Organisation and had become one of them, an enemy of the gorons, and an enemy of her. Dad, big and square and in some ways not a bad guy at all.

Dad, standing pressed against the wall just like the man Cook a minute ago, with a vespa moving in on him, stinger pushed forward between its legs.

"Don't talk to me about Dad." By now the vespas would be all over the dome. Some people would see them coming and shut their doors. Others wouldn't.

"What kind of mood will the vespas be in?" Bryn asked her. His eyes were quite cold as he looked at her. Had he stopped loving her or something?

Worried, she answered him truthfully. "They'll be scared, so they'll attack on sight because of that. And the dome's rather like one of their hives, so they may see people as intruders. They don't mean to be hostile, you know."

He gathered up the two guns and gave one to Susanna. She looked as though she knew how to use it. She knew everything, the bloody woman. Then he stared at her again, and for the first time she felt a little scared.

"Just tell me one thing," he said. His voice was as cold as his eyes. "Did you deliberately summon up these vespas?"

What could she say? "Of course not, Bryn. They sniffed out the pheromones in here."

"I just hope you're telling the truth." He left her and stepped cautiously into the corridor. She pushed past him, just in case. The corridor was empty of people, but a vespa squatted on the floor about ten meters away. Bryn shot it and it exploded horribly. They sometimes did that if the beam went in too easily, like at a joint, and heated up the insides. "Come on!" he shouted, and began to run down the corridor. They came across several vespas just around the corner, buzzing and smashing against a closed door. Bryn and Susanna fired at them together, sharing the destruction. Then glass began to shatter and the vespas flew through, and she heard more screaming from the other side.

"Careful where we point these things!" Bryn shouted. So Susanna didn't think of everything, after all.

Most people had gotten wind of the danger and they'd closed their doors. She could see them through the glass walls, sitting tight and looking scared. Nobody seemed to have pistols, and there was no sign of the Security people.

It was depressing, the way Bryn and Susanna worked together, covering one another at awkward corners, moving systematically around the corridors, sometimes firing simultaneously as though they were telepathic or something. Maybe she should have let that vespa take Susanna while she had the chance.

Becoming despondent, she drifted away from them down a side corridor, emitting a calming influence and gathering a small following of quiescent vespas. This whole thing could turn into a personal disaster. The vespas weren't doing as well as she'd hoped. Where were the screaming crowds, the zooming attackers? If a couple of hundred people died it'd be seen as a disaster too huge to blame one girl for. But if only a handful of people were killed they'd be talking murder. She knew bloody well Bryn suspected her of being at the bottom of it. And he might not forgive her, ever. He'd conveniently forget that she saved his life a few times, and instead choose to remember that she'd killed four men in Edlin's office. Not to mention Sabin. Bryn had been radiating disapproval ever since she shot that bastard yesterday.

At least the gorons had made their presence felt in the service dome. The Samaritans would tread more carefully from now on.

She realised that for some seconds she'd been staring at the words DIRECTOR OF ENGINEERING. Dad's office. She looked through the slack door.

Her heart thumped.

Dad lay on the floor; she could see his head and shoulders sticking out from behind the desk. She pushed her way through the drooping valve and laid a hand on his face. It was still warm. Well, it would be, wouldn't it? She shoved her hand down inside the neck of his uniform, trying to feel a heartbeat. Everything was terribly still in there. He was dead. No doubt about it.

She would not cry.

She heard a clicking and a scrabbling. She wheeled around. A vespa perched on the back of a chair in the corner of the office, watching her. The vespa that had killed Dad. Six other vespas waited for her outside.

She smiled at them through the glass. Funny how when you wanted to act friendly, you went the whole hog. She thought welcome, she extended her hands and acted welcome. One by one they scrambled into the office. They stood around her, waiting.

Now she thought: Kill . . .

Instantly everything was confusion. She backed out of the door hastily and watched from the other side of the glass wall. Seven vespas whirled and fought in a fearsome maelstrom of snapping mandibles, jabbing stingers and thrashing wings. Chairs crashed to the floor, papers fluttered everywhere, cupboard doors flew open and contents were scattered. She flinched involuntarily as a vespa thudded into the other side of the glass. Gradually the battle condensed into a struggling heap beside the desk.

Suddenly it was over. Vespas backed off. Five dying vespas lay twitching under the desk. The survivors began to preen themselves noisily. Cautiously she re-entered the office.

She should do something about Dad. It wasn't right to leave the poor guy lying on the floor like that. At least she should clear some of the litter off him and lay him out straight. She began to gather up the scattered papers, then stopped.

One of her paintings lay on the floor nearby.

No doubt about it; it was her work. A picture of the five domes of Samarita at sunset, all crimson and silver. She'd been quite proud of that one. Martha had sold it to a family heading out to Deganwy, so she'd said.

So she'd said . . .

A cupboard door hung half-open; the painting had spilled out of that, along with others. She flipped through them; all her paintings, all ones Martha had supposedly sold to people leaving Goronwy. And she'd had the money for them; she'd spent it on food. So who had paid for them?

She sat on the floor beside her father's body, and at last she began to cry.

CHAPTER 32

BY THE TIME THE LAST OF THE VESPAS had been tracked down and shot, fourteen humans were dead, including those in Edlin's office. All of Samarita was in shock. For the first time in fifty years, people had been exposed to the unpredictable dangers of living on an alien world. Now a number of them were heard to talk longingly of Mother Earth. The killing of the female embryos had become common knowledge, there was a feeling of communal guilt, and it was clear that life on Goronwy would never be the same, for humans or gorons.

The last stronghold of the vespas was the office of the Director of Engineering, where Security forces found five. The creatures attacked immediately with a strange kind of desperation, unlike their normal deliberate approach with stinger pushed forward. Sharp mandibles and foreclaws were brought to bear, and twice the Security team fled the length of the short corridor before plucking up the courage to return and resume battle. Glass flew in all directions, reinforcements arrived, and eventually the vespas lay dead and dismembered around the office.

They found Mistral lying over the body of her father behind the desk. When they rolled her over her eyes were open, unfocused and staring fixedly. They thought she was dead. Then they saw blood flowing freely from cuts to her head and body. The power was still out, so they sent a runner for medical assistance. Susanna arrived within a couple of minutes. When Mistral saw her, her eyes came alive and she began to scream and struggle. She was subdued with a transdermic. The stretcher team arrived soon afterward and Susanna accompanied her to the hospital.

Meanwhile Trevithick was being questioned by Tillini in Edlin's office. The bodies of Edlin, Carstairs, Brassworthy and Cook had been laid in a row against the wall and covered with blankets. Tillini stood against the balcony valve, huge head slightly bowed in recognition of the low human ceiling. Rob Mauser leaned against the door valve, pistol in hand.

"For God's sake let me go and see how she is!" shouted Trevithick again.

"Susanna has gone to deal with the matter," rumbled Tillini imperturbably, "and she will report back in due course. Nothing you can do will affect events. I fail to understand your excessive concern for this girl, when a number of more worthy humans have died. So answer my questions, please. Now that Susanna has gone, perhaps we will have answers of a less flippant nature."

"She told you. Edlin held us at gunpoint. He and the others are responsible for sending fraudulent reports to Earth. It's been going on for years. Others were doing it before Edlin came."

"Yes, yes. That is none of my business. I want to know how and why the vespas penetrated the dome."

"You already know that!" Trevithick was beside himself with anxiety and frustration. What had happened to Mistral? Was she still alive? The Security runner had talked about extensive injuries. Had she been stung by a vespa? "They came in through the balcony door valve, soon after the power failure."

"Yes, but why? They've never done this before. As you know, the power was switched off by goron terrorists. An unusual coincidence that the vespas should then attack, I think."

"I'm not familiar with goron or vespan mentality."

"You're more familiar with gorons than most, Trevithick. You've been living among them for many days now."

"The goron language includes pheromone signals. I suppose it's possible they could incite vespas to attack. I doubt it, though."

Mauser spoke. "What about Mistral Greene? She's kinda weird. Could she be at the bottom of this?"

"Of course not."

"She's cute in a funny kind of way, wouldn't you say, Bryn?"

"I'm not trying to protect her, if that's what you mean."

The questioning went on and on. It became obvious that neither Tillini nor Mauser had any clear idea of Mistral's powers or Bryn's involvement, but that their suspicions were aroused.

In the end Trevithick's patience ran out. "To hell with you!" he shouted. "Shoot me if you like. I'm going to see how Mistral is." He took hold of Mauser's gun arm to pull him away from the door.

It was fortunate that Susanna arrived at that moment.

"Getting a little impatient, are we?"

"How is she?"

"She'll live," said Susanna briefly. "Mostly cuts, a few bruises, no broken bones. Luckily we don't need power to handle that. She's in shock, though. Ralph's dead."

"Oh, God."

"There'd been a lot of activity in his office. Dead vespas everywhere and she was lying among it all. Poor kid. Maybe she'll be able to tell us what happened one day, but my guess is it'll be a while yet."

Tillini said, "This is very unfortunate. I had hoped that Mistral would be able to reason with the gorons in the service dome. If such is not the case then you must do it, Trevithick. You know these creatures. As I understand it, they have activated the lock that isolates the dome from outside. We cannot break in. The only alternative is the tunnel Mistral dug into the sewer. I suspect that's how the gorons got in."

"Tunnel? What tunnel?" Trevithick feigned ignorance.

Tillini let it go. "I don't want to send an armed team up there except as a last resort. There's too much delicate equipment in there for excitable humans to be waving lasers around. If you could settle the matter simply, without damage, we will be prepared to forget previous differences."

Susanna laughed. "That's very decent of you, Tillini. Can he trust

343

you? We haven't found out who killed Marik Darwin yet. And then there was Gary Docksteader. And others going back over the years."

Tillini addressed Trevithick. "I cannot understand this woman, so it is better to ignore her. You will talk to the gorons?"

"I'll do it. Just show me where this tunnel is."

"You don't give anything away, do you, Trevithick? Mauser will take you to the entrance. By the way, do you know why the gorons cut off the power?"

He thought for a moment. "My guess is they're flexing their muscles and giving us a strong hint to get off their world. There's no better way to do that, than to cut off our power. Life in Samarita depends on it."

"They will not do it again," said Tillini. "We will strengthen our security."

"But it won't matter any more, not after what's happened at Ladysend." He explained the contents of the warpwire to Earth. "So we've recommended to Earth that we pull out," he concluded. "We'll let the gorons have their world back."

"You have done well," said Tillini after a pause.

It was impossible to read the face of a muscan, but Trevithick got the impression Tillini meant this sincerely.

Which was worrying.

He'd been expecting to find rotting stoag carcasses in the tunnel, but there were none. Who had cleared away the residue of that battle? Surely not Security. Possibly the stoags themselves. Possibly they fed their casualties to the vast mother stoag in much the same way as old gorons committed themselves to Lady.

The sewer was dry. He made his way toward the service dome by flashlight, wary of any lurking and aggressive stoags that might have been left behind as guards. Ever since Wilfred had attacked Sabin so fiercely he'd viewed the beasts in a different light. An animal of such size and weight, with heavy paws equipped with claws for digging, would be a fearsome adversary in a culvert such as this. They were not always the gentle vegetarians that Mistral had originally led him to believe.

A disk of light glowed ahead and soon he was climbing through an open hatch into fresh air. The service dome was smaller than the others and open-plan. Much of the skin was translucent. Large open areas housed the sewage treatment plant, the reverse osmosis plant and distillery, the hydroponics farms, the engineering workshops and the power station. Behind them rose the storage areas, built like outsize shelving and extending three quarters of the way up the dome's height.

The power station was fed by external solar panels and consisted mainly of storage batteries and switching devices to ensure fluctuating demands were met at all times. A number of gorons sat quietly on the low wall bounding this area; their stoags, some twenty of them, rooted among the hydroponics vats nearby. Some thirty humans sat in disconsolate attitudes on the concrete floor, watched over by four gorons and four stoags. Near the storage area elevators a lone stoag lay motionless.

Trevithick shouted and waved. A goron hurried to meet him.

"Bryn Trevithick! It's good to see you."

"I wish I could say the same, Gaston. What the hell have you guys gotten yourselves into?"

"It was all Mistral's idea," he said proudly. "We were to cut off the power, which would paralyse the domes. She told us humans were very dependent on electricity, unlike us. She didn't say what she was going to do next, but I could tell it involved fighting. Has it happened?"

"Yes. Did she tell you why?"

"Revenge!" he intoned wide-eyed, as though it were a hosanna. "We will avenge ourselves on the humans. Then Goronwy will be ours again!"

"Of course it will," he said impatiently. "You don't need revenge to make that happen. A lot of humans have died pointlessly."

"What an honour, to die at the hands of Mistral!"

It was a waste of time, trying to impress a goron with death rolls. "Mistral is badly hurt herself."

That one hit home. "She will live?"

"I thought you didn't care who lived or died."

"We need Mistral. She is unique and she must not die. She must lead us through the difficult times ahead."

He eyed the earnest little man. "She'll be going back to Earth with the rest of us," he said gently. "I thought that was what you people wanted."

"Mistral will not go to Earth. She knows we need her."

"Maybe." He looked around the dome. "Well, Gaston. What are we going to do about this? Have you had enough of revenge for the time being?"

"I don't know. Would you think so? It will be good to get back to our normal work. First I must show you something." He led Trevithick over to the storage areas. Each storage cell was about five meters high by five wide and twenty deep, of modular construction built to fit into starships. Some were full of imported items a project would not normally produce for itself, others contained the cast-off junk of fifty years. They ran the width of the dome and were stacked dizzily high.

"What happened to the stoag?" asked Trevithick. The motionless animal was dead. And it had died in some agony too; its neck was arched back and its teeth bared in a fixed snarl.

"That's what I wanted to show you. I would not want your people to drink this nectar unknowingly." He indicated a nearby cell where a mass of stage scenery had been stored; backcloths, props, even what looked like parts of a medieval castle. Behind this were stacked a few grey drums on which the word MACRO-NUTRIENTS was stencilled, followed by the letters N-P-Mg-S-K-Ca with a percentage for each. He recognised the drums from his tour on Annecy. They were Outward Ho issue, probably produced colonially.

"The stoag drank this? It's not nectar, Gaston. It's fertiliser for the hydroponics fields."

The goron looked puzzled. "I saw the word nutrient there, and the stoag was hungry. Liquids are for drinking, aren't they?"

"Not always." There was a spigot knocked into the base of the

346

nearest drum and a bowl beneath it. "Human liquids come in many forms."

But macronutrients were not usually shipped in liquid form.

He picked up the bowl and sniffed the puddle in the bottom. "How much of this stuff did the stoag drink?"

"Very little."

He found a flask, filled it with the liquid and corked it. "I'm going to take this for analysis. I don't like the look of it. It's been contaminated in some way. Make sure nobody else drinks any." On an impulse he went to the hydroponics area, opened a tank lid and pulled a lettuce from its bed of medium. He laid the lettuce on the concrete floor and poured a little of the liquid over the leaves. Within a minute the leaves had begun to deliquesce into a brown slime. He stared at it in horror. If this stuff had been used in the hydroponics fields it would have wiped out Samarita's entire supply of fresh food.

"You're frightened, Bryn."

"No, it's all right. I just let my imagination run away with me for a moment, that's all. Now, I'd like you and your people to go back the way you came and disperse. It's possible that our Security forces may want to take action against you, and I wouldn't like that to happen."

"You mean revenge doesn't stop? Each side takes it in turn?"

"Well, yes. Now get your people out of here and we'll talk later."

The gorons left quietly, the stoags followed, and within five minutes the power was back on and the service dome back in operation.

"It could be some kind of herbicide, but I have a nasty feeling it's much worse than that."

Susanna held the flask up to the light. "I'll run a few tests."

"Can you do it right away? Everything's wrong with this stuff, Susanna. If it's what the label says, it should be powder, not liquid. And they tell me that stoag died almost immediately; I mean, herbicide can be poisonous to animals, but not that poisonous.

While you're checking it out I'll run through the shipping inwards records. I'd like to know where it came from and who ordered it. There's enough in those drums to wipe out every living thing on Goronwy."

He used the terminal in Susanna's lab and worked in reverse chronological order. Shuttle arrivals on Goronwy were rare; one per year at most. Cell units were many and varied, however. They averaged over two hundred per shuttle, each cell having its own manifest. In general cells were addressed to departments; occasionally two departments would share a cell. Trevithick ran a search on Fertiliser. In recent years shipments would be addressed to Jonathan Cook, the late Director of Sustenance.

He found very little fertiliser was being shipped in. That made sense; by now Samarita was almost self-sufficient; fertiliser was a by-product of the sewage plant. Only special macro-and micronutrients were needed these days. Had the drums deteriorated and deliquesced over decades?

An hour later, quite unexpectedly, he found what he'd been looking for.

He'd missed it the first time around because the shipment had not come from Earth. One year ago, twelve drums of macronutrients had been imported from the Outward Ho colony on Deganwy. That much made sense; Deganwy was in the same system as Goronwy so it was a much shorter haul than shipping fertiliser from Earth. The drums had arrived in a cell booked to Martha Sunshine, which accounted for the theatrical oddments in the same cell.

Susanna was back, looking over his shoulder. "A split shipment? Just make sure the drums were charged back to Sustenance, Bryn."

He glanced at her quickly. There had been something odd in her voice. He called up the waybill details. "No, they weren't. I guess it was an oversight."

"And I guess Jonathan Cook didn't need them. Prepare yourself for a shock, Trevithick. You want to know what's in those drums? Trent's Vivicide."

"Christ! That stuff was outlawed years ago!" Trevithick himself had been partly responsible for it being taken off the market. Trent's Vivicide was the most effective herbicide known to humans. It was absorbed through the leaves and killed plants within minutes, becoming inert within three hours. Its disadvantage, discovered after extensive use, was that it also attacked animal life forms of a certain genetic structure. Humans and other Earth animals were immune, fortunately. "I understand they used it here to clear bush-trap from the construction areas," he said. "But that was fifty years ago. It was banned ten years ago. Why would we bring it in last year?"

Susanna put her arm around his shoulders as he stared at the images on the screen. "Ask yourself whose consignment it came with. Ask yourself who's property it's sitting among right now. And the mislabelling wasn't done here on Goronwy, Bryn. See what I'm getting at? Now ask yourself who knows people on Deganwy well enough to have them mislabel a banned product."

"Not Martha."

"Martha, yes. The very same. Our Director of Entertainment who's been negotiating with Deganwy over *Barker Sam*. A cool customer disguised as a red-hot Momma."

"I can't believe it. Why would she want twelve drums of Trent's? What would she gain from wiping out our hydroponics?"

She shook his shoulders gently. "Bryn darling, use your commonsense. Goronwy life forms all have a similar basic genetic structure. And the stoag died. Just imagine what a few drums of Trent's tipped down that sewer would do to Lady. Remember what Ralph Greene said? The sewer could act as a giant hypodermic for administering drugs to Lady sub-cutaneously?"

"Okay, I remember you telling me. I just can't take it in. So you're saying Martha Sunshine has shipped in the means to kill Lady, but she hasn't done it. I still don't get it."

"Bryn, my love. You and I are going to pay a visit to Martha Sunshine right now, and we're going to interest her in a theory or two. Oh, and bring that pistol."

The three of them sat around the coffee table in Martha's office. It was an interesting room; the walls were covered with holograms of theatrical personalities that had visited Goronwy over the years, all mouthing and smiling in their little alcoves. If asked—Trevithick knew to his cost—Martha would turn up the sound on any hologram and they would hear fulsome platitudes spouting forth.

He was content to let Susanna do the talking.

"A bad business, the vespas getting in," she was saying. "It's not just the cost in lives. It's the loss of goodwill between us and the gorons."

"Do you really worry about that kind of thing, darling?" boomed Martha. "Hell, we'll be off this godforsaken rock before long."

"All of us? I imagine some will be staying."

"What the hell will they live on? Samarita isn't self-supporting, and humans like their creature comforts. You have to exploit a world before you can scratch a living from it. You know that as well as I do."

"Maybe Outward Ho would help out," said Susanna. "After all, they're already on Deganwy, so why not move in here as well? Two colonies in the same system can't be bad."

"Outward Ho?" Martha examined her fingernails.

"Of course, they'd have to wait for the gorons to all die off. That could take thirty years. And that would be a pity, really, because it'd mean all those Samaritans who might otherwise have stayed, would be gone by then. So Outward Ho wouldn't have a ready-made nucleus of colonists already here."

"I guess they wouldn't," said Martha slowly. "Too bad."

"But if Lady were to die really soon, the goron males wouldn't have anything left to live for and they'd all jump into the rotting remains. Which would mean Outward Ho could move in right away without bringing the wrath of the Galaxy down on its head."

Now Martha's plump face creased into lines of laughter. "You know, darling, you're absolutely right! Maybe if you warpwired Outward Ho and suggested it, they'd cut you in. You're in the wrong business."

"There's just one drawback," said Susanna lightly. "Lady isn't going to die quickly. Not unless somebody speeds things up."

"A good way," said Martha, playing along with it, "would be to accidentally crash a copter into Lady Herself. That might do it. Then again, the abdomen might live on. I'm not sure what the ethical position would be, if that happened."

"It might be easier simply to pump poison down the sewer. That wouldn't be so easily detected. It would have to be something quick acting, fatal to Lady but relatively harmless to humans."

Martha heaved her bulk to her feet, chuckling. As she leaned forward, gigantic breasts almost spilled from her low neckline. Like Susanna, she was rarely seen in uniform. "Remember Trent's Vivicide? What a pity it was banned. You could kill an awful lot of Lady with a few drums of Trent's. I believe they used it to clear this site. Excellent stuff on bushtrap."

"It so happens Bryn came across a few drums of Trent's today," said Susanna quietly.

Martha waddled slowly around the table and came to a halt behind Trevithick, leaning over him and putting her arms around his chest so that her breasts rested on the back of his head and neck. "Did you now, Bryn? And where did you find them?" Her arms tightened around him.

"In fertiliser drums in one of your storage cells, actually," he croaked nervously, wishing he could handle this as well as Susanna.

She let him go suddenly. "Fertiliser drums? My God, that could be a costly mistake. We'd better warn Jonathan Cook. We would-n't want him pouring the stuff into the hydroponics."

"Jonathan's dead."

"Good grief yes, I forgot. And Edlin and the other members of the stay-at-home committee. I'm sure you've tumbled to their stalling tactics by now. Ivor's been keeping me informed." A shadow crossed her face. "And now he's gone too. Well, at least there's nobody around to dispute that warpwire we sent off. So that should pretty well wrap things up here, so far as the Organization's concerned."

Trevithick said bitterly, "You must have been delighted about that warpwire. It really clears the decks for Outward Ho, huh?"

"Always pleased to be on the side of law, order and good-looking men."

Susanna said, "Bridget Booker committed suicide. She couldn't face being responsible for the death of all those goron females. Can you?"

"Suicide, huh? Poor old girl." She looked genuinely sorry. "That's the price you pay for taking life too seriously, darlings."

"It would be nice if we didn't have to, wouldn't it?" Susanna herself was looking unusually serious. "But there have been an awful lot of deaths since you came here. Are you going to retire wealthy, happy in the knowledge of a job well done and mouths well shut? Or will you get the occasional twinge of conscience in the middle of the night? How much has Outward Ho paid you for preparing Goronwy for colonisation, Martha?"

She laughed, breasts wobbling. "'Confess, confess', she cried. This is just like the last act of one of our amateur dramatics."

"I work directly for the Organisation HQ, Martha. If I had a badge, this is the moment I'd whip it out. I've known for some time there are two groups of bad guys here. There's the Procrastinators, Edlin and his committee and their predecessors, who don't kill people—even female gorons—but who've done everything else in their power to hinder any cure for Lady. And there's the Pirates.

"I wasn't sure of the Pirates' identity until recently, but they're a ruthless bunch of cut-throats, believe me. They kill gorons and humans, anyone who stands in their way, and they'd like to kill Lady but they can't make it too obvious. They tried to use subtlety by enlisting Marik Darwin to whip up goron resentment, but that failed so Marik was disposed of. The Procrastinators have been playing into their hands by making sure Lady isn't cured. The Pirates may be smaller in number than the Procrastinators but they always stood a better chance of winning out in the end because they had Outward Ho behind them."

"All of Outward Ho?" said Martha, wide eyed. "The full majesty?"

"A small group of influential people on Deganwy, mostly muscans. And now the Organization's leaving, they'll be moving in. You can bet the touring cast of *Barker Sam* will include a few well-chosen shakers and movers when it arrives. So the only thing left, is for Lady to die quickly and cleanly. Trent's Vivicide would be ideal."

"Author! Author!" Martha clapped vigorously. "An impressive script, Susanna."

"But they're using you, Martha. Don't you understand? Outward Ho is run by muscans. Apart from you the chief Pirates here are muscans: Tillini, Murdo and Vorda. Once you've outlived your usefulness they'll get rid of you like they got rid of Marik Darwin. They don't think the way we do. They act with a horrible kind of logic, and they use humans to do their dirty work. They're a blight on the Galaxy, and I can't understand how a human can sell herself out to them!" Susanna had risen to her feet on the last words, pink-faced.

Martha strolled over to her desk and sat on it, skirt riding up, big thighs spreading under the weight, fat calves swinging. "You can't understand, huh?" Now her face was pink, too. "Maybe that's because you're beautiful, Susanna. You didn't spend half your life playing fat people's parts in lousy amateur shows, and playing them for laughs, yet. People laugh at you because you're witty, but it doesn't matter how witty I am, they'll laugh at me because I'm fat. Except the muscans. How much of the work in your department is cosmetic surgery, Susanna? Make this girl prettier by straightening her nose, make that guy more handsome with a hair transplant? But what can't you fix? Fat. Blubber. Flab. Destructive behaviour like eating too much. What can you do about that, huh? Carve me like a turkey? The hell with humans and their crazy standards!"

And she wriggled until her skirt rode up to her waist. She jerked at her neckline and her breasts tumbled out. "The hell with you!" she shouted. "Look at me! Is all this human?"

Susanna said quietly, "You underestimate yourself, Martha."

"Oh, sure I do. But Doctor Trevithick is the expert here. Give me your opinion, Bryn."

He regarded her, trying not to see the bloated exhibition of bitterness or the killer hidden underneath. He tried to see Martha Sunshine, the bouncy, vital Director of Entertainment who'd charmed him in the past. And after a moment he succeeded.

"Really, Martha, I've always thought you looked great," he said mildly. "You must have known that, surely?"

She blinked, slid down from the desk, pulled her skirt down and her bra up. "And I'm a great goddamned actor as well. But I don't want the part you're offering me, Susanna. You see, there's no point in thinking about it now, not with *Barker Sam* coming in, and everybody getting ready to leave. We're all going to be too busy to worry about trivialities. So let's forget our differences, shall we, and try to enjoy our last days on Goronwy."

Trevithick stared at her. She smiled back blandly. Then he heard Susanna laughing. "What the hell, Bryn," she said. "It's better than Tillini's jail. Come on, let's see how Mistral's doing."

"Bless you, my children," said Martha Sunshine the killer.

CHAPTER 33

THE SHUTTLE ARRIVED fifteen days later. Trevithick and Susanna joined a crowd of some four thousand at the grandly-named Goronwy Spaceport to watch. The spaceport was, in fact, an area of cleared bushtrap and aeolus five kilometers to the west of the domes. No buildings, just blackened soil. The shuttle sat on its tail of flame and squatted toward them out of a pale blue morning sky.

"It always looks as though it's going to land right on top of you," said Susanna cheerfully. "One day it will. It's just a matter of time."

Trevithick had been so busy since receiving the reply to his fateful warpwire that he'd hardly had time to consider the overall picture. Earth HQ had authorized him to act as chairman of the local Board of Directors and to oversee the evacuation. They'd also insisted that Susanna sit on Board meetings with full voting powers. A Organization starship would arrive in orbit in thirty days. The shuttle presently arriving would leave in twenty days, loaded with personnel and all the equipment that it could hold.

And that would be the end of the Samaritan project on Goronwy.

The shuttle, bright silver with the huge words OUTWARD HO emblazoned on the hull, touched down gently a couple of kilometers away, shuddering with the thrust. The engines died, the dust settled. Ear muffs and goggles came off and excited conversation started up.

"Nice of Outward Ho to lend us their Deganwy shuttle for the evacuation, don't you think, Bryn?" remarked Susanna. "A touching example of cooperation between corporate giants."

"My heart bleeds. They've got all the *Barker Sam* cast and equipment on board, and there's a small deputation coming to talk to us at this afternoon's Board meeting. But otherwise, it's almost as though they're speeding us on our way."

Susanna said thoughtfully, "They must have moved fast to get *Barker Sam* all packed up. And why would they bother, with everybody leaving here in a few days? It's not just a one-night show. It has a continuing plot going on for ten days or so. Uncommonly good of Martha to organize it all, just for the pleasure of the departing Samaritans. It stinks, Trevithick. And there's little we can do about it."

He watched the elevator descend from the base of the hull. Squat vehicles trundled out, hauling trains of loaded wagons. It was the first indication of the great size of the shuttle: those tiny centipedes crawling away from its belly. "Time to go," he said, turning away.

At this moment a distressing event occurred. He'd already noticed a woman glancing at him from time to time. She looked vaguely familiar but he couldn't place her. She was heavily built, wearing brown overalls; her face was plump and pale, her eyes protruded slightly. She looked to be about forty.

In half a dozen quick steps she was at his side, grasping his forearm and goggling up into his face. "Bryn Trevithick, aren't you? You don't know me. I'm too low on the totem pole for you to bother." She stepped back a pace as though to get a better view of him, although still holding onto his arm. "So you're responsible for us all being thrown out of our homes. I expect you're very pleased with yourself."

Annoyed, he jerked his arm free. "I'm sorry you feel that way. But if you don't like the idea of leaving your home you shouldn't have joined the Organization in the first place. You know all Samaritan projects come to an end."

"I was born here. I had no choice. My kids were born here. You're uprooting us and shipping us out to God knows where like a herd of cattle. You bastard. You bastard! Everybody knows it's you. You're the one who persuaded the Organization to close us down."

"We'd have been closed down in any case, sooner or later."

"Not with Manning Edlin in charge, we wouldn't. But now he's dead, and Cook and Brassworthy and Carstairs, all the ones who fought for us and gave us hope. Now they've died for us. You have blood on your hands, Trevithick, and everybody knows it!"

Susanna stepped between the woman and Trevithick as it looked as though she was about to attack him. "Just shut up and piss off, will you?" she said forcefully.

But people were beginning to edge closer, muttering. It looked as though an ugly situation might develop.

"And there's going to be more blood on your hands if you try to get us into that shuttle!" shouted the woman, looking around for support. "I tell you, Trevithick, we're not going to take it! You're going to have a revolution in Samarita!"

"Bryn!" Susanna had started up their ATV. "Hop aboard. You won't do any good here."

It went against the grain, but she was right. The muttering had escalated into shouting and a number of fists were clenched. He threw a leg over the little vehicle and Susanna gunned the engine. "A nasty moment," he observed, heart pounding as they sped away.

"There'll be others. You're too polite for this kind of thing, Bryn. Those people aren't interested in reasoned argument; they just want to kick somebody's teeth in. And I don't want those teeth to be yours. Maybe you should take a lesson or two from Tillini on how to handle opposition."

He had to laugh. "I'll have a word with him at this afternoon's Board meeting."

"It's worrying, though, the way they've made martyrs out of Edlin and his gang. I just hope no new leaders crawl out of the wood-work." She slowed, swung the vehicle in a half-circle and stopped. They looked back.

The crowd were all facing in the same direction, but they weren't watching the unloading of the shuttle. They'd stopped an approaching ATV and two people were standing on top of a loaded truck, waving their arms as they addressed the multitude.

"We're in for a rough ten days," said Susanna.

It was a very different Board of Directors that met that afternoon. Gone were the ranks of the Procrastinators, their places taken by rather nervous-looking deputies. A welcome addition from the aesthetic point of view was Susanna, sitting between Trevithick and Janet Starseeker. Martha Sunshine was there too, at the request of Tillini.

"I call the meeting to order," said Trevithick, the memory of the crowd at the spaceport very fresh. No doubt they'd have wrapped up their impromptu meeting by now. Would they disperse, or would they head this way in a mob?

The meeting started with an involved discussion on the evacuation schedule. Everybody had problems with it. Nobody stood any chance of getting everything packed and loaded on the shuttle by the projected departure date. "Then leave it behind," Trevithick was forced to say again and again. "We can't delay the starship."

The situation had been worsened by the death of Ralph Greene, who would normally have organized dismantling and shipping of much of the equipment. His deputy, although much respected as a proximation whiz, was next to useless as a manager. His feebleness caused outbursts of anger among people needing decisions before they could plan ahead.

Trevithick and Susanna did their best, but an air of negativity prevailed. Indeed, thought Trevithick, the Board was like a microcosm of Samarita itself: a bunch of whingers bent on preserving an impractical status quo. He found himself wondering how Manning Edlin would have handled these people. And now he was in the chair . . . He drifted into an erotic fantasy, feeling the warmth of Susanna's thigh against his. Ivor Sabin's words came back to him: The power lies here with me. Did sex and power always go hand in hand? He gazed around the table; in a minute he'd call a halt to the bickering and make a ruling or two. The power lies here with me.

But it didn't, really.

He'd known it all along. Everybody around the table knew it. You could tell, by whom they deferred to, and whom they glanced at when making a point. His own power was a tenuous thing, bestowed by faceless people light-years away, fragile, easily broken by a chance thread of light from a laser pistol.

The real power lay with Martha Sunshine and the muscans, Tillini, Murdo, Vorda.

"I think we might see the delegation from Deganwy now, might we, Bryn?" said Martha when the various combatants paused to draw breath. "We can go on for hours arguing like this, but there's no point in being impolite to people who've been kind enough to help us."

It was unanswerable. "Bring them in," he told the man nearest the door.

The delegation consisted of three purple-robed muscans, who introduced themselves as Bajin, Felto and Yed. Yed was the head honcho, it seemed. There was a pause while people scuttled around looking for muscan chairs to accommodate them. Eventually Yed was seated at the table opposite Trevithick, with Bajin and Felto sitting immediately behind in arrowhead formation. The three exchanged nods and gestures with the muscan members of the Samaritan Board, but ignored the humans.

Trevithick was expecting the worst, but was unsure what the worst might be. "Welcome," he said. "It's always good to receive visitors from another world. I hope you enjoy your stay here on Goronwy, and on behalf of the Board I'd like to thank the people of Deganwy for making their shuttle available to us." He tried a feeble smile. "Our projects don't stay long enough anywhere to warrant a permanent shuttle."

"Yes," said Yed. At least it spoke in the human tongue. "We have a specific reason for this visit, of course."

"I assumed such was the case." Apprehension was making Trevithick sound pompous. Susanna nudged him. "So, what can we do for you, Yed?"

"We were sorry to hear of the problems your colony has been facing in recent days. Withdrawal of Earthaid and the threat of closing down, a brief reprieve and new hopes, only to be dashed when it was found that false information on progress had been sent to—"

"Hold it!" Trevithick wasn't going to let Yed get away with that. "A couple of points. First, this is not a colony; it's a Samaritan project of limited duration. Second, how did you know about the false information?"

"It is common knowledge," said Yed. Martha was smiling openly at Trevithick.

"All right, go on," he said to Yed.

"As I said, we were sorry. And we would like to help. We have already placed our shuttle at your disposal, but we can do more. We are aware that very many of your employees would like to stay on Goronwy. Who can blame them? This is their home. Such a personal upheaval is not a thing Outward Ho likes to see. Such misery, such tragedy. So many hopes left behind, and the unknown still to be faced."

Yed uttered an odd droning noise. It was echoed by Bajin and Felto, and briefly by Tillini, Murdo and Vorda. It was the muscan demonstration of sympathy.

"They knew all that when they signed on," snapped Trevithick. He was getting a little tired of this particular issue.

"So on behalf of Outward Ho, we have come to offer our help. We are prepared to fund this project ourselves for so long as any of your employees wish to stay on Goronwy. In due course Lady will die and, in the absence of intelligent life on Goronwy, Outward Ho will officially take possession. Your employees will automatically become members of our new colony. They need never leave. And without the gorons and the attendant phero-mone problem, this will be a much more pleasant world to live in."

There was a stunned silence. Martha Sunshine—who was one of the few present not stunned—was the first to speak. "That is a very generous offer, Yed."

Ignoring Susanna's restraining grip on his thigh, Trevithick lurched to his feet and shouted, "You can go to hell!"

"But doesn't this solve all our problems, Bryn?" asked Martha, eyebrows raised in surprise.

"It makes a gift of Goronwy to Outward Ho, with ready-made colonists already in place! How long do you think Lady will last, when the only people left here are those with a vested interest in killing her off as soon as possible?"

"Lady's incurable and infertile. There are no more foetuses on the way. She doesn't matter any more, Bryn. I'm sorry, but that's the truth of it."

He stared around the table, not really expecting any support, but to his surprise a number of people met his eyes; a hopeful sign.

Janet Starseeker said, "Excuse me, but I do think we still have a duty to Lady and the surviving males. I would like to put forward the motion that we evacuate as planned, but leave behind a small group of Organization people to help Lady and the males through their final years as best we can."

"According to recent estimates," said Martha, "that may be as long as fifty years. Don't you think you're being unduly stubborn, Bryn? You're sacrificing the happiness of several thousand people to a principle. Loosen up, darling."

He felt Susanna's warm breath against his ear. "Back off gracefully, Bryn," she whispered. "The bloody woman's right."

"But if you need convincing, Bryn," Martha continued, "just come out onto the balcony for a moment."

She walked over to the balcony door and activated it. As the valve opened, the chanting of thousands of voices filled the boardroom. She beckoned to Trevithick. He followed reluctantly, passed through the valve and joined her outside.

Below them a huge crowd had assembled. As soon as they saw Trevithick the chanting broke up and became a swelling roar of anger. Rocks began to patter against the wall of the dome, fortunately far below them, but the meaning was obvious.

"And they don't know about Outward Ho's offer yet, darling," said Martha. "What will happen when they hear you've turned it down?"

The announcement of Outward Ho's offer caused much rejoicing among the inhabitants of Samarita. It never occurred to people that it might be rejected. After all, why should it? It was so obviously the best solution from all points of view. So everybody would become employees of Outward Ho? So what? It was just another faceless corporation from somewhere in the Galaxy. And it was the biggest and most prestigious of the colonization outfits, with an excellent pension scheme.

And it was comforting to know there was another Outward Ho colony in the same system. No doubt exchanges of personnel would be arranged between Goronwy and Deganwy. That would be interesting.

Within a few hours everyone was sold on the idea of working for Outward Ho. Trevithick's grudging announcement accepting the offer was a formality. Immediately afterward he left with Susanna in her copter, and soon they were sitting on the chesterfield in her cottage, drinking mead and watching the setting sun turn the lake to crimson.

"Sulking," said Susanna. "That's what we're doing. We've accepted defeat with bad grace, and we've run off for a damned good sulk. That's what I'm doing, anyway. I don't know about you. For all I know you've been heavily bribed and you're sitting there gloating."

"No such luck." He took a deep drink from his mug. "God only knows what the Organization will think of me after this. I've lost them a few thousand excellent people."

"Good grief, you've changed your views on the quality of our staff, haven't you?"

"Well, all right, but the Organization doesn't know the truth. And I don't feel like telling them."

"I'll tell them. They trust me. And they trust you too, after you blew the gaff."

"They didn't trust me when they fired me."

She stared at him. "Fired you? They never fired you, Bryn. Murdo and Martha cooked up that notice of dismissal between them. I thought you knew."

After a pause for amazed reappraisal a thought occurred to him. "Was Edlin involved?"

"I don't think so. It may have come as a genuine surprise to him. He would have been uneasy about your Confessional, but there wasn't much he could do about it. Martha and Murdo knew a good man when they saw one, though. So they acted accordingly. And all the time your nasty little friend Ivor was running between three camps. His biggest loyalty was to Martha, because he knew Martha had Tillini on her side. He was no hero, little Ivor."

This brought a mental image of a young woman sitting beside Sabin in a goron shack, plotting murder. "How was Mistral this morning?" he asked.

She hesitated. "Pretty good. She's coming out of it. It really was a rough passage for her, Bryn. She'll be okay to see you in a day or so. Sorry I've had to keep you away, but she needed complete quiet and continuous therapy. I'm glad to say she showed signs of regaining her foul temper yesterday."

"I wanted to see her about the possibility of Tillini bringing charges against her over the vespa attack. I'm sure Martha suspects something. We have to get our stories straight."

"My guess is, Tillini will drop the whole thing. He'll do what Martha wants, and she's a funny kind of person. On one hand she's a ruthless killer, and on the other . . . Well, I do believe she has a soft spot for you. And possibly for me and Mistral too. She's got what she wants, so she sees no reason to do anything vindictive. Anyway, it wouldn't be easy to build a case against Mistral. Her only involvement was in Edlin's office, and all the witnesses to that are dead, except you and me, thank God."

He thought about it, gazing out of the window at the lake. After a moment, Susanna began to cuddle close, running her fingers over his thigh. He said, "Do you realize we haven't seen any gorons out there feeding Lady?"

"Too bad," she said absently, otherwise engaged.

"No, really. Why have they stopped feeding her?"

She swung toward him, and he saw with a shock that the blue eyes were bright with tears. "P-piss on the bloody gorons," she faltered. "I'm the one that needs comforting right now. Do it, Trevithick!"

"What's the matter?"

"Never mind what's the matter. Just let's say somebody walked over my grave. Listen, do I have to take this dress off myself or are you going to be a gentleman and do it for me?"

He fought a fearsome premonition and put it behind him. He stood and unclipped her belt, then pulled the dress over her head and tossed it onto a chair. Then there was a delay, while a certain amount of hugging and kissing went on. Finally he completed the job and stood for a moment watching her in dumb admiration. Then she undressed him, except for his socks. He'd noticed that before; she never could be bothered to take his socks off. They clasped each other fiercely and tumbled in a well-organized fall to the chesterfield, and what happened after that was pure mindless joy.

Daylight came eventually and he rose and went to the window. The sun threw the shadow of the cottage across the beach, and the premonition returned. The goron coracles were nowhere to be seen, and as he turned from the window he caught Susanna quickly wiping tears from her eyes.

She knew he'd seen her. She rolled off the chesterfield and stood, and yawned, and stretched, gloriously naked. She locked her fingers behind her neck and favored him with a smoldering glance of outrageous lust. She said:

"Don't ask any questions. The only thing that matters is that you always remember me like this. Now let's go back to bed."

CHAPTER 34

THEY FLEW BACK TO SAMARITA THREE DAYS LATER at the urgent request of Janet Starseeker, who was having difficulty making sense of the equipment inventories and suspected Outward Ho intended to take full advantage of the confusion. Instead of taking the route over the mountains, Susanna flew past the goron caves and into the canyon. Dipping low, she hovered near Lady Herself. The torso had fallen forward until the head was resting on the surface. As they watched, one of the stunted arms twitched feebly.

"I don't think Outward Ho will have long to wait," Susanna remarked.

"Did they have anything to do with Lady's sickness, do you think?"

"No. We all know it's been coming on for years. They'll hasten her end with the Trent's Vivicide, but death comes to us all in one form or another, my love." She keyed in a fresh altitude and the copter rose clear of the canyon.

He swallowed; his throat felt constricted. "What are you and I going to do?" he asked clumsily.

"Do? We're going to organise those good Samaritans who want to leave, and we're going to get them and their possessions onto the shuttle."

"No, I mean . . . After. The two of us, I mean."

The copter lurched slightly. "It's all in the lap of the gods, isn't it, Bryn? Everything is. Surely you noticed how little control we have over events here."

"Susanna, answer me."

"Please don't let's talk about it. Let's take it as it comes, huh?"

Those days at the cottage had brought home to him how much he depended on her love. "Listen, if you want to stay here, I'll stay. If you want to go back to Earth, I'll go with you. If you want to go anywhere else in the Galaxy, I'll go there too."

She reached across and took his hand. "You can't say fairer than that. And I love you too, very much. But we both have jobs to do and—" she swallowed "—other loyalties. Now, let's work out how we're going to handle things in Samarita. We'll have to establish a presence otherwise we'll find Outward Ho robbing the poor old Organisation blind. We'll need to update all the inventories and get those bastards to sign for everything left behind, then the Organisation can bill them. Okay?"

"I suppose so," he said gloomily. "I don't feel very practical today."

"Neither do I, so before we update the inventories we'll call in at my apartment and screw our brains out. How does that suit you?"

"Better."

It was late afternoon before they finally reached Susanna's office, dazed with love. The corridors were full of people hurrying to and fro with boxes of possessions; others sat at their terminals looking a little lost. It was a return to reality with a thud.

"I have a couple of things to do at the hospital," said Susanna. "See you back here in a while. You can use my terminal."

He called Janet Starseeker for an update on the inventories. Then he called Murdo and had a staff listing put in foreground, with instructions that each person mark it according to whether they were staying or leaving. One by one the marks began to appear. He scrolled through the list. Some of the decisions were surprising; people whom he'd thought were staunchly Organisation were opting to stay. The way things were going it looked as though Outward Ho was going to have a very healthy colony here.

Half an hour later Susanna reappeared, leaning against his back and looking over his shoulder. "Works out at about two-thirds staying, so far," she said. "More than I expected."

"We should have known. People are loyal to the place they think of as home. Not to a nebulous bunch of bureaucrats back on Earth."

"I guess so."

He realised she was trembling. Concerned, he stood and put his arms around her. People in the corridor passed by with scarcely a glance through the glass wall. They had more important things to worry about than the Director of Ecology and the Manager of Health Services locked in an embrace.

"It's all right," he said, patting her rump as he might comfort a child he was hugging. Then his attention was caught by a smartly-dressed young woman coming down the corridor. She wore a royal blue jacket over a white blouse with a red and blue silk cravat, with a short blue skirt. At first he thought she was a stewardess from the shuttle, but there was something about the way she walked; that dancer's stride, swaying yet balanced . . .

"Oh, my God," he said.

Susanna detached herself from his arms and watched Mistral approach. She said with a catch in her voice, "This is the classic Cinderella scene, Bryn. I . . . I just hope I can handle the fairy godmother role."

Mistral's hair had been shortened; it swung shoulder-length as she walked, revealing a perfect face; the slanting green eyes, the slightly tilted nose, the firm chin. And the wide brow and high cheekbones . . .

With no trace of scarring.

As she walked toward them, people turned and watched her go by. She was smiling to herself, well aware of the effect she was having but hardly able to believe it. She stopped outside the glass wall and looked through. The faint smile widened, became confident, became radiant as she saw Trevithick. She winked at him and walked on down the corridor.

Susanna said, "I couldn't tell her what I was going to do. She wouldn't have given permission. Would you believe she hated me when she found the scar was gone? That was the biggest part of the therapy, to get her to accept that she had no excuse for acting like a jackass any more. A jennyass, technically speaking, I guess.

When you're beautiful, you've got responsibilities." Her own face was sad. "You have so much power, you see."

"Why didn't she come in here?"

She took his hand. "I told her not to. I wanted a chat with you after you'd seen her."

The premonition was creeping back. "I always thought you couldn't stand the sight of her," he said lamely, trying to stave off any fateful turn the conversation might take. "It was good of you to do this for her."

"I didn't do it for her, Bryn. I did it for you."

The premonition returned in full measure.

"She doesn't need to be beautiful for me."

"No. She needs to be good for you. Not bitter. Not all twisted up inside. She needs to be kind. Sensible. And she couldn't be like that, the way she looked before. You do see that, don't you, my love?"

"You're going away, aren't you?"

"I want you to understand." She drew him through the door valve out onto her balcony. "I doubt if people are monitoring the bugs today, but you never know. Okay, listen to me. You think Outward Ho have won, don't you? In that tiny mind of yours, you're convinced they'll have Lady killed off within the year, and all the male gorons too. And then they'll come in with the heavy machinery."

"Yeah," he muttered. "Something like that."

They watched a group of gorons near the bank of Lady. They stood gazing at her surface, listlessly. There was no sign of the usual bustling activity. Upturned coracles lay nearby like a row of dead turtles. A barge was tied to the bank, apparently abandoned.

"I don't see why Outward Ho should have everything their own way, Bryn. Mistral's staying, of course. They'll try to make her fit in; they don't like mavericks wandering around outside their colony sites. But they'll fail. You see, Mistral is stronger than anyone on Goronwy. She can control the stoags, the vespas and . . . the men. It's only a matter of time before she starts getting the better of the muscans, too. She's unique, Bryn. She's too hot for anyone to handle . . . except you. And you hold the power of love over her."

"She could go off me, you know." It was a poor argument. "And anyway, there's no need for you to go."

"How can I stay, loving you the way I do? I don't know what route Mistral will take, but there's a very good chance she's going to finish up on top here, with absolute power over the new colony. And you know the dangers of absolute power. Somebody's got to control her, and you're the only person who can do it, Bryn old buddy."

"Susanna, I've never been able to control her."

She led him back into the office. "Look, here she comes again. Bring her in, sit her down and talk to her, and let nature take its course. When I say let nature take its course, I mean within the bounds of propriety; there are a lot of prudes out there. All right, my love? Oh, and look after her. For all her power she's only flesh and blood and a laser can do a lot of damage. Be seeing you." She slid her arms around him, kissed him slowly and thoughtfully, then let him go and stepped out into the corridor.

Mistral entered, smiling.

"Got you all to myself now, haven't I," she said.

It took five more days to load the shuttle with two thousand people, their personal possessions, and all the equipment that Outward Ho would not be taking over. Trevithick threw himself into the work and Mistral proved to be an able assistant, studiously hiding her sex appeal under yellow Organisation coveralls and making no demands on him. Susanna was nowhere to be seen. Trevithick inquired after her whenever the opportunity arose, but nobody seemed to know where she was. On the afternoon of the fifth day, as he and Mistral were checking equipment through onto the shuttle elevator, he caught sight of Martha Sunshine.

A temporary shelter had been set up near one of the shuttle's legs. A milling crowd of evacuees said their goodbyes here before being passing through to the personnel section of the elevator. Martha stood among them. She saw him at the same moment.

"Bryn!"

Somewhat reluctantly, he joined her. "Who are you seeing off?" he asked sourly.

"I'm not. I'm leaving."

"Leaving?"

"Didn't you know, darling? Little Martha has outworn her welcome on this world."

"You're not serious." He stared at her. Now he noticed a heap of boxes nearby labelled SUNSHINE. "What happened?"

She glanced over her shoulder, a practised gesture of melodrama. "Well, nothing yet. But I'm not kidding myself. There's a big muscan presence at the top here, and its going to get bigger. There won't be room for a big human presence, meaning me. So I'm taking the money and running."

"Literally?" The forthright world of big business was always a puzzle to the academic Trevithick. "You mean they've actually paid you off?"

"Don't look so shocked, darling. I did them a lot of big favours. And now I want to find my place in the sun and enjoy life. After all my hard work, it would be a waste to end up burned in half like Gary Docksteader and Marik Darwin, wouldn't it?"

"You killed both of them, didn't you?"

"What, personally? Little me?" She clapped a hand to her breasts in a dramatic gesture of surprised innocence.

"Gary was working on Lady's aging process and he was helping you with your theatrical stuff at the same time. I suppose he chatted to you about his research and you reckoned he was getting too close. You were in the storage dome with him the day he died."

"So you reckon I slung him over my shoulder and carried him outside past the guards, and dumped him in the middle of aeolus field? Stretches belief, Bryn."

"No, you probably called Tillini."

"That would have been simpler."

"You're a ruthless goddamned woman."

"But sexy, huh? You said so yourself, in as many words. And that did me good and—" she reached out and patted his cheek "—maybe it saved your life. They tell me you're staying on here. A word of advice from Auntie Martha. Watch your back. Sorry to hear about Susanna, by the way."

His heart thumped. "Sorry to hear what about Susanna?"

"Well, her going back to Earth and all that."

"Have you seen her?"

Martha glanced up at the dark underside of the shuttle. "She boarded a couple of days ago, they tell me." When she looked at him again there was an unexpected sympathy in her eyes. "Too bad. Don't think in terms of leaping aboard and searching for her, Bryn. It would only prolong the agony."

A loud hailer rasped instructions. "Sounded like they're calling your group," said Trevithick woodenly.

"I can't tell you how glad I'll be to get off this godforsaken rock. My only regret is I'll miss the opening night of *Barker Sam*. You should see it, Bryn. Take Mistral along. Make the most of what you have. Some guys would kill for it. Believe me, I know all about killing. Well, so long."

And she took hold of him before he could back off and kissed him firmly on the lips, pulling him into the cushiony expanse of her body. Then, chuckling, she wiggled fat fingers at him and trod in stately fashion toward the elevator.

Mistral, who had been checking off some equipment, approached as he stood there lost in thought. "I saw her kiss you. I told you she wasn't so bad, didn't I?"

He was in shock. "She's appalling. She's absolutely the worst. She's sold out every human being here. Have you forgotten what she did to you? The art show?"

"The show was a flop because my paintings were no bloody good," said Mistral levelly. "Nobody was buying them except my dad, didn't you know? All Martha did was to show me the truth I wouldn't have seen otherwise, because I was so blind jealous of Susanna."

She'd grown up. They stood watching the evacuees rising smoothly into the shuttle. In another two short Goronwy days the shuttle would lift off, taking all the loyal Organisation employees home, including Susanna. Most of them were aboard now, getting settled in for their ten-day journey to the starship. A few undecideds remained in the domes, time running out for them.

Then he suddenly remembered. "Lath!"

"What?"

"Lath Eagleman! We left him at Ladysend. He can't look after himself, and Outward Ho won't want him, that's for sure. We should put him on the shuttle!"

She took his hand. "Come on. We'll take a copter." They made their way to the parked ATV and drove to the copter pad. Susanna's ambulopter was there. Trevithick explained the situation to the Security man, obtained the keys, and within minutes they were rising above the domes. Lady lay beneath them, a glistening ribbon in the sunlight.

"Look!" exclaimed Mistral.

Trevithick tilted the nose down for a clearer view.

A wide split had appeared in Lady, running diagonally from one bank to the other. Trevithick descended until the copter hovered a scant two meters above the surface. Sunlight shone obliquely into the crevasse, revealing water rippling about four meters down.

"She's breaking up," he said heavily. "This split looks as though it might go right through to the bottom."

A group of gorons stood on the bank, gloomily regarding the stern of a barge protruding vertically from the crevasse. Trevithick keyed in one hundred meters and the copter rose and skimmed downLady. As they flew further south Lady began to look like a dried-out mudpan, with cracks breaking desiccated flesh into polygon shapes. A stink of decay filled the tiny cabin.

There was no doubt about it; no possibility of a last-minute cure. Outward Ho wouldn't be needing the drums of Trent's Vivicide.

Lady was dead.

Ladysend looked the same. Somehow he'd expected everything to have changed; memories of his last visit here had taken on a dreamlike quality. The blackened remains of the school lay beside

Bridget's apartment but the rest of the buildings were still intact. The goron huts were all there too; with the little men sitting in the sun all around. Three gorons left their fellows and approached the copter as Trevithick and Mistral sat in the cabin surveying the scene.

"Who are they?" he asked. The family resemblance of gorons was strong. "I don't want to insult them by not recognising them."

"Morgan on the left. Tresco the bargee." She stared. "And the other one's Calder. What's he doing here? You remember Calder, who went through the canyon with us?"

"Yes. A miserable little toad. When we got to the beach he just went off without a word."

The gorons gathered on Mistral's side of the cabin, looking in. "I'll just slip up to Bridget's apartment for a moment, okay? You can ask them about Lath." She stepped to the ground, spoke briefly to the gorons, then hurried off toward the tall building.

Trevithick got out and shook the tiny goron hands. Their faces looked strange; then he realised they were not wearing human expressions any more. "It's good to see you again," he said.

"Lady's dead," said Morgan. "It's nobody's fault. Your people tried. Thank you."

"But Bridget Booker killed the females," said Calder.

"She didn't know," said Morgan. "I killed them too; all of Clan Birthcare did. We should have trusted our instincts, but we didn't. I think it was the first time Lady had ever produced females, so how were we to know?"

Trevithick asked, "What are you going to do now?"

"Some people said we should commit ourselves to Lady," said Morgan. "But what is the use of doing that if Lady is dead? She can't accept us. On the other hand, what is the use of our lives if she is dead? We've talked about it a lot."

"We shall probably talk about it until we die," said Tresco. "My barge sank and my stoags ran away. The last time you saw me I was useful. Now I'm nothing."

"Have you come to help?" asked Morgan. "We need advice. Humans are able to live without purpose. We need to do the same for a number of years. Will you show us what we must do? We miss Bridget so much."

Trevithick regarded the earnest little faces helplessly. Other gorons were getting to their feet now, and walking slowly toward them. He fancied there was supplication in their eyes. A flash of colour attracted his attention. Mistral was descending the steps from the apartment, all long legs, the muscles of her thighs prominent. She'd changed out of the yellow coverall into her old, short red dress. She must have left her bag of possessions up there on the previous visit.

He had the sense of things closing in on him.

"We'll try to help," he said.

Mistral arrived, smiling, perfect white teeth and bright green eyes. "I know you like me better in these things. Now everything'll be like it used to."

"We're looking for a human," he said to the gorons. "Lath Eagleman. He was with us when we came before, and he got left behind. Have you seen him?"

"We've seen him," said Morgan. "He stayed with us. Then he walked away."

"Which way did he go?"

The goron pointed west. "Two days ago."

"He can't look after himself," Trevithick explained. "He's sick. In the head, I mean. Did anyone go with him?"

"No."

"Did he take any food, or nectar or anything?"

"No," said Morgan regretfully. "At the time I thought it was foolish, but humans never listen to us."

"If you think we're strange," snapped Mistral, for once losing patience with the gorons, "you should try talking to a muscan some time. So you let poor Lath wander off alone? You should have known better, Morgan. And you a member of Clan Birthcare, too!"

The sun was dropping toward the western plain. "It's too late to go looking for him now," said Trevithick. "We'll take the copter first thing in the morning. When we find him we'll take him straight back to Samarita. There'll still be time to get him onto the shuttle."

"If we find him," said Mistral pessimistically. Then she brightened. "Still, it means we have the evening to ourselves for the first time for ages. We can sleep in Bridget's apartment."

He hesitated. "Bridget's apartment? This is hardly the time or place to—"

"Don't be such an old fuddy-duddy. It's a beautiful evening in a beautiful place, and you've got a beautiful girl here with you. She seized Trevithick's hand. "Come on, let's go for a walk along the beach first! You do think I'm beautiful now, don't you?" she asked anxiously.

"Yes." He allowed her to draw him toward the beach.

"And what's more," she said in a thrilled whisper, "I'm not wearing any underwear!"

"Oh, for God's sake. You haven't changed at all."

As the ripplegrass gave way to sand, she turned and faced him. "You don't want me to change. You like me this way. I can tell, you see. I know exactly how you feel, even though you've been trying to avoid the truth this last few days. I've always known. So kiss me and let's get this bloody walk over with, and get to bed."

As a sop to his pride he insisted they walk as far as the little cove at the end of the beach, but that was a mistake because the sight of a sandy hollow between rocks brought back happy memories to Mistral. She sat down, the setting sun gilding her legs, and looked up at him. "Come on down here," she said.

When he hesitated, fighting it, she chuckled and lay back, wriggling down so that the skirt rode up. With an inward groan Trevithick knelt beside her and kissed her while her urgent hands worked at his clothes. Then, in a few short violent moments, he surrendered to superior forces.

When she'd recovered her breath and composure, she said quite calmly, "Just accept it, Bryn. We'll both find it so much nicer that way. She's gone, and neither of us will ever mention her again."

And in that moment, like a sad elegy, they heard the sound of a violin playing the slow movement from Mendelssohn's violin concerto.

They stood, rearranging their clothes. "He's over the other side of those rocks," said Mistral.

They climbed the rocks circling the cove and found Lath Eagleman in the shadows on the far side, still playing, gazing down at the water with eyes that were not quite empty. The sea was calm, the waves slow, lifting and dropping the level of the dark water lazily.

"She is coming," he said, without looking at them. "She always comes at this time. She likes my music."

Trevithick's scalp prickled. Was Lath speaking of the long-dead Brighteyes? Did she materialise from the waves in that fractured imagination of his? "We have to get you back to Samarita, Lath." He tried to take the bow away.

"No!" He jerked away like a child with a toy, cradling the bow and violin protectively. "Go away!"

"Let him play until it's dark, Bryn," said Mistral. "We're not going back until morning anyway. Come and sit here with me." She'd found a shelf of rock; she patted a space beside her.

He sat down and considered Lath, and the water, and the girl beside him. The music played on; Lath sounded a little better tonight. He found he'd slipped an arm around Mistral. The evening was warm and the rocks on the far side of the cove sparkled in the crimson light of the setting sun. The sea rose and fell dreamily.

Things could be worse.

The shuttle would leave and the colony would settle down, and Outward Ho would pour in all kinds of equipment to make it a good place for people to live in. Industries would start up; mining, manufacturing and the various service industries. Outward Ho never kept a tight rein on things; they allowed private enterprise to flourish and took their profit in taxes. In due course Samarita would be a city and Ladysend would be a resort area and a fishing port.

Did it really matter that muscans would be pulling the strings? Surely not, provided humans could lead happy and productive lives. Only a racist could get upset about a detail like that. And anyway, there was Mistral, so Susanna had assured him. Between them, he and Mistral could probably keep the muscans in check.

The music played. "She comes," said Lath. "My little mermaid."

"Look, Bryn," whispered Mistral, leaning forward. "Look!"

There was a rock near the middle of the cove. He'd been watching it idly for some time. Sometimes it was clear of the water, then a wave would lift gently over it. Now there was something lying there. In the fading light he thought it was some kind of Goronwy mud-skipper; it seemed to be propping itself up on a pair of fins near its head. Then he realised the shape was all wrong, and he saw the creature for what it was.

As Lath had said, it was a little mermaid.

It was about fifteen centimetres long, with a humanoid head, torso and arms. From the waist down it was dolphin-like with a smooth tail ending in tiny flukes. It lay still, its head turned toward Lath, its eyes shadowed.

"You don't suppose . . . ?" said Mistral.

"It could be. It could be!" A wild excitement was growing in him. "Remember Clan Birthcare was on strike for ten days? Nobody was checking on the foetuses. She could have slipped through then. She must have!"

Mistral waded out, gently took hold of the little creature and brought her back to the rocks. She didn't struggle. Lath continued to play, and she watched the movement of his bow as she lay in Mistral's lap.

Trevithick pondered. She would need to be hidden and well protected for a while; Mistral and the gorons could handle that. He'd get a warpwire through to Earth explaining the situation. Once the existence of the female became public knowledge there wouldn't be a thing Outward Ho could do about it. Samarita would have to be evacuated almost completely, with just a small group left to help raise the female.

"They'll still need us," said Mistral, following his thoughts.

He stood. "Come on. Let's show her to the gorons."

Mistral laughed. "Won't they think we're just the greatest guys!"